## A NOTE ON THE AUTHOR

**JAY McInerney** came to prominence in 1984 with his first novel *Bright Lights, Big City*. He is the author of six further novels: *Ra som*, *Story of My Life*, *Brightness Falls*, *The Last of the Savages*, *el Behaviour* and *The Good Life*, two short story collections, and e non-fiction books on wine, one of which was the acclaimed *A Hedonist in the Cellar*. He writes a wine column for *Town and Country* and is a regular contributor to the *Guardian*, the *New York mes Book Review* and *Corriere della Sera*. He lives in Manhattan Bridgehampton, New York.

jaymcinerney.com / @JayMcInerney

# THE
# GOOD LIFE

B L O O M S B U R Y

LONDON · OXFORD · NEW YORK · NEW DELHI · SYDNEY

Bloomsbury Paperbacks
An imprint of Bloomsbury Publishing Plc

50 Bedford Square                1385 Broadway
London                           New York
WC1B 3DP                         NY 10018
UK                               USA

www.bloomsbury.com

BLOOMSBURY and the Diana logo are trademarks of Bloomsbury Publishing Plc

First published in Great Britain 2006
This paperback edition first published in 2016

British Library Cataloguing-in-Publication Data
A catalogue record for this book is available from the British Library.

ISBN: HB: 978-0-7475-8090-4
TPB: 978-0-7475-8453-7
PB: 978-1-4088-7696-1
ePub: 978-1-4088-2254-8

2 4 6 8 10 9 7 5 3 1

Typeset by Newgen Knowledge Works (P) Ltd., Chennai, India
Printed and bound in Great Britain by CPI Group (UK) Ltd, Croydon CR0 4YY

MIX
Paper from
responsible sources
FSC® C020471

To find out more about our authors and books visit www.bloomsbury.com.
Here you will find extracts, author interviews, details of forthcoming
events and the option to sign up for our newsletters.

FOR JEANINE

Who rescued me that day
and many days thereafter

In middle age there is mystery, there is mystification. The most I can make out of this hour is a kind of loneliness. Even the beauty of the physical world seems to crumble, yes, even love.

—JOHN CHEEVER

Cataclysmic events, whatever their outcome, are as rare and transporting as a great love. Bombings, revolutions, earthquakes, hurricanes,—anyone who has passed through one and lived, if they are honest, will tell you that even in the depths of their fear there was an exhilaration such as had been missing from their lives until then.

—ANA MENENDEZ

# PART ONE

# Indian Summer

1

S    ummer used to be as endless as the ocean when she was a girl
     and her family rented the gray shingled cottage on Nantucket.
     Now, she found it hard to believe she was already back in Man-
hattan and the kids were in school and she was already racing home,
late again, feeling guilty that she'd lingered over a drink with Casey
Reynes. The kids had been home for hours after their first day in first
grade, and she had yet to hear about it.

Women blamed themselves; men blamed anything but.

This was Corrine's interpretation of the guilt nipping at her high
heels as she cantered up Hudson Street from the subway, passing the
hand-lettered sign in the window of their Chinese takeout: FRESHLY
GROUNDED COFFEE. Guilt about leaving the kids for so long, about not
helping Russell with dinner, about attempting to restart her long-
dormant professional life. Oh, to be grounded herself. Seven-fifteen
by her watch. Still attuned to the languorous rhythm of the summer—

they'd just closed up the house in Sagaponack four days ago—she'd barely had time to kiss the kids good-bye this morning and now the guests would be arriving at any minute, Russell frenzied with cooking and child care.

Bad mother, bad wife, bad hostess. *Bad.*

When she had yearned to be a mother, imagining what it would be like to be a parent, it had been easy to conjure the joy . . . the scenes of tenderness, the Pietà moments. What you don't picture are the guilt and the fear that take up residence at the front of your brain, like evil twins you didn't bargain for. Fear because you're always worried about what might go wrong, especially if your kids were born, as hers were, three months early. You can never forget the sight of them those first few days, intubated under glass, veined eggshell skulls and pink writhing limbs—the image stays with you even as they grow, reminding you of just how fragile these creatures are, how flimsy your own defenses. And guilt because you can never possibly do enough. There's never enough time. No matter how much love and attention you lavish on them, you're always afraid that it will never be enough.

Corrine had become a connoisseur of guilt; not for her the stabbing thrust of regret for an ill-conceived act—but, rather, the dull and steady throb of chronic guilt, even as she'd done her best to rearrange her life around her kids, quitting her job to take care of them and, over the past two years, working highly flexible hours on a screenplay and on a project that was the obverse of a busman's holiday—a start-up venture called Momtomtom.com, which had been on the verge of a big launch this past spring, when the Internet bubble started to deflate and the venture capital dried up. This afternoon, she'd spent four hours making a presentation to a possible backer, hustling for seed money for the Web site. As these prospects dimmed, she'd been trying to set up meetings on the screenplay, an adaptation of Graham Greene's *The Heart of the Matter.* And here were the theoretical bookends of her existence, the maternal and the romantic—the latter submerged and almost extinct. In fact, that had been her secret intention in writing this script: to try to rekindle the romance and fan it back to life.

4

Corrine hadn't wanted to be one of those mothers who paid someone else to raise her kids; for the first five years, to the astonishment of her friends and former colleagues, she'd stayed at home. Manhattan was an existential town, in which identity was a function of professional accomplishment; only the very young and the very rich were permitted to be idle. The latter, like her friend Casey Reynes, had their charities and their personal assistants and inevitably managed to convey the impression that all this constituted an exhausting grind. Russell had initially supported her maternal ideal, though, as the years went by and their peers bought vacation homes in the Hamptons, he couldn't consistently disguise his resentment over their straitened finances, or his sense that his stay-at-home wife had become translucent, if not invisible, within the walls of their loft—a nanny without salary.

Writing a screenplay was, in their circle, code for being unemployed; finishing the first draft failed to produce the sense of accomplishment she'd expected. A screenplay, after all, was a kind of theoretical object, a recipe rather than the meal itself. And thus far she hadn't had much luck in assembling the ingredients. So when the kids entered preschool last year, she had tried to turn her obsession with child rearing into a profession—formalizing the body of knowledge she'd acquired as a full-time city mother into a viable on-line resource. If that plan didn't work out, she would have to return to the job marketplace, as much for her own self-esteem as to defray the $34,000 tuition for the kids.

A homeless man was encamped in the shadow of construction scaffolding across the street from her building—a rarer sight than it would have been ten years ago. A young, dirt-caked slacker with a ragged goatee, a bull terrier on a leash, and a paper coffee cup at his feet. As Corrine hurried past, he said, "Hey, beautiful. I need a blow job. I need a place in the Hamptons. I need a movie role."

She paused, registering the humor—and her husband would have loved this, storing it away with all the other anecdotes he used to illustrate his wife's hilarious singularity—but instead of laughing, she was thinking about *needs*. What we need in order to make life bearable.

5

Suddenly coming to her senses, the panhandler gaping at her.

"I need romance," said Corrine, dropping a dollar in the wishing well of his cup. "Whatever happened to the romance?"

She burst into her apartment, aching for her children, who over the course of the interminable afternoon might have died, dashed their heads against the edge of the coffee table she kept vowing to replace, been kidnapped, or forgotten her entirely. Corrine would have been less surprised at any of these scenarios than she was to see Hilary on the sofa, playing with the kids.

"Mom, guess what. You won't *believe*! Aunt Hilary's here."

Her daughter, Storey, loved to deliver news and make announcements.

It's true—she wouldn't believe. Last Corrine knew, her little sister had been in L.A. She'd tried calling as recently as last week, only to be told the number had been disconnected. And now here she was in TriBeCa, reclining on Corrine's couch with Jeremy in her lap. No matter that Corrine had seen her dozens of times in the intervening years: Hilary was preserved, in Corrine's mind, semifrozen at the age of fifteen, the last year they'd shared a domicile, so that it was always a surprise to see her as a woman, and a pretty convincing one at that. Only a few evanescent lines at the corners of her eyes hinted that she'd passed thirty a few years before.

The first thing Corrine did, pure reflex, was to scoop Jeremy up into her arms and hug him, but instead of clutching her, he squirmed.

"Hey, sis." Hilary rose from the couch, stretching lithe and cat-like in her leopard top. As if to preserve Corrine's illusion of her youthfulness, she still moved and dressed like a teenager, and had the body to carry it off. "Thought I'd surprise you."

"I'm . . . I *am*." Corrine belatedly hugged her sister with the arm not holding Jeremy—a sister sandwich, with her son—their son?—in the middle. Surprised, yes, Corrine thought . . . although at some point unpredictability becomes a pattern. "You look . . . great," Corrine said.

"Thanks."

"Aunt Hilary's been in *Paris*," Storey said.

"Paris?"

Jeremy squirmed out of Corrine's grasp and dropped onto the ottoman.

"Well, actually I came from London today, but I've been in Paris for the past two weeks."

"She met Madeline," Storey said, holding up her favorite book. "Can you *believe* it, Mom? Aunt Hilary *knows* her. Why didn't you tell us she knows Madeline?"

"I had no idea," Corrine said, casting a reproving glance at her sister. "Although, actually, now that I think about it, I'm not surprised at all. Your aunt Hilary knows just about everybody in the whole world."

"The *whole* world?"

"Your mom's just making a little joke."

It was true—you couldn't watch a movie or open a magazine without Hilary dropping intimate remarks about the two-dimensional icons therein. Why shouldn't she know Madeline?

"Aunt Hilary saw her at the Eiffel Tower with Miss Clavel and the other little girls."

"What's so great about Madeline?" Jeremy asked. "She's just a little girl."

Just like Hilary to tell Storey she was acquainted with a fictional character, fiction being her great specialty. Corrine didn't want Storey getting mocked for relating this triumph at school. She was feeling ambivalent enough about the Fluffies—the fairylike creatures that she had conjured up for the kids when they were three, who had their own biographies and their own little house in the kids' bedroom. They'd been through this once before when Hilary claimed to be great friends with Barbie—to whom she bore more than a passing resemblance.

"Corrine," Hilary said, "why are you looking at me that way?"

"What way?" Storey demanded. "What way is she looking at you? Mom, what does she mean?"

Jeremy was bouncing up and down on the sofa.

"Have you got a place to stay?"

"Collin has this loft in SoHo? But I have to call his neighbors for the keys. I think I may have the wrong number or something."

As if, Corrine thought, she was supposed to know who Collin was. Some fucking drug dealer, minor English aristocrat, or bass player, if experience was any guide. She gestured toward the couch. "You're welcome to the guest suite." Theirs was one of those old tunnel-style TriBeCa lofts, shaped like Manhattan itself, long and skinny, the most space they could find for the money back in 1990, when the area was still considered remote—an eighteen-by-eighty-foot rectangle with a single bathroom carved out of commercial space in the seventies. They'd walled off first one bedroom in the back and then another when the children were born, and kept telling themselves, as the years slipped past, that they'd probably move by the time the kids needed separate bedrooms. Which they did now. The experts said six was the age, but somehow all of the possible solutions seemed to require more cash than they commanded.

Russell was calling out from behind the kitchen counter. She wondered how he was taking this.

"Can Aunt Hilary give us our bath?" Storey asked. "Please please please."

"I suppose so," said Corrine.

"Race you to the bathroom," Storey told her brother.

"We will *walk* to the bathroom," Corrine said, grabbing hold of the back of Jeremy's shirt. Last week, he'd slipped and bruised his forehead—so Corrine reminded herself as she tried to justify the note of irritation in her voice.

Russell, meanwhile, was in his cooking frenzy in what they called the kitchen, retaining the nomenclature of residences with discrete rooms, flailing away with his ten-inch German chef's knife, juggling his beloved copper pots and French steel pans, which weighed as much as the unused dumbbells in the bedroom closet, the heft of which seemed to her to have as much to do with the macho aesthetics of amateur chefdom as with heat distribution. Cooking was a new sphere of masculine competition; Russell and Washington and his chef friend Carlo had lately taken to comparing notes on butchers and cutlery the way they used to deconstruct stereo equipment, garage bands, and young novelists. For fifteen years, Russell had been perfectly happy with their Calphalon pots, a wedding present from Macy's, until Washington told him the sous-chef at JoJo said they were for pussies.

She kissed him on the cheek. "I promise I had no idea," she whispered. "I haven't spoken to her in weeks—months, probably. You're not furious, are you?"

"Don't worry, she exonerated you."

She put a finger to her lips. Russell seemed incapable of speaking at any volume but loud, a characteristic ill-suited to loft living.

"At least she didn't show up with some head-banger or felon in tow." She put her arms around her husband's ribs. "Is she going to spoil your perfect seating chart? I don't see how we can—"

"No big deal," Russell said, chopping away at a leek.

Corrine could hardly believe her ears. Russell was a maniac about his dinner parties. He was capable of throwing a tantrum if Corrine added someone at the last minute. It was one of the few areas of life in which he was prissy. When he put on his chef/host hat, everything had to be just so. Not to mention the fact that he'd grown tired of the saga of the prodigal sister-in-law, although he wouldn't admit it.

She shook her head. "You mean you won't have a heart attack if there's an uneven number at the table?"

"Actually, Salman canceled this afternoon. And then Jim called and said Cody Erhardt was in town and would I mind if he joined us."

Now she understood. "Did Salman have an excuse?"

"He's got a deadline and he leaves on his book tour tomorrow."

Corrine could tell he was disappointed, though he liked to act as if having Salman Rushdie over to dinner was no big deal. That was one of the things she hated about New York, how you were supposed to be cool and take for granted the awe-inspiring people and events you'd fantasized about back home in Altoona or Amherst. By the time you were behind the velvet ropes or sitting at the front booth, you were probably too jaded to admit how lucky you felt or to enjoy it the way you once imagined you would have.

Corrine was actually relieved, since in the absence of their illustrious guest, the evening would be more relaxed. It wasn't just Salman and his heady aura of celebrity; his new girlfriend was absurdly beautiful, to the point of being a socially disruptive force. The last time they'd had dinner together, Russell made an ass out of himself trying to amuse her; and besides, they'd been friends with Salman's wife, the mother of his youngest child. Corrine didn't believe everything she read in the tabloids and she refused to take sides in marital disputes, but this one hit a little close to home. And she was still worried that a bomb might go off in his vicinity, although supposedly the fatwa had been lifted. The people who wanted him dead weren't the forgive-and-forget type. She'd always been nervous when Russell hooked up with him in London, and she could never quite relax when they saw him in New York. In the early days, when he was holed up in London, surrounded by armed guards, Russell had had a fax number that went through Scotland Yard or MI5. It was all very James Bondian, which, of course, appealed to Russell's sense of adventure, but after spending a week with him in London a few years ago, making the rounds of book parties and running into Salman almost every night, she found it kind of absurd. If the Iranian secret police or whoever the fuck they were had any clue, all they would have to do would be to stake out the fashionable cocktail party circuit for a few nights and they'd have him. Martin Amis's launch party? Hello? It was lucky, of course—and made you feel a little safer, like maybe these fanatics weren't that dangerous outside their own countries. Salman had certainly been very conspicuous around New York in the last year, and nothing bad had happened yet.

"I'm sorry, honey. Are you terribly disappointed?" She kissed his cheek as he squinted at an open cookbook.

"It'll be nice to see Cody," he said. At least Erhardt's films hadn't alienated any Muslim fundamentalists, as far as she knew, although she recalled Christian fundamentalists had picketed one of them. Russell had published a collection of three of his screenplays a few years back. He was a hero to those who believed that his peers from the class of 1969, those legends responsible for the brief renaissance between *Easy Rider* and *The Deer Hunter,* had sold out and succumbed to the demands of the marketplace and the debt maintenance on their houses and wineries. Or died, if not young, then in the full flower of excess. Among the cineasts who could name three Japanese directors other than Kurosawa, those for whom the modern indie era began with *sex, lies and videotape,* Erhardt was revered as much for his intransigence and his noble failures as for the films he had actually written or directed, although at least one of these was acknowledged to be a classic.

It suddenly occurred to her that he'd be a great director for her screenplay of *The Heart of the Matter.*

In what seemed like one of those moments of semipsychic marital communion, Russell said, "I think Jim said he'd sent him a copy of your screenplay."

"That would be—he'd be great," Corrine said. Not that she was about to bring it up at dinner . . . not unless he did. She had a horror of appearing pushy or mercenary, a legacy she blamed on her WASPy New England heritage—a worldview in which business and pleasure were strictly segregated. She knew that this was a quaint notion and thoroughly contradicted the very essence of social life in Manhattan.

These dinner parties were always preceded by Sturm und Drang—Corrine almost wondered if it was worth it. Tonight's suspense had begun to build when Washington had called to say that his wife, Veronica, was sick. So Russell had invited Carlo, who, besides being a chef, a fact that could only increase the level of angst and adrenaline, belonged to that class of gregarious New Yorkers with phantom spouses. "Married singles," Corrine called them.

"Since we know Carlo won't bring his wife, why not invite Martha Stewart," Corrine said, "and really make yourself fucking crazy?"

"Carlo will love Hilary," Russell said. "Hard to say which of them is more likely to start groping the other. Actually, she seems fairly sane and balanced for a change. Plus, she's keeping an eye on the kids. And you should've seen how happy they were to see her."

"She hasn't even spoken to them in three months."

He paused in his chopping and looked up. "A little testiness there?"

"Just an observation." The subject of her sister was fraught with . . . well, with being fraught.

"Maybe she's sensed some, I don't know, ambivalence on your part."

"What's *that* supposed to mean?"

"I don't know. It's just . . . I think we're *all* still trying to figure out the dynamics of this particular extended family."

She watched his hands, wincing at each stroke of the glistening blade. Russell was such a klutz; he shouldn't be allowed to wield this ruthless German cutlery—witness the scars from his culinary adventures. "Are you saying I'm insecure?"

Russell put down the knife and embraced her, holding his wet hands away from her back. "Actually, it's the typical family drama. You love your little sister, but she happens to drive you insane."

Corrine allowed herself to be mollified, even as she tried to remember the last time Russell had hugged her. She should mark it down on her calendar, along with her increasingly infrequent periods.

"Do we have any thyme?"

She checked her watch. "Almost seven-thirty."

"Not *time*," he said. "Thyme."

"What are you trying to say?"

"The herb? *Thyme?*"

She glared at him. God, she hated how tense and snippy he got before a dinner party. Why did he bother? Why not just order in Chinese like normal people or expense-account something preprepared from Dean and DeLuca?

"How the . . ." She lowered her voice. "How would I know? *Thyme*—I'm not even sure what the hell it is. The kitchen's your domain. Gourmet cooking is part of your recipe for the good life, not mine. And don't blame me because you invited your chef friend and now you're all wigged-out."

Thyme? The only thing she knew about thyme was that it was part of the title of that Simon and Garfunkel song.

"Sorry," he said.

"In other words, you're not asking me a question. You're telling me that we don't have any *thyme* and hoping I might fetch you some."

"Do you think you could pop around the corner?"

Corrine sighed. She supposed this might be preferable to witnessing the escalating panic of the home chef, but she wanted to explore the subject of Hilary a little further.

Actually, no, she didn't. "So who's coming, exactly?"

"Carlo—"

"I still don't understand why you invited him. Unless you can only entertain under pressure."

"Carlo doesn't expect a four-star meal. He's just grateful to be invited to someone's home. Everyone else is too scared to cook for him."

"Well, I'm glad you're so relaxed."

"I'm fine."

"Who else?"

"Nancy Tanner—"

"I like Nancy." Nancy was the perennial single girl of their set. Five years ago, Russell had published her first novel, a story about a perennial single girl, and it had become a surprise best-seller. Corrine had become nostalgic for the days when Nancy's anecdotes about disastrous dates had seemed less like material she was trying out for her next book or talk-show appearance, but she always said, when called upon to defend her, that she'd earned it. Scrapping for years, jammed into a walk-up studio in Yorkville, blue-penciling articles about acne and dating and diets for young women's magazines as her twenties turned into her thirties, surviving on canapés and cigarettes, intermittently investing her hopes in some wildly inappropriate suitor. Even lying about her age, which had become a gossip-column tempest— who could blame her? Women like Casey hated Nancy because she was pretty and thin and refused to play by their rules and because they assumed she must be after their husbands. Finding her own life increasingly circumscribed by the rituals of middle age and motherhood, Corrine liked knowing somebody who was still running around drinking too much and screwing strange men. Some of them might be married, but Nancy never poached on her friends. And she could always be counted on to say or do something embarrassing at the dinner table—nearly a lost art here at the beginning of the new century—particularly since Washington Lee had quit drinking. A few months ago, at their last dinner party, she'd told Paul Auster that he ought to read John Grisham "to bone up on plotting."

Actually, Nancy was a lot like Corrine's little sister, except that Hilary hadn't yet written the book, or made the transition to act two—still the party girl at the age of thirty-whatever: the girlfriend, the traveling companion, the bit-part actress with the movie-star social life. If Corrine wasn't mistaken, Hilary would be thirty-five on her next birthday—the scariest one for single urban women, what Nancy had called in a recent article "the female equivalent of the two-minute warning in football." Time left, but not all that much. Bio clock ticking away.

"And of course the birthday boy and his dragoness—Jim and Judy. And Washington, and now your sister."

"Don't seat those two together—Washington and Hilary, I mean. They'd probably go at it right under the table."

"Where's the phone?" Russell asked, his head whipping around the wreckage of the kitchen. "I've got to ask Carlo about the meat." Sometimes she wondered how he didn't hurt his neck jerking his head around like some demented robin frantic for worms.

"What are you cooking?"

"*Poitrine de veau farcie.*"

"Sometimes you can be such a fag. What's that in American?"

"Stuffed veal breast. It's kind of a retro dish."

"Sounds a little heavy. It's, like, seventy degrees outside."

"Hey, summer's over."

"Then why are you wearing a polo shirt?"

When Corrine stuck her head in the bathroom, Hilary was in the tub with the kids. She opened her mouth but found herself speechless, unable to think of an appropriate response. If her talk with Russell had made her self-conscious about her feelings for her sister, she nonethe-

14

less had a sudden terrifying premonition that Hilary had come to take her children away from her, and she wanted, needed, right *now,* to lift Jeremy up out of the tub, away from his . . . *aunt* was the word that had formed in her mind. But, of course, Hilary was more than his aunt—and that was the crux of the problem.

She tried to narrow her indignation to focus on the inappropriateness of Hilary's body, which wasn't the body of an aunt or a mother, but that of a starlet, of a fantasy object in a magazine. Would it be any less inappropriate if her six-year-old son were in the tub with a figure more boyish? Jeremy, however, seemed oblivious, his back to his naked aunt's tits, holding a Pokémon figure in each hand. And what about Russell, who might at any moment walk in to check on things? *Things.* That was what they were—she was seeing through Russell's eyes now—like objects with a separate existence from the owner's. She felt she had some sudden insight into the male psyche—the objectifying power of their lust.

She tried to remember the last time she'd seen her sister naked. Were her breasts always so *pronounced*? So *there*? She caught herself looking for scars. Living in L.A. all these years, of course she must've had them done. Something Hilary was likely to do anyway. As if she could read her sister's mind, Hilary began to soap her breasts and looked up at Corrine, innocent and unself-conscious, or provocative.

"I thought I'd better clean myself up for your company."

Will they be treated to a glimpse of your breasts? Corrine wondered.

Storey, who'd been humming, broke into a warbling song:

> *When you say good-bye*
> *It doesn't mean you'll die*
> *So don't cry*
> *When you say good-bye*

"That's a nice song," Corrine said.
"I just invented it."
Where did she come up with this stuff?

"This is Pikachu," said Jeremy, holding up a Pokémon, an obsession that had killed off the dinosaurs.

"How do you do, Pikachu?"

"Mom," Storey said. "Aunt Hilary knows the Backstreet Boys."

"I'm sure she does," Corrine said. "I'm sure she does."


Corrine was dressing when Russell, wearing his Chez Panisse apron, barged in to announce the arrival of Washington Lee.

After all these years, she still thought of Russell's entrances as being abrupt, almost slapstick. Crash Calloway. She usually found this endearing, though, Russell's physical lurchiness offsetting some of his more effete pretensions. She looked at her watch. "Remember when Washington always arrived two hours late?"

"That was before he stopped drinking. Now he wants to eat at six-thirty and be home by ten."

It was kind of sad, the extinction of that bright genie that came out after Washington had had a few. Corrine didn't particularly go for black guys as a rule, but the glimmer in his eye was when he was hitting his stride, the naughty confidences he drew you into, the outrageous and obscene comments always delivered with dry aplomb, his way of playing on your fear of being an uncool white person but then letting you off the hook at the last minute, allowing you to laugh *with* him at *them*. . . . She missed the bad old Washington, the one who wobbled to his feet as the dessert was served to quote swatches of poetry in a variety of languages before screwing one of the guests in the bathroom. It was all highly amusing, until the moment it became merely sloppy, a moment that came earlier and earlier in the evening as time went by and which became less and less charming after he married Veronica and they had a baby. Then he'd finally stopped, cold turkey, and while he was a less unpredictable element, she missed that spark, the demonic gleam. . . . The lights grew dimmer as they hit their forties and some of the lights had been extinguished altogether.

Russell pulled off the apron and rummaged in his closet. "Any idea how long Hilary's staying?"

"Haven't had a chance to ask." She glanced over at him. "You don't *really* mind, do you? God knows we owe her."

"I *like* Hilary," Russell said. "I'm crazy about Hilary." He held up one of his stripy English dress shirts. "What do you think? With a blazer and jeans."

"Very Upper East Side at home for the evening," Corrine said, smiling at the pride Russell took in his slightly fuddy-duddy, contrarian form of dress, particularly since they'd moved downtown. He was one of the few humans south of Fourteenth Street who didn't own a pair of black jeans.

"Maybe she can do some baby-sitting," he said. "I mean, not that I think of her as a natural in that department. On the other hand—"

"Let's not get into the other hand," said Corrine, nodding to indicate Jeremy, who was suddenly in the door.

"Hey, Dad," he said. "What's faster—a Ferrari or a Porsche?"

"It depends," Russell said.

"Jimmy Clifton's dad has a Ferrari, but Asher Gold's dad has a Porsche."

"Ferrari," Russell said.

"I thought so. Thanks, Dad."

This was one of the perils of raising kids in New York, she thought, at least if you were trying to subsist on less than two hundred and fifty grand a year. Ferraris and Porsches. When they had first moved to TriBeCa, it was a frontier village populated by artists, musicians, and families that couldn't afford space uptown and didn't mind traveling ten blocks for groceries, but in the last few years it had been overrun by Wall Streeters and celebrities and Kennedy princes. If they'd owned their loft, they at least would have profited from the gentrification, but by renting, they had missed out on the boom. Although their rent was for the moment stabilized, they lived in fear of paying market price for the space. She'd tried to persuade Russell to look at houses in Brooklyn or even Pelham, a not-too-distant refuge of the middle-aged culturati that had some unrestored houses and decent public schools, but he was determined to make his stand in Manhattan, claiming he was too old for Brooklyn and too young for Pelham—a typical Russell observation.

"How do I look?" Corrine smoothed her hair back and faced him.

"Great," he answered without looking.

"How would you know?"

He turned away from the mirror, where he was fixing his collar. "That dress isn't my favorite."

"What's wrong with it?"

"Too stretchy across the top. It makes you look flat."

"I *am* flat." She pictured Hilary's breasts, their volume and thrust.

"No you're not." He seemed to take this personally, as if she were devaluing marital property. For her part, Corrine was quite happy with her endowment and secretly believed that cup size had an inverse ratio to IQ. "Well, thirty-four barely B doesn't exactly count as stacked."

"You asked my opinion, my love."

"Go see if Storey's in her pj's yet. Since I've got to change."

While she didn't necessarily share Russell's opinion on the dress, she now felt self-conscious—a bad way to start out an evening. Suddenly, it was all about tits.

"Hey, Mom," Jeremy said. "Can humans transform themselves?"

"What do you mean, honey?"

"I mean, can they change into other things?"

Puzzled, she finally looked away from the vanity and saw he was playing with one of those Transformer robots that can be converted into trucks and tanks and planes. "That's a very good question, honey."

"Well, can they?"

"Better ask your father."

# 2

Everywhere he looked, there was a black Suburban with smoked windows, idling curbside or double-parked, like a crocodile lurking beside a riverbank. Yesterday, this same vehicle, or one identical to it, had been standing outside his gym, but when Luke approached, it had disappeared into the current of uptown traffic before he'd thought to take down the license number. Though he hadn't noticed anything when he flagged a cab outside the New School, the black hulk had been behind him since they'd come up from the underpass in front of Grand Central, trailing him up Park, making the turn onto Eightieth and then onto Lexington, passing slowly as his cab pulled to the curb outside the apartment building where his daughter was meeting her psychiatrist.

When, a few minutes later, he confided his suspicions to Ashley, who was surprised, if not necessarily thrilled, to see him standing on the sidewalk, she rolled her eyes with that exasperation that she seemed to reserve for her credulous father.

"Do you know how many black Suburbans there are in the city? Half the girls in school get picked up in them."

She was right, of course. In the last decade, they'd become as ubiquitous as Lincoln Town Cars, the hypertrophied stealth vehicle of urban wealth.

"You realize I've got study group at Bethany's house in a few minutes?" she added impatiently.

"Actually, I thought maybe you could blow her off and we'd go to Starbucks or something."

She seemed to weigh this option for a moment. "It's our first one. After the summer and all."

"Well, then, I'll walk you over," he said, trying to hide his disappointment.

"I think Mom may be right," she said as they headed west on Eightieth. "You've got too much time on your hands."

This remark he chose to ignore. "How was school?"

"Okay."

"You happy with your teachers?"

"Uh-huh."

"So you think I gave enough money to the capital fund last year?" He still couldn't get over the fact that one of the mothers had informed Sasha, over lunch last year, that in order to get the best teachers, a girl's parents were expected to give at least ten thousand on top of the tuition, which was almost thirty. Or that in the end he'd caved in. On the Upper East Side, charity tended to entail this kind of cost-benefit analysis.

"I guess."

As they walked toward Fifth, the conversation limped along in this fashion—like a pedestrian with a stunted leg.

He left her at the door of the limestone Beaux Arts town house. "Your mom and I are going out tonight."

"I know," she said, turning in the doorway. "To the benefit at the zoo. Didn't Mom tell you I'm going, too? She had an extra table, so I invited some friends."

. . .

Letting himself into his apartment, Luke sought out his wife, who was being groomed by her hair and makeup team, and stood outside the master bedroom, reluctant to enter this buzzing, fragrant enclave. In recent years, he'd felt less and less at home in their bedroom anyway, and spent less and less time there. His alleged snoring, his midlife, middle-of-the-night, enlarged prostate–induced trips to the bathroom, the differences in their schedules—all of this added up to many nights on the daybed in the library. When he left his job, he had imagined that this would change, that the sexual fervor of their early years—or at least the companionability of their middle period—might be revived; but if anything, he spent fewer nights in the marital bed than when he was still working, and sex was strictly by appointment. Unfortunately, he still wanted her. To be relieved of that specific desire might be a blessing, as apparently it had been for other long-married husbands of his acquaintance.

Standing in the doorway, observing her in the midst of her pre-party regimen, he was reminded of Bismarck's remark about law and sausages—feminine glamour was something you didn't necessarily want to see being made. At one time, Sasha herself was strict as a bride on her wedding day about segregating their toilettes, banishing him from the bedroom in the days when she still did her own hair and makeup, but she'd long since ceased worrying about preserving that part of her mystique for him.

She was one of those celebrated beauties—women for whom the drape of a garment and the shape of the eyebrow were subjects of advanced study, who submitted themselves not only to trainers, hairdressers, and stylists but even unto the scalpels of surgeons in pursuit of a feminine ideal that they, in turn, took their modest part in shaping after their pictures appeared in the party pages of *Town & Country* and *W*. She was, in one sense, a professional beauty. In fact, Luke was still proud of her on that purely superficial level, of making an entrance with Sasha on his arm.

The hairstylist was aiming a huge blow-dryer at his wife's skull, which was somewhat disconcertingly exposed and pink—memento mori—in the jet of hot air, while her colleague dabbed at Sasha's eyes with a little brush. Finally, the stylist noticed Luke standing in the doorway and turned off the dryer.

Opening her eyes, Sasha looked at him in the mirror. "Oh, Luke, there you are. Do you think I have too much shadow?"

Her voice had shadows, husky and abraded by years of smoking—but all the more attractive for that. People were starting to say she sounded like her pal Betty Bacall. Even in this intermediate stage of preparation, she could provoke his desire, and at this moment he almost held that against her.

"Depends. Are you trying to look mysterious or slutty?"

"I thought so," Sasha said. "Let's lighten up on the shadow, Yvonne."

Although renowned for her fashion sense, courted by designers and doted on by their assistants, a perennial on the Best Dressed list—she would be sitting in the front rows once Fashion Week commenced in a matter of days—Sasha still trusted Luke's judgment on matters of basic taste and proportion, perhaps an instinct left over from the days when she dressed and groomed for him alone, or at least most especially for him.

"What are you wearing?" she asked as the hair dryer resumed its howl.

"A strapless tulle gown from Dolce & Gabbana over a push-up bra."

"What?"

"My tux." This was practically tautological—the benefit was formal.

"*Duh*. I mean which tux?"

"The Anderson & Sheppard."

"Luke, you've been wearing that thing for ten years. It's starting to shine."

"And I'm hoping to wear it another ten."

"Not to mention that it hangs on you." She turned to the girls. "Luke's lost fifteen pounds since he quit his job, which, as far as I'm concerned, is the only good thing that's come out of this whole finding-yourself kick, losing that business-lunch paunch, though I'm starting to suspect he must be having a fling. Darling," she said, "can't you wear the Ozwald Boateng I bought you in London?"

"When I'm younger."

The garment in question was cut like a cigar tube and made him look like an Oscar nominee advised by an overzealous team of stylists.

"Now that he's unemployed," Sasha said to the girls, "Luke's working on his sense of humor."

He sat down on the bed and sank slowly into the fluffy depths of the duvet. "And what will you be showing to stunning advantage?"

"Don't worry. Oscar lent me a gown from the showroom."

"I wasn't worried."

"Well, I'm just telling you what a thrifty little hausfrau you have."

He took some comfort in the verb, with its imputation of possession.

"It's *beyond*," Sasha said.

"Just *wait* till you see it," Clarice said.

"It's to die," the other one said.

"Totally to die."

The blow-dryer started up again.

He looked around as if to reacquaint himself with the room. While the public rooms were austerely neoclassical, in the style that had become fashionable in their little corner of the world in the nineties, the bedroom was a pastel nest, the inner chamber of a queen bee, all padded and layered in patterned and quilted fabrics from Fortuny, Scalamandre, and Brunschwig.

"Can you think of any reason," he asked once the blow-dryer stopped, "why anyone would be following me?"

"What do you mean?"

"I mean I keep seeing the same black Suburban everywhere I go."

"He's also working on his paranoia," Sasha announced to her groomers, "now that he has all this time on his hands." She turned to Luke: "Maybe you should be writing a thriller instead of some book about samurai movies." Back to the girls: "He spent a year in Tokyo when he was working for Morgan and bought into the whole Bushido thing. Of course, all the investment bankers like to think of themselves as Toshiro Mifune in *Yojimbo*, fearlessly slicing down the competition. That whole *Art of War* thing. He's rented a little studio over on Seventy-sixth to write, but I think he's probably using it to entertain exotic women. Or maybe to look at Internet porn."

"Just trying to stay out of your way, dearest," Luke said.

She wasn't actually worried about him straying; only about his self-imposed sabbatical. Although he'd determined six months ago that they would be able to maintain their current opulent manner of living for some years to come, even if he failed to resume working, she was alarmed at the prospect of a declining standard of living, or even a static one. Were it up to her, Sasha would have been perfectly willing to trade back the fifteen pounds he'd lost for the seven-figure income without a second thought, and, in fact, the market slide of the past spring had suddenly seemed to bear out her fears. As yet, he hadn't confided the extent of their losses, but he was the principal investor in an independent film-production company that was, he suspected, on the verge of collapse after an overambitious expansion into broadband, which he himself, as their former investment banker, had encouraged back in the days when they were shoveling money at every twenty-five-year-old with a laptop and a business plan.

Whatever her concerns about her monthly allowance, Sasha seemed slightly embarrassed at having a husband whose place in the community was no longer clearly defined. He thought of himself as a ronin, a samurai without a master, and somehow he imagined she would share his excitement about this freedom, that she might find it romantic, even sexy, to have a husband who wasn't just another suit.

As part of his program of exploration and personal improvement, he'd planned to spend the summer traveling through Europe with his family, but Sasha had been loath to miss out on the social season in Southampton, as had their daughter, who seemed to believe that an hour spent without her friends was a hideous waste; in the end, they'd settled for two unhappy weeks in Italy.

"They have a term for guys like Luke," Sasha announced. "Men who cash out their winnings early and leave the table. There're dozens of them around town. *Walking ghosts.* That's what they call them. Isn't that good?"

"Hell, I wish I could retire," said Clarice, pointing her blow-dryer at the ceiling. "I mean, isn't that like everybody's dream?"

"Luke, I think we've found your next wife."

To her credit, Clarice blushed.

"What's this about Ashley going to the benefit?" He would have preferred to have this conference in private, but his irritation drove him forward. "I really wish you'd consulted me about this. I can't see why she needs to attend these kinds of events at her age. Especially on a school night."

"We had an extra table and I thought it would be nice for her to host her friends. Don't be such a stick-in-the-mud."

"She's thirteen years old, Sasha."

"Fourteen. I seem to recall you moping around at the birthday party last month."

"And if you'd had your way, it would have been her Sweet Sixteen. Isn't she precocious *enough,* for Christ's sake?"

"What's the harm? It's important to socialize her."

"Prepare her for a life of charity balls?"

"She'll be with her friends. She's going directly to Bethany's house and changing there, so we'll meet her at the zoo."

"Just because Bethany's mother lets her dress like a slut and hang out till dawn."

Luke had finally realized how seriously his wife's ambitions for their daughter diverged from his own three years ago when he'd picked up the Sunday *Times* magazine one morning and discovered a full color picture of her standing in front of their building in a Gucci trench coat, under the headline YOUNG FASHION PLATES OF MANHAT-TAN. He should have made a stand then. Or somewhere along the way. Instead, he had allowed it to happen while he spent most of his waking hours making a career that bankrolled a style of living that he did not, he suddenly realized, find amusing.

The other reason he was upset about Ashley's presence at the benefit was that this "extra table" would have cost at least ten grand.

After changing into the tux, he drifted out to the rarely used double-height living room—which seemed to be holding its breath, as if awaiting a crew from *Architectural Digest* or *House & Garden* to set up and shoot it—checking out what appeared to be a new Christian Liagre daybed he was almost certain he hadn't seen before, then remembered Sasha threatening to update the decor with some contemporary pieces if they couldn't redecorate this year. "The whole Biedermeier neoclassical look is so mid-nineties," she'd concluded. For that matter, he wondered if he recognized the carpet—was it the same Tabriz or Shiraz he'd been walking on for years, or had it been replaced recently? For some reason, it looked different.

The light was going fast, the days getting shorter, although the heat of summer lingered in the air outside. From the window, Luke looked out over the water towers of Fifth Avenue to the park, studying the senescence of the daylight, which seemed almost viscous, ready to coagulate—trying to register that perfect moment of transition from day to evening, that instant when the light, in dying, was most nearly itself.

It was the hour of anticipation and preparation, the still pivot between the activities of the day and the promises of the night. He felt as if he was waiting for something to happen. Something miraculous. Something other than the gala beginning of another officially sanctioned autumn season. Wasn't that the promise of the city—that anything could happen—the possibility of riot and reinvention? Or had it been revoked somewhere along the way . . . while he was in the Hamptons this summer, when he was still working downtown and wouldn't have noticed? When he'd turned forty?

Finally, Sasha stood framed in the doorway, vibrating, it seemed to him, with the knowledge of her own creamy beauty, her hair a golden helmet, wearing something that looked like a rippling golden sheet secured over one shoulder. Diana the huntress.

Jesus, he thought. She looks edible.

"So? Isn't the dress *beyond*?"

"Definitely."

"Isn't it to die?"

"Well," he said, having never quite gotten used to this figure of her speech, though he heard it a dozen times a day. He pulled her toward him and raised his hand to stroke her forehead.

"*Luke,*" she said, squirming out of his grasp. "My *hair.*"

The elevator doors opened on Luke's floor, revealing a tuxedoed Tupper Carlson, ruler of a downtown brokerage house and the president of the co-op, descending from the penthouse with his great blue heron of a wife, notable for her stick legs and prominent beak. (Five years ago, with his application pending before the co-op committee, Luke had given five thousand to the Audubon Society, on whose board she aptly sat.) Her pencil-thin, sinewy arms and knotted hands were at odds with her taut glazed-porcelain face. Sixty-year-old arms and hands, forty-year-old face. Dr. Baker her Praxiteles, as Sasha had once remarked.

"What a lovely dress," Sasha said.

"Oh, this? I found it in the closet. I can't even remember where I bought it."

"It's *beyond,*" Luke said, smiling stupidly.

This regal couple always conveyed a certain irritation when forced to share the elevator, having largely insulated themselves from unexpected infusions of humanity with their chauffeur-driven cars, private jets, and private clubs. As board president, Carlson had been responsible for replacing the elevator man with a control console and video system at the door, which allowed the doormen to regulate the destination of the elevator—presumably to spare Carlson the discomfort of sharing the cramped conveyance with a representative of the lower orders, although he'd justified the change in economic terms. It was also Carlson who, in order to prevent the lesser rich from infesting the building, had raised the cash-purchase requirement from 75 to 100 percent, and the net-worth requirement from double to triple the purchase price of the apartment, although Luke had circumvented these mandates by borrowing half a million from his firm and then, after his application was approved, repaying it by taking out a secret mortgage. Everybody did it, of course, except for those like Carlson, who were so rich that they sneered at the tax deduction.

It seemed to Luke at this moment, as they silently descended, that Tupper's demeanor was even more citric than usual, as if he knew about some of Luke's recent market losses, which wasn't impossible, given his position in the financial community; the only thing more distasteful than a man of declining means to someone of his caste and temperament was such a man who held shares in one's co-op.

"After you," Luke said when the doors finally opened.

Fifth Avenue was clogged with limos and Town Cars, but after ten minutes they had nearly reached the entrance, where blue police barriers funneled them between the scrum of paparazzi and curious civilians into the Central Park Zoo. As their driver tried to ease over toward the curb, he was cut off by a black Mercedes, followed closely by a black Suburban.

"There it is again," Luke said.

"There what is?"

"The black Suburban."

"For God's sake, Luke."

"And if I'm not mistaken, that's Melman's Mercedes," he said. "The way I hear it, his thugs are completely out of control. A cab sideswiped one of his cars the other night and they opened fire right there on Seventy-third Street. He had to make some calls and spread some cash around to keep that out of the papers."

"I don't know what you're babbling about."

The two cars inched forward ahead of them. Three hulks in suits jumped out of the Suburban while it was still moving. The two cars docked in front of the entrance. A fourth bodyguard leapt from the front seat of the Mercedes, conferred with the others and reconnoitered the crowd, then finally walked back to the car and tapped gently before opening the rear door.

From his window, Luke glimpsed Bernard Melman and his escort—not the wife but the daughter, Caroline, from his first marriage. Melman, a head shorter, was intermittently visible, or at least the skunklike white stripe of his pate was. Luke glanced over at his wife, who was checking herself out in the mirror of her compact, apparently unaware of Melman, who was rumored to be on the brink of a divorce, his wife having taken up residence in their Palm Beach house.

Finally, their car nosed up to the entrance. Sasha tugged Luke's bow tie down at the corners, imparting a less rigid, more insouciant look. He jumped out of the car and held the door open for Sasha, who elicited a hue and cry from the photographers. Sasha took Luke's arm and marched forward, amid calls of "Sasha, over here." "Smile, Sasha." "Who are you wearing?"

Luke let Sasha set the pace as she paused in front of her favorite photographers, letting her step out ahead, and admiring her himself: a figurehead braving the dark waves of paparazzi surging and yearning on either side of her, illuminated by flashes of lightning.

"Come on, Luke, give us a smile."

Amazing, he thought, trying to summon a semblance of a smile, that one of them remembered the name of Sasha's husband. The benefit circuit was the realm of wives; husbands were merely the bankers, black-and-white shadows of their brilliantly plumed mates.

"Just one by yourself, Sasha."

Luke stepped away. Sasha rolled her eyes and pursed her lips apologetically, as if to say, What a bother. But she obliged the photographers' every request.

"One more. This way."

"That's the third great lie," Sasha said when she rejoined Luke. "When a photographer says 'Just one more.'"

"Only if you're a beautiful woman."

"Well," she said, rewarding him with a smile all his own. "Around here, the competition is mostly geriatric."

Finally, they were past the gauntlet and sheltered by a tented tunnel that emerged into the courtyard of the zoo. Luke announced himself to one of the young women with clipboards who flanked the inner entrance—all of them in black, alert, ready at a moment's notice to be either slavish or slightly imperious, as the situation demanded. She repeated his name interrogatively, as if testing its validity.

"Here are your place cards, Mr. and Mrs. McGavock," a second young woman said, then whispered something to the first.

"Get me a drink, darling," Sasha said. "I'm going to say hi to the girls." She gestured toward a group over near the seal pool.

At the bar, Luke stood behind a redheaded socialite known for her wit. "I was married to Tom for six months," she said to her girlfriend. "It was a case of mistaken identity, basically. Someone said he was the biggest prick at Time Warner and I misheard the verb."

She'd said the same thing to Luke at a previous benefit, when she was still married to the man in question, who had subsequently moved into the Carlyle when the couple split. Word was that he'd left her after catching her with her head between the legs of his partner's wife. To which one listener replied, "Yeah, but why did he leave?"

Carrying the two drinks, he looked around for Sasha and caught sight of her huddled with Melman, the only man present to whom even the movie stars paid court. He watched from a distance as Sasha whispered in Melman's ear and the deputy mayor waited respectfully for his moment. Melman was perhaps not quite as small as Luke liked to imagine him, although the hulking bodyguards who accompanied him everywhere—which some saw as an affectation to underline his importance—did nothing to make him seem taller. Bernie was one of the few corporate raiders of the eighties to have flourished in the subsequent decade. Time travelers from that era would scarcely have recognized the socially prominent philanthropist who was practically this evening's unacknowledged guest of honor. Although he had left in his wake a Hoxsey's army of disappointed investors and wrecked companies, it was said that he had never been on the wrong end of a deal, and, unlike some of his peers, he'd never been indicted. Very few people had the knowledge or the interest to evaluate his arcane financial dealings, and his victims tended to dwell in the outer provinces of the republic, where goods were manufactured, or in the arid regions of corporate finance, far from the gossip columns and society pages of

Manhattan. During his early years in New York, he had been caricatured as a barbarian and a parvenu. His current eminence and good press stemmed as much from genuine admiration for his vast fortune as from fear of his power and influence, which now included certain branches of the media. The rumors of his impending divorce seemed plausible—Melman and his wife hadn't been photographed together in months. There was also, Luke knew, a certain buzz surrounding his friendship with Sasha. They had been spotted lunching together recently, not at the Four Seasons or Aureole or one of the consecrated stations of their mutual circuit, where their presence would be so conspicuous as to merit no reproach, but at a dowdy Italian spot on Third Avenue in the Fifties. Sasha had explained the rendezvous plausibly enough—she was hitting him up for a big donation on behalf of the ballet, on whose board she served—if not the unlikely venue, where they might have believed it was unlikely to see anyone they knew. Luke found it more than curious that his wife, of all people, would have chosen to dine anonymously with such an illustrious acquaintance, rather than showing herself off from a choice banquette in the Grill Room or on the sidewalk in front of La Goulue. As it turned out, some helpful soul called in the sighting to the *Post*'s "Page Six," which reported it the next day with the comment that the restaurant in question hadn't seen such glamorous diners since Kennedy was president.

# 3

ow's it going in here?" Russell asked, sticking his head in the kids' bedroom.

"Dad, it's just girls, okay?"

Storey, naked and pink, was showing Hilary her wardrobe—the various outfits spread out on the bed. Hilary had a towel wrapped around her chest and another around her head. In this refuge of dewy femininity, Russell felt like an intruder—a hulking male animal. "Mom wants you in your pajamas," he said, as if uncertain of his own authority, and retreated to the living room—or so he thought of it, having grown up in suburban "colonials"—loft living presenting certain problems of nomenclature. Jeremy was wrestling with Washington, who, for all his dangerous proclivities, was remarkably good with kids. Unlike Russell, he was looking very downtown, black suit over a black shirt with a seriously long and pointy collar—black on black on black. Ever since his bald spot had taken over, he'd been shaving his head.

"Yo, Crash, you better change before the other guests get here."

"I *am* changed," Russell said.

" 'Scuse me, bro. I thought you'd just gotten back from guest lecturing at some fu—" He stopped short in deference to Jeremy, who was now on his shoulder. "—some freaking prep school."

"My Transformer can change into a battleship," Jeremy said.

"Now *that's* cool. If only your dad could be as hip as you are."

Corrine came out as the guest of honor emerged from the elevator with his wife. Jim Crespi was turning forty-five, although he could have passed for thirty-five in his vintage sharkskin suit and his record-store clerk's glasses. He proffered a bottle of Cristal to his hostess.

"You're not supposed to bring a present," Corrine said, unsettled by such extravagance from a man facing bankruptcy.

"Jim believes in cutting back on the necessities," Judy said, "but he can't imagine drinking Moët." Her fresh Jean Seberg haircut emphasized the fierce planes of her face, which seemed too taut to accommodate a smile.

"Let's open it," Jim said, "before the bank repossesses it."

It was hardly an auspicious moment in their lives, the production company he'd founded and taken to such heights having collapsed this past spring in a heap of lawsuits. When it became clear that Judy wasn't going to throw the usual surprise party, due to heightened domestic tension verging on violence and legal counsel, Russell had stepped in. By his own account, Jim had nearly everything tied up in the company, and Judy, who sold multiacre apartments to very wealthy clients, deeply resented the fact that her husband had squandered his fortune, although, like most fortunes of the era, its existence had been more virtual than actual. When she'd first met him, Jim had been the wittiest and the sexiest man in the room, in almost any room, riding the success of the little indie movie that had grossed fifty million; he had dated half a dozen of the most sought-after women in town, including at least two whom Corrine would have been pleased to see him settle down with. But perhaps because Judy reminded him of his mother, he'd somehow fallen in love with the only one his friends universally disliked, who, after selling him an apartment, proceeded to make him miserable until he married her and then made him more miserable still. It was hard to tell if this latest trouble was terminal, since the marriage, viewed from the outside, had been on life support for years, despite having produced two healthy, well-adjusted children. Since Jim was Russell's friend and Corrine had no independent communication with Judy, she couldn't really tell; Russell was reluctant to pry, or perhaps it was more relevant that both he and Jim were men, bound by the code of heterosexual masculine stoicism. Whenever she asked Russell how Jim or any of his other friends were doing, the answer, invariably, was "Fine."

The gathering achieved critical mass with the simultaneous arrival of Carlo and Nancy, stepping out of the elevator together like some kind of binary visual joke, a one and a zero; Michelin man Carlo bearing bags full of cheeses, greens, and oils, and stick-skinny Nancy in her Pucci, carrying yet another bottle of Cristal. Carlo joined Russell in the kitchen while Nancy attempted to communicate with the children, who could tell that she had no real interest and therefore ignored her accordingly.

Corrine put the children down when Russell gave her the fifteen-minute warning; they demanded a story from their aunt.

"Aunt Hilary's busy with the grown-ups."

"She promised us a story," Jeremy said.

"She promises a lot of things, but I'm the boss around here."

"Are you mad at Aunt Hilary?" Storey asked.

"I love your aunt Hilary. She's my sister."

"But sometimes you seem mad at her."

"I'll send her in to say good night," Corrine said, for once happy to pull their door shut behind her.

"When I got to Hollywood, the studios were dead," Cody Erhardt was telling a rapt audience, "but they didn't know it. They kept making Doris Day movies right through the sixties. Then *Easy Rider* came along and they finally realized they didn't have a fucking clue. They rolled out the red carpet for anybody who had long hair and a film degree. Me and Marty and Peter and the gang. That's when the kids took over the administration building. *Chinatown, Five Easy Pieces, The Last Picture Show, Shampoo.*"

After Hilary named his own contribution to the list, Corrine caught her eye, signaled toward the children's room.

Erhardt shrugged—an approximation of modesty.

"Didn't you know Ashby?" Hilary said.

"Did I know him? He practically lived in my guest room. If I could remember half of the shit we talked about . . . Well, the whole thing lasted six, seven years. I knew the glory days were over the afternoon I went to Frank Mancuso's office and saw that Market Research had moved next door to the head of Production. That was all she wrote. I could give you the exact date if I had my journals. Or it might have been the day that *Jaws* opened wide. But then, Steven was a mole, just pretending to inhale, playing for the other side."

"Hilary," Corrine said, "the children would like to borrow you for a moment."

"Forget cultural stereotypes," Washington was saying when the sisters returned from settling the children. "Girls are *vicious*, man."

"You had to have kids to figure *that* out?" Nancy Tanner asked.

"I'm taking Tamara to a birthday party on Park; it's the usual fucking madhouse, baby-sitter late, crosstown traffic, so I arrive half an hour late. All the other little girls have already formed into packs. And even her friends treat her like some leper, simply by default, because they need a scapegoat, someone to vent their nastiness on. Salt and bile and everything vile. That's what they're really made of. Except for Tam, of course."

"They're just really clannish at that age," Corrine said, somehow afraid the whole racial issue was about to rear its head. She didn't want the fact that Tamara was the product of a black father and a white mother to be the real reason for her social banishment, even though she always immediately suspected exactly this kind of injustice.

"If you think it's something they grow out of," Nancy said, "try being the only single girl at a big dinner party on Park Avenue."

"Or Brentwood," Hilary added.

"The veal, she is here," Russell announced, carrying a steaming tray to the table and presenting it with a flourish, dipping it ostentatiously in Carlo's direction. "Why don't we just pass it?"

"Looking good," Carlo said. "Nice glaze. That's the sign of a chef who knows how to make a sauce."

"Oh my God," Nancy said, "my *eyes* feel fat just looking at that thing."

Corrine stood up to help with the side dishes.

"Russell has decided it's fall, despite the weather."

"And that's pink Peruvian salt in the little black dish," the host pointed out.

Washington looked appalled. "Pink Peruvian *what*?"

"And the other one's *fleur de sel* from Guérande."

"Would a line of either," Nancy asked, "do a girl any good?"

"This is such an amazing view of the towers," Judy said, motioning toward the downtown skyline framed in the window. Possibly, she was trying to make up for remarking on her last visit that if they put fifty grand into the place, they'd have "a nice cozy little loft." Her clientele would consider this raw space, with its exposed wiring, patched walls, and undulant wood floor. Judy had gotten their own loft renovated, trading favors with designers and contractors she worked with.

"It's nice at night," Corrine said of the view, "but the thing is, we're in shadow half the day."

"What are we drinking?" Jim asked, holding up the bottle.

Oh, Jesus, here it comes, Corrine thought: the wine speech.

"It's a Super-Tuscan," Russell said. "Sangiovese and cabernet. We discovered it on a trip a few summers ago. It's produced at this beautiful hilltop estate outside Greve."

"What makes it so super?" Nancy asked.

"Throw back six or seven glasses and you'll be flying," Jim said. "Able to leap tall buildings."

"A few more and you'll be impervious to pain," Carlo added.

"Here's to superpowers," Hilary said, raising her glass.

"It's a technical term," Russell explained somewhat peevishly, "for new-style wines grown in the old Chianti region."

Carlo piled veal onto Nancy's plate while taking the opportunity with his free hand to squeeze her waist. "Hey, baby, we gotta put some meat on those bones."

When Corrine returned with the asparagus, her sister was in the middle of one of her movie-star stories.

"So, we're on this loch, you know, in Scotland. And in between takes, he strips off his clothes and dives in, swims around for a bit. And, you know, the water's like forty degrees. Then he climbs out and walks across the fucking heather. Heather, gorse, whatever they call it. The best boy and the gaffer are sitting there gawking. They can't believe what they're seeing; it's like a fucking tree trunk. And he notices them staring and he stops and says, 'What are you fucking looking at? *Yours* doesn't shrink in cold water?'"

Corrine had definitely missed something. "*Who's* this?"

"Next you're gonna tell me he can dance," Washington said.

"It's actually true," Cody said.

"Wait a minute," Corrine said. "When did you ever make a movie in Scotland?"

"How about a little suspension of disbelief?" Jim said.

"It *is* true," Nancy said.

"*What's* true?"

"What? You've, like, seen the *organ* in question?" Russell asked.

"Actually, no," said Nancy apologetically, as if at a loss to explain how she had failed to get up close and personal with this particular penis. "But I have a friend who, uh, sampled the goods. And hobbled for three days afterward."

"Well, then it *must* be true," Russell snorted.

"Do I hear the sound of masculine insecurity?" Hilary asked.

Seeing Russell blush, Corrine came to his rescue. "Russell has nothing to be insecure about."

He rewarded her with a look of sheepish gratitude.

She almost added, At least not that I can remember, since she wasn't sure when she'd last come into physical contact with the subject of this allusion.

"That's sweet," said Nancy. "Of course, Corrine hasn't been doing a lot of comparative analysis over the last twenty years."

"Really," Hilary chimed in. "We're not too sure about her expertise in this area." The party girls showing a flash of slutty solidarity.

Corrine laughed with the rest, although she resented the implication. How did they know what she'd been up to? She was sick and tired of playing the role of model wife for their friends, for whom Calloway was a byword for marital stability—or was it stagnation? Everyone had long since forgotten their separation, their decade-old troubles; she wanted to jump up and remind them, say, Hey, remember when I fucked his best friend?

She wanted to say that people have secrets—even secret lives. True, her own portfolio of secrets was slim and yellowing with age. A long flirtation with Duane Peters that stopped just short of consummation. And, long ago, Jeff Pierce, Russell's best friend and alter ego . . . the bittersweetness of that love sealed forever by his death. Hardly a day went by—no, that wasn't true. The saddest thing of all was that many days did go by without her thinking of Jeff, though she had for a long time afterward. She and Russell had survived that revelation, barely, partly because she'd downplayed it, made it sound like a one-off, an accidental crime of opportunity. She'd thought of Jeff again tonight while listening to Jim, who had some of the same reckless charm, that Dionysian air of passionate excess, although Jeff had a streak of self-loathing that counterbalanced his egotism . . . and anyway, it all began to seem faintly ludicrous—like long hair—beyond a certain age. Fame, however, could extend that horizon almost indefinitely—especially for men. Cody Erhardt, for example. Who was a little overweight and currently a little drunk.

"I grew up in the era of the existential hero," Erhardt was saying, pounding the table with his fist. "We'd inherited modernism and we were running with it. The quest for meaning in a meaningless universe. *Breathless, La Dolce Vita, Taxi Driver.* We took up the challenge when the novelists retreated to their universities and their metafictional masturbation. It was a tag-team event between rock and roll and the, if you will excuse the expression, cinema—the search for authenticity. That was back in the seventies, when you guys were watching *Sesame Street*. Seven years ago, I saw *Pulp Fiction* and I thought, Fuck me, I'm over the hill. That's it. That was pretty much the birth of the ironic hero. The whole wink-and-nudge school of directorial sensibility. The glorification of the inauthentic and the ersatz. Everything I believe in's thoroughly out of date."

Was it her imagination, Corrine wondered, or was there a little cross-table chemistry between Jim and Hilary, who seemed to be aiming her Hollywood reminiscences in his direction.

"I had a part in that movie," she was saying. "Just a walk-on. I was the girl who gets out of the cab just before the motorcycle chase scene."

"I remember that," Jim said. "But what exactly was the dramatic justification for your toplessness?"

Hilary threw a piece of bread across the table at him. "I wasn't."

"If only," Carlo said. "Jesus." Staring at Hilary's chest, he seemed genuinely moved by this hypothetical vision. His large appetites were part of his charm, though probably not to his wife. He seemed, to Corrine, like an octopus—reaching out with one hand for the bread and meat, smoking with another, drinking with yet another, while simultaneously groping the nearest females in sight, drawing everything toward his mouth, which couldn't possibly be big enough. . . .

"Thank you, Carlo." Hilary dipped her head, a minibow.

"I'm sorry," Jim said, "what I meant to say was, What was the justification for your *not* being topless?"

How in the hell, Corrine wondered, had she never noticed it before? It was all about tits. Ever since she was thirteen, Hilary had been bigger than Corrine—but when had she become such a *C*?

"You're an *actress*?" Judy asked, looking sourly at Hilary.

"Not really. I just have a lot of friends in the business."

"You got me babe," Cody offered.

"Because if you're thinking my husband can put you in a movie, think again. He's in Chapter Eleven."

"Hilary works in a gallery," Corrine said, piercing the silence that followed this remark. "Dade-Grenfeld, on Doheny. It's actually one of the top galleries in L.A." She suddenly felt protective of her little sister, eager to make her sound like something other than a blond-bimbo party girl, starlet, amateur hooker. . . .

"I did until recently," Hilary added cheerfully. "Actually, I'm kind of taking some time off at the moment. I'm working on a novel."

Russell was rolling his eyes, but Corrine thought, Why not? It sounded about as plausible as any of Hilary's other ambitions. She realized that she not only hadn't caught up on her sister's recent movements; she was afraid to ask, fearful that she would be called upon to be her sister's keeper, a thought shot through with guilt as she reckoned how much she owed Hilary. The children, in fact. How could you ever repay anybody for *that*?

"I have no doubt you'll find someone to give you half a million for it," Washington said. "First novels, especially first novels by chicks, are the book equivalent of Internet stocks, untainted by sales histories, unwritten first novels being the purest form of speculative, faith-based publishing. If you had a publishing track record, now that would work against you. But having none, you'll find arms and doors open. We just paid over four hundred grand for a chick who published her first story in *The New Yorker*'s summer fiction issue."

"Well," Hilary said, "first I have to finish it."

"No, no, don't do that. Once it's finished, the limitless promise of the hypothetical novel will be circumscribed by your execution, and then later by its sales history."

"You know," Russell said, "one of my authors—a well-known, critically acclaimed novelist—he plays golf every weekend with a bunch of doctors. One Saturday, this brain surgeon, top of his class at Johns Hopkins, he turns to him between holes and says, 'Hey, I'm thinking about writing a novel in my spare time. Maybe you could give me a few pointers.' My guy stops the cart and says, 'You know, that's a hell of a coincidence. Because I've always wanted to see what brain surgery is really like. Maybe you could show me the basics, help me get started.'"

"I feel the same way," Carlo said, "when some fucking editor asks me how to make pesto."

"I'm not trying to, like, write *Anna Karamazov*," Hilary said.

"It's more commercial . . . kind of *Valley of the Dolls,* a girl in Hollywood kind of story."

"Just stick to the West Coast," said Nancy. "I don't need any competition."

"And don't let her fuck the writer," Jim said. "Unless she's Polish."

"So, are you in New York for a while?" Carlo asked, leering theatrically into Hilary's cleavage.

"That remains to be seen," she said.

Corrine exchanged a worried look with her husband.

Judy said, "It must be so hard, starting from scratch at your age."

"Actually, I have lots of friends here," Hilary said, casting a glance at Jim, who suddenly looked nervous and skittish.

Helping Russell clear the plates, Corrine suddenly realized how desperately she needed to pee, at which point she also knew she was probably a little buzzed; certainly she'd had more than usual. The bathroom door was locked, so she took the opportunity to check on the kids, who were sleeping soundly, Jeremy as still as death beneath the covers, Storey pinwheeled across her bed, having thrown off all of hers. The bathroom door was still closed, and she looked down the hall, taking inventory of the guests; she had just concluded that Hilary and Cody were missing, when they emerged from the bathroom, bright and innocent and slightly amused by something, possibly themselves.

When she returned from the bathroom, Jim was advancing a new theme: children as the new social accessory. "So we're sitting on Gibson Beach, chatting away with Davis, who has his kid, Dalton, for the weekend. When who comes churning up the beach, all breathless, but Victoria."

"Victoria is Davis's ex," Corrine said, annotating for Hilary and Carlo.

"Who cheated once too often on Davis," Jim said, "who finally threw in the towel and divorced her, the mother of his child. The child who sees said mother only on those rare occasions when she's stopping off at home to change between parties, 'cause otherwise she's trolling the social ponds of Manhattan and Palm Beach and Southampton for eligible men."

"That's the point of this shtory," said Judy slurringly. "The *bad mother*."

Looking over at Judy, Corrine realized that she was drunk, her face the color of a boiled lobster.

"No," Jim said wearily, "the point is a larger sociological lesson about the culture. About the way we live now, if you will. So there's Davis on the beach with his son, exercising his weekly custodial rights, when his ex races up the beach as if she'd just gotten advance notice of the Second Coming and wants to share the news with everyone on the beach."

"Oh, *please*," said Judy. "I call that overwriting. Jim can't just *tell* a story. He has to *overtell* it."

Jim assumed the air of Job and continued. "So anyway—beach, child, two ex-spouses. 'Davis, quick, I need Dalton,' she gasps. 'What do you mean, you need Dalton?' asks Davis. 'Caroline Kennedy's having a party,' she says. To which Davis responds, understandably, 'So? What does that have to do with Dalton?' 'It's a party for kids,' says Victoria."

"I don't have to listen to this," Judy said, rising to her feet, swaying and nearly capsizing before she gripped the back of her chair.

"Darling, it's just a story. A funny story about two—"

"I think we all know what it's about."

"It *does* sound like Victoria," Russell said, rising in concert with Jim.

"Don't roll your eyes at me," Judy shouted, supporting herself on the back of the chair. "Our kids happened to enjoy that party. You think I don't know you've been telling people I'm a bad mother? Well, maybe you think Hilary'd be better at it. Helen fucking Keller could see what's going on here. The little looks. The little footsie. Was she the one you fucked in L.A. last year? Maybe you ought to have kids with *her*. We know she's fertile, though she doesn't seem all that damn interested in her biological offspring, does she? Kind of a masculine idea, donating your genetic material and moving on? Is that the kind of mother you want? You think Russell and Corrine are such perfect parents, the golden couple, the ideal goddamn family, Corrine the perfect mother—well, at least my children are *mine*. I didn't need to borrow eggs from my slutty sister. They're my children—*mine*—and you'll never take them away from me, not in a million bazillion years. . . ."

Eyelids drooping, shoulders slumped, she appeared to be on the verge of passing out; but instead, she suddenly launched herself in the direction of the elevator, as fleet and agile as a gazelle, dodging Jeremy's tricycle and disappearing from view.

"I'm so sorry," Jim croaked. "Let me see if I can . . ." He hesitated and peered toward the entryway, where they could hear the sound of the elevator door clattering open.

"Let me," said Russell.

Corrine was stunned. She did not understand how she figured in the equation of the Crespis' marriage, or why her convoluted reproductive history had suddenly become the focus of Judy's tirade.

"No, please." Jim touched Russell's shoulder and then turned to the table. "Please excuse us. My wife's not herself."

They sat in silence as he followed, albeit more slowly, his wife's exit, no one saying a word until they heard the elevator door close for the second time.

"Did I miss something?" Carlo asked.

"Two affairs," Washington said, "one miscarriage, and ten years of deepening domestic misery."

"Sounds pretty standard," Cody said.

"Well, I'm suddenly feeling a lot better about my marriage," Carlo confided.

"I'm feeling a lot better about being single," Nancy added.

Russell said, "At least we didn't have to sing Happy fucking Birthday."

"So who's going to the fashion shows this week?" Nancy asked.

Later, from her reclining vantage on the couch, Corrine counted thirteen wine bottles and three water bottles on the table, looming over the bloody wineglasses, the overflowing ashtrays, the remains of the panna cotta, and the wreckage of the cheese plate with its oozing Camembert and pocked Stilton. Still life with heartburn.

Suddenly, she wondered if Judy and Jim were fucking each other's brains out at this very moment, if strife was the corollary of great passion, an elaborately theatrical form of foreplay, if the relative tranquillity of her marital life wasn't really a joke.

She was still amazed, and somewhat saddened, by Judy's assertion that she and Russell were such a model couple to their friends, even though Judy had only floated the idea in order to shoot it down. Because they once, actually, had been a kind of ideal, the golden girl and boy. She wouldn't have put it that way herself, but she heard it over and over again from their friends—all about the college sweethearts who'd sailed off into the world together. For many years, they were the example that everyone pointed to, the haven of domesticity for their single friends and later a harbor of solace and inspiration to which they returned when their first marriages foundered.

"You people have got to update your taste in music," Hilary said. "Is Russell even aware that Jimmy Carter is no longer president? I think they ought to print an expiration date on CDs. I mean, sure, *Blood on the Tracks* is great—"

"It's the music we played in college," Corrine said, suddenly indignant, "the sound track of falling in love." At that moment, they were listening to Squeeze's "Black Coffee in Bed," which had come a little later, the early years in New York. "Elvis Costello is still hip, isn't he?"

"You got to hear the Strokes." Hilary was sprawled beside her sister, holding her wineglass up to the light. Russell was in the bedroom, making a phone call to Australia, trying to catch up with one of his authors.

"Just out of curiosity," Corrine said, "did you ever fuck Jim?"

"That still doesn't justify the way she acted tonight."

Corrine laughed. "I like the idea of an immoral act gaining legitimacy in light of subsequent events."

"I kept thinking that after you left college, you'd stop talking like that. It's been—what, twenty years?"

"I keep waiting . . ." Corrine was about to say something about her sister's rampant promiscuity but decided to let it pass.

"For what?"

Corrine lifted herself up out of her deep slump in order to facilitate a serious discussion. "I don't know. It's not like I have it all figured out."

"I know you think I'm like a total flake and a slut and—"

"No, I don't think that."

"Well, anyway, I've been thinking a lot about what I want to do with my life. And for one thing, I'd like to be closer to the kids. More involved, you know?"

This declaration chilled Corrine to the bone.

"I mean, after all, I'm their biological mother. I want to see them more and I want them to get to know me. And frankly, I'm tired of L.A. and that whole phony scene. New York is so much more real, you know?"

"I think there's just as much phoniness here," Corrine said, unable to express her fear and therefore focusing on the peripheral issue. It was as if, in the course of being attacked by a slavering wild dog, she'd started to speculate about the possible danger of fleabites. "If you really get down to it. It's just not as formulaic."

"They've become real little people," Hilary said. "With, like, these real personalities and all. Do you know that Jeremy was correcting my grammar earlier? And Storey, she reminds me of how I was at that age."

It was all Corrine could do to restrain herself from screaming at this point; late as it was, she was grateful when the phone rang, the more so when it proved to be Jim, urging her to come out and meet him and Cody, who wanted to talk about her screenplay.

4

Surveying the glossy humans encircling the seal pool, Luke felt excluded, an old lion exiled from the pride to which his daughter now belonged, and it was probably too late to do anything about it. How had he let that happen? The last he remembered, she was seven. They had their own language back then, which was more or less the native tongue of Princess Land—where she claimed to have lived before descending to earth, a place populated entirely by girls, all of them princesses.

He spotted Guillermo Rezzori in a huddle of tuxedoed bankers over by the penguin house. Guillermo waved him over, but Luke waited until he'd extracted himself from the group.

"What's the matter," he asked, embracing Luke, and kissing his cheek—a gesture Luke was never quite able to take for granted, although he admired its insouciant Latin stylishness. "You look terrible."

"Thanks."

"We need to talk about the Shooting Gallery. Meet me for breakfast?"

"I don't do breakfast anymore. One of the benefits of retirement."

"You don't have to eat. We'll have coffee. Windows on the World at eight."

"All right." In fact, Luke had already planned to meet his accountant next door, at the World Financial Center, at nine.

"So, where's Sasha?"

"Off flirting."

"With whom?"

Luke shrugged.

Guillermo nodded gravely. "I happened to notice." He'd always presented himself as a great cynic, and relished tales of heterosexual folly, especially when they involved his closest friends. "Come downtown with me after this, tell me all about it. We'll make a strategy. There's a new club I need to check out."

"I fail to see how watching you cruise young boys is likely to make me feel any better."

Guillermo frowned, looked around to see who might be within earshot. He touched a finger to his lips. "Please," he whispered. "We're uptown now."

Guillermo lived a double life, believing that his sexual identity could only hinder his career in the financial world. He maintained two distinct groups of friends, Luke being one of the few who straddled lists. Luke had been his mentor at First Boston, where he'd arrived, fresh out of Harvard Business School, ambitious and scared and barely conversant in English. His foreign accent and manners had helped preserve his disguise on Wall Street: His stylishness and obsessive privacy could be attributed to his Colombian birth and upbringing by his colleagues, who viewed the world beyond Manhattan primarily in terms of investment and vacation opportunities. As far as they were concerned, he'd arrived at Harvard from nowhere—impossibly distant from the grid of prep schools, colleges, and prosperous suburbs with which they were familiar. He'd taken a brief stab at marriage with a Harvard classmate who was fully apprised of his past, and although the marriage didn't take, it remained a convenient point of reference for Guillermo—a MacGuffin to divert suspicion from the real story. While Luke had come to admire his talent and drive, it was only after he'd left the firm that they had become intimate friends, Guillermo pursuing his friendship with the same tenacity he applied to making deals and cruising bars—eager to reveal himself in all his tortured complexity. For all the energy he spent in concealing himself, he desperately needed someone on the other side to appreciate the arduous, artful ingenuity of his performance, and while many of Luke's college and Wall Street friendships were already fading, he and Guillermo had become, it would seem, the best of friends.

"I've got to find my date," he said.

"Who's the lucky girl?"

"Very pretty. Currency trader. I actually find her attractive."

"See you at the table," Luke said.

He experienced a bittersweet stirring of middle-aged desire while staring at a clutch of gangly young women—a grove of tawny, whippety limbs, bronzed over the long summer in the Hamptons, before suddenly recognizing his daughter among them. In makeup, tottering on spike heels, she looked almost old enough to be here. In the past six months, she had suddenly, frighteningly, blossomed, shooting up and shedding the extra pounds that had crazed Sasha with the specter of a chubby daughter—hence the yoga lessons, the personal trainer, the dietary supplements. He tried to compose himself as he made his way over. On a sudden impulse, he stopped short, half-concealed from the girls behind another group.

"They think they're so goddamn smart at Chapin."

"Can you believe she's hooking up with him? I mean, he goes to *Hewitt*. I mean, *really*."

"Who'd go out with a Hewitt guy?"

"Everybody's father's some supermogul and not smart—"

"Yeah, like when he graduates he'll be living on his parents' ranch in Aspen as a caretaker."

"*If* he graduates."

Luke finally interrupted this symposium. "Hi, sweetie."

"Hey, Dads," she said, looking down at the ground. She had recently reached the age at which having parents was an embarrassment. "You know Bethany and Amber."

"Of course." In fact, he had known Bethany's mother, Mitsy, quite well shortly before he got engaged to Sasha, and much as he'd enjoyed it at the time, he was horrified when his very own daughter had started running with hers. Tonight, Bethany looked like an expensive hooker with her raccoon eyes and her tiny leopard-print dress. And Amber—a jewel with a prehistoric bug inside. He was nothing if not morbid tonight.

"Long time since we've been here together," he said to his daughter. "You used to love the red pandas."

Ashley looked stricken at this reference to her recent childhood; Bethany and Amber giggled.

"What about your homework? I trust you got it done this afternoon?"

"*Dads.*"

Her friends tactfully averted their eyes.

"School's just started. We don't have any yet," she said, looking away. The final humiliation, for both of them, being that he'd backed her into a lie.

"Okay," he said cheerfully. "You girls have fun. But I'm taking you home by ten."

His daughter rolled her eyes in farewell.

He had been sitting at the table for twenty minutes when Sasha finally appeared with Casey Reynes, their eyes all glittery and bright. Casey, Amber's mother, was one of Sasha's druggy friends. Luke had somehow been under the impression that coke had largely disappeared from their circle a decade before, and was uncertain whether his wife's indulgence was a recent revival of an old party habit or if he simply had failed to notice it all these years, as he apparently had failed to notice so many other things while he was so single-mindedly pursuing his career.

Sasha took a chair at the other end of the table between Casey's husband, a partner at Goldman Sachs, and an actor invited to punch up the mix, a young man who was obviously exciting Guillermo's interest. Luke himself was seated between Trinnie Johnson and Guillermo's date, Sloane Cafferty, a fierce young trader a few years out of Radcliffe, who was morbidly fascinated by his ronin status.

"What do you *do* all day?" she asked as the waiters served the salad course.

"I read," he said. "Today, I went to the Whitney and looked at the Hoppers. And then I went to a class at the New School. Socratic Humanism."

"What's it about?"

"About? I suppose it's about being human."

"Don't you miss, you know, being in the game?"

"Not really. To tell you the truth, by the end, I really hated my job."

"Guillermo says you would've been running the firm in two years if you'd stayed."

"Luke's writing a book," said Casey, jumping into the conversation. "You know, I really should introduce you to my friend Russell Calloway; he's an editor at one of the big houses. Very intellectual. He's married to my best friend, Corrine."

Yet again, Luke wished he'd never announced his intention to write. It sounded like such a dreadful cliché, and the fact that he'd failed to accomplish anything in that direction made him feel increasingly fraudulent when the subject came up. True, Japanese cinema had been a passionate hobby for years, and he'd spent hundreds of hours watching videos of samurai movies and making notes, but the notion of actually writing something grew more remote with each passing month. Instead, he consulted reference books and sought out rare videos on the Internet. The secret ambition that had animated him in his twenties, the one he had not announced—to write a novel—seemed even more implausible. He was discovering that it was difficult to adjust to the solo formlessness and fluidity of his days after spending half a lifetime enslaved to the rhythms of the financial markets, engaged in the rigidly structured rituals of corporate enterprise.

Today, besides going to the Whitney, he'd gone to the gym, read the *Times* and the *Journal* more or less cover to cover, spent an hour trading on-line and tinkering with his account, made an appointment to see his accountant downtown, watched *The Rosie O'Donnell Show,* browsed for an hour in the Madison Avenue Bookshop, had lunch at Serafina with a copy of the new Salman Rushdie novel, masturbated, taken a nap, gone to his philosophy class at the New School, seen Ashley, and walked the three blocks to his apartment to dress for this evening. Sometimes he was surprised how easy it was to fill a day and sometimes he was horrified.

"What are your goals?" he asked Sloane, turning the question back on her. "Where do you want to be in twenty years?"

"I don't know, I guess I'd like to be running my own fund."

Looking into her eager eyes, Luke tried to remember when all of this had stopped making sense to him.

Certainly that would have been the acceptable route, leaving the firm to run ten or fifteen billion by himself.

Letting his attention drift across the table, he heard Web Reynes giving the actor the definition of a player. "Basically, to be a player, you need a hundred million," he was saying. "I mean, that's where it all gets kind of interesting."

The actor looked frightened, even as he nodded.

Web caught Luke listening in on them.

"Wouldn't you say that's pretty much true?"

Luke shrugged. "I'm afraid I'm not in the club."

"There ought to be a word for it. I mean, millionaire's become so meaningless—everybody's a millionaire."

"How about *centenaire,*" Luke said. "The hundred-million club."

"Not bad," Web said, smiling. "I took some Latin at Exeter."

The conversation was blessedly truncated by the speeches and awards portion of the evening. *Who has done as much for this city. Needs no introduction. Cause dear to our hearts.* Luke looked across the table at Sasha just as she exchanged a glance with Bernard Melman, who was seated at the table behind her.

. . .

Over the course of dinner, Sasha repeatedly beckoned the waiter to fill her wineglass and huddled confidentially with the actor. At one point, she noticed Luke watching her and stuck out her tongue, then held out her glass for more chardonnay. Her laughter carried across the table as if she were determined to be the life of the party. He caught snatches of her conversation, her voice metallic and shrill. *Isn't it to die?*

When the band started playing, she rose from her seat. "I'm in the mood to dance," she said, looking at Luke. "But my husband is looking at me censoriously. And he's not much of a dancer anyway. Perhaps you'd take me for a spin," she said to Guillermo, who replied that he would be delighted. Luke watched as they walked out to the open area of the pavilion.

After listening to Sloane discourse about the euro, he looked up to see Melman cutting in on Guillermo with the air of a suitor supremely confident of his welcome. Guillermo retired with a chilly bow to the billionaire as Sasha took his hand and shook her hips to the band's approximation of "All I Wanna Do." Although he looked slightly ludicrous, Melman was, if anything, a little more confident than most of the other paunchy middle-aged men who'd been coaxed out onto the dance floor.

Luke excused himself from the table and went off to look for Ashley, exchanging greetings with friends and acquaintances before finally spotting her at the so-called children's table, taken aback to see her deep in conference with Anton Hohenlohe. All of the young men at the table were at least a decade older than Ashley and her friends, and Hohenlohe, a friend of Sasha's, was closer in age to the mother than the daughter. To his admirers, he was a stylish boulevardier, a living link to a lost continental world of Ferraris, Côte d'Azur casinos, and polo. His great-grandfather had supposedly been closely associated with mad King Ludwig II of Bavaria, Wagner's patron. Depending on one's point of view, New York society was increasingly meritocratic or just increasingly nouveau riche; but Hohenlohe was considered a representative of the venerable tradition of aristocratic leisure. He was ubiquitous in Paris and Palm Beach as well as New

York, and rumors of sexual malfeasance seemed only to enhance his mystique.

He'd turned up here after a sojourn in Hollywood, where he'd first come into his inheritance and set himself up as a producer. The motion-picture business had a tradition of hospitality toward rich young men who wished to share their wealth in exchange for sex with aspiring actresses. If the girl whose night with him ended in the emergency room of Cedars-Sinai with nearly toxic levels of Rohypnol and cocaine in her bloodstream and some very nasty bruises had been without connections, or if Hohenlohe himself had been more established in the community, the incident probably would have been hushed up or allowed to fade away, but under the circumstances, he decided that Los Angeles wasn't truly glamorous.

Luke was appalled that this was Sasha's idea of suitable company for their daughter and her friends—she, after all, had set up the table, which Luke had paid for. He watched as Ashley threw back her head and laughed at some remark of Hohenlohe's, her manner and gestures reminding him all too much of her mother—a resemblance that was sealed when she lifted a champagne flute and tilted it upright between her lips—afraid that if he went over to the table he might lose control of his temper and further alienate his lately surly daughter. It occurred to him he could solve two problems at a single stroke, interrupting Sasha's dance with Melman in the name of urgent parental business. He would tell her that he was taking Ashley home immediately and, if possible, send her over to make this announcement to their daughter herself. He was counting on his righteous indignation and Sasha's vestigial sense of guilt to work in his favor, but when he spotted her among the dancers, he began to wonder if guilt was a concept with which she was familiar.

To the tune of "Bootylicious," one of the season's hits, Sasha was grinding her pelvis into Melman's, her hands on his shoulders. Even more than her posture and the burlesque motions of her hips, it was the expression on her face, a kind of liquid abandon combined with an intense focus on the eyes of her partner, that made the scene so lurid to Luke, and, he realized, looking around, to a great many of the assembled guests. Any other couple might have engaged in a similar display without attracting quite so much notice, but the eminence of both parties guaranteed them an audience; it was as if a spotlight followed them, illuminating their every gesture, and casting giant shadows that magnified the pantomime of their desire.

Without a context, the dance might have been innocent enough. But clearly, this was richly contextualized. It was in the eyes of the riveted tribe, the pity with which they regarded him, unable to keep from looking even as they wished at all costs to avoid his gaze . . . in the way he saw women whispering to their neighbors. The community knew how to interpret this performance because they had been prepared for something like it—a confirmation of the buzz and rumors. This, if nothing else, was what Luke learned tonight—that his suspicions, far from being paranoid, were pretty general throughout the 10021 zip code, where even the clueless husbands seemed to know.

And it was not so much the suggestive rhythm of her hips as the fixity of her glassy gaze on her partner that seemed so damning. Luke could either put an end to this by cutting in on the dance or he could walk away and postpone the reckoning. But he couldn't continue to stand here watching and being watched, so he retreated to the back of the tented area to compose himself. Leaning against the railing of the snow monkey enclosure, he regarded the sign attached to the fence.

### SEPARATE LIFESTYLES

Male snow monkeys have larger canine teeth, a fuller mane of hair, and weigh 20 percent more than females. Females remain with the group in which they were born for life. Males leave when they reach sexual maturity and may join several different groups during their lifetime.

There was no sign of these anthropomorphs, male or female, and Luke turned away with an urgent sense of finding his daughter, of saving her somehow.

She was laughing at something Hohenlohe was whispering in her ear, and from a certain liquidity in her posture, Luke could tell she was drunk. He approached unobserved and put his hand on her shoulder. She looked up, the blurred giddiness of her expression coming into a wary focus at the sight of his face.

"We're going home," he said.

The expression she directed at him over her creamy shoulder was like some terrible composite of a petulant seven-year-old's and her mother's worldliest smirk. For all of his own indignation, he was shocked by the look of loathing—the glower of a drunken fourteen-year-old—deforming her beautiful face.

"Let's go," he said, steeling himself and glaring at Hohenlohe.

She turned away, took a swig from the champagne glass, and rose slowly to her feet, attempting to convey a sense of outraged dignity as she struggled to establish her balance. Hohenlohe, observing proper form, rose beside her, napkin in hand, while her friends averted their eyes and bowed their heads.

"I assure you I was—"

"We were just having a conversation," Ashley said.

"You can finish it when you're eighteen," Luke said.

"It's not like this is the first time I've had, like, a glash of sampagne."

"Aren't we sophisticated? How many *glashes* have we had tonight?"

Amber and Bethany giggled nervously.

"Just because you're having a lousy time," she said.

"We'll finish this conversation at home," Luke said, taking her hand and leading her away from the table.

"I hate you," she muttered once they'd passed out of earshot.

At that moment, a seal rocketed out of the pool, glistening in the artificial light against the backdrop of the trees and, above them, the cream-colored pueblos of Fifth Avenue, splashing down sideways and sending a luminescent wave over the edge of the wall. The night air was perfectly balanced between the heat of summer and the cool of the approaching autumn as they walked out, alone together, among the partygoers. The women were beautiful in their gowns, or at least glamorous in their beautiful gowns, their escorts rich in this richest of all cities, and Luke had never felt less like one of them, reminded now of the figures he'd seen this summer in Pompeii and Herculaneum, frozen in their postures of feasting and revelry.

# 5

velyn's gave every appearance of a dive—being so drab as to make some visitors nostalgic for a lost Greenwich Village. I thought this kind of place was extinct, you might say, if on a whim or in order to get out of the rain you had descended eight steps down from the sidewalk and pushed through the door, squeezing past the regulars slouched on the dull, pitted mahogany bar till you reached the dining room, which was the length of a subway car and slightly wider. At nine o'clock, half the tables would be divvied up between tourists and aging bohemians who remembered the proprietress as an Off-Broadway diva, and who in their time had been drawn here by the legend of the Abstract Expressionists and Beat poets who were said to have lurched about the premises for a season or two before settling on the Cedar Tavern. No photos or memorabilia commemorated this golden age; the walls were bare, except for a few land- and seascapes, possibly Italian, of the kind purchased on a forgotten holiday. The very name, for Corrine, conjured a lost era of half-remembered night crawls and predawn revelry, the riotous codas of book parties and gallery openings and movie premieres, the fuzzy preludes to a dozen youthful hangovers. Surprised as she'd been to get Jim's phone call, and by the notion of a postmidnight script meeting, she was nearly as surprised by the venue. She never would have come out if Jim hadn't insisted, if Russell hadn't encouraged her. It was ridiculous really, although kind of a typical Hollywood power play, and if Corrine had had a higher opinion of herself, she might have suspected it was a come-on, but Cody pretty much had his pick of gorgeous young actresses, not to mention Corrine's vixenish sister, who pointedly had not been invited to come along. Anyway, Russell had said what could it hurt and speculated that maybe it was less about the script and more about Jim needing some feminine comfort and counsel.

By 1:30, the tourists and diners were long gone, replaced by the vampires, many of whom she imagined might well have remained in place since she'd last set foot in here seven or eight years ago—the restaurant people just getting off their shifts, the line chefs and managers, the musicians and the made guys and the character actors who specialized in playing made guys, along with the kinds of directors and writers who had not yet been to rehab or who were in between visits and wanted to get down, sometimes in the company of A-list actors, without fear of reading about it in the gossip columns the next day. All of them waiting for the Duke, a vaguely reptilian-looking fellow with slicked-back silver hair. She couldn't remember if Russell had discovered his service first, or maybe it was Washington, but the packets he dealt not so very discreetly had extended countless evenings well past natural, legal limits.

Some of the gossip columnists were here, too, in an unofficial capacity—whatever happened at Evelyn's was off-the-record; it was like one of those watering holes on the savanna, at which the zebras drank unmolested beside the lions. Evelyn would have banned anyone who molested a fellow drinker or committed any untoward behavior to print. Corrine remembered that Monday nights were always busy. The Evelyn's crowd rested up over the weekend, Friday and Saturday being amateur nights. Evelyn herself—a big overflowing woman with chipmunk cheeks who was never seen to move from her spot—sat lumpishly at a table in the back with a few haggard-looking friends. Cody was sitting at her table, although there was no sign of Jim.

He stood up and wobbled over. "Alone at last," he said, kissing her cheek.

"Where's Jim?"

"His leash got yanked. Shall we get a table?"

She had a notion that she'd been set up, but then decided that if what he was looking for was sex, he would've summoned Hilary, or Nancy, or one of a tag team of adoring women he must surely have at his disposal. Besides, she was already here. "Why not?" she said.

Choosing a table in the back room, he held out a seat for her and sat down beside her. She was aware of Erhardt's reputation as a pussy hound; he'd been married twice, both times to actresses, although this hadn't prevented him from engaging in more and less publicized affairs. So here they were, meeting at a dive after midnight, with Erhardt flagging down an entirely unnecessary drink.

"I've always heard you two were the perfect couple. You and Russell. Ivy League prince and princess."

"There's no such thing as a perfect couple," she said.

"My point exactly."

"Ah, so that was your point. I was wondering."

"Marriage is difficult," he said. The arrival of the waitress seemed to cheer him; he waved the hovering figure in, like one of those guys with flashlights beckoning a 747 forward on the runway, watching his drink as it was lowered to the table, as if to make sure it didn't fly away. "She's a professional," he said after she left.

"Who, the waitress?"

"She does parties after hours for five hundred an hour."

"How is she?"

"I'm not into that kind of thing. Though I've been to some of the parties."

"I hear you're into leading ladies," Corrine said.

"To direct an actress, you have to put her on a pedestal, make her into a goddess. You have to fall in love with her a little so the audience will fall in love with her a lot. It's what you might call an occupational hazard."

"At least you're well compensated for it."

"Some of these crazy bitches—not nearly well enough."

Erhardt had a vast repertoire of scowls and facial tics with which he carried on his own side of the conversation when forced to dam the torrent of his own speech and listen; unlike most of the directors of his generation, who seemed to believe that beards conferred on them a certain intellectual gravity, he'd always been clean-shaven, and thus unable to mask his impatience with the generally misguided and imprecise opinions of his interlocutors.

"So, Jim said you were interested in talking about *The Heart of the Matter*."

"Already we're talking business."

"As opposed to what?"

He sighed, threw his arms over the back of his chair, assuming the lecture position. "You know, Greene divided his fictional output into two categories, one of which he called 'entertainments.' And the story that eventually became *The Heart of the Matter* was originally conceived as one of these, a kind of suspense puzzle, this upside-down procedural in which the crime and the criminal were known and the mystery, for the reader and the criminal, lay in identifying the detective who was pursuing him. And of course you've got the skeleton of that structure in the novel as written, Wilson, the not-so-secret operative spying for the Home Office on poor old Africa hand Scobie. But eventually old Graham decided to go a different route and write a *novel*, with all the complexity and moral ambiguity that that word implied for him. Which is a long-winded way of saying that *The Heart of the Matter* doesn't exactly qualify as the kind of entertainment that plays in Peoria. Not exactly boy meets girl, loses girl, gets girl back."

Corrine tried to model her face into that of a good student absorbing instruction, although she was familiar with the contents of this speech.

"Neither are any of your films," she said.

"Who was it who described the three-act structure as boy meets girl, boy and girl get into a pickle, boy gets pickle into girl."

"You?" She was beginning to wonder about the agenda. What exactly were they doing here?

"Okay," he said after a revivifying swallow. "I've been thinking about this book for years. I love the idea, but I've got some questions right from the start. Let's just put aside the whole Catholicism can of worms for a moment. We've got Scobie, the honest policeman in a corrupt colonial African hellhole. Too honest to be trusted by his careerist drone peers. His wife, Louise, a nag and a drag, whom he's too decent or too passive to shed himself of. Do you think he loves her?"

"He loves her in a way."

"You're equivocating," he said, waving to Abel Ferrar across the room.

"He pities her."

"Exactly. The problem I have is if you make her too pathetic, which I think Greene does, and, as I say, you've been incredibly faithful to the master, then you eventually lose patience with Scobie. Instead of being noble, he just looks like a fucking masochist. If you make her *too* sympathetic, of course, then you tip the balance of sympathy away from him when he starts to fuck the little shipwrecked girl."

Corrine's sympathy had always been with Scobie, whose nobility broke her heart. That's what made her want to do the movie—his fierce, unforgiving morality, his refusal to put his own needs or desires first. An honest policeman forced to compromise his honesty for the sake of his wife's happiness . . . trapped between two women . . . trying, impossibly, to do right by both of them and finally acknowledging the impossibility.

"There were times," she said, "writing the script, when I measured Russell against Scobie and almost hated him. Russell, I mean." Why was she saying this? she wondered, looking at the residue of her most recent glass of wine, remembering suddenly that the screenplay had been Russell's idea—he was the one who'd suggested it to her. But she definitely had Cody's attention. He'd stopped squirming in his seat and was leaning forward to listen. "Because I couldn't imagine him, in the same situation, being as tortured as Scobie. True, he had been unfaithful to his wife, but he hated himself for it, and finally killed himself because he couldn't bear to let either one of them down."

"No, no, no. He killed himself because he'd committed a mortal sin. It's all about his relationship with God. A Catholic God. I've got some real problems with Scobie's Catholicism. But it's crucial. The women are just place markers, ciphers, empty vessels of neediness. Scobie is—"

"Don't insult Scobie. I love Scobie."

"You love him because his erotic map, if you can even call it that, is essentially female. He's a chick. He needs to be loved; he needs to be depended on. It's the dependence of the two women that binds him to them, his need to be needed. Their essence is irrelevant."

"That's a pretty sexist reading."

"Oh, please. And here I was just beginning to think you had an original mind."

"I'm not a knee-jerk feminist. And I don't have much use for either of the women."

"Exactly," he said. "The women are black holes of neediness."

She wasn't sure whose point had been won here.

He noted her confusion. "What I'm saying is that this is actually a fairly special case. Scobie doesn't love the way most men love, and he doesn't cheat the way most men cheat."

"Why *do* most men cheat?" she asked. "I'm curious."

"Why ask me?"

"Because you're such a perceptive observer of human nature. And you're a man."

"Because we yearn for the unknown."

"Strange pussy."

"If you will. Because men are romantics. Scobie's not. He's a realist. Don't laugh. You think I'm kidding?"

"How do you define *romantic*?"

"Unrealistic expectations. A yearning for the infinite. Dissatisfaction with the actual. The actual being the familiar. The body of the woman you've already slept with. When you fuck a strange woman, you're searching the void for meaning."

"Oh, please."

"Surely you'll admit that women are the realists. Let me give you an example. Right now, I have a yearning for a bottle of burgundy. Long ago, back in, oh, probably 1993, I had a bottle of '71 La Tache, and I've been trying to recapture that bliss ever since. I've swilled dozens—nay, hundreds—of bottles of similar stuff in the last decade and paid thousands and thousands of dollars for the privilege, and not only have I never recaptured the glory of that experience, most of the stuff tasted like rotgut—thin and bitter and ungiving, the vinous equivalent of Greene's portrait of pruney old Louise. But the next time I'm faced with a wine list, I'll order burgundy, hope triumphing over bitter experience, still seeking that primal and quite possibly illusory ecstasy of the '71 La Tache."

"I know exactly what you mean," Corrine said. "The last time Russell asked me how I was feeling was 1993, but I keep talking to him anyway, hoping to recapture that experience."

"How about a bottle of wine?" he said.

"That's about the last thing I need." She looked at her watch. "I have two kids at home. I have to get up at seven."

"Don't hide behind that maternal thing."

Trying to attract service, he waved both of his arms over his head.

She'd already had more to drink tonight than she had in years, but she was sort of enjoying this, partly because she was drunk. And how often did she have a chance to get drunk with a fucking legend? On the other hand, she didn't want to get so shitfaced that she'd find herself in an awkward situation.

He excused himself to go to the men's room. When he finally returned, he pulled his chair up directly beside hers and threw his arm around her, exploring with his hand.

"Thanks, that's my left breast," she said. "I've been looking for it all night."

"If I said yes right now, would you go home with me and the waitress?"

63

She tried to gauge whether this was a joke. His gaze was glassy and intense through the thick frames of his glasses. "I thought you weren't into that kind of thing."

"I lied."

"You're serious?"

He nodded slowly.

"You're saying, if I fuck you and the waitress, you'll direct my screenplay?"

"That appears to be what I am saying."

"What's to prevent you from changing your mind in the morning?"

"I won't. I give you my word, right here."

"Flattered as I am, I don't believe you'd base your decision on whether or not I fucked you. And if you did, I could hardly trust your judgment. Could I?"

"You underestimate your own attractions."

"I think you've got me mixed up with my younger sister."

"No, her attractions are very superficial. I know. I've been there."

"You must feel very special."

"It would be interesting if I had an option check in my pocket. Just to see if you'd be tempted."

"We'll never know, will we?"

"I enjoy posing these moral dilemmas," he said.

"Are they often successful?"

"I'm usually disappointed," he said, "to discover how easily and cheaply people will sell their souls. I actually admire your integrity."

"So that was a hypothetical," she said, throwing him a rope.

"It might have been," he said, not deigning to take it.

Good save, she thought. She wasn't entirely certain how serious any of this had been. Directors as a class were congenitally manipulative, and Erhardt was obviously a real mind-fucker, but somehow she wasn't all that offended.

"Did you get Jim to call me over here just so you could hit on me?" she asked, genuinely curious. In a strictly theoretical sense, she found the idea kind of amazing.

He paused to consider this, then shrugged. "Motives are usually mixed, don't you think?"

Riding home in the cab, she decided that she was more flattered than offended. It seemed to have been a very long time since she had seen herself as an object of desire. The night before, after she was in bed, she'd felt a stirring of the old impulse, which had been dormant for many months, if not years. She'd put down her book and rolled on her side, stroking Russell's hip. He'd grunted appreciatively. But when, after a few moments, he failed to put down his manuscript, she'd retreated to her own side of the bed. Sex had become a yawning chasm between them. Once upon a time, they'd had the freedom of each other's bodies—knowledge that had since been lost along the way. Like all married couples of long duration, they'd experienced the ebb and flow of physical intimacy, though by now the tide had been out so long, she'd begun to doubt its return. After all this time, she felt awkward and self-conscious and she didn't know how to return her body to him. Every sexless day that passed made it more difficult to resume the old intimacy. At one time, before the kids came along, they'd had sex every morning—a routine established after they had found themselves too tired at night.

She sensed acutely that it was her own fault. From the time she'd been pregnant, she hadn't wanted to be touched. And she definitely hadn't wanted to be touched after the children were born, feeling defective in the wake of their radically premature birth—why hadn't she been able to hold them longer? Or rather, it wasn't that she hadn't wanted to be touched—she hadn't wanted to be fucked, which was, to Russell, the point of touching. Physical affection was, in his mind, foreplay. He didn't seem to have any use for the sort of tenderness that didn't lead to orgasm. And this fact made her more reluctant, more resentful. She'd felt herself tensing up whenever he stroked her arm or kissed her ear—because she knew that these gestures were not ends in themselves. And he, in time, had started to withhold them.

Who knows, she thought as she paid the driver and climbed out, almost tripping as her heel slipped from the curb, pausing to look up at the huge monoliths looming above her . . . after all this time, he may have stopped wanting me. It occurred to her that she wasn't growing any younger. She was still thin; her tits were still more or less in place, not least because there wasn't that much of them. But she was almost forty-two. What if she started wanting him again, only to discover he no longer wanted her?

She'd watched him as if from a great distance . . . lying on his back on the far side of the bed, his manuscript hovering above his face. It all seemed so sad and foolish. Lying two feet from her husband, and wanting him in the old way, she'd felt as shy as a virgin. The white sheet between them like a blank page she couldn't find the words to fill.

# PART TWO

## That Autumn

6

A sh Wednesday. The debris—the paper and sooty dust—had surged up the avenues and stopped at Duane Street.

Staggering up West Broadway, coated head to foot in dun ash, he looked like a statue commemorating some ancient victory, or, more likely, some noble defeat—a Confederate general, perhaps. That was her second impression. Her first was that he was at least a day late. Yesterday morning, and well into the afternoon, thousands had made this same march up West Broadway, fleeing the tilting plume of smoke, covered in the same gray ash, slogging through it as the cerulean sky rained paper down on them—a Black Mass version of the old ticker-tape parades of lower Broadway. It was as if this solitary figure was re-enacting the retreat of an already-famous battle.

He paused to lean against a Mercedes coated with the same dust, a yellow respirator dangling from his neck like a talisman, the creases of his face highlighted by the gray powder. She thought somehow that for all his dishevelment, he looked familiar, though she couldn't say why.

His knees showed through the ripped legs of what until recently had been a pair of dress slacks. The hard hat looked anomalous, and indeed, as he tilted his head back, it fell to the curb, exposing a dark tangle of hair, streaked with the ubiquitous talcy ash.

Corrine approached slowly, afraid she might scare him, a little spooked herself—the street and sidewalks deserted, as if they were the last two people on earth. "Are you . . . all right?"

Corrine held out a bottle of Evian; she was just about to give up, when he raised his hand and reached for it. Both his hands were raw and bloodied, seeping wounds still wet beneath the dusty grime.

After draining the bottle, he seemed to take note of his surroundings, turning his head in both directions before finally looking back at Corrine. He stared at her for an uncomfortably long interval, like someone untrained in the social graces. "You're the first person I've seen," he finally said.

She supposed he was in shock or something. She detected the molasses residue of a southern accent. *Seen* sounding almost like *sane*.

"Unless I'm imagining you."

"No, no," she said. "At least I don't think you are. It's hard to tell, though. What's real, I mean."

"Can you still smell it here?" he asked.

"The smoke?" Corrine nodded, looking up at the milky plume that arced south by southwest above the office buildings of Broadway.

"Have you been . . . digging?"

He wet his lips and looked back down in the direction from which he'd come. "I was supposed to meet my friend Guillermo at Windows on the World."

She nodded encouragingly. "Yesterday?"

"Was it yesterday?" He seemed to be puzzling out the time frame.

"Tuesday." She realized she'd sidetracked him. This might be the first chance he'd had to tell his story. For the past twenty-four hours, they'd all been telling their stories—accounting for their whereabouts and testing their own reactions in the telling. "The eleventh," she said.

"The morning of the eleventh. I got down there just before nine. I was supposed to meet Guillermo at eight, but I left him a message saying I couldn't make it."

"You were lucky," she said.

He nodded slowly, as if considering an idea that hadn't occurred to him before. "I called him late the night before and left a message canceling. Not canceling—postponing. Until ten. But I never followed up. The thing is, what happened was, I had a fight with my daughter that night, and I was coming downtown to meet my accountant at nine—his office was in the World Financial Center. But I just didn't feel like waking up that early, so I left him a message. Postponing the breakfast. But who knows if he got it? Eight o'clock yesterday morning."

She nodded tentatively, trying to take in the details. Sirens wailed from the direction of the West Side Highway. A Boston terrier with a white mask dragged its owner into view around the corner on Duane Street. They looked like a pair of bandits—the dog with its white mask, the owner with red kerchief fastened behind his head, concealing his nose and mouth. She should probably be wearing something herself, she realized.

"When I got out of the cab," the ashy man was saying, "people in the plaza were looking up and pointing. I didn't really think about it, not until I was in the elevator of my accountant's building. Somebody said there'd been an explosion in the tower. I was in the accountant's office, reading the *Journal,* and I suddenly thought, Wait a minute, maybe Guillermo didn't get the message. He might not have checked. I tried to call him on his cell phone, and then Number Seven was evacuated. I'm calling him over and over as I'm walking down the stairwell from the twenty-seventh floor. Then I'm on West Street, looking up at the smoke, and redialing him when I saw the jumpers. That's the last thing I remember, bodies raining down on the plaza. Falling slowly and then suddenly exploding like rotten fruit on the concrete.

"Next thing I know, I'm lying on my face in the blackness. I can't breathe and I can't see, and my entire body is aching from the inside out. I don't know if I'm blinded or there's just no light, but finally I make out a yellow glow in the distance and I start crawling toward it. Then some people pulled me into the lobby of a building."

71

"Did you reach your friend?"

"After the second tower came down, I went back. Because I thought he might be in there in that monstrous pile and it was my fault. I couldn't bring myself to leave. I just stood there on the edge and then, I don't know, I got in a line, behind another guy. I just took my place, passing along pieces of the debris. Someone gave me a hard hat." He paused and examined the cut on his arm. "Once in a while, I stopped working to make a call. Then my phone went dead."

"Phone service is completely screwed up," Corrine said. "You shouldn't assume—"

"This morning, there were volunteers down there with phones. I couldn't reach him." He shrugged. "Mailbox full." He shook his head. "A hundred-something floors up. If my daughter hadn't gotten drunk, if my wife hadn't been . . . If I hadn't fought with the both of them. Windows on the World at eight."

"Have you talked with them? Does your family know you're safe?"

He nodded, directing a disconcertingly intense gaze upon her. Not the look of a lecher, more the unself-conscious stare of a child. "You look familiar," he said.

"Corrine," she said, holding out her hand.

"Luke," he said, taking her hand as he glanced back over his shoulder. "Is this really happening?"

"I think so," she said. "It's all kind of unbelievable, though."

"I keep wondering if I ever actually regained consciousness."

She held his rough hand and kneaded it cautiously.

"You made it," she said.

"I know what it is," he said.

"What?"

"You look like Katharine Hepburn."

"What, spinsterish and flinty?"

"In a good way."

"You're delirious." Actually, she recalled Russell saying the same thing. Centuries ago. "Do you want to wash up? We're right up the street. I just came out to check on a neighbor."

He shook his head. "I should get home."

"You'll have to walk up to Fourteenth. Everything's blocked off below that. And even then . . . I don't know if there are any cabs."

"Thanks," he said.

"Please," she said, feeling embarrassed in the grip of his gaze. "For what? I didn't do anything. Not compared to what you've been doing. . . ."

"Actually, you did," he said.

Corrine jotted her name and her cell phone number on the back of a receipt from Odeon. "Do me a favor," she said, her voice breaking. "Will you just let me know . . . well, that you made it home safely. Would you do that for me, please?"

It was in many respects a typical encounter on the day after, one of thousands between stunned and needy strangers, the kind of thing she might have recalled months or years later when something reminded her of that time or someone asked her where she'd been that day.

7

To Luke, it seemed nothing short of miraculous that you could still pick up the phone and conjure up moo shu pork, shrimp toast, and fried dumplings, that men from Shaolin and Shanghai were fanning out on mountain bikes through the streets and avenues above Canal, bearing the sacraments of a New York Sunday night in plastic bags slung over their handlebars. This much of the metropolitan idea, at least, was intact. Smoking a cigarette under the awning of his building as the doormen politely ignored him, he counted five of them racing their bicycles across Seventy-seventh Street, ministering to the shaken populace at the end of this apocalyptic week.

Under the pretext of buying the foreign papers, Luke had come outside to smoke. After all these years of berating Sasha for her smoking, he was stubbornly unwilling to admit he'd picked up the habit on the breaks between digging.

He followed one of the deliverymen into the building and exchanged a fifty-dollar bill for his family's traditional Sunday meal from Pig Heaven, carrying the bags up in the elevator and setting up in the kitchen, calling Sasha and Ashley from their separate corners of the apartment even as he found his thoughts tending downtown. With his body clock so out of whack, downtown in flames, the schedule of office life now a receding memory, Luke didn't think he would notice Sunday as such, didn't think he would feel the usual suck of low-grade depression. Hard to believe that the rhythms of the week could be so internalized that this particular Sunday would register as anything except the fifth day of an entirely new calendar. Perhaps the muted feeling of letdown had as much to do with the sense of receding crisis, as when, a few days after the funeral of a loved one, the narcotic of shock wears off and the sense of surviving from moment to moment gives way to the realization that you will simply have to carry on with the routines of daily life as if nothing had happened.

He knew he was lucky to be alive—but he felt distinctly unworthy of this gift. These last few days, instead of light and blessed and spared, he'd been feeling borne down by the burden of it as the roll call of the noble, hapless victims unscrolled on television and in the papers. He'd been scared shitless most of the hours he'd spent downtown and haunted by nightmares ever since, but he felt so utterly useless up here on Seventy-seventh Street that he now wished he'd stayed. As if he belonged somewhere, even inside that toxic cloud, behind the blue police barriers—a feeling he hadn't had in a long time, since he'd become bored with his job and disaffected with his life.

"Pig Heaven!" he called to his family.

As the son of a minister, Luke had been required to go to church until, at the age of fourteen, he'd fled north to prep school, and if for a few years he'd been sinfully proud to listen to his father intoning the service, leading the songs, and instructing their neighbors in the paths of righteousness, that pleasure had been supplanted in later years by a vague embarrassment and increasingly by a profound desire that his father's profession might be carried on out of sight of his friends—in an office or a factory, say—especially when he started addressing the issue of civil rights from the pulpit, thereby alienating a portion of his flock.

"Ladies? Dinner!"

Being the minister's son had complicated his own participation in the required delinquencies of adolescence. Luke was gifted enough to skip sixth grade, with socially disastrous results; for several years, he found it difficult to insinuate himself into the pack of older boys with their facial and pubic hair, and his attempts to do so tended to be awkward and ill-judged, often resulting in detention, without permanently changing his outsider status. He came to dread the Monday-morning return to school, which inevitably tainted the pleasures of the preceding day, as well. For years, the ticking clock of *60 Minutes,* which he watched every Sunday night with his parents, seemed to him to signify the end of his brief weekend respite from careless hazing and academic boredom. This vague looming dread persisted long after he'd become a track star and a member of the group that smoked cigarettes down by the river, and was reinforced in his early years on Wall Street when the Sunday-night clock ticked, ticked, ticked toward an eighty-hour week of Hobbesian warfare.

Various secular rituals had been devised to replace church, to fill out the hours and dull the anxiety of the Sabbath, with its muted intimations of mortality: brunch, museums, galleries, and, finally, the family meal of Chinese food in the kitchen.

"Ashley? Sasha! God*damn* it!"

Finally relenting, he fetched them from their respective bedrooms. Ashley at her computer, instant-messaging, her head bobbing to whatever was playing on her headphones, and then, startled by the touch of his hand on her shoulder, typing "POMS"—*parent over my shoulder*—and reluctantly unwiring herself. Sasha was sitting in the lotus position on the master bed, talking on the phone, nodding and holding up an index finger. These iterations of domestic life somehow failed to comfort or inspire in him a sense of gratitude for his survival. Returning home on Wednesday evening after walking for two and a half hours, he'd felt a great sense of relief and enjoyed a brief and tearful reunion with his wife and later his daughter. But already that *intensity* of feeling was fading, replaced by the more familiar sensation that his presence was somewhat superfluous. And being here, so far away from the epicenter, made him feel almost guilty.

"Please let's not watch the news," Sasha said, plucking a spring roll and examining it critically. "I don't think I can take any more of this right now. And that includes *Sixty Minutes*."

"I'm not hungry," Ashley said, slouching onto a stool alongside the kitchen counter.

Luke wasn't particularly hungry himself, but the idea of the Sunday-night meal—just about the only one they had together, alone in the house without Nellie, the housekeeper off in Brooklyn for the night with her own family—now seemed more important than ever. On the other hand, he had to admit that on Wednesday, Nellie, God bless her, had seemed grateful and overwrought, welcoming him on his return. He picked up a fried dumpling and dipped it in soy sauce. "It's kind of amazing, when you think about it," he said. "We just take it all for granted most of the time—phone service, elevators, delivery food. . . ."

"I was just talking with Sophie Painter," Sasha said. "They're moving out to their house on the island and enrolling the kids in Hampton Country Day."

"How do you feel?" Luke asked his daughter. "Are you scared about being in the city?"

She shrugged. "I don't know."

"Because that's an option," he said. He looked across the counter to gauge Sasha's reaction, but she wasn't showing her hand.

"All my friends are here," Ashley said.

"So far they are," Luke said. "We don't really know what's happening or who's going where yet." For several months, he'd been entertaining a vague notion of starting over someplace else. Sasha's resistance had always been the obstacle, but it seemed to him his own restlessness and sense of dissatisfaction had been validated by the current events.

"At the very least," Sasha said, "this seems like an awfully good argument for prep school next year."

"Or maybe it's an argument for sticking closer together." This was an ongoing debate, with Sasha and Ashley on one side and Luke on the other. He wasn't ready to see his daughter leave home, perhaps because he'd done it himself, so eagerly, and in his mind his departure for prep school marked a gradual, if undramatic, estrangement from his own family. He'd taken Ashley on a tour of New England prep schools over the summer without acceding to the inevitability of the plan.

"This stuff is swimming in fat," Ashley said, poking a chopstick into the moo shu pork.

The note of teenage world-weariness set him off. "Guillermo's buried under that rubble, for Christ's sake," Luke said. "I might've been there myself. I *should* have been there. Who gives a damn about fat?" He didn't know what to think when he saw the tears welling in her eyes, or how to react when she stood and bolted from the kitchen.

"For God's sake, Luke. That girl spent all day Tuesday not knowing whether you were alive or dead. She was beside herself. She thought she'd lost her father. Has it occurred to you that it was hard for us, too? She's traumatized. We all are. We were worried sick about you."

He waited for some physical manifestation of this sentiment, wanting his wife to touch him, embrace him . . . trying to find it in himself to reach across to her, but the pathways of intimacy were clogged from disuse, stopped up with the debris of old resentments, which these catastrophic events had failed to dislodge. For a brief moment, though, it had seemed that the force of the blast downtown had cleared it all away. They'd fallen into bed on Wednesday and fucked as if their lives depended on it, clinging to each other in the dark. The next morning, she'd discovered the bruises, footprints on his back—apparently he'd been trampled while he was sprawled in the darkness—and she had actually cried.

Luke now sought out his daughter, who was lying on her bed, staring at the ceiling. She turned away when he sat down beside her and stroked her forehead, which, he noticed now, was lightly speckled with nodes of acne—this observation inspiring a fresh wave of guilt and tenderness. She, in fact, had saved his life, however indirectly and unintentionally.

"I'm sorry, baby, I didn't mean to blow up like that."

"Everything's falling apart," she said, sniffling, hiding her face, her amber hair sprayed across the pillow.

"That's why we have to stick together."

"Okay," she murmured unconvincingly.

He wanted to take her in his arms, but he was held back by a sense of her exquisite teenage fastidiousness, her new hypersensitivity to touch and his own awkwardness with her budding womanly form. "What if I read to you?" he said. He tried to remember how many years it had been since he'd done so.

"I don't know," she said, her tone suggesting that she was willing to be persuaded.

"One of the old stories," he said, sensing an opportunity, a glimmer of susceptibility to old certainties and the simple pleasures of childhood. When she failed to object, he walked over to her bookshelf, diverted from his quest for a familiar volume by a curiosity that yielded to alarm as he examined some of the strange new titles. When had *Gossip Girl,* the Vampire Chronicles, and *Sex and the City* taken their place alongside *Stargirl, The Chocolate War,* and *Are You There God? It's Me, Margaret*?

Selecting a tatty old standby, he sat down beside her on the bed and started to read: "'*Where's Papa going with that ax?' said Fern to her mother as they were setting the table for breakfast.*"

A snort of recognition issued from the pillow.

"'*Out to the hoghouse,' replied Mrs. Arable. 'Some pigs were born last night.' 'I don't see why he needs an ax,' continued Fern, who was only eight.*"

Ashley turned to face him. "I always thought of Gran's farm when we read that. I liked imagining you growing up that way, with all the animals."

"Actually, we didn't move to the farm till I was eight or nine. We lived in town before that."

"I wish we went to visit more often. We used to go a lot more."

"I'm glad you like my family."

"Seems like I like them more than you do."

"*As if.* "

"I'm serious."

"I mean, you ought to say," he said, already regretting this schoolmarmish fastidiousness, "'It seems *as if* I like them more than you do.'"

"Whatever. Sometimes I think you're a little ashamed of them or something."

"That's not true."

"Well, Mom is."

"I wouldn't say that."

"Right." Lying back on her pillow, she rolled her eyes. "Whatever you say, Dad."

"Shall we read a few chapters?"

"How come you don't have a southern accent?"

"I have an accent." *Ah hev an ex sint.*

"A little. You did just then. Not like Uncle Matthew."

"Well, *darlin'* . . ."

This elicited a faint smile.

"Uncle Matthew, now, he's lived there his whole darned life. I've been up north amongst the Yankees more than half my life now."

She brushed the hair away from her face to reveal an expression of bemused tolerance, her mouth set in a tight smile intended to be ironic. Luke was careful not to examine her too closely, and when he glanced down at the end of the second chapter, she was asleep, breathing softly through her mouth.

Cautiously, with a tenuous sense of entitlement, he retreated to the master bedroom; his breakthrough as a father and the memory of Wednesday night awakening a nostalgic chord of warmth for his wife. He found Sasha sitting in front of her vanity in a peach teddy, brushing her hair. He watched her examining herself in the mirror, unaware of his presence; her wistful and unguarded expression arousing a certain tenderness commingled with lust. She jumped when he placed his hands on her cool shoulders; he'd almost forgotten the silkiness of her skin. Lowering his face into the fine mist of golden hair, he felt her shoulders tensing against his touch, but he persisted, burrowing into the soft, fragrant skin beneath her ear.

"Did you talk to Ashley?"

He nodded. She held the brush in midair with palpable impatience. He took it from her and began to brush her hair from behind.

She sighed and dropped her arm to her side, tolerating this gesture. "I'm sorry," she said. "On top of everything else, I've got my period."

"Since when has that stopped us?" he said, trying to sustain his mood. If anything, it usually made her more passionate, or so he seemed to recall. It could be so simple; if only they could cross that line once more, he imagined he could win her back and even forgive her.

"I'm just really feeling tense right now."

In the face of her resistance, he felt the promptings of a less generous impulse, the desire to ravish and possess her, to reclaim what had once been his. He reached down with his free hand and cupped her breast.

"Maybe tomorrow," she said, removing his hand.

Looking at her clenched face in the mirror, he stopped brushing and held out the brush to her, like a general passing his sword to the conquering enemy, a formal gesture of surrender.

Sasha had once been an ambitious, wide-eyed girl new to the city, a beauty who was determined to be more than an ornament. They'd met at an otherwise-dreary Park Avenue dinner composed of his senior banking colleagues and their shopping wives. One of these was a contributing editor to *Vogue*—a largely ceremonial title—who'd encountered Sasha when she submitted her annual piece on her favorite stores; an assistant editor in the features department, just two years out of Hollins College, Sasha had been assigned to turn the words on the manuscript page into prose. Rather than get all fuddled on the phone, the woman had invited the young editrix over to her apartment, and if at first she'd looked a little *too* pretty, after a painless hour in which Sasha had convinced her that the many emendations and excisions of the text were mostly her own ideas, the woman decided she'd discovered a fresh new extra girl for her parties.

Luke was smitten from the moment he saw her, in a borrowed dress from the wardrobe department. Her perfect features had all the virtues of youth—he hated to admit it now, but her face had acquired character and true beauty only when she hit her thirties—and he found her coquettish manner thoroughly charming. She also had a filthy mouth, and, as he discovered later, she knew how to use it; this seemed to him a brilliant counterpoint to her wholesome southern blondness. And as southerners, they had a language and a culture in common. After having proved to himself that he could hold his own in New York, he couldn't help feeling comforted and drawn to this gorgeous compatriot.

Before they sat down to dinner, she'd told him about her quirky girlhood in Charleston, surrounded by eccentric aunts and uncles. Later he was to discover that her father had gambled away his small trust before disappearing when she was three—a fact that allowed him to excuse and sympathize with her ferocious ambition. Her background eventually caught up with her claims for it a few years after they were married, when her mother landed a Florida sugar baron and became a grande dame of Palm Beach, with Sasha the devoted stepdaughter.

She needn't have embellished her background for Luke. Far more decisive was her performance when she went home with him that night. Though he'd enjoyed a fairly extensive and varied erotic career up to that point, he had never been quite so thoroughly seduced and ravished. In his bedroom, she seemed more like the star pupil of some fabled seraglio than an art major fresh out of Hollins, an academy for proper southern young ladies. It had taken him many years to come out from under that spell.

If anything, it was her appetite for the more innocent pleasures, her provincial's enthusiasm for everything the city had to offer, that had made him love her. She wanted to see and do everything; she dragged him to the ballet, the museums, and the theater. She'd even tried to interest him in jazz, an art form he found formless and annoying. Still, he admired the effort. The few spare hours his job had afforded him previously had been spent in restaurants, at the Racquet

Club, and in the artier movie houses that were still a feature of the New York landscape, and he felt grateful to be introduced to the wider wonders of the metropolis.

When had the dewy sheen of youthful exuberance hardened into the glossy shellac of sophistication? He knew it was partly his fault, being seven years older, with ambitions of his own. The same thing happened, he supposed, to all of the eager boys and girls drawn to the brilliant glow of the city from Charlotte, Charlottesville, Pittsburgh, Pittsfield, and Des Plaines; from Buxton, Kingston, Birmingham, and Bellingham. They gained their citizenship at the expense of their amazement. In the long run, the spectacle and chaotic grandeur of the city, like the sun, were too overwhelming to view with the naked eyes of wonder. They donned their two-hundred-dollar sunglasses, looked straight ahead when they walked down the street. When was the last time that any of them had even looked at those towers at the tip of the island, really? The same thing had happened to Luke, though he retained some of his capacity to be amazed—if only at the rapidity with which Sasha had become the epitome of a certain rarefied type of urban sophisticate, a process no doubt accelerated by her mother's sudden leap in fortune and social standing. Having once been happy enough to spend holidays with Luke's family in Tennessee, she suddenly began visiting her mother in Palm Beach and insisting they accompany her and her new husband to Aspen at Christmas.

He was a willing enough coconspirator in this transformation; he'd encouraged her to join boards and involve herself with charities, until eventually he realized, on the evidence of his massive overdrafts and glimpses of the party pages in glossy magazines, that they were traveling in circles where she was an intimate and he was a guest, the indulgent, if slightly anonymous, husband of the famous beauty. He had to admit that for a long time he'd felt proud to be able to finance this version of the good life.

Suddenly, she was flying by private jet to parties in Palm Beach while he worked fourteen-hour days. Somewhere in the middle of this transition, Ashley had come along. Sasha had said she wasn't ready, that she was too young, but he'd finally convinced her. As her husband, and, so far as he knew, the sole recipient of her sexual favors, he was titillated and selfishly flattered when she told him she wanted a cesarean in order to preserve the tone and integrity of the orifice that had given him so many hours of delight, but later he would look back on this as a very inauspicious beginning to family life. Nor, in retrospect, did the other rationale for her preplanned cesarean grant much comfort, especially when she divulged it in clarion tones across a dinner table one evening: "My mother was sixteen hours in labor with me and said it was the most painful thing she'd ever experienced. You think I was going to subject myself to that when I could have a sedative, some intravenous Demerol, and wake up a few hours later with a nice clean incision and a few stitches?"

Motherhood might have worked. Certainly Ashley's arrival distracted her and had given them a point of common reference, but he couldn't help realizing after a few years that the full-time nannies saw more of their daughter than Sasha did. In matters of child rearing, her ideal seemed to be the nineteenth-century English nobility.

Sasha had objected strenuously to his sabbatical and resented the idea of his becoming a fully engaged parent, as if they were rivals in this field—even though she didn't especially want to pick Ashley up from school, or take her to museums and movies. What discouraged him even more was that she clearly didn't understand his desire to find a more satisfying use of his talents and energies. Of course, he'd waited just a little too long to become a full-time husband and father; they both seemed a little bewildered by his sudden availability. Sasha's busy and glamorous life seldom required his participation, nor did it leave much room for anything else. And now that his daughter had plunged into the choppy waters of adolescence, he found himself watching from the shore, shouting advice that was lost on the winds.

While he'd made more than enough to weather a couple of years without cutting back too much on their massive expenditures, Sasha confounded him with the pronouncement that you weren't really rich until you had your own jet.

He retreated to the library, the ghetto of his masculine prerogative. After Sasha and the decorator had paneled and furnished it in their own interpretation of English men's club style, he had filled out the bookshelves, which had once graced a Scottish castle, with his own books and bric-a-brac: mementos of his academic, business, and bachelor life, none of which, he realized as he looked around now, had really quite personalized it. The gun rack over the fireplace with his matched sidelock Purdy twenty-gauges and the samurai sword he'd bought back from Tokyo. A collection of tombstones—Lucite slabs commemorating mergers and IPOs—occupied one corner of the leather-topped partners desk; the other was devoted to family photographs in the requisite Tiffany sterling frames: his father in mortarboard and robe on his graduation from Yale Divinity School, his mother on horseback. Somehow, his own family had been segregated here in this one room.

He dialed his mother's number in Tennessee, another Sunday-night ritual.

"I almost called this morning," she said. "I had a terrible dream last night. I dreamt that your phone call Wednesday was a dream. In last night's dream, when I woke up, I found out that you hadn't called, and when I called the apartment, Sasha told me you'd died in the towers."

"I've been having nightmares myself. I keep seeing the face of this woman in the rubble. Except that she didn't have one. Her face had been burned off. Then suddenly, she has Guillermo's face. And he's asking me where I was."

"My poor Luke."

"Tell me something mundane and bucolic."

"Emily Dickinson's pulled a tendon and that idiot Dr. Reed wanted to put her down."

Afterward, swiveling in his Bank of England chair, he caught sight of the biweekly deposit Nellie made of the contents of his pockets before she took the clothes downstairs to be picked up by the dry cleaner: coins, a matchbook from "21"—and a receipt on which was written in perfect Palmer longhand the euphonious name Corrine Calloway above a phone number. That angelic apparition floating above West Broadway, whom, in his delirium, he'd briefly and wishfully imagined as the last woman on earth—or the first.

"Hello?"

"Corrine? It's Luke McGavock. I met you, I think it was on Wednesday, as I was lurching uptown. You were kind enough to hydrate me and more or less reassure me about the continuing existence of life on the planet. I just wanted to thank you."

"I should thank you. Your example inspired me. I've been volunteering down here the last couple of days."

"Down where?" he asked.

# 8

The air was charged as if by the electricity of an imminent storm—by the suspense of the increasingly urgent and unlikely search for the living, by the thick proximity of the dead, by caffeine and the hallucinatory buzz of sleeplessness. The volunteers went about the mundane tasks of food and beverage preparation with a kind of syncopated exigency, animated by the fierce gravitational pull of the black hole several blocks to the north—shouting out to colleagues a few feet away for more sugar packets, more ice, darting between the coffeemaker and the coffee urns, racing a shopping cart full of soft drinks and sandwiches north on Broadway toward the smoking ruins as if in response to imminent famine . . . or so it seemed to Corrine as she showed Luke around the soup kitchen.

What is now called Bowling Green, she explained, was the spot where Peter Minuit purchased the island of Manhatta from the original inhabitants; later, it was the colony's first marketplace—where the precursors of Wall Street traders shouted figures in guilders, buying and selling flour, horses, salt pork, sugar, rum, and slaves. All the essentials. Subsequently, the little plot was dedicated to sport and leisure. For a few years, a gilt equestrian statue of George III had stood here, until a drunken Revolutionary mob had ripped it down, stripped off the gold leaf, and melted the rest down for musket balls, "some of which," she added, "presumably ended up maiming and killing King George's soldiers."

"Are you a historian?" Luke asked at the end of her recitation.

She felt herself blushing. "I did a little research the other night."

Across the street, beyond the U.S. Customs House, Battery Park, its bigger, greener cousin, spread out toward the river. In the seventies, as the massive Twin Towers of the World Trade Center rose a few blocks to the northwest, casting the area into afternoon shadow, the city restored the bedraggled little park, which this week had become the site of one of several improvised relief stations for the rescue operation under way in the wreckage.

Corrine had discovered the soup kitchen through her friend Casey, who'd gone to the Ralph Lauren boutique to do her bit for the city's traumatized economy, just as the mayor had advised everyone to do. Her exhausted but exhilarated salesgirl had explained how she had been up all night working at a soup kitchen down at Ground Zero, which conversation Casey had mentioned in passing to Corrine, who called the salesgirl and got the cell-phone number of a guy named Jerry, who'd started the operation—the salesgirl letting it be known that it was only because Casey was such a good customer that she was doing so. Everyone wanted to volunteer, to get close, to work off the shock, to feel useful, to observe the carnage, to *help*. Corrine had to admit that her own motives were so compound and complex, she could hardly begin to analyze them. Alongside dozens of city agencies, a vast network of private philanthropic organizations was being reconfigured to direct money and energy toward the scene of the attack. After the initial exodus of thousands from downtown, the flow of bodies had been reversed as thousands more had attempted to reach the site, only to be turned away at the police barricades.

Corrine showed Luke what there was to see of the Bowling Green relief station, an open-fronted tent with a few folding tables and coolers. At the other end of the cobbled square was the police van, headquarters for the men of the Brooklyn South precinct who'd been deployed on the second day to seal the area and enforce security, one of those movie-location vehicles on loan from a production company; and, in fact, at certain moments it seemed to Corrine, though she felt petty for even thinking this, that Bowling Green and the entire zone had the self-conscious air of a movie set, with all the same accoutrements—walkie-talkies, catering tables, muted hysteria. The firemen and the ironworkers were the stars, unapproachable, eyes glazed and fixed on a point in the distance . . . especially the firemen, and you gave them their space—you didn't speak to them unless they spoke to you.

She introduced Luke to Jerry, a hulking, bullet-headed carpenter who looked like Telly Savalas in *Kojak*. He'd rushed downtown the first day and returned the next day with a coffee urn and a van full of food. He had already explained to Corrine how he had cadged fifty cases of Coca-Cola products from a Brooklyn distributor and traded ten of those to the National Guardsmen occupying Battery Park in exchange for two canvas tents with frames and then swapped ten more to the Salvation Army, which had set up behind the AmEx building, for five cases of Sterno.

"Luke was working on the pile the first day," Corrine said, eager to establish that her new friend was not, despite his Bean boots, chinos, and rugby shirt, some Upper East Side dilettante.

To her surprise, Jerry embraced Luke—engulfed him, really—and thumped him on the back.

"God bless you, brother. Welcome to our humble operation. We're trying to do our little bit. We just got this generator this morning." He pointed to the throbbing two-wheeled contraption out on the cobblestones. "When I first got here, I had to unscrew the base plate on the lamppost to get a power outlet. That's one of the things you know if you grew up in the city, and you don't sound like you did, Luke. It's all about knowing where the juice is. You got to know who to call. Where to go for a generator or a bus or a permit. Where to get a hundred respirators and twenty tanks of propane. In New York, it's all about knowing how to connect the wires. Now more than ever. You got any drag in city government? Because these bastards from the Parks Department were sniffing around this morning, threatening to evict us."

"I know the Parks commissioner," Luke said. "I could make a call."

"The man's got juice," Jerry said, throwing a hamlike arm around Corrine. "Where'd you find this fucking guy?"

"On the street, actually."

She felt a strange pride in her new acquaintance, with whom she had a certain tribal sense of identity, affinities of background and education that weren't supposed to matter anymore, at this leveling moment. But wanting Jerry and the cops and the ironworkers to like her or at least not dislike her or make her feel guilty of some kind of slumming, she wouldn't dream of bringing certain of her friends around, and for that matter, she didn't really feel like sharing the experience. But Luke didn't seem to be blowing her cover.

"Let me introduce you to my friend, Captain Davies," Jerry said, nodding toward the big cop ambling across the cobblestones from the command post—who, unlike the volunteers, seemed to evince a kind of professional lassitude, conserving his energy for a moment of actual crisis—trailed by a patrolman Corrine hadn't seen before. She liked Davies, with his gruff humility, his stylized, purely formal flirtatiousness. A pink-skinned Brooklynite attached to the Brooklyn South, he cut a wide swath in the cluttered tent, his walkie-talkie and blocky Glock, nightstick and flashlight and cuffs jangling and clanking on his hips. He wasn't likely to sneak up on a perp, nor to have an easy time making it down the aisle of a bodega. Until a few days ago, the chances of their sharing a cup of coffee together would have been astronomically remote, but by now Corrine knew a great deal about Davies's family, his boat, and the intricacies and inanities of the NYPD pension plan.

Luke shook hands with Davies, who introduced the new guy,

Spinetti, a young patrolman in his twenties, dark and well built—a body familiar with Nautilus and StairMaster. Both men wore elasticized black ribbons of mourning over their badges.

"Luke's been digging," Jerry told them.

"A few hours is all," Luke said.

"More than I been doing, pal," Davies said. "I'm just sitting on my ass out here so I can't take this hero stuff already. I'm coming out of the station house this morning, woman comes up and hugs me. I don't even know what city I'm in anymore when I wake up in the morning. People coming up on the street and thanking you? They used to spit on us. Sometimes I think I must be in Kansas. If I wanted to live in fuckin' Kansas, I'd pack up and move."

"Personally, I think, you know, it's nice finally getting some, whatever, respect," Patrolman Spinetti said tentatively, as if disagreeing with the captain was to go out on a limb.

"When the shit came down," Jerry said, "you guys responded to the call."

Davies shrugged. "I hate to tell you, but I was sleeping in that morning."

"In some ways, it's been great this week," the patrolman said. "The radio's almost silent. No calls. No gang fights, no domestics, no stickups. Like even the punks are in shock."

"Yeah, well, somebody forgot to tell those assholes who looted the stores under the plaza. A few hours after the buildings come down, they're scooping up Rolexes and cameras within sniffing distance of the rubble."

Corrine had heard about that, but already it was clear that these stories weren't going to be part of the narrative of heroic acts, random acts of kindness, last words to loved ones on cell phones, bizarre coincidences, missed planes and buses that, had they been caught, would've carried the passengers to certain death, as well as the obverse—the last-minute shift changes and uncharacteristically early arrivals at the office. Such as Luke's phone call postponing breakfast at Windows on the World. What would he make of this miracle? Would it change his life? Persuade him to marry his secretary? Travel to India to find a guru? Move back home, down south, to care for a dying relative?

Corrine was showing him how to use the coffee machine just as a wave of National Guardsmen descended, so she let him handle pouring while she moved to the warming trays to dispense the ziti that had arrived from a restaurant on Mott Street. The upstate reservists—polite, close-shorn, burly men from Buffalo and Rochester and Utica, wearing stiff new camo uniforms—sat at the two picnic tables or stood inside the tent, blowing at their paper cups and plates, nodding deferentially to the cops, who, in turn, lowered their voices and made room for the silent crew of ironworkers that came through shortly after three, begrimed and beatific in their exhaustion.

It was after four in the morning when the tent finally emptied out. Jerry sent the three young women from Ralph Lauren home, enlisting Spinetti to drive them uptown. Luke declined the ride and lingered on with Corrine, cleaning up after the big rush.

Eventually, they joined the boys outside at the picnic table. The heat of the day had dissipated hours ago and the air was cool; it might have passed for a beautiful night if not for the acrid stench of the smoke churning the sky to the north.

"Back on the night shift," Jerry was saying. "After wasting my working life in bars and clubs, I finally get a civilian job, and here I am on dawn patrol again. In the winter, I never *saw* daylight. The last club—I never actually met my boss, the owner of record, but I talked to him once a week on the phone from Attica, where he was a guest of the state. The most important duty was delivering a bag of cash to Brooklyn on Wednesday and Saturday nights. After I closed up the club around five, I drive the cash to a restaurant in Flatbush with a loaded nine-millimeter Sig-Sauer in the glove compartment. I leave the Sig in the car, knock on the back door, and usually it's opened by my friend Dino, who's like five three in his lifts and missing a piece of his ear. We might drink a sambuca or two and discuss the Knicks or the Mets. Sometimes I leave the place at dawn with a new suit or a car stereo—swag from the latest truck hijack or cargo interdiction at JFK.

And one night, the performance bonus is—excuse me, Corrine—a complimentary blow job from the chippie occupying the seat next to Dino."

Corrine wasn't offended—although she preferred not to dwell on this image.

"I'd worked in the clubs for fifteen years and finally decided I had to get the fuck out. It's crazy. It's no life. I wanted to be a civilian. I had experience as a carpenter, but I didn't want to do the four-year apprenticeship for the union, so I went to Dino and he took care of it. Got my union card as a master carpenter and started out at twenty-eight an hour, as opposed to fourteen."

"Nice of Dino," Corrine said.

"He owed me," Jerry said. "They all owed me." He suddenly leaned over the picnic table and asked, looking at her plaintively, "Do you think things balance out? I mean, can a good deed—deeds—compensate for a bad one? You know—that karma thing."

She glanced over at Luke to see if she'd missed something.

"I lied for them, perjured myself. Some poor fucker, black guy, got the shit kicked out of him by my bouncers, he was in the hospital for two months last year, and as far as I know he's still doing physical therapy. White. Darin White. Bad enough going through life called White when your skin's the color of burnt toast. I testified, said I saw it happen, saw him go off on my guys, that he was crazy on PCP or something and started the whole thing, even though I was busy in the office at the time with a stripper and it was my boy Tiny who was cranked up and went crazy on the kid for no reason and the others jumped in and just started whaling on him. I came out just in time to see the last kick. We dumped him in front of the ER at Beth Israel half-dead."

"I remember that case," Luke said.

"Fucking tabloid circus. Al Sharpton all over the shit. They told me to disappear until they came up with a plan, so I hid out in this basement office, a secret wine cellar from Prohibition days. The cops searched the premises while I smoked weed and watched videos behind three feet of stone and the tabloids ran pictures of Darin White in traction, looking like a fucking mummy in those bandages. So what about you, Luke? Why'd you quit your job? You get tired of busting pension funds and throwing the little people out of work? Isn't that how you LBO guys make the big bucks?"

Luke smiled. "It's not as glamorous as it sounds."

"But why'd you quit?"

"It stopped being fun," he said almost interrogatively. "Ten years ago, we were like cowboys, making it up as we went along, riding in with guns blazing. Eventually, it became, I don't know, business as usual."

"So," Jerry said, "did you put away enough to stay retired?"

"Depends what you think is enough. My wife thinks you need a jet. I have a friend who says you need a hundred million to be a player."

"Are you a player?"

"Jesus, Jerry," Corrine protested.

Luke shook his head. "Afraid not. Tell you what, though, there'll be fewer players after the markets reopen in a few hours."

"You really think it's going to be bad?" Corrine asked.

"A bloodbath."

"No, that was last week," Jerry said bitterly. "Let's not confuse fucking red ink with the real thing."

Corrine found Jerry's anger a tonic. Just beneath the surface of his altruistic pragmatism was an undercurrent of rage—not an inappropriate state of mind just now. She sensed that if he hadn't been able to throw himself into relief work, his energies could easily have turned violent.

Davies emerged from his van and waddled over to join them, clanking like the Tin Man, taking a seat at the table and accepting a cigarette from Luke.

They sat in silence as the darkness began to seep away, watching as the silhouettes of office buildings emerged against the dingy backdrop of the predawn sky. Corrine registered a moment of perfect stillness, a silent pause marking the transition from night to day, which was punctuated by the distant, rising growl of diesel engines and the percussion of steel on steel, the relentless work resuming.

This morning would carry a different sound, a distant rumbling underground from the subway tunnels on either side of the park, followed by the faint, swelling tattoo of leather soles and heels on concrete stairs as the first wave of office workers surged up and spilled out onto Broadway. Men and women with briefcases, backpacks, and portfolios, early risers come to restart the great wounded machine of Wall Street. Receptionists and hedge-fund managers, retail brokers and risk and liability managers, systems analysts and janitors. And suddenly the spell would be broken, the sense that nothing existed outside this sacred, ravaged place.

"I can't imagine going into the office today," Luke said, "or tomorrow or the next day. But then again, I can't imagine *what* I should be doing. What are we supposed to do now?"

She knew exactly what he meant, and was reluctant to leave Bowling Green, but, in fact, the answer in her case at this very minute was that she had to go home and get her kids ready for school.

"Look at them," Jerry said. "It's like nothing happened."

"They're doing what they have to do," Davies told him. "It's a good thing."

Jerry shook his head. "Well, they should show a little goddamn respect."

"Hey, life goes on. That's the object, isn't it? Showing the bastards they haven't crippled us."

"A little respect is all I'm saying."

At that moment, a man emerged from the mouth of the subway entrance, a briefcase in one hand and an American flag in the other, holding it aloft as he took his place in the silent parade of commerce.

# 9

The smell of bacon wafted into the kids' bedroom, making Corrine faintly nauseated. She tried to get them to eat fruit in the morning, which was hard enough without Russell frying up crispy strips of salted pig fat.

Storey wouldn't budge. She wanted to wear her gray flannel Jacadi jumper, the one Casey had bought for her birthday, which was at the bottom of the laundry hamper.

"Sweetie, it's dirty and wrinkled. Besides, you wore it your first day at school last Monday. Technically, that would make two days in a row, since you haven't been back since then. You don't want to wear the same outfit again, do you?"

"Why can't you wash it?"

"Storey, it's seven-thirty and we're about to be late for school."

She hesitated, arms folded imperiously across her Little Mermaid pajama top, weighing the arguments. While she was fetishistic in her attachment to two or three articles of clothing, including the jumper, she was also a stickler for punctuality. Her parents' chronic tardiness was a constant source of mortification. On the other hand, the gray flannel jumper could be a cover story—an objective correlative of the general anxiety.

"Are you nervous about going to school?"

Storey tugged at the waist of her pajama top and studied the picture of Ariel.

"Do you want to talk about what happened last week?"

"Maybe I could wear the tartan skirt and the black turtleneck," Storey said.

"Good idea."

With an air of world-weariness, she removed her pajamas. "That means I have to wear tights."

"I'm sure we can find a clean pair," Corrine said, digging through Storey's drawers. Several dirty pairs were balled up at the bottom of the underwear drawer. She smoothed one out on the bed and handed it to Storey.

"They're dirty."

"You didn't seem to mind the fact that the jumper was dirty."

She took the tights between her thumb and forefinger. "Are you going to pick us up from school?"

"Probably Jean will."

"Probably?"

"Definitely." More than ever, at this moment, they had to be reassured about routine, to feel secure and informed. Although Storey, thankfully, seemed more concerned about her wardrobe.

"I can pick them up."

Corrine turned to see Hilary framed in the doorway, stretching her arms over her head, catlike. "Jean's on duty anyway."

"I want Aunt Hilary to pick us up."

"We can get ice cream," Hilary said. "Won't that be great?"

"If you want, you can go along with Jean," Corrine said. Not a chance in hell that Corrine would entrust the fetching of her children to her sister. If Hilary met a cute guy in the next few hours, or found some great new shop, the kids would be on their own come three o'clock. As it was, she'd nearly killed them even before they were

97

born. Thinking about all this, Corrine could barely restrain herself from snatching Hilary's hand from Storey's head.

"You've got beautiful hair, baby."

"Just like my mom's."

"Well, yes." Hilary glanced at her sister. "It does run in the family."

Corrine shot her a look. In the past week, there'd been a dozen similarly ambiguous references in front of the children, and Storey was a water witch in the detection of undercurrents.

"One of the Fluffies is missing," Storey informed Hilary.

"The who?"

"The Fluffies."

"They're kind of like fairies," Corrine explained.

"That's their house," Storey said, pointing to the dollhouse beside her bed. "They come out at night. Grown-ups can't see them. The daddy's missing. Like Dylan's daddy."

Corrine winced, inadvertently making a "Let's not pursue the subject" face.

"I still can't believe he's gone," Hilary said.

"Missing." Corrine vigorously shook her head.

Hilary rolled her eyes.

"Quarter to eight, girls." Russell was standing in the doorway, naked except for the towel around his waist. What the hell was that about? Showing off for Hilary? She examined his body critically— barrel chest, a few graying hairs amid the dark thicket. A hairy swelling at the waist, not quite a pot—more like a Frisbee. Not bad for a man his age, but not necessarily, if that's what he was hoping, a body to arouse lust in a younger woman.

"Thanks for the bulletin," she said.

"What's a bulletin?" Storey wanted to know.

"In this case, an officious and unnecessary announcement."

"Kind of like you want to shoot a bullet *in* somebody?" Storey was deeply aware of how clever she was being.

"That's really cute, honey," Hilary said, pinching her cheek. "You are such a smart thing."

"Kind of like," Corrine said, and then, seeing Storey's reaction, she said, "No, honey, that was just a stupid little joke of Mommy's." Walking on fucking eggshells. "Is Jeremy ready?"

Russell nodded.

"How come Daddy's not dressed?" Storey asked.

"That's a very good question. Maybe he wants everybody to check out his washboard abs, or it could be his favorite jumper's dirty."

*"Mom!"*

Russell retreated in confusion. Maybe she'd been too hard on him—maybe he just wasn't really thinking about his state of relative undress. He'd been walking around in a daze the last week, with one of his best friends missing and presumed dead. She had to remind herself that Russell tended to internalize these things and that he'd seen everything up close—walking down Greenwich Street, glancing up to see the first plane a few hundred feet overhead just after he dropped the kids off at St. Luke's and then returning to the loft, watching from their window the, as he put it, "not-quite-tiny-enough" figures jumping out of the tower eight blocks away, close enough to distinguish between men and women. That was what seemed to have upset him the most, though no one else was really talking about it—there was almost a news embargo on the jumpers. Russell said he stopped counting after twenty-seven. . . .

Terrible as it might sound, she couldn't help hoping that if nothing else, this might draw them together again by stripping away his veneer of jaded sophistication. Two decades in the city had hardened him; she missed the sensitive and insecure boy she'd met at Brown, the bookish hick from Michigan who wrote poetry, including a cycle of twenty-one sonnets to Corrine on her twenty-first birthday, who loved Dylan Thomas and Scott Fitzgerald and all the sad, doomed young men of letters, who was intimidated by the preppies and the native New Yorkers on campus.

Even as she tried to deal with the kids' anxiety, she was worried sick about his.

When she and Storey finally emerged from the bedroom, Jeremy and Russell were curled up on the couch, watching cartoons. She would have been more impressed by Russell's willingness to sit in front of the Cartoon Network if she hadn't known that he enjoyed it almost as much as his son, if she thought he was making a sacrifice. She'd rather cut off her nose than watch a cartoon. It never ceased to amaze her that a man who had "Dover Beach" committed to memory and read Wittgenstein for pleasure could happily while away hours watching Daffy and Tweety and the Powerpuff Girls.

She led Storey over to the couch. "Okay, Coco Chanel here is finally ready for school."

"Who's Coco Chanel?"

"Right," Russell said, rising like a zombie. "Come on, Jeremy, let's go."

Jeremy ran over to his mother and clutched her tightly, his eyes filling with tears as he burrowed into Corrine's crotch. "I don't want to go."

"What is it, honey?"

He shook his head.

"Are you scared?"

He nodded. In fact, he had been anxious last Monday, his first day at the new school, and had often resisted preschool, clinging and crying in just this fashion. Somehow, she found it reassuring now that he'd been a reluctant schoolgoer even before the eleventh.

Storey now grew concerned for her brother's peace of mind. "Don't worry, Jeremy. The terrorists only attack skyscrapers. And our school is only three stories high."

This sounded as logical as anything Corrine herself could have come up with, or as anything they *had* come up with so far in the way of reassurance. Storey was at her best when assuming the role of her brother's keeper. Older by thirty seconds, she was deeply conscious of this seniority.

Corrine and Russell exchanged a look, a query of mutual helplessness.

"There's nothing to worry about," she said, feeling like a baldfaced liar. "It's all over now." Never had she felt quite as dishonest as a parent as in the last few days, trying to comfort the children, when she felt absolutely no comfort or security herself. The old certainties were pretty thoroughly discredited. What were you supposed to say—Don't worry, be happy?

"But Dad works in a skyscraper," Jeremy said, suddenly spotting the flaw in Storey's earlier bromide.

"It's a small skyscraper," Russell said. "More like a high rise."

Jeremy looked puzzled.

"Daddy will be extra careful," Corrine said.

"Where are *you* going?" Storey demanded.

"I'm going to a restaurant to get some food and drinks for the rescue workers," she said.

"Can I come?" Jeremy asked.

"No, you have to go to school."

"If I can't go with you," he said, "then I want to stay home."

"Nobody's going to be here."

Corrine looked at Russell, who seemed to have tuned out of the conversation. "Dad, do you have anything to say about this?"

"About what?"

"About Jeremy going to school."

"I think, well, I think Jeremy should go to school. I think it's important to reestablish the routine."

"But I don't want to go."

"You have to go," Storey said, "or else you'll miss all the lessons and then you'll get behind and then you won't get into college."

"I don't want to go to college."

"Come on, guys," Russell said. "We don't want to be late."

"Hey, Dad," Jeremy blurted, "did all the terrorists die? Because they were on the planes?"

"Because if they all died, they can't attack us," Storey said. "So we should all go to school and don't worry."

"Well, that's a good point," Corrine said cautiously. Anything to get them off to school. Time enough to nuance this response later, to hint at the existence of other malevolent souls out there.

Outside, she hugged them all on the street, trying not to communicate her own sudden sense of dread, sparked by the acrid tang in the air and the sight of a platoon of Guardsmen on the corner of Duane Street.

"It's still on fire," Jeremy said, pointing at the plume of smoke that filled the sky to the south, tilting toward the east.

"So, Russ, you'll call Jean and make sure she can get into the city? . . . Russ?"

He nodded.

"I'll be on my cell. And I should finish my shift by four. Wait, do you have your license? And the copy of the lease?"

He looked blank. "I don't have the lease."

"Russell, for God's sake, we talked about this."

She waited while he went back upstairs, again checking her own purse to make sure she had her driver's license as well as the second copy of the lease on the apartment, official correspondence showing her residing at this address—they needed this stuff to cross the police barricades, to prove they resided here in the war zone. The license because it had her picture, and the lease because, like most residents of Manhattan, she had a license from her home state, where she hadn't lived for twenty years, the logistics for getting one in the city being too tedious and grueling. Her Massachusetts license showed the address of her mother's condo in Lenox, while Russell's was from Michigan. She'd explained all of this the last couple of days to various out-of-town cops who'd volunteered to take over the secondary and tertiary policing duties of the city. On the thirteenth, she'd had a bitch of a time getting back home after meeting Casey uptown for a drink. The barricades had moved down from Fourteenth Street to Canal in the last day or two, but inside the restricted zone, proof of residence was still required.

As they waited for Russell, the Levine clan descended from the penthouse with Todd in his Grace Church School uniform. After a dispute about a water leak, the Calloways had gone without speaking to them for more than a year, but in the last few days the animosity had given way to a spirit of wartime camaraderie. Astonishingly, they'd all shared a meal up at the Levines' that first night, at their request.

"You guys holding up?" Ray asked, the very image of a downtown ad guy with his salt-and-pepper goatee, black turtleneck, and black jeans.

"We're fine," Corrine said.

"Any word on your friend?"

She shook her head. "Not since he rode off on his bike after he saw the first plane hit."

"I might have done the same thing," Ray said, shaking his head solemnly, "if I hadn't been uptown with a client. Can we walk you up to the border?"

"We're just waiting for Russell. He forgot his copy of the lease."

"Rebecca forgot hers on Friday. She finally got through by showing her Prozac bottle. It was the only thing in her purse that actually had our address on it."

"I could have whipped out my Xanax and my Ambien," Rebecca said, "but he looked like some farmhand and I didn't want to blow his mind." She sold ad space for Condé Nast, apparently a very stressful job.

"Have you got phone service yet?" Corrine asked, thinking the kids had heard all they needed to about Rebecca's pharmacopoeia.

"It was on when we got back last night," Ray said. "We spent the weekend in Amagansett. I told Rebecca she should stay out there with Todd."

"I'm not going to hide," Rebecca said. "I'm a New Yorker. And so's my kid." Indeed, Rebecca had the bluntness as well as the high polish that Corrine had always associated with native New Yorkers—although even she had been deeply shaken and tearful that first night; Corrine was a little sorry to see that she was regaining her tough-girl swagger. Even after twenty years, Corrine thought of herself as something other than a New Yorker, or at least she had until this past week.

"Well, it's nice to have the option is all I'm saying," Ray said.

"Mom's feeding the rescuers," Storey said.

"What's this?" Rebecca asked.

"It's nothing, really, I'm just doing a shift at this soup kitchen down at Bowling Green."

"Oh my God," said Rebecca. "That is so great."

"It's just a little coffee and doughnut station I heard about."

"You must give me the number," Rebecca said.

"Rebecca wants to meet a fireman," Ray said.

"Have you seen the Bradfords?" Corrine asked, inquiring after their upstairs neighbors.

"You'll love this," Rebecca said. "They checked into the Sherry-Netherland as displaced persons. They're living it up uptown, room service and Frette sheets changed daily—courtesy of the city."

"That's terrible," Corrine said. "I mean, it's not like our building was damaged."

"They were going on about the air quality," Rebecca explained, "but really it's a paid vacation."

"Actually," Corrine said, "I do wonder about the air."

"They used asbestos in the first seventy floors of the south tower," Rebecca said. "Or maybe it was the north, whatever. Before the law changed. So that's just part of what we're breathing down here. And they're telling us it's perfectly safe?"

Jeremy had struck up a conversation with Todd. "Is your school in a skyscraper?" he asked.

"It's got four stories," Todd said. "Dad says it's the best school downtown by far."

"Well, *one* of the best," Rebecca said. "There're *lots* of good schools in New York."

"Is *their* school good?" Todd demanded.

Russell finally arrived, his timing better than usual, from Corrine's point of view. And then something surprising happened, something that made her question her assumptions about the immutability of character just when she had imagined the Levines' reverting to type; after she'd once again hugged her husband and children goodbye, Ray stepped into the family circle to give her a hug, and then, Rebecca, in her steel gray Dolce & Gabbana two-piece armor, followed suit.

Flabbergasted, she looked at Russell to get his reaction, but evidently he hadn't registered this little miracle on Hudson Street.

"You be careful," Ray said.

"Thanks, Ray," she said. "I will. And you, too."

Once all of them had said their good-byes, the Levines headed west to Church Street, while Russell led the kids up Hudson and Corrine walked toward the ghostly plume of gray smoke hanging there in the pale blue sky.

# 10

t had probably been twenty years—years of foie gras with poached pears, curry with mango chutney, and other culinary yin and yang, fat and sweet permutations—since Luke had actually bitten into a peanut butter and jelly sandwich. Corrine had thrust one at him, and he was astonished by the sweet, acidic lash of the grape jelly, the gluey peanut butter sticking to the roof of his mouth, the host of emotions and memories this now called up.

"What's the matter?" Corrine said.

"I have this thing where I absolutely have to have the jelly come to the very edge of the bread," said Karen, the Ralph Lauren girl. "And right to the corners. Every bite has to have jelly."

Luke exchanged a look with Corrine, a look referencing the girl's youth, her *sportiness,* the bright primary palette of her disposition, but that perhaps said more about the two people who were exchanging it. Corrine was standing beside her at the sandwich station, both of them wearing plastic gloves.

"I was obsessive about it. Used to drive my mother crazy."

"Do you realize," Corrine said, "that Smucker's has a patent on the crustless peanut butter and jelly sandwich?"

"No fuckin' way," Patrolman Spinetti said. "Excuse my French. That's like having a friggin' patent on apple pie."

"No, really, they do."

This, Luke thought, was just the kind of weird thing Corrine would know, realizing, too, how odd but exhilarating it was that he should think he knew this about her, after just a few days working beside her. But it was true: She *was* a repository of quirky facts and arcane erudition; this was one of the things he admired about her. The other night, when they went for a walk in Battery Park, she'd told him that a hummingbird's heart beats a thousand times a minute.

"I like mine with the peanut butter spread on both slices of the bread," said a young Guardsman, the squareness of his head accentuated by the flattop cut.

"Then it would get all over your hands."

"No, I mean both pieces on the inside."

"It's a rather disgusting invention, no matter how you make it," said Yvonne, an angular young Frenchwoman with bright orange hair who had showed up with baguettes and charcuterie. She was slicing the last of the baguettes open; finishing a pile of cigar-shaped sandwiches—*jambon, fromage, saucisson.*

"You're insulting our national dish," Karen said.

"I hate to disagree with a beautiful lady," the square-headed Guardsman said, "but the cheeseburger is our national dish."

"Which is why," Corrine said, "the average American has twenty pounds of undigested meat in his intestines."

"That is so gross," Karen said.

"You're all wrong," Jerry said, holding up a can of Campbell's condensed chicken noodle soup. "This is it. Our national dish."

Once upon a time, these had been the two staples of Luke's diet— peanut butter and jelly and chicken noodle soup.

"I tried volunteering for the other soup kitchen, the gourmet one David Bouley started." These were the first words from Clara, an older woman with a mass of graying hair, black-lacquered nails, and a sour mien, who stood at the coffee machine. "But they said they were fully staffed—unless, I guess, you're a model or a movie star. I don't expect they're serving condensed soup over there."

This diet kept transporting Luke back to his childhood—sudden flashbacks of cafeterias and kitchen-counter lunches, comfort food trailing memories that weren't necessarily as comforting as advertised. The mnemonic power of a simple sandwich. One bite could take him back to a picnic with his mother—a day of riding, the smell of manure and cut grass, the simple joy of possessing her for the day. Buried within the same peanut butter sandwich was a fourth-grade taste of impending doom, when Chuck Johnson, who'd been held back a year and was as big as a teenager, waited for him at the tetherball court while he masticated slowly in the cafeteria, having challenged him to a fight in second period. Chuck had called his father "a nigger lover" because he'd spoken out against the Confederate flag at the courthouse. Luke responded by calling Chuck a Neanderthal, and Chuck didn't need a dictionary to recognize an insult when he heard one. This exchange ended with Luke lying sprawled on his back, looking up at the tetherball hanging from its pole, gasping for air as his classmates howled and cheered.

"You know, when you gave me that sandwich," he told her later, "if I acted strange, it was because it took me back thirty years."

They were sitting on the steps of the Customs House, looking back at the glow of the lighted tent: the improvised domestic diorama—women serving and men eating.

"I had this sudden image of my parents' kitchen in Tennessee—the avocado green refrigerator, the round pine table, the ladder-back chairs with rush seats. I was twelve, maybe thirteen. I'd skipped school that afternoon. My mother was supposed to be on her volunteer shift at the hospital and my father was away at some conference in Knoxville."

In his adolescence, he had come naturally into possession of a secret life, come to covet privacy, to enjoy the freedom of the empty house—the illusion of independence conjoined with the security of home. Not least because it was the safest, most comfortable place to indulge the new imperative of masturbation.

After hiding his bike behind the house, he told her now, he'd assembled the ingredients of his afternoon repast; Wonder bread, a jar of Skippy and another of Welch's grape jelly. Leaving a satisfying mess on the counter, he sat down at the table to eat, weighing and ordering his options: He could go directly to his room, dig the *Playboy* out from its hiding place behind the World Book encyclopedia set, and find instant relief. Or he could prolong the anticipation and start in his parents' room, explore the treasures of their drawers: his father's medals from Korea, his mother's underwear, the little circular rotating calendar with the help of which she practiced the rhythm method. The happy trance of the act that these investigations inspired was interrupted by the sound of car doors in the driveway. He heard his mother's laughter, then the tap of boots on the flagstone walk.

"Don't tell me you were caught in the act?" Corrine said, wincing in sympathetic anxiety.

He shook his head. He wasn't sure why he was telling her this, something he'd never even told his wife, except perhaps that she had been more or less responsible for resurrecting the memory.

"Then I heard another voice that I recognized. It was Duck Cheatham."

"Duck?"

He shrugged. "It's a southern thing. I had friends called Boo and Bear. Even went to school with a kid named States' Rights. Duck and his wife were friends of my parents. For a while, they did everything together, including vacations. We always spent Christmas Eve at their house before we all went to midnight Mass at my father's church. My brother and I hung out with their kids, and everybody used to joke about Mom's special friendship with Duck. If you were at a cocktail party and wanted my mother, all you had to do was look for Duck, who was a good head taller than most people in the room, and there she'd be. And they rode together all the time, something my dad and Duck's wife weren't interested in."

Her brow wrinkled in half a dozen folds, and what appeared to be an intense sympathy made him feel justified in sharing the story. He handed her a cigarette from his pack of Marlboro Lights. They'd both started smoking again, a response to stress, a harking back to the uncomplicated pleasures of youth, which was reinforced by the habits of the cops and Guardsmen. A way of punctuating and dividing up the long intervals of waiting and inactivity, it was also a shared habit, a kind of communion. Whatever the initial impulses, this recidivism provided them with a context for loitering and conversation.

"So there I was with my jeans around my ankles on my mother's bed."

She laughed, expelling two plumes of smoke through her nose. "Sorry, I just suddenly pictured you."

"I panicked. Then I pulled myself together and listened. I could hear the murmur of voices downstairs. I thought about retreating to my own room, but I couldn't, safely anyway, because the floorboards in the hallway would give me away. We lived—my mom still lives—in an old farmhouse, and it's impossible to sneak around without rousing the dead. So I'm creeping across the floor as stealthily as I can toward the door and trying to decide what to do, when suddenly I hear them on the stairs."

"Oh no."

"All I can think of is the closet. The door's partly open, so I slip in and pull it closed behind me."

"Oh God."

"I heard them come into the room and fall into bed."

She took his hand and clutched it.

"Sorry," he said. "I don't even know why I'm telling you this." But the pressure of her hand and her look of concern seemed justification enough. "I stayed in the closet. Fifteen minutes, half an hour, I don't really know. Eventually, they got dressed and she walked him downstairs." She squeezed his hand tighter. "When I heard them outside, I went to my room and climbed out the window, not for the first time, and dropped into the backyard. Then I sneaked through the back pasture and hid in the barn, which, I realized almost immediately, was a bad idea, because Mom practically lived in the barn. She's a horse person. So I circled the tree line of our neighbor's pasture and came out on the main road, waited until I saw the bus pass by, and then I walked up the driveway. I didn't know how I'd be able to face her. I shouted hello from the front door and shot up to my brother's room. Matthew was already home. When she called us down to dinner, I tried to act as if it had just been another day. But the minute I walked in the kitchen, I remembered the peanut butter and jelly and bread, and there was no sign of any of it. She'd obviously cleaned up. I waited for her to say something, but she never did."

"You never talked about it?"

"God no. Not to her. Not to anyone, really. I hadn't thought about it in years, not until you handed me that sandwich."

"You poor thing. That must have been . . . Fuck. What happened? Did they keep seeing each other?"

He shrugged. "There were rumors, of course. I don't really know for certain. Eventually, Duck went bankrupt and his wife divorced him. Then of course he shot himself."

"Why 'of course'?"

"I don't know, it's another southern thing—how you'd expect the story to go. I'm not sure if it ever came out in the open, the thing with my mom. I don't even know if my father suspected."

"He was a minister?"

He nodded. "Yeah, a pastor. He died last year."

"Do you miss him?"

He shrugged. "I left my job three weeks later."

Of course, he had made the connection before, but hearing himself say it now, it sounded so obvious.

"I'm sorry about the sandwich," she said, leaning over and kissing his cheek. "But I'm glad you told me." She kissed him again, this time on the lips. Suddenly, grudgingly, he registered a commotion from the direction of the green.

Jerry's Pathfinder was parked on the cobblestones outside the tent; half a dozen vividly painted, pneumatic women in tight T-shirts and halters were climbing out, strippers recruited from the club where Jerry's girlfriend worked.

"The girls are back," Corrine said.

"I guess we should resume our posts."

"Oh, *now* you're suddenly feeling the call of duty."

For a moment, she seemed genuinely jealous.

"Do you go to those places?" she demanded.

"Once in a while, I used to. It was a client entertainment thing. Honestly, it doesn't do it for me."

"Are you just saying that because it's what you think you're supposed to say?"

"No, really. I find it awkward. And frustrating. Generally speaking, I fail to find it stimulating—and if it was, what exactly am I supposed to do with my . . ."

"Erection?"

"I was going to say 'excitement.'"

"No need for euphemism."

"But, yes, exactly. I mean, what is the fucking point of that?"

"Svetlana tells me at her club there's a special Boom Boom Room where you can relieve the pressure, so to speak."

"That's good to know."

"Have you ever been with a prostitute?"

"I can't believe you're asking me this."

"Well, who else am I going to ask? I'm curious about these things. It's not like I can ask my friends' husbands. I'm a middle-aged mother. I don't know why, but talking to Svetlana, I just suddenly realized there's a whole secret world of male sexuality I know nothing about." She looked up at him expectantly. "So?"

"I'm not going to answer that."

"So you have?"

"No, I—"

"Was it exciting? Or just sleazy?"

"For most of us, sleazy *is* exciting. That's kind of the whole point."

"Have you done it more than once?"

"I didn't say I'd done it at all. I was merely pointing out that sleazy, dirty, nasty, whatever you want to call it—that's the appeal of professional sex."

"Are hookers really better at it than the rest of us?"

"I couldn't say."

"Come on."

He sighed. Her curiosity was amusing, even stimulating. What the fuck, he thought. "Once," he said. "In Hong Kong. On a business trip."

"And?"

"Honestly? It was great."

She slapped his shoulder hard, playfully. "She was good?"

He nodded.

"What did she do that was so special?"

"I'm not going into detail."

"Why not? Did she blow you?"

"You're unbelievable."

"No, I'm just curious."

"Have you ever heard the expression 'She could suck a golf ball through a garden hose'?"

"Wow . . . I mean, no. But that sounds good, I guess. Actually, it sounds painful, but I assume that's really good. From the guy's point of view, I mean. So you think sex is like, say, tennis or chess—practice makes perfect?"

"Well, why wouldn't it be? One thing I can tell you is that young women are highly overrated. They don't know shit."

"Being middle-aged, I'm glad to hear it."

Holding her gaze, he felt the urge to lean over and kiss her.

"I think we better go back to the tent," she said.

# 11

The bomb scare came as a relief.

Cocooned within two and a half walls of books, his office window framing the towers of midtown—a dozen vertical targets in the sky—Russell was sitting at his desk, in front of his computer screen, when his assistant, Roger, rushed in to announce that the building was being evacuated. Disruption and uncertainty were the new norms. The Dionysian gods enshrined in picture frames on his walls suddenly seemed almost quaint: bleary, bearded John Berryman; Keith Richards sweating onstage; the signed publicity still from *The Shining* ("To Russ, who gives good book, Jack") and the author's photo of his long-lost friend Jeff Pierce, the doomed look in his eyes even then, an expression that seemed appropriate to the mood of the moment.

He'd spent a good part of the morning answering E-mails from around the globe—assuring everyone that he'd survived. He'd deleted five copies of Auden's "September 1, 1939," and three of Yeats's "The Second Coming," as well as two copies of an E-mail labeled "SATAN'S FACE?"—an image of smoke pouring from one of the towers, a scene in which it seemed possible to descry a grinning demonic visage. And yet another image, supposedly taken from the observation deck of the north tower, allegedly recovered from the rubble, with a tourist posing against the endless vista while behind him a plane headed straight for the tower.

The city had never seemed so fragile. Bomb threats, chemical scares, viruses biological and virtual. The sound of sirens had become endemic, or was it just that he noticed them now? No rumor was implausible. Last Thursday, the wind had shifted and carried the smoke uptown, well into the Fifties, and the sense of stunned relief that had seemed to prevail among those who found themselves alive on Wednesday had given way to anxiety and public craziness, as if the electrical-fire, oven-cleaner smell carried with it some psychotropic substance—Russell saw people shouting on street corners, talking to themselves, couples fighting bitterly on the sidewalks. It reminded him of 1979, when he'd arrived in a nearly bankrupt city that felt on the verge of collapse, fraught with trash and peril.

Today, just when some resumption of the normal rhythms seemed possible, the computers had gone crazy; Roger had explained that a new kind of virus was rampaging through the Internet, infiltrating their system—whether another prong of the terrorist attacks or the work of opportunistic hackers, no one was certain, although, sadly, the system had been working well enough at 3:17 this morning to receive the E-mail now frozen on his screen:

Haven't heard from you since the 11th & can't help wondering if you would ever have made the effort to find out if I was alive if I hadn't called you that day. Just because I survived doesn't mean I'm okeydokey. Or that I can sleep at night or that I don't listen for the next explosion & the sirens. Or that I don't wait every night for you to ring my buzzer. Correct me if I'm wrong, but wasn't that you who used to buzz after you'd been out to dinner at Balthazar with Susan

Minot or cocktails on the Upper East Side with John Guare or the National Book Awards dinner with your wife (whose name I'm not supposed to mention—I can see how you wince when I do, like it's the name of God in some religion where they aren't allowed to speak it). Wasn't that you who used to stagger up the stairs & expect me to service you without so much as a "Hey, Trish, how you doing? How was your day?" It sure looked like you, but then I was down on my knees and my angle was bad, so maybe I was wrong. Maybe that was somebody else. Maybe that guy got crushed under the rubble. The fact that you are not returning my calls or E-mails makes me question the depth of your feelings for me, not to mention your basic human decency. Would you treat a friend or business associate this way? I even began to worry, stupid me, that something had happened to you afterward, like maybe you'd been hit by a taxi or you'd been a mensch and gone down to Ground Zero to help with the rescue effort and fallen into a hole or something, but then I saw you throwing back martinis and being terribly witty & charming with that ugly wrinkled redhead at the Four Seasons, so I guess not. I'm still hanging on by a thread, thanks for asking.

I have feelings, too, you know. And given all that's happened, I am rethinking my life and the role of the people in it, and I was stupid enough to hope that maybe you were, too. That maybe you were finally going to admit that you weren't happy in your present situation.

I'm tired of being treated like a no-maintenance sexual resource. I'm tired of waiting for your call, waiting for you to show up at the door, never knowing if I will see you again. I don't plan to wait forever. I think you know me better than that, although I'm beginning to wonder if you know me at all.

Trish had been his assistant for a brief period a couple of years ago, and though he'd resisted her overtures and her air of lubricious availability for as long as she was sitting outside his office, he succumbed one night after a long, drunken PEN dinner when Corrine was visiting her mother and the nanny was spending the week with the kids, calling her at midnight and climbing the five flights to her tiny walk-up on McDougal Street. This had established the pattern, and while he always regretted it in the morning, he somehow learned to live with the guilt, as we get used to any hardship through repetition, and would find himself calling her again a few weeks later or simply showing up on her doorstep after a night of public festivity. But his behavior seemed truly appalling to him now, when he was forced to calculate the value of his spiritual and emotional resources, which had never before felt so fragile or essential.

He could easily have been in the mall underneath the World Trade Center, picking up his reading glasses—it was the location of his oculist, and the Gap where they outfitted the kids, their regular destination for many of life's necessities—or standing in the plaza, hit by a jumper, or simply gaping when it all came down on top of him. Or for that matter, he might have rushed down after the fact, as Jim had done, to see if he could offer help. He oscillated between feeling grateful for being spared and feeling guilty that at no point in the hour or so between the impact of the first plane and the collapse of the first tower had he experienced that altruistic impulse, though he'd been only ten blocks away from the disaster. He would have liked to believe it was a concern for his family that had kept him riveted at his window, watching the spectacle. These days, his job seemed fairly stale and pointless, the sum of his accomplishments far smaller than he'd once imagined it would be. What seemed worth preserving was his family.

He'd been meaning to write or call and tell Trish as much, but he was afraid of her reaction—knowing all too well her obsessive nature and the violence of her passions—the very qualities that made her so sexually enthralling.

Washington appeared at the door. "Let's bail, chief."

Their building seemed an unlikely target—an undistinguished office tower in midtown, home to a publishing conglomerate owned by Germans, a brokerage house, two accounting firms, and an ad agency, but he looked around the office, wondering what, if anything, he should take with him. His first editions were all at home. And at this point, his collected correspondence made for a pretty bulky set of files.

Empty-handed, he followed his colleagues down the hall toward the elevator. The evacuation was orderly, everyone waiting patiently for the elevator, speaking in undertones, trading rumors: *Anthrax at Condé Nast . . . Special Forces in Afghanistan . . . Gold bullion at Ground Zero . . . Nimbda virus in the E-mail . . .*

"Yo, man, tune in." Washington was tugging at his arm.

"What?" Russell said.

"I said, 'How are the kids holding up?'"

"They're doing okay. Yours?"

"We've had a few nightmares. They call it 'the big fire,' good neutral nomenclature. Basically, they're taking their cues from us. The kids who are hysterical are the ones whose parents are shoving them under the bed every time they hear a plane overhead. Kids are sponges, basically. Incredibly absorbent, ridiculously expensive sponges." He paused, looked up at the floor indicator over the elevator. "Fuck it, let's take the stairs."

Russell followed him to the stairwell.

"Veronica wants to leave the city," he said, holding the door for Russell.

"That was Corrine's first reaction."

"Maybe it's time."

"You? In the suburbs?"

"It's not about me anymore. It's about the kids, Russell."

Voices echoed through the stairwell as they descended.

"Actually, I've been thinking about it myself," Russell said. Which, incredibly, was true, although for years the *burbs* had been for him and Washington alike, as for most of those who'd grown up there, a punch line that required no introduction, one they continued to laugh at even after marriage and parenthood had domesticated them. Among the simple articles of their faith, along with a disdain for commerce in its purest forms, was the belief that lawn care and commuting were incompatible with the higher pursuits, that the metropolis was the source of the life force.

Washington nodded. "This shit isn't going to stop. It's only a matter of time before they hit the water supply or the subway."

Their progress was slowed by a clot of office workers on the eleventh floor, including a hysterical woman whose voice reverberated through the vertical labyrinth of concrete.

"For the love of God, what do these people want? What did we do to them?"

When they finally reached the sidewalk, the block was teeming with displaced office workers; cops with megaphones were directing them away from the building. The crowd parted before a twisted figure in a wheelchair, for a police van nosing in from Third. The mood was one of disciplined retreat, the general crisis seeming for the moment to have instilled a sense of collective identity and purpose on the anarchic impulses of the urbanites. The enforced intimacy of sweating bodies was strangely comforting. Russell found himself pressed against a beautiful, nameless girl he recognized—dark and delicate, of Indian extraction, he imagined—from shared trips on the elevator, enveloped in her musky scent. Was this to be the legacy: wartime couplings, sudden intimacies, frenzied couplings in stairwells and broom closets? Suddenly, inexcusably, he felt the same erotic possibility hovering in the smudged air as he once had when he was in his twenties, even as the dark woman was sheared away from him.

They joined the pedestrian current flowing east along Fifty-first toward Second, and, as if by instinct, went straight to Billy's, a smoky, wood-paneled former speakeasy and a frequent refuge from the purple-white fluorescence of the office. Russell was surprised to hear Washington order a martini; he'd been on the wagon for almost three years.

"Desperate times."

"Carpe diem," Russell said, not knowing how else to react.

"No word on Jim?"

Russell shook his head.

"You want to talk about it?"

Russell shook his head again. "What's to say?"

"I know how tight you guys were. Sometimes I think he filled the hole Jeff left behind."

Russell nodded, determined to keep his composure.

"I expect Judy's enjoying her role as widow and martyr."

"Jesus, man. That's harsh." Russell would never allow himself to express this sentiment, at least not now, although he had to admit he'd felt it on the several occasions he'd talked to her in the last several days. And he was grateful, at that moment, for the blasphemy.

"The poor bastard."

"Maybe it's not the worst way to go."

"I wasn't thinking about his death," Washington said. "I was thinking about his life."

Their drinks arrived.

Washington held his up to the light, sniffed it, and sipped. "How's Corrine?"

"I don't know. I've barely seen her. She's working at this soup kitchen down at Ground Zero."

"She always had that Florence Nightingale thing going on."

"I'm about to remind her that charity begins at home."

"I think we're witnessing the beginning of the end of the whole idea of the city," Washington said. "Technology was already making concentration irrelevant. Terrorism will make it impractical."

"This is why you're moving?"

"Veronica wants to get me out of here. I don't really have a choice. Not if I want to save my marriage." His face assumed a slightly comical, hangdog expression.

"What happened?"

"Came home at three-thirty the other night, redolent of whiskey and pussy."

"Ouch."

"Or so I'm told. Memory doesn't quite serve. I went out for dinner with Slansky and he's looking at the wine list and I thought, Fuck it, I could be chopped meat tomorrow. Why not eat, drink, and be merry? Two bottles and a few hours later, I found myself at Evelyn's, sitting on a bar stool next to Nancy Tanner."

"You fucked Nancy?"

"A gentleman doesn't fuck and tell."

"Was that the first time?"

"First I remember."

"God, after all these years. How was it?"

"As best I can remember, pretty good."

"Does Veronica know it was Nancy?"

"No. Not that it matters much. I've been pure as the driven snow going on three years, but there's a lot of history here, and Veronica's just been waiting for me to slip." In the old days, Russell had been fascinated by his friend's unself-conscious philandering. Despite his recent hiatus, Washington still liked to say that men had four needs: food, shelter, pussy, and strange pussy. Whereas Russell believed there were two kinds of men—those who cheated, and those who felt guilty afterward—and that he was irrevocably one of the latter. Until Trisha, he'd strayed only once, but he was endlessly curious about this bottomless subject of marital infidelity in its myriad variations. For years, he'd counted on Washington to provide him with a sense of his own comparative virtue.

"So Veronica gave you an ultimatum?"

He nodded. "It's been a topic for a long time now, but recent catastrophic events, personal and historical, seem to have converged."

"Which topic, Westchester or strange pussy?"

"Connecticut, actually. Range Rovers, golden retrievers, Barbour jackets. That's me on the back nine in white golf shoes. A Connecticut Negro on the clay court. Veronica's made an appointment with a Realtor in New Canaan for next weekend. Since the morning of the twelfth, the Realtors be busy up there, baby."

Whether or not to leave had become a mainstay of Manhattan discourse in the last week. He and Corrine had discussed it, of course, and while they hadn't come to any conclusions, it seemed their positions in this debate had reversed. For years, she'd brought it up routinely, whereas his stock answer had always been that John Cheever might still be alive and well if he'd just stayed put in Manhattan. But these past few days, she'd surprised him by expressing a desire to cast her lot with the city, even as she acknowledged that they had to think of the kids—she who had never seemed quite comfortable calling New York home, who could never stop using the word *house* when she really meant *apartment*.

"It makes sense," Washington said, sounding like a man trying hard to persuade himself to come to terms with a fait accompli. "We'd save forty K on tuition alone."

"You'll pay twenty-five or thirty in property taxes," Russell said, although he was conscious of the fact that he was advocating a position in which he was losing faith, his opposition largely rhetorical, his ostensible defense of staying in the city no more spirited than Washington's case for leaving. Middle age and parenthood had long ago begun to erode his sense of invulnerability. Recent events had accelerated that process.

"Come on," Washington said. "I can't be all alone out there in the land of plaid pants."

"I might take the number of that Realtor."

"Time was, I used to say I'd rather die in Alphabet City than survive in Mount Kisco. But I can't think that way anymore. As parents, we don't really have the luxury of cynical bravado. I think Veronica's right. The party's over. Time to leave."

"Didn't we say that in '87? That the party was over?"

"Hey, we had a good run."

For all of Washington's moral relativism, for all of his failings as a husband and his gleeful misanthropy, in fatherhood he had discovered his one true faith. His devotion to their kids was acknowledged even by his detractors, and was a source of wonder to Russell. Russell wanted to be swept up in that rapture, to be the kind of man who would make any sacrifice for his children. He hoped it wasn't too late. Somehow, he'd sensed a shift of power in the direction of his wife. She seemed to have been invigorated by the disaster, whereas he felt paralyzed.

Washington ordered a second martini and the conversation drifted to business, Russell bemoaning the sales figures of a first novel for which he'd entertained great hopes. Washington had an even bigger nightmare; the author of their lead nonfiction title for the spring, an inspirational business memoir, had been indicted in a false-accounting scheme. And the books on their fall list, regardless of merit, were almost certainly doomed. They both remembered how the Gulf War had killed book sales in '91. It would be nearly impossible to get TV and radio coverage for months to come; this past spring, hardcover sales had already gone down almost 40 percent in the wake of the unending presidential election and the stock market slump.

"We gots to get in the nine/eleven business," Washington said. "You see that woman on the news this morning? Wife of the guy who tried to take on the hijackers over Pennsylvania."

"Todd Beamer," Russell said.

"Articulate. Pregnant. Widow of an American hero. Sounds like a book to me." It was just the kind of topical, commercial, exploitative concept that they both normally sneered at.

"Not exactly our kind of publishing," Russell said. "More a Simon and Schuster, HarperCollins instant-book thing."

"Yeah, well, maybe it should be. I've got some feelers out."

"I wouldn't be surprised if she's agented up already."

When Washington waved for his third martini, Russell said, "If Veronica's on the warpath, I don't think you want to be diving head-first into the martini shaker." He had a long history as Washington's caretaker—carrying him out of bars, pouring him into cabs, covering for him with Veronica and their bosses. Then, three years ago, Washington had quit drinking, without benefit of counsel or institutional support—an impressive display of willpower.

"Just one for the road, chief."

Russell didn't want to be his best friend's keeper. At moments like these, he just wanted to be twenty-five again, when heedlessness and reckless abandon constituted an aesthetic program. Much as he knew Washington shouldn't be drinking at all, it was just so fucking *uncool* to be the one to say so.

. . .

After a truncated afternoon at the office, he took the express to Canal. At the barricades, he showed his driver's license and his lease. The cop, who wore a New York State trooper's uniform, was unfamiliar with the map of downtown, unconvinced by the Hudson Street address.

"Where's this supposed to be?"

"Five blocks south," Russell said. "Across the street from Nobu."

"What the hell's a Nobu?"

"It's a restaurant."

"Any good?"

"If you like raw fish."

The cop looked him over before handing back his documents.

"Once a year's plenty for me," he said, turning to his partner and winking. "On the wife's birthday."

Preoccupied as he was, saddled with gloom, Russell was two blocks away before he registered the joke.

Storey raced across the loft to greet him, while Jeremy remained on the floor between the couches, hypnotized by his Game Boy. Corrine was on the phone, pacing outside the kitchen.

"Daddy, Daddy," Storey said, climbing into his arms. "I got a hundred percent in spelling."

"I should hope so," Russell said.

"Hey, Dad?" Jeremy called out, looking up from his game. "I've got a really good joke."

He carried Storey over to the kitchen.

"Russell's home. I'll talk to you later." She put down the phone and pecked at his cheek. "Everything okay?"

"We had a bomb scare at the office."

She scowled and put a belated finger to her lips.

"Jeremy, come quick," Storey shouted, seeking, as always, to draw her brother into the social circle. "Daddy had a bomb at his office."

"Not a bomb," Russell said. "A bomb scare. It's a false alarm. They thought there might be a bomb, but there wasn't."

Jeremy frowned. "Why did they think that?"

"Somebody made a phone call saying there was."

"Why?"

Rolling her eyes, Corrine lifted Jeremy into her arms. "It's just some silly people playing a trick," she said.

"That's a mean trick," Storey said.

"Why did they play a trick?" Jeremy asked.

"Tell Dad your joke, Jeremy," Corrine said.

"Oh, yeah. Dad, what does it mean if a husband is unfaithful?"

Russell tried to maintain a neutral demeanor as he glanced at Corrine, who looked smug.

"I don't know," he said. "What does it mean?"

"Well, if he goes to the store and he takes a label that says 'low-fat' off something and sticks it on the real ice cream, the fat kind, and takes it home for his wife to eat. That's what it means."

Russell puzzled over this, relaxing slightly, wondering what it could possibly signify.

"What would be the point of that?" he finally said. "Then he'd have a fat wife."

"Yeah," Jeremy said, chuckling. "Pretty good trick, huh?"

He risked another look at Corrine, whose face reflected his own bemused puzzlement. Perhaps the joke didn't mean anything.

"I've got the kids' dinner ready," Corrine said. "I walked all the way to the Gristedes in the Village and back with the groceries. The market's still closed. They're not letting any trucks in."

When the phone rang at 1:30 that morning, Russell was in bed, alone, his wife out smearing peanut butter on the wounds of the city.

"Russell, I'm really sorry to call so late. It's Veronica." She paused, as if to extend the interval of hope before asking the inevitable question. "You haven't seen Washington, have you?"

"It's all right," he said. "I wasn't really asleep." For just a moment, in the dark, he could imagine himself transported back through the years to a brighter moment—for him, if not Veronica—when these calls were a regular feature of life, when Washington had invoked his name as a dinner companion without warning him, or when he'd actually been at Washington's side, chasing through the night in their quest for the elusive heart of the city, which throbbed like a bass guitar line, just audible somewhere around the next corner, behind the next door, just ahead, down the next set of stairs. . . .

# 12

Corrine was working with Svetlana, a tiny, nervous creature with large spherical breasts and a wide, worried face, showing her how to make peanut butter and jelly sandwiches. Svetlana was dubious. "It looks gross," she said.

"You've never eaten one?"

She shook her head. "We had no such thing. We had caviar, not peanut butter. My father was a colonel in the army."

The good old days—when Corrine had nightmares about nuclear holocaust.

Svetlana dutifully donned the plastic gloves, handling the peanut butter as if it were a toxic substance. An exotic dancer who worked at the same club as Jerry's girlfriend, Tatiana, she was taking time off while recovering from her latest boob job. She hoped to double her income when she returned to work.

"Do you enjoy it . . . the dancing?" Corrine asked. Of course, what she really wanted to know was whether she slept with the customers.

Svetlana seemed to find the question naïve. "It's job," she said. "Until I get my green card." After successfully constructing two sandwiches, she seemed to gain confidence and decided to elaborate. "It's very simple when you dance. You have the power. Men are very simple. Like children. They want candy. You have candy. You understand? I don't think I have to explain this to you."

"I understand," Corrine said. A thought that had been nagging her suddenly came into focus: Was Russell having an affair? She realized she'd been trying to suppress the suspicion for months, but it would explain a great deal—certain absences, physical and otherwise, inappropriate outbursts of cheerfulness, a certain severing of the links between emotional stimulus and response, his failure to initiate sex. She stepped out into the open air to consider this possibility; she didn't really notice the police car pulling up, until Hilary stepped out of the door on the passenger's side, wearing a tube top and a little black bolero jacket.

After waving good-bye to her driver, she turned to survey the scene and spotted Corrine. "Hey, sis."

"What are you doing here?"

"Doing my part."

Corrine felt acutely that her terrain was being trespassed upon, and she distrusted her sister's motives, though it would seem petulant to say so. "Well, it's not like you can just . . . I mean, we're pretty fully staffed right now."

"I'm sure I can find some way to help out." She peered into the open-fronted tent, empty except for the volunteers—half a dozen young women who appeared to be trying to make themselves look busy. Jerry had disappeared for the moment. "So this is it?" Hearing a note of disappointment in her sister's voice, Corrine felt obliged to justify their mission.

"It's a little slow at the moment," Corrine said. "You just missed the midnight rush." Although she resented her sister's appearance, she nevertheless wanted the place to seem like a vital and bustling part of the relief effort.

"Where's the, you know, the Ground Zero?"

"It's a few blocks that way," Corrine said, pointing.

"I sort of imagined you'd be right on top of it."

"We take food to the site." In fact, Corrine had not yet gone in herself, imagining that as a privilege to be earned, not taken for granted, as much as she wanted to see what it really looked like. "We provide a little oasis where they can get away a little bit. And we feed the cops and the National Guard."

"Not the firemen?"

"They kind of keep to themselves," Corrine said, suddenly seeing the operation through her sister's eyes, and finding it somewhat marginal and inessential, removed from the terrible center of things.

But then Hilary found something to engage her interest. "Who's *that*?" she said, nodding toward Luke as he climbed out of the Pathfinder.

"He's one of the volunteers," Corrine said, trying to keep her voice neutral.

"Maybe I'll stick around."

Although she hardly knew the man, Corrine didn't want her predatory sister glomming on to him. Besides, she'd been hoping to talk to Luke tonight, hoping to get a little more of his story.

"Hi, I'm Hilary," she said as he approached with a bag of ice in either hand and a confused look on his face.

"Luke," he said.

"This is so wonderful what you're doing down here. I really admire your . . . I think it's really, you know . . . great."

This barely articulate accolade flummoxed its recipient.

As if, Corrine thought, Hilary's vocabulary did not include terms to cover the impulses of charity and altruism, immediately recognizing her own lack of charity toward her sister. Why was it always like this?

Corrine showed her sister the basic routine, but Hilary kept asking when they were going to Ground Zero, drifting off to talk to Luke and Jerry. A short while later, Corrine looked up from the warming trays, to see her climbing into a cop car, presumably the one in which she'd arrived.

129

Captain Davies, who'd been examining the dinner selections, was also watching. "Your sister seems to have made a friend."

"She always does," Corrine said, "although she usually goes for the bad guys. Seems like all my life I've been watching her jump into fast cars with fast boys. Cops didn't usually enter the picture until later, in the wee hours, after the wreck, or the busted party. Then we'd go pick her up at the police station. I don't know why I still worry about her after all these years. Was that one of your guys?"

Davies shook his head. "O'Connor, Brooklyn North."

"Well, I'm sure they'll find lots to talk about."

"Oh, yeah. He probably wants to tell her all about his new baby girl."

Around three o'clock, a wave of Guardsmen descended and Corrine got caught up in the rush, making sandwiches, putting the drinks on ice, chatting with everyone as they came through. When the tent finally emptied, she stepped out into the moonlight and stretched, wondering if the wind had shifted or if she had simply become inured to the acrid stench of the ubiquitous smoke.

Luke joined her on the cobblestones, holding out a pack of Marlboro Lights. She took one, which he then lit for her.

"Guillermo smoked," he said.

"Your missing friend?"

He nodded.

"Are you still blaming yourself? About him?"

"How could I not?"

She couldn't think of anything to say that might assuage his guilt.

"What's really fucked up is that I think I blame my wife and daughter, too. Although in a sense, they saved my life."

"Was he your best friend?"

"I don't know. I suppose so." He took a long drag on his cigarette. "You lost somebody, didn't you?"

"My husband's friend, really." She said this in order to put her claim on the collective reservoir of grief in perspective—she hated exaggeration and self-dramatization—and also because she felt the need

130

to bring Russell into the conversation. "I mean, he was my friend, too, but he was one of Russell's closest friends."

He nodded, blew out a perfect smoke ring. "How is he? Your husband, I mean."

"Well, of course he's devastated."

Luke nodded sympathetically.

"Actually," she said, "it's kind of hard to tell how he is. I mean, I can imagine how he must be feeling. I know him, and I know he loved Jim. And I know how I feel and even how I'd feel if I were him. But I can't really tell. I can't get him to talk about it."

"Give him time."

"Has this . . ." She nodded in the direction of Ground Zero. "Hasn't this made you feel closer to your wife? Isn't that the natural impulse—to cling together?"

He consumed an inch of cigarette, the ember casting an eerie glow on his somber face, as he considered this. He dropped his cigarette and ground it into the cobblestones. "You'd think so, wouldn't you?"

# 13

The presence of the dead was most palpable in the hours after midnight, their spirits hovering in the canyons. It was better, feeling them around you, than seeing them in your sleep uptown. There was something demoralizing about the sunrise—the daylight inappropriately cheerful and mundane. Darkness, with its enfolding intimacy and its mortal intimations, was more suited to the time and the place, more conducive to mourning, to rumors, to shared confidences and bravado. The nights had turned crisp, an improvement on the balminess of the first two weeks.

He was smoking in front of the tent when Captain Davies walked over from the trailer after checking in for his shift at midnight.

"Haven't smoked in twelve years," he said, "but I'd take one now."

Luke shook out a Marlboro and lit it with his Bic.

"I was thinking about my friend Danny O'Callaghan. Fireman. Chain-smoker. Almost killed him. Finally gave it up last year. I heard he was missing and looked for his name when I checked the list at the precinct ten days ago. There were some other friends on the list, but no Danny. I go back to my desk, feeling like at least *he* fucking made it. Few minutes later, I realize I'd been looking under the C's. I went back downstairs and checked the O's, and there he is. I was just thinking I should have a smoke for Danny boy."

Ever since Luke had called the Parks commissioner and won the soup kitchen a stay of execution, Jerry considered him a master of the juice. Now he was calling chefs and maître d's to round up food that Jerry picked up in his Pathfinder, driving back and forth across the checkpoints. A hundred steak dinners from Smith & Wollensky. Fifty penne *pomodoro* from Lupa. Eighty burgers from Union Square Café. Lamb chops *Scottaditti* from Babbo. Jerry, meanwhile, had conjured other basics, cases of Sterno, long underwear, hard hats, ice, and coffee. Feeding a stream of transit cops, sanitation workers, welders and salvage guys, and once in a while a couple of firemen. They were like ghosts, in another place even when they stood in front of the coffee urns.

Luke joined Captain Davies and Jerry on the cobblestones of Bowling Green, where they were taking their ease in green faux-leather office chairs requisitioned from One Broadway, across the street. To the northwest, the night sky glowed yellow, illuminating the columns of smoke and steam.

"If this keeps up, I'll have to retire next year," Davies said. "And so will a lot of the guys. All this fuckin' overtime, eighty-, ninety-hour weeks, I won't be able to afford not to. Retirement pay's pegged to your last year's take-home, and I'm never going to have another year like this again. You don't have any choice."

"Doesn't sound so bad," Jerry said. "Work on your fishing. Spend time with the family."

"Bad for the fish," Davies said. "Bad for the force, too, losing half their senior officers. And I'm not sure my wife's really thrilled about it, either. Last thing she wants is me underfoot all day."

"Since I stopped working," Luke said, "my wife's been furious. She doesn't know what to do with me. I thought I was going to become a real family man. Took up cooking—which turns out to have come in handy this week—but she didn't appreciate that at all. 'We're surrounded by the greatest chefs and caterers on the planet,' she says, 'and you have an MBA in corporate finance, and you're suddenly going to buy an apron and puzzle out the mysteries of coq au vin?' She thinks I'm trying to show her up. Accused me of invading her space. But I'm not sure she even knows where our kitchen is located."

"I read somewhere," Davies said, "that in Polynesia, somewhere like that, the men sleep in one big hut and the women sleep in another."

"What about sex?"

"Sex? What sex? I'm a married guy."

"I hear everybody's fucking their brains out uptown," Jerry said. "There was an article in one of the papers today."

"At least something good's coming out of this," Luke said. "Posttraumatic sex."

"Don't tell me," said Major Donahoe, a pink-skinned, silver-haired insurance adjuster who commanded a National Guard contingent camped out in Battery Park. "I don't know how you boys do it down here in *New* York. I was up at the Armory on Lexington Avenue, where they got that Center for the Missing yesterday, and you know how warm it was, all those skimpy halter tops and T-shirts and short shorts. Jesus Christ, we got some women in Syracuse, least we call them women, but they don't look a goddamn thing like that. In fact, I'm beginning to wonder if you got a whole 'nother species down here that you're keeping to yourselves. Planet of the Babes. Another one on every block. What percentage of the chick population down here is in the fashion-model business? I mean, you must have passed some local legislation against fat and ugly. Shipping the losers upstate in the middle of the night. Come on, admit it. I don't know how you boys can stand looking at all that pussy all day long. I'm pretty sure it would drive me crazy. I know it would sure as hell drive my wife crazy, with me spinning my head in every direction like a drunken owl. All this outrageous trim, I think I . . ."

The thought died as Corrine approached across the cobblestones.

"Don't mind me," she said.

Donahoe just nodded and tilted his head toward Corrine. "Hey, I rest my case."

At three, Luke rode out on the Cushman with Corrine and a Guardsman into the night, stopping at several checkpoints to hand out sandwiches and sodas, finally coming to a halt at the edge of the pile, a chaos illuminated by banks of spotlights floating in the air, where huge grapplers loomed in the smoke and gnashed their teeth like dinosaurs, dipping and lifting their heads with forty-foot beams clenched between their jaws, jets of flame spurting into the air in the wake of the debris. Tiny figures clambered up and down the jagged slopes of the wreckage, antlike lines of men stretching across the rubble, which extended out of sight in the distance.

Luke was mesmerized by the filigreed beauty of the exoskeleton of the south tower, its Gothic arches rising eight or ten stories above them, strangely lacy and delicate and comforting in the unnatural movie-set light. As they sat in silence trying to take it in, he felt his body go cold, a tingling in the extremities of his hair and a sinking in his gut. It was the same place he'd seen that first day, and yet different. The relief operation infinitely more complex, mechanized and specialized, no longer animated by hope. He was looking at a mass grave. When he turned away and looked at Corrine, he saw tears coursing down her cheeks.

"Everyone says it's so small when they see it on TV," she finally said.

He shook his head.

"Actually, it's huge," she said. "It's the biggest thing I've ever seen."

# 14

When the National Guard came through, men from the north with lusty appetites and small-town manners, Corrine couldn't help feeling old and unattractive as they thank-you-ma'amed her, saving their banter for the younger girls. After they'd wiped out the sandwiches, Jerry called his friend Nick at the Salvation Army, looking for cold cuts, but they had nothing to spare. Checking with Meals on Wheels, he was told the truck wouldn't be back downtown until the next afternoon, when the main offering would be five-gallon bags of baked-bean soup. So, with five volunteers on hand, Jerry decided to drive uptown for supplies. The donation can out front held twenty-seven dollars and change.

"Would you mind riding along with me?" he asked Corrine.

"No, I'd love to."

They were just heading for the Pathfinder when a black Suburban with a WTC Relief pass on the windshield pulled up on the curb beside the green and the driver called, "Yo, Jerry."

He hopped out, a wiry little man in an NYFD T-shirt, and saun-
tered over, black ostrich cowboy boots splaying out beneath his jeans,
another laminated pass bouncing on his chest.

He exchanged manly hugs with Jerry, their cheeks brushing first
one side, then the other.

Jerry turned to her. "Corrine, this is my friend Dino."

The man made a courtly little bow. "A pleasure." Then he looked
at Jerry. "Just thought I'd check out your operation."

"Nothing much," Jerry said. "Just a tent or two and a couple of
tables."

"Hey, don't be so modest. This is very impressive, what you done
here. A very good thing. So show me around."

"What you see is what you get." Jerry ushered him into the tent.
"This is Katie, Svetlana, and Cynthia."

They all nodded cheerfully.

"Hey, girls. It's a wonderful thing you're doing here." His tone
suggested that his sanction and blessing were somehow official, as if
he were speaking from a position of authority. He took a Styrofoam
cup and helped himself to a cup of coffee, which he sweetened with
two sugars and two packets of Sweet'n Low, holding the empty en-
velopes up in front of Jerry's nose. "You should get some Equal, the
stuff in the blue packs. This shit is carcinogenic." He examined the
tray of sandwiches and lifted the lids of the warming trays to check
the hot entrées, then took a seat at the picnic table and glanced
around as Corrine replaced the lids.

"So how do you pay for this shit?" he said.

"Mostly donations. I'm a little out-of-pocket."

"That's no good." Dino reached into his pocket, peeled a hundred-
dollar bill off his roll, and handed it Jerry, who waved it away.

"Take it, go on." He shook a Camel filter out of his pack and
tapped it against the table. "You should do a little fund-raising. You
got your five oh one c three?"

"Come on, Dino, we got three coolers and a coffee machine here.
What do you think, I'm the fucking Red Cross?"

"That's what I'm saying. You could expand, serve the community
better with some real funding. Get some gas, some kitchen equip-

ment. Tell you what, maybe I'll drop the forms off the next time I'm in the neighborhood."

"You don't have to do that, Dino."

"Hey, it's no problem. Like I said, I can take care of it for you."

Jerry nodded glumly.

"Keep up the good work," he said as they embraced outside the tent. "I'll see you soon."

They watched him drive away, waving, and climbed into the Pathfinder. "Is he from the fire department?" Corrine asked.

Jerry laughed through his nose.

"He's more like the one who starts the fires."

"What fires?"

"You don't wanna know."

"That was a good idea about setting up a nonprofit."

"Corrine, believe me, Dino doesn't know the meaning of non-profit and he's never had a selfless thought in his life."

"So he's the—"

"He's the one who dictated my perjury."

Corrine was dumbstruck to think that anyone would try to exploit this tragedy on a systematic basis, but of course she was notorious for her naïveté. "What are you going to do?" she asked.

"What I'm not gonna do is set up any five oh one c three," he said.

TriBeCa was still locked down, so they took the FDR up to Fourteenth and drove across to the Food Emporium on Union Square, where Jerry double-parked right out front. "Charity has its perks," he said, tapping the WTC Relief pass on the dashboard. "Just ask the Red Cross officials in their BMWs."

"You don't seem to like the Red Cross much," she said.

"They been on my shit list ever since they refused to barter for coffee. I was offering three cases of Sterno. The bitch told me she needed invoices, said they had to go through official channels. And how many millions pouring into their coffers in the past week?"

Jerry saw himself as a guerrilla of the relief effort, trading respirators for propane, scrounging up forty pounds of buffalo wings from a buddy who managed some West Side sports bar. This forced retreat into the traditional economy for cold cuts obviously seemed faintly distasteful, a failure of ingenuity. He resented these uptown forays, these glimpses of a city insufficiently mindful of the crisis.

Inside the door of the Food Emporium, he grabbed a shopping cart and wheeled straight to the deli section, right up front, casting a covetous eye on the squarish pink hams and yellow cheeses, the logs of salami, and the big turkey breasts in their fishnet brassieres, while Corrine took a number.

"Look at all that," he said, nodding toward the glass. "We could stock the tent for a week—even two. Except we'd need refrigeration. Actually, we need it anyway, I gotta call that woman at student services at NYU—what was her name—see if she could hook us up with some."

After all the hours spent downtown at the relief station, Corrine felt like an alien in this extravagant, brilliantly lit intersection of supply and demand, amazed to discover the old consumer rhythms were still intact.

An old lady with a four-footed cane pressed her face against the glass in front of them.

"How's the roast beef today?" she asked. "Is it lean?"

"Very nice," said the fat man in the hairnet behind the counter.

"Because I don't want it unless it's lean."

A nasal voice piped up behind them: "Oh, for Christ's sake, lady, just get the roast beef." The complainant was a twitchy youth in a warm-up jacket and camo cargo pants, his sneer adorned with a wispy nimbus of facial hair. Jerry turned to stare at him and was still staring when a second counter attendant called out his number.

"What's on special?" Jerry asked. "I got a lot of hungry rescue workers downtown."

To Corrine, this sounded a little self-righteous, but maybe he was angling for a discount.

"We got the turkey breast on special at four-ninety-nine."

"Give me ten pounds of that."

Corrine could almost feel the kid seething behind them as the deli woman patiently shaved slice after slice of white meat, the big ovoid slowly disappearing into the whirling blade. When she removed the butt end and said, "Let me get you a fresh breast," there was a groan from behind them. After she'd weighed out the two towering stacks on the scale, she said, "Let me just print up the total." She winked at Jerry, her cheeks as pink as the ham in the case. "And then if I was to slice an extra pound or two and just kind of seal it up with the rest, I don't think the manager's gonna know the difference."

"For Christ's sake," the adenoidal voice protested.

"You're very kind," Jerry said to the woman. "And after that," he said, with what seemed to Corrine a certain malicious relish, "I think I'd like five pounds of Virginia ham."

"Oh, fuck me!"

Jerry turned slowly, seeming to expand in volume as he did so. Corrine had always thought she wouldn't want to see him really mad and now she was certain of it. There was something wounded and angry in him.

"I'm feeding people who are digging day and night down at Ground Zero. What's *your* emergency?"

"Well, aren't you fucking *special*."

For a man his size, he had a very quick right hand. She was pretty sure she heard the sound of his knuckles glancing off the kid's cheekbone, and something else, a cracking sound, just as the kid went down, wobbling and sinking to his knees.

"All *right*," said the fat man behind the counter.

From the knot of customers around the deli counter came the sound of hands clapping. Jerry took a bow.

The kid was writhing on the floor, holding the bloody remains of his nose. "You fucking prick," he muttered. "I'll fucking kill you."

Jerry turned to the deli lady. "That was five pounds of Virginia ham, if you don't mind."

The boy struggled to his feet, slowly straightened himself, his right hand cupped beneath his nose. "You bastard," he honked, or at least that's what Corrine thought he said.

. . .

140

"If I really *was* a Jew bastard," Jerry said when they were back in the car, "I would have kicked his fucking anti-Semitic ass right out the door. You heard that, didn't you?"

"Maybe," Corrine said. "It could have been."

"Maybe kicking him was a mistake," Jerry admitted.

Certainly, Corrine thought, that was where he had lost the sympathy of the crowd, which surveyed him with a collective horror when he finally looked up to draw breath.

"I don't know, I'm just so goddamn angry. Jew bastard, *you* bastard—what's the difference?'"

Corrine shrugged. "I thought you were Italian?"

"My mother was Jewish."

She wondered if the punk at the supermarket knew that the faith passed matrilineally.

# 15

The doorman let him in. The loft had always seemed strangely uninhabited—like a show house, a model unit, a generic late-model, postartist SoHo loft. Very little of Guillermo was visible from the doorway, just vast expanses of white wall and walnut floor, with intermittent mesas of dark wood and outcrops of beige and taupe upholstery. Partly, this was a deliberate strategy; he liked to do up a place and then flip it, which strategy called for a certain impersonal, Olympian mode of decor and tended to minimize the possessive imprint. The open kitchen was equipped with restaurant-quality stainless-steel appliances, of which only the Sub-Zero refrigerator had ever served its intended platonic purpose. Luke wasn't sure which would be creepier, if he'd been overwhelmed by a sense of his friend's presence and spirit, or this—that he didn't really feel it at all, Guillermo having left so little of himself behind here in his ostensible final earthly abode. He'd bragged to Luke about spending $300,000 just gutting and decorating the place, and that a friend at Condé Nast had promised him a spread in *House & Garden,* which would help Guillermo sell it at a massive profit. But then he heard from a kid whom he described as "a former trick," who worked in the art department and whom he'd run into recently at Boy Bar, that the magazine's design director was reluctant, having asked, after his scouting tour of the loft, "What's the caption, 'Another fag with too much money'?" What had hurt Guillermo the most about this remark was the fact that he prided himself on his robustly masculine taste. He had been aiming for a sort of cultivated hetero look, not least because he entertained clients there, and had envisioned his apartment in the mold of an early sixties bachelor pad, the kind of place where the Hathaway shirt man entertained Pan Am stewardesses. Of course, he'd hired a decorator, but he'd micromanaged the details himself, choosing the art and the fabrics, many of which had been shipped from Italy and France, and believed the result to be quirky yet somehow classically modernist. The old wine press from Tuscany in the corner beside the bar, for instance—what was faggy about that? Guillermo had wanted to know. There was nothing blatant or formulaic in the place, as far as he could see, no nudes by Mapplethorpe or Herb Ritts, no fussy handbag collection—so he had raved to Luke a few weeks before.

At least the bedroom had a few visible traces of the owner—pictures in ebony frames on the ebony dresser: his parents and his sister and a single picture of his freckled all-American wife, a memento of the failed experiment; and, much to Luke's surprise, one of the two of them shirtless on the deck of a yacht in Gustavia harbor, Luke potbellied and flabby beside the lean and sculpted Guillermo. The room was immaculate, the bed made. On the bedside table, a volume of Deepak Chopra and a copy of *Underworld,* the virgin spine of which cracked smartly when Luke paged through it. In the drawer, a vial of Ambien and one of Viagra, as well as a Lufthansa sleep mask. In the mausoleum of the master bath, resisting the urge to catalog the extensive collection of pharmaceuticals, he found what he was looking for—a toothbrush and a hairbrush, although, like everything else in the apartment, they bore no sign of use.

. . .

At Lexington, they climbed out of the cab and walked down toward the Armory. Hundreds of solemn pedestrians milled on the sidewalk, viewing the makeshift gallery that had sprung up on the walls of the curry houses and the lampposts on either side of the avenue—the faces of the missing glancing back hopefully and artlessly in photographs taken at weddings and graduation ceremonies, now hanging above impromptu shrines of flowers and candles.

By now, though, this fiction of the *missing* was becoming harder to sustain. These people were missing in the most radical sense. They weren't wandering around the streets. He had seen that rubble, walked on it . . . his throat constricting and eyes welling all over again as he moved now with Corrine through the crowd, looking at the names and faces on the posters. The posters were not really queries so much as memorials—simulacra for bodies that would never be found, for the corpses that would never be viewed in open coffins before being laid to rest in consecrated ground. MISSING . . . *Two earrings in left ear . . . pinstriped suit with yellow tie and pocket square . . . lightly freckled . . . tongue stud . . . silver wedding ring . . . crescent-shaped scar on right calf . . . birthmark the shape of Puerto Rico on left arm . . . ankle bracelet . . . tattoo of the Grim Reaper on upper right arm.* In one photo, a middle-aged man stood next to an elephant.

Beneath a picture of a fireman: *Last seen on Channel 7 News clip Tues 9/11. Clip filmed at St. Vincent's Hospital. He was treated and most likely returned to Ground Zero.*

Tears were streaming down the face of the man standing on the sidewalk in front of this poster, a muscular Hispanic man in a double-breasted mohair suit, who looked at Corrine and said, "It's my son."

"You got to believe," said his companion, a dark pretty woman with stunning brown eyes.

A pockmarked boy with a scraggy ponytail and four tiny rings in his right ear leaned against the wall of the Armory, holding his dog on a leash, a sign hanging from his neck: PLEASE FEEL FREE TO PET MY DOG. IT MAY MAKE YOU FEEL BETTER.

The pretty Hispanic woman was now hugging the father as he

wept inconsolably. "They'll find him. He's coming back to you. You must believe."

Up ahead, some kind of disturbance—a black man in short dreads locked in a strange embrace with a white guy.

"They're dead," he shouted as the other man struggled to hold him. "What's the matter with you people? They're fucking gone. They're already cremated, crushed and incinerated like garbage, and we won't even have a fucking bone to bury. It doesn't have to make sense. People die. People in the Middle East get blown apart every day and we read about it in the *New York* fucking *Times* or the *Post* while we're sitting at Starbucks drinking our white-chocolate mocha."

The white guy himself looked wild with grief. "It's okay, man."

"It's not okay. My mother died a nasty, horrible death, leaking out of every orifice. Was that fair? Did that make sense? Did I make a fucking *poster*?"

A space had opened around them, ringed with solemn spectators sharing an expression of mournful indulgence. You might have expected someone to register outrage or censure, to hit him or tell him he was full of shit. But these people had already seen hundreds of permutations of grief over the past fortnight.

Finally, carried along with the crowd, they arrived at the door of the Armory, where a stocky black cop intoned, "Families only. Families only beyond this point."

Luke tried to speak. Corrine clutched his hand and gave him a look of encouragement. He cleared his throat, reached into her shoulder bag, and held up the hairbrush and the toothbrush for the cop to see.

# 16

When she moved to the city, no matter how hard she'd worked that day or how little she'd slept the previous night, Corrine always felt her pulse quickening as darkness fell and the walls and cubicles of office life dissolved and anything seemed possible as the disparate workday tribes spilled into the streets and the bars and restaurants to mingle and preen, to boast and hunt.

Night beckoned—friends calling, and friends yet to be made. She dreamed of the chance encounter or conversation that would reveal what she really wanted to do with her life, of meeting the stranger who would *be* what she wanted to do with her life. That brief season—her first year after Brown, when Russell was studying at Oxford and she was a single girl in the undiscovered and boundless city. Even after they'd married, she felt the electricity and promise of the Manhattan twilight into which they plunged as a couple, Russell's golden

Labrador expression—you could almost imagine the wagging tail—ever expectant about the restaurant, movie, or play, the concert, gallery opening, or book party. It was a *collision* of friends, for in those days parties were not organized so much around specific occasions or the promotion of a product as they were a function of irrepressible conviviality.

For several years, her motherly duties had left her with a deficit of nocturnal energy and curiosity about the world outside the walls of her loft, her yearning having been incarnated in the flesh of her children, not that she didn't sometimes remember and miss the sense of anticipation out there. But more often, she felt anxious about the lures and snares that her husband might encounter between office and home, the beautiful women in restaurants, at bookstore readings and screenings, at the parties he claimed he needed to attend. She herself was very happy to be in bed by 10:30 with a novel or biography. Now, however, like someone whose house has been broken into and ransacked, she was feeling wounded and vulnerable. Her initial desire to flee the city, clutching her babies, had partially subsided as she'd felt herself drawn beyond the barricades by an impulse no less compulsive than the old restlessness. She felt strangely at home at Bowling Green, near the epicenter of the trauma that had ruined their sleep and clouded their dreams.

A schedule had taken shape at the relief station—eight to four, four to midnight, midnight to eight. Jerry had set up a work roster on a clipboard. He directed them at their tasks, sent them out on scavenging missions, found a job for everyone. He was one of the men who had risen to the moment while others remained dazed and helpless, gaping at their television screens. As long as he was focused on the logistics of relief, he seemed to have an answer to every question. Then there was Luke. Like her, he seemed compelled to spend his waking hours at Bowling Green, to have found the simple chores of the soup kitchen to answer some profound need. The kids were asleep, and somehow the zone was more alive in the dark hours, the work she was doing more urgent, the sense of isolation and containment more complete. Then it was truly a world apart.

*They also serve who only stand and wait.* What was that from? Russell would know. She'd meant to ask him last night but had stopped short, seeing his vacant look as he sat in front of the television, watching the news. At first, she'd imagined that if nothing else, this thing would draw them together as a couple, as a family; that had seemed the only possible good that could come out of it. But after the first spate of phone calls, when they'd found each other and gotten the kids from school and absorbed the initial shock of disbelief, he'd become, if anything, more withdrawn.

Even before the eleventh, long before the eleventh, he had been growing increasingly preoccupied and short-tempered, and now she'd have to repeat a question three or four times before she got his attention, which was probably, she had to admit, another reason she was drawn to the night shift. Her conversations with Luke were more engaging than any she'd had with Russell in years. Of course, she realized it was a kind of wartime intimacy, the camaraderie of strangers in a lifeboat, but it underlined how distant from Russell she'd felt these last few months. Hell, years.

It was exhilarating, too, behind the barricades, flirting with the cops and the Guardsmen—that old frisson between men and women. "That's part of your job," Jerry had told her. "I had a girl come up the other day and apologize that she was still wearing makeup from her job, like it was frivolous or something, and I told her, 'Hell, smear it on. Put on that lipstick, babe.' These guys need a little cheering up. Why the hell do you think we discourage male volunteers?"

New volunteers continued to arrive, sometimes far more than were needed, especially in the daytime, which was another reason she preferred the late-night shift. Tonight, though, seven of them had showed up for the midnight shift, and she'd felt slightly resentful. Katie, a pretty little ponytailed hippie girl from Brooklyn, had immediately claimed the coffeemaker, the center of the operation, where everyone was living on caffeine. A cranky piece of machinery dating back to the Lindsay administration, it heated slowly, and overflowed frequently, requiring constant attention and fifteen minutes to run through its groaning cycle, the coffee then transferred to insulated plastic urns, which always seemed to be running perilously low.

She and Katie exchanged little bits of their lives over coffee in the predawn hours. She was, of all things, an herb gardener in Prospect Park and quickly announced her desire not to work with meat products, if possible. She seemed an unlikely New Yorker, with her sweet chipmunk face and Heidi braids, someone who should be living in Colorado Springs or one of the Portlands. She'd made up little sachets of essential oils, peppermint and lavender, that she handed out to anyone with a mask or a respirator as a prophylactic against the smell, the stench that Russell complained permeated her clothes and her hair and her skin.

Corrine checked the sandwich station, which was looking somewhat depleted, and started digging through the boxes of supplies for peanut butter and jelly and generic white bread, taking a young actor with complicated hair and multiple earrings as her apprentice. She found plastic packages of presliced ham and salami, as well as a huge block of yellow cheese, in one of the coolers and had Nico hack off slices of cheese with one of the dull knives scavenged from God knows where, while she laid out an assembly line of open-faced bread and ham.

The others skulked around like new kids in a school yard, all with a quietly desperate air of wanting to look occupied, not quite sure whom to report to or how to make themselves useful, until finally Jerry drifted over from the police van, exuding an air of significant exhaustion, looking to Corrine as if he hadn't slept since she last saw him, sixteen hours before. He paused in front of the open tents and surveyed his troops, then waved to Corrine, his gait like that of a man trying to keep his balance on a storm-tossed deck as he approached her table.

She told him that Russell had talked to his chef friend Carlo Monsanto, who would have fifty pasta dinners ready for pickup in the afternoon.

"You're a star," Jerry said. He turned then to address the newcomers, eagerly awaiting their instructions as Corrine herself had not long ago. "Anybody with cooking experience here?"

Two hands went up, a young man in an NYU sweatshirt and a white-haired woman who looked like Grace Paley.

"Because you won't be needing it here," he said.

Jerry set them to opening the cans of chicken noodle soup, adding bottled water, and heating the large pots; loading the coolers with soft drinks; collecting and bagging the empty cans and bottles.

Three Guardsmen in brand-new camo outfits came in for coffee, followed shortly by a couple of sanitation workers. The Guardsmen were griping about the fact that their guns were locked up in the park—some agreement between the city and the federal authorities.

"What if something did happen?" said a chubby corporal. "It's like showing up at a gunfight with a knife."

"You'll have your gun soon enough," his sergeant said, "when they send you overseas to fight the towelheads."

Jerry sat down with two transit cops, one of whom said that if any of the subway tunnels under the rivers gave way, the water could flood the system all the way up to Harlem.

Jerry disappeared for half an hour and eventually reappeared with Luke, driving his SUV up onto the cobblestones and parking by the tents. They unloaded a gas grill and some propane from the back and set it up in an unoccupied corner, and before long all the male volunteers, Guardsmen, and cops drifted over to check out this new piece of equipment and to offer advice about its operation. Within minutes, the smell of grilled meat filled the tent. The smell of burning fat, after an hour of working with slimy cold cuts and smearing peanut butter and jelly on bread, was making her nauseated, and Corrine knew she'd lose it if she didn't get some air.

A few minutes later, Luke joined her on her bench across the street. "Are you all right? You kind of bolted just then."

"Just felt a little queasy," she said. "I used to have issues with food. Suddenly, it was like it was all coming back to me. After lo these many years."

"That doesn't surprise me." He shook a cigarette out of his pack and lit it with his Bic. "I just had another little time warp myself, smelling those burgers on the grill," he said. "Fourth of July, big cookout with my girlfriend's family at Henderson Lake. I was fifteen. Hot dogs and burgers and chicken on the grill at their summer house. It had been a very big deal, my spending Fourth of July weekend with them and not with my own family and because we had this tacit agreement—my girlfriend and I, that is—that we were going to do it that night. And then this buzz spread through the clan, the adults whispering to one another, a sudden sense of alarm communicating itself to the kids. Someone started banging on the door of an upstairs bedroom. Finally, they got a ladder from somewhere, put it up against the side of the house while the women herded the children to the front yard. Joanie's father went up the ladder and climbed in a second-floor window. Her aunt had killed herself, her unmarried aunt Eileen, slit her wrists in the bathtub while we were throwing a football and laughing in the yard, waiting for our burgers. That was the first death I really remember, that made any impression on me, even though I barely knew the woman. I've been to lots of cookouts since then, but I haven't thought of that in years." He paused and took a drag from his cigarette. "Not exactly a food issue, I guess. Still, all sorts of weird memories seem to have been churned up lately."

As soon as he said this, she felt it was true. Odd fragments of the past had been suddenly uncovered, jutting above the surface like fossils revealed by an earthquake.

"I guess you didn't get lucky that night," she said.

"Actually, I did. I hate to say it, sounds terrible, but I remember realizing at the time that it worked in my favor. She dragged me into the cabana shortly after the police arrived. I had nothing to compare it to at the time, but the proximity of death seemed to, I don't know, turbocharge the sex."

"There are probably thousands of people having sex all over the city right now. Clutching one another, reaching out for a stranger. I mean, more than usual." She suddenly felt awkward, worried that he would think she was being flirtatious or suggestive, which she hadn't meant to be—even as she experienced an unexpected intimacy with this attractive man.

He nodded in a distracted way, looking out over Battery Park, and she wondered whom he was thinking about—not the long-lost girlfriend, she suspected.

"So what about these food issues? If you don't mind my asking. Seems like we ought to know if you're a poisoner or a radical fruitarian."

"It's okay," she said. "It's better if I talk about it, actually."

"I was just about to take a walk up Broadway," he said.

"I think they can spare me for a few minutes." She followed him around the edge of the park, past the raised butt of the fat bronze bull she'd once posed beside after getting hired as an analyst at Merrill. Still poised to charge up Broadway, it pointed its huge head toward Wall Street, that narrow chute between office facades a couple blocks away. "I used to work over there," she said, pointing to an office building on the north side of the street.

"We were practically neighbors," he said. "I used to work at Morgan. We could've passed each other on the street."

"It was a long time ago," she said, "another lifetime, the bull market of the eighties. Even though I never really felt like I belonged, there were moments riding that wave when I could almost suspend my disbelief. Then it all came crashing down. Not like this, of course, but the crash of '87 seemed, I don't know, cataclysmic at the time."

"I remember."

"Personally, it was a real disaster."

"Personally is maybe the only perspective we have."

"My . . . Russell . . ." Why, she wondered, had she hesitated over the word?

"Your husband."

"My husband was on the verge of engineering this leveraged buyout of the publishing house he worked for. It was crazy. He was an editor, making like thirty thousand a year, and suddenly he's maxed out our credit cards and got Bernie Melman as a partner."

"Bernie Melman?"

"You know him?"

"Friend of my wife's."

Something in his expression made her pause.

"I think he's sleeping with my wife, actually."

"You think?" She felt a strange sympathetic thrill at this intimation.

"I'm not sure exactly how far it's progressed. Far enough that it's a topic of conversation in our overheated little zip code. Far enough that I think he's been having me followed. Kind of ridiculous, isn't it—the illicit suitor having the husband trailed by private detectives? But that's his style. He's always gone in for a certain amount of corporate espionage, and I guess he has to keep his staff busy."

"Why would he have you followed?"

"Well, I suppose it would be convenient for him if it turned out I had a mistress. That's one of the good things about being down here. Behind the barriers. No private detectives in black Suburbans. You know what's really strange? His first wife was actually named Sasha. My wife's name."

"You sure you're not just being—"

"Paranoid?"

"I mean, there are a lot of black Suburbans in the city."

"So everyone tells me. It doesn't matter anyway. I don't have anything to hide, except maybe embarrassment. The mortification of the cuckold."

"Russell had a thing with this girl. An investment banker. Come to think of it, I'm pretty sure she worked for Bernie Melman. God, that whole time was so insane, I haven't thought about it in years. The only way I can is to write the whole thing off as a kind of mass hysteria we got caught up in, Russell most of all. Imagine, he's afraid he's going to get fired, so he decides to buy out the company. And he probably would've pulled it off, if not for the crash. But when the financing fell through, he was pushed out of the deal that eventually emerged. And along the way, we separated. Then his best friend—our best friend, actually—died a few months later."

This was a bare summation certainly, but she'd just met him, after all.

Coinciding with Jeff Pierce's death, and the onslaught of the new epidemic that had killed him and the revelation of mutual infidelities,

153

the crash of '87 spelled the end of their collective innocence. Visiting Jeff in Silver Meadows, where he was in rehab, being treated, as he said, for "an *excess of excess*," they somehow failed to notice that the tracks on his arms were being replaced by the lesions of Kaposi's sarcoma. Carried away by the epidemic. Did that qualify as self-inflicted?

And their own destinies? They'd participated in the binge and contributed to their own undoing—certainly Russell had. But this thing, this was as absurd a deus ex machina as a sneak attack from Mars. Wasn't it? Surely they weren't responsible for *this*.

"But you got back together," Luke said. "In the end."

She nodded. The market, and the city, had recovered, soaring to heights that made the bull run of the eighties seem quaint in comparison, and what of the lessons that were supposed to have been learned? Only the styles had changed, SUVs replacing stretch limos, platinum replacing gold, new money aping the unshowy habits of the old, as if the only lesson of it all was that the sins of the previous decade had been sins against taste; the belief seemed to prevail that if you didn't flaunt it in a tacky way, the lightning bolt wouldn't find you. But she refused to believe that anyone deserved to die for the collective hubris.

She knew that Russell had felt he'd been left behind, relatively impoverished and marginalized in the new boomtown. After a brief stint in Hollywood, he'd gotten another editing job, while she had gone to law school and then to the DA's office, quitting when the kids came along, reducing their income as their expenses soared, stranding them like paupers in a city of zillionaires, and she knew Russell resented that. Would this new apocalypse strengthen them, or reveal the weakness of their foundations?

"Are you scared?" she asked.

"Of course."

"Of what? Dying?"

"Not so much of dying. Of dying before I discover the point of my existence. Before I accomplish something."

"Surely you've accomplished something."

"I've facilitated the movement of capital around the globe like a bee mindlessly carrying pollen. Financial markets are autonomous. Markets, if they work correctly, supersede the will and whim of individuals. Which would seem to make me, my career of the past nineteen years, more or less irrelevant."

"But markets don't work perfectly; there are always information gaps and friction. Which is the whole point of the Street. Of people like you—like you used to be."

"Well, I decided there had to be something more important that I could do. Now I'm certain of it—I can't, after all this, imagine going into the firm every day. But I have no fucking idea what it might be. I've been thinking about Guillermo, wondering what he might have done if he'd known how little time he had left. What did he leave behind? A few friends and a beautiful loft."

They were walking alongside the graveyard of Trinity Church, where, she seemed to remember, Alexander Hamilton was interred. She stopped and looked in at the blackened and tilting stones. "I just realized there aren't really any graveyards in Manhattan. I mean, barely. This one and a few other old churchyards that have survived. It's like the dead have been banished to the boroughs and New Jersey. You know Père-Lachaise in Paris, that huge cemetery? Every weekend, the Parisians walk and picnic among their illustrious dead. We don't have the space or the time for the dead."

"We do now," Luke said, nodding toward the smoke emanating from the new graveyard.

"So what do you do with your days when you're not making peanut butter sandwiches?"

"I'm writing a book."

"Really?"

"No, in fact, not really. It's what I say, since Manhattan abhors idleness."

"I know, I know," she said, amazed somehow to hear this coming from a man.

"I haven't really touched it since June. And I doubt I will."

"What would it be about if you *were* writing it?"

"I think it would be about the samurai film. I have hundreds of pages of notes. It's not as if I haven't been circling it. But I can't really claim to be writing. I'm beginning to wonder if it's not too late, at my age. In college, I thought I wanted to be a writer. I smoked Gauloises and lugged *Ulysses* and *Being and Nothingness* around the Williams campus. Investment banking—that was about getting my bearings, making some money before I started my real life. You know, make a few bucks and sail off to Europe or Burma. Like Hemingway, Graham Greene—"

"I can't believe you said Greene. I love Greene," she said. She'd been expecting to hear Faulkner or maybe Walker Percy. "I've actually been working on a screenplay of *The Heart of the Matter.*"

"Old what's his name . . . Scobie. I loved that book."

"It's still good."

"I just meant I haven't read it in years."

"You should."

"So you're a screenwriter?"

She laughed. "Hardly."

"I thought that was the proper term for people who write screenplays."

"Oh . . . I see what you mean. More of a mother who's written two screenplays than a screenwriter. I just . . . it sounds very glamorous. I just can't really think of myself as a *screenwriter.* I actually sold one, years ago. Story of an idealistic young woman corrupted by Wall Street. Well, *almost* corrupted by Wall Street. But then of course—not. Saved by her conscience in the third act. Universal bought it, but it never actually got produced. No, *The Heart of the Matter* is a labor of love."

"You're a Catholic?"

"Only by marriage. And you're a southerner?"

"Only by birth."

"I thought it was something like Catholicism—more or less indelible."

"Don't we all come to New York to invent ourselves from scratch?"

"We try. But I'm beginning to think our past always catches up with us in the end. Nobody's sui generis."

He looked at her skeptically. "Do you always talk like this?"

"Like what?" she asked, blushing. She knew what he meant; Russell used to call her on it in the old days.

"Like, I don't know, a professor of logic."

"I've been accused of it."

"Tell me about those food issues," he said as they approached the checkpoint.

"I haven't talked about that in years."

"Not even to your shrink?"

She'd been certain he was going to say *husband*—and was relieved that he hadn't. "You see before you one of those rare New Yorkers who don't have a shrink. Which probably proves I'm not a New Yorker at all—still an old-fashioned New England WASP. Unless you count six months of marriage counseling."

"Did it work?"

"I thought so at the time," she said, realizing with a kind of thrill—the thrill of contemplating a dangerous stunt, a backflip from a high diving board while your parents aren't looking—that she wasn't sure, now, all these years later, if it had worked. Was her marriage working? Noting that she'd used the singular pronoun, wondering what the hell she was doing, though of course she knew what she was doing—she was just surprised that she was doing it.

"But we were talking about food," she said, stepping back from the edge of the diving board.

"Okay."

"What's that supposed to mean?"

"I'm just agreeing with you. It's just a kind of verbal filler, a way of saying I'm listening."

"Okay."

"Exactly. So you were saying?"

"Well," she began.

"If you'd rather not, I understand."

"No, I want to," she said. "So shut up and listen." Somehow, this

157

seemed more flirtatious than anything she'd said yet, but she pressed on. "I've always had these little hang-ups, I guess you'd call them. For the longest time when I was little, I'd eat only three things: bananas, link sausages, and Cream of Wheat. I literally couldn't swallow anything else. When my parents tried to get me to, especially if it was meat that wasn't a sausage, I'd just sit there chewing and chewing for hours, and if I tried to swallow, I'd gag. I guess I must have gotten over it eventually; I can't remember when that period finally ended. And then I went to prep school."

"Ah, yes," he said.

"Why do you say 'Ah, yes'?"

"Sorry."

"I guess you've heard this story before. It is kind of generic, like the lesbian crush or the dashing older man. Anyway, to make a long story short, I became obsessed with my weight and eventually they sent me to a hospital where I had to learn how to eat again and get over my body-image problem."

"And did you?"

"Mostly. But I still wonder, why do we have to be hungry, why do we have to eat all the time? Sometimes—over the years—I've had these little relapses. There are emotional triggers, blah, blah, blah—" She stopped in her tracks, smiling at him brightly, her vision blurred by tears. He hesitated, taking a step back toward her and reaching for her, lowering his arms as she leaned away from him.

"I'm sorry, I didn't mean to pry."

"No, it's not . . . it's not your fault."

"Well. I'm—"

"I think that's why I couldn't have a baby."

He didn't say anything, for which she was grateful.

"I never really admitted that before," she said, wiping her eyes.

"I thought you'd mentioned children yesterday."

"Twins. My sister's eggs. My husband's, ahem, sperm. My womb. Very complicated." She started to walk again.

"The one who was here yesterday? Hilary?"

"I know it's probably irrational," she said, "but sometimes I'm terrified that she's going to want to claim them someday. That was the first thing I thought when she turned up on our doorstep. Right before . . . all this."

"She didn't really strike me as the maternal type."

She was suddenly conscious of the din, the roar of diesels and the clanging percussion of steel on steel.

They stopped just in front of the barricade at Pine Street, by the Equitable Building, beyond the chain-link fence that had been thrown up recently. Three huge banks of lights hovered above the invisible carnage, illuminating the shifting clouds of gray smoke that sifted into the sky. From within the murk, the grapplers rising above the ruins, dipping and disappearing again, unleashing further spumes of smoke. They stood silently, looking through the mesh of the fence for what might have been several minutes, or longer.

"You said you had a daughter?" she finally asked, after they started to retrace their steps.

"Thirteen. No, fourteen. I keep forgetting. Wishful thinking, I suppose. One of the things I looked forward to about not working was spending time with her. But she won't let me in. I wish I could just take her away. Get her out of here. But I'm afraid it's too late."

"She's only fourteen."

He looked out into the smoke beyond the barricade. "Fourteen in New York is like twenty-seven in normal human years."

"God, I hope not."

"And where would I take her, anyway? She'd be getting the same message from the culture in Tennessee or Alaska—live to spend, dress to kill, shop and fuck your way to happiness—it's just transmitted more rapidly here."

As jumbled as this was, she thought she knew exactly what he meant. Jeremy asking about Ferraris and Porsches popped into her head.

"The truth is, I dread going home in the mornings," he said. "I start to panic whenever I think about going back uptown. I feel like as long as I stay here, nothing else will happen. To the city. To me. I'm afraid of what comes next."

The sky to the east was salmon-colored above the anonymous office towers of lower Broadway. Corrine was reminded of those riotous nights when the dawn had caught them unawares—unwelcome as a visit from the police, signaling the end of the revelry. She felt her own sense of dread and melancholy, emerging from the long nocturnal suspension of belief. Remembering, dimly, that the night was never long enough when you were falling in love.

# 17

How were you supposed to trust your judgment when your sense of proportion and balance had been shattered, when the governing body that generally checked your emotions was overthrown, anarchy threatening to break out at any moment? At a time when you might find yourself breaking into tears with no ostensible cause, what did it mean that the sight of a certain face could lift you up and make you believe that what was left was worth saving? Or else that it could all go to hell, all of it except for you and her.

Did he feel this way because of what was happening around him, or in spite of it?

It wasn't as if he could compare the course of his feelings to a hypothetical narrative in which planes hadn't crashed and towers hadn't fallen, in which they weren't both, like the rest of the population, in a state of shock. In that narrative, they never would have met, something that was now, for Luke, almost unimaginable and certainly undesirable. His sleep was ravaged by images of carnage, but his daydreams featured the two of them as the last survivors, walking cinematically out of the smoke and rubble of an even more comprehensive cataclysm. This had been a recurring fantasy of youth—the only scenario in which he could imagine the girls he desired having anything to do with him: a disaster that wiped out the entire population, except for two, he and his beloved, tiny figures walking away from the ruins of Babylon into a vast, blighted landscape.

Luke began to wonder if whatever good he was doing downtown was morally canceled out by the pleasure he derived from being there.

Once again they were awaiting, and trying to postpone, the coming day, sitting on a bench in Battery Park and watching the sun rise over Brooklyn, lingering as the rosy penumbra diffused into a steely October sky. The smoke was still thick around them, but they were seldom aware of it. It had become the air they breathed.

"Do you think she's still having an affair?"

"At this point, I really don't know."

"Being here every night—don't you think you're giving her an awfully long leash?"

"I think *enough rope* is the operative cliché."

"Lately, I've been wondering if Russell hasn't been having an affair."

"What makes you think that?" He tried not to betray undue interest in this possibility, even as his pulse quickened.

"I don't have any evidence, if that's what you mean. It's just a feeling."

"Wouldn't it make more sense for you to work the day shift, when he's at the office?"

"That's what Russell was asking this morning."

"What did you say?"

"Just that I like it better at night. The kids are sleeping, so I don't miss them. And that this is where I need to be. I didn't say this, but I suppose I don't feel very close to him right now." She suddenly turned to face him. "Why? Are you implying something?"

"What might I be implying?"

"I don't know—that it has something to do with you?"

He shook his head vigorously.

"Well, actually, goddamn it, I suppose it does. That's the bitch of it. I think it probably does have to do with you." She reached for his hand and squeezed it.

He leaned across the bench and kissed her. He was surprised how easy it was, and how much he liked the way she tasted, her mouth a kind of living, briny delicacy with an earthy note, a taste almost of truffles, hinting of further and deeper pleasures, which were also suggested by the slow caress of her tongue when she hesitantly brought it into play, although he felt that he could be happy with just this, exploring the variations of this kiss for a very long time. He had forgotten, if he ever knew it, that a kiss could be so absorbing and satisfying in its own right, something to be savored . . . an end in itself rather than a stop along the way to one's ultimate destination . . . even as he felt the increasing pressure of a nascent erection.

He hadn't been certain whether he would make the transition from liking her and admiring her—liking the way she looked and laughed, finding her quirky and sensible at the same time—to wanting her. Somehow, he hadn't expected, if it came right down to it, to respond to her viscerally. He'd imagined that many of the qualities that drew him toward her—intelligence, a sense of humor, shared values— would prevent him from seeing her as an object of sexual desire. For all of Sasha's high polish, she projected a voracious, exhibitionistic sexuality, which clearly distinguished her from the *nice* girls in the room. No one had ever said of Sasha that she was *nice*. Ultimately, you knew she wasn't, and this made her dangerously attractive. One of those women who needed to communicate their desirability, a hypothetical availability—at least until recently he had imagined it to be hypothetical—to every man they encountered, she had the heart, and the manner, of a courtesan. Her more attractive dinner partners inevitably left the table dreaming of the myriad ways that Sasha could make them happy if only she weren't married, if only a tenuous and reluctant grip on propriety didn't restrain her. It was almost pathological, her need to provoke desire, although Luke had to admit it worked on him as well as on the others—that it had helped keep him in the marriage all these years. He had stopped respecting her, but he still wanted her. Once he had finally admitted this to himself, it had become even easier to want her, simply to lust for her, and act on it, to think of her as a geisha to whom he happened to have proprietary rights.

By contrast, Corrine seemed unselfish and morally taut, which Luke had imagined, when he first met her, might protect him from being fatally attracted to her. For some time now, he'd reassured himself that she was not a particularly sexual creature. But the first kiss cleared away his doubt, even as it promised to complicate his life. It was a ridiculous time to fall in love, inappropriate, somehow; certainly inconvenient, given the fact that they both were married. But he couldn't stop exploring her mouth—almost shocked at the intricate figures and tropes performed by her importunate tongue. Without conscious effort, he followed her lead, feeling himself engaged in a rhythmic lingual waltz. The juiciness of her mouth and the gentle pressure of her hand on the back of his head—this is *sex,* he thought, his left hand cupping her shoulder until she drew it downward and placed it on her breast.

He sensed they were embarked on a course that would entail secrecy and deception; meanwhile, if only for the moment, he was pleased to indulge his pleasure.

Corrine eased herself out of his embrace by degrees, pulling away with a gasp and then coming back in to chew and peck at his lips, dodging away again as he tried to reciprocate, suddenly straightening herself on the bench and folding her hands primly on her lap.

"It's too late now," he said, seizing her arm. "Now I know you're not a prude."

"Is that what you thought?"

He shrugged, dipping down and nipping her lips.

"I was beginning to think so, too. I mean, that's how I was beginning to think about myself for the last few years."

He laid his head in her lap. "I don't want to go home."

"Where shall we go?" She stroked his hair. It occurred to him that such casual ease was almost as intimate as the kiss. There was something almost postcoital in the pose. "Somewhere, you know, far away."

"Zanzibar."

"Or Mandalay."

"Do you think about leaving the city?"

"At first. But now I think I want to stay."

"Are you cold?"

"Not at all. Are you?"

She shook her head, looking down at him as she raked her fingers through his hair, which suddenly seemed, to him, terribly coarse. "Do you sleep together?"

"Not in a long time."

"Me neither."

"Usually, I sleep in the daybed in the library, or in my studio."

"I'd love to see your studio. Your little in-town pied-à-terre."

"Come now."

She seemed to weigh the request. "Don't think I'm not tempted," she said finally. "But I think—"

"I didn't mean—"

"You didn't?"

"I'm not sure what I meant, really. I just don't want to leave you."

He wasn't sure what he wanted. If he was ready to be unfaithful. Ample justification doesn't in itself recalibrate one's sensibilities. After more than fifteen years of marriage, it might take time.

# 18

He took the bag from the man in front of him on the line, cradling it in his arms. The zipper split open and he found himself staring at a woman with no face, only a charred, featureless black mask. Then the bag started to move in his arms. Looking down again, he saw Guillermo's face looking up at him.

Luke bolted up from a deep chasm of sleep and found himself in his studio. He felt drugged, weighted and tied to the sofa, trussed, like Gulliver, by a thousand tiny threads. A brilliant panel of sunlight showed beneath the drawn shade over the unoccupied bed, dispelling the grim spell of his dream. He was fully dressed, his clothing rank with the downtown smell of smoke and ash. Lately, he had favored the sofa, in an effort to outwit his insomnia and his general dread. If he lay down here, he could pretend to be merely resting, temporarily dallying, rather than actually courting sleep, and often, in this surreptitious manner, he was able to lose consciousness.

Three-thirty by his watch. When had he fallen asleep? What day was it? As the most recent instance of the recurrent nightmare began to fade, it was gradually replaced by a sense of well-being as he recalled his hour on the park bench with Corrine that morning.

Resisting the urge to sink back into sleep, he raised himself up, straining against the weights and ropes of the long week, his limbs and joints stiff and sore. This, he supposed, was what age felt like.

The answering service picked up when he phoned home. It had been—what?—almost two days since he'd spoken to Sasha. He'd planned on surprising Ashley after school, but it was too late now. The prospect of checking his E-mail seemed even more depressing than that of facing his family; besides, he didn't have to check to know what his investments were doing. On a whim, he called his mother.

"I'm having nightmares," he told her.

"You always did."

"Now I have a reason," he said testily. Why did he always get so irritated with her?

"I don't know why you don't come home and spend some time on the farm," she said. Fresh air, she believed, was a universal panacea, and, in fact, she'd made a calling out of her belief in the curative power of horseback riding.

"How are your patients?"

"You know we don't call them patients."

"It must seem very far away to you there."

"We feel it," she said. "But not the way you do. Is there any news of your friend Guillermo?"

"No news, Mom. Just guilt and nightmares."

When he hung up, he decided to walk over to the apartment and face the girls, taking a loopy diversion through the park. He ambled over to the Great Lawn, where couples lay on blankets in the green expanse and where, as if to prove that life went on, a softball game was in progress. On the path to the reservoir, spandexed runners with pillowy white feet dodged around him and made for the cinder track. A beaky merganser surfaced out of the murk, blinking, swiveling his head back and forth like a tourist emerging from the subway. The afternoon sun poured a slick of rippled silver across the gray water. Rising to the east, the rectilinear fortresses of Fifth Avenue; to the west, the fanciful towers and battlements of Central Park West. The city up here untouched and seemingly untroubled.

Entering the apartment, he paused to look at the family photographs in Tiffany frames in the front hall, which seemed almost unfamiliar to him, all of the frames shivering from the monotonous bass line emanating from Ashley's room: a head shot from Sasha's modeling days; the three of them in ski clothes at Aspen, and again at his parents' a few Christmases ago; one of Sasha with Sting; another of Sasha with Bill Blass, as if they were part of the family.

He strolled down the hallway to Ashley's room, encouraged that he recognized the tune, "Gin and Juice," a hip-hop favorite among private school gang bangers. He knocked and, after waiting what he judged a respectful interval, opened the door.

He would be haunted by the image, unable to erase it, though in the first moments he had trouble composing and interpreting the elements of the tableau. A boy standing, a girl sitting on the bed amid fuzzy stuffed animals in pastel shades. The boy's head tilted back, his hands cradling the blond head at his waist. He didn't recognize the boy, his sandy hair slicked back, the grooved trails of the comb distinctly visible. The girl was his daughter, her head rocking back and forth in a contrapuntal rhythm to the beat of the song. He wasn't sure how long he stood there.

The boy finally sensed a presence and turned, panicking as he saw Luke, his hands flying to adjust and conceal himself, a flash of pink flesh as he spun away and struggled with his jeans, Ashley looking up, annoyed, then turning to see her father in the doorway.

Later, he would picture her expression as she looked at him then, her wide eyes and swollen lips, hoping to analyze it in such a way that he could finally put the image to rest, to separate out the purely abstract surprise that modulated to fear, as well as the reflex of guilt from the specific sadness, so he imagined, of knowing that she would never look the same to him again.

"Oh my God," she said, burying her face in her hands.

Luke looked at his daughter—and registered, if perhaps in its last moments, the only love he'd ever believed was indestructible, the one untainted by lust or self-interest, the love that he believed would finally restore his own innocence and redeem his gray and shriveled soul.

The boy stood with his hands in front of his crotch, frozen in terror. He was taller than Luke, with the broad chest of an athlete, but they both knew that at that moment it would be no contest. Feeling the violence rising within him, Luke realized he had to leave the room. He turned to his daughter, who was hunched on the bed with her arms wrapped around her knees.

Later, he will wonder if he uttered the words *you slut* or merely heard them in his head as he turned on his heel, walking down the hallway and out the door without a destination in mind but with a clear and purifying image of himself as a solitary wanderer, a tortured figure at large in the streets of the mournful city.

# 19

'm worried about Ashley. She hasn't said so in so many words, but I think she's really shaken. She's been . . . I don't know, strange. Fragile. I'm going to take her out to Sagaponack for the weekend. I think she really needs to get out of the city."

They were sitting in the library—his turf, insofar as any part of the house was. Complete with defensive weaponry, shotguns and sword, should he be required to defend his castle.

He'd been waiting when she returned from her committee meeting. She was dressed with her usual casual grace, black leather jeans and a black cashmere pullover, her hair brushing her shoulders with a hint of terminal flip, which she accentuated in the evening. Trimmed once a week at Frederic Fekkai—with the kind of precise edge that looked as if it could cut flesh. An awkward formality prevailed between them. He hadn't yet told her about what he'd seen in Ashley's bedroom the previous day, and wasn't sure he would. He was holding it in reserve—he wanted to assess the domestic situation first.

"Am I invited?"

"Of course you're invited," she said. "I wasn't sure if you were done saving the world yet."

"I'm not saving anything. If anything, I'm giving you a little space. And myself some time to think. Although it's nice to do something that feels vaguely useful."

"You have an MBA, for Christ's sake. You practically restructured the debt of Argentina."

"They're about to default again, actually."

"You're a financial genius. Anybody could make sandwiches for the firemen."

"Is this a plea to come home?"

"Of course I want you to come home. I want us both to get on with our lives. I don't know what you think, but—"

"It's not just what I think. Everybody we know thinks the same thing. Especially after your little display of dirty dancing at the zoo."

She pinkened at this. He'd left the apartment before she rose that morning, and in the days and weeks that followed, it had been easy to avoid the subject of Bernie Melman, public events having eclipsed the private realm.

"I admit I may have had one too many glasses of wine that night."

"An example your daughter was emulating. It makes me wonder what happens when you have two or three too many. Or a couple lines."

She rolled her eyes, intending to imply that the charge was ridiculous, an old canard. "Well, that's all in the past."

"Have you seen him since?"

For a moment, it was clear she was going to play dumb and ask whom he meant, but she changed her mind. "No, I have not."

He believed her, somehow confident he could still tell when she was lying.

"Look, we've all been traumatized," she said. "I think this is a good time to make a fresh start. I've been thinking a lot about us."

"Come to any conclusions?"

"Just that we should try to be good to each other. That's all. And build on that."

"Does that mean you're keeping your options open?" So far, he hadn't pressed her; he hadn't asked the hard question. He wasn't entirely certain what was holding him back, whether it was a fear of hearing the truth, or of forcing her to lie—or a sense of resignation verging on indifference.

When her cell phone chirped from her purse, she couldn't quite disguise her relief. "Let me just see who this is. It might be Trudy about the benefit. Given . . . you know, everything that's happened, we're probably going to postpone." She pirouetted, walked into the living room. "Hey, I was just telling Luke it would be you."

He wasn't even sure if he loved her anymore or if, except for a daughter, they had anything in common.

"Trudy just had a brilliant idea," she said, returning to the library, all cheery and bright and practical. "She asked about you, so I told her about your charitable work, and bing! Genius idea! We could do a joint benefit for the ballet and your soup kitchen. You'd probably want to incorporate as a five oh one c three, but Judy could take care of the paperwork."

"Why the sudden interest in the soup kitchen? You've got that oversized smile, the one you use for small children, lame dinner partners, and gossip columnists."

The smile disappeared. "My, my," she said, sinking into the side chair across from him. "That's a little harsh. Let's try to remember that charity begins at home."

"As does fidelity. It's the centrifugal force that holds domestic life together." Realizing, as he said this, that he himself was under the influence of the centripetal pull of illegitimate desire.

"Look, the charities are scrambling madly. All the fall benefits are up in the air. Yasmin has just postponed the Alzheimer's. No one wants to seem insensitive, but people have a hard time thinking about the ballet or the opera when five thousand people are missing, however many it is. So the chairs are desperate to link up with some kind of nine/eleven–related charity."

"For Christ's sake, it's just a couple of tents with some warming trays and a coffee urn."

"Well then, it sounds like you could use funds to expand your operation."

"I don't even know if we'll still be there next week. They could shut us down at any minute."

"Then call the mayor. This is what I mean: With your talent and your connections, you could be doing something bigger than passing out sandwiches. It's not as if I'm asking for myself."

"I don't know. I'll talk to Jerry."

"Who's Jerry?"

"Jerry started the soup kitchen. He's that carpenter I told you about. It's his call."

"What if I talk to him?"

"Be my guest. I'll give you his cell number."

"The other thing—Trudy was wondering if you could get her a pass or something down to Ground Zero."

"A pass?"

"Don't act so self-righteous. People are curious. They want to see it. The Portmans got a tour yesterday—you know he's a big Republican donor—and they said it was very moving. I said I'd ask, that's all," she said, suddenly backing off. She stood up, walked over, and put her hands on his shoulders. "I'm supposed to meet the Traynors at Swifty's for a bite," she said. "Will you join us? Just the four of us."

"I don't think so."

"I can't bear for you to hate me."

"I don't hate you, Sasha."

"Can we try to be good to each other?"

"I've been trying all along."

She leaned over and kissed him on the cheek.

"Where's Ashley?"

She looked at her watch. "She's with the tutor; then she's going to Amber's for dinner. I told her to be home by eight. Maybe you could take her down to your little soup kitchen, Ashley and some of the girls. It might be good for them."

"Was that her idea?"

"I suggested it. I'm sure she'd be happy if you asked." She paused, tugging at a strand of hair. "What did you two talk about yesterday?"

"We didn't really talk at all."

"She said she'd seen you. She seemed a little, I don't know, nervous. When I asked her how you were. I told her she should be proud of you, that you'd been down in the middle of it all, helping out, that you were probably a little shell-shocked. That you'd seen some terrible things."

Terrible things indeed. "I can't recall you asking me what I'd seen."

"Well, I can imagine."

"I'm not so sure about that."

"Oh, stop being a martyr. Has it ever occurred to you that after doing everything in your power to avoid being like your father, you're finally reverting to type? I mean, that was the first thing that occurred to me when you said you were quitting your job. Next thing I know, you'll be enrolling in divinity school. Or maybe you can be like your great-great-whatever grandmother and write letters to the relatives of all the victims."

This was an allusion to his father's great-grandmother, who after the Battle of Franklin had buried hundreds of Confederate dead in the family graveyard and then spent years writing letters of condolence to their families.

"I remember the day I first told you that story," he said, "you had tears in your eyes."

She looked at him suspiciously. "You've met someone, haven't you?"

"What makes you say that?"

She continued to study his face. "Because you're trying to push me away, just when we should be drawing together. I'm just as shaken as you are. I've been having nightmares. Has it ever occurred to you that I might need you more than the people downtown? Why won't you let this be a fresh start? Eveybody's reevaluating their lives. Asking themselves what really matters."

"At our age, fresh starts are harder to come by. History accumulates. Just because we've been attacked, that doesn't give everybody a clean slate. I can't just forget everything that's been going wrong with us just because we're scared about the future."

She knelt in front of him and put her arms around him, kissing his neck, teasing his earlobe with the tip of her tongue. "Maybe I can help you forget," she whispered. "It's been too long." Her right hand moved from his shoulder to his lap, reaching for his zipper.

"Much too long," he said, feeling somewhat revolted. "I've been waiting a long time for you, and now you'll have to wait for me."

When she pulled his zipper down, he pushed her hand away.

"Fine," she said, rising to her feet. "You go hang out in the rubble with the good girls. We'll be in Sagaponack."

She turned and left the room, leaving him to regret his intractability as he wondered if perhaps she was capable of changing after all, if she might be ready to come back to him just at the very moment he'd given up on her, as he savored the unfamiliar taste of marital guilt.

# 20

The stillness of 3:00 a.m. was sullied by a conflict among the volunteers over who would make the next trip to the site, half a dozen of them engaged in a tug-of-war over a shopping cart loaded with supplies.

"You can go next time."

"Who put you in charge?"

"Why don't we all go?"

"We can't all go. It's supposed to be two people. That's what Jerry said. They're not putting on a fucking show."

"Well, I've been here for seven hours."

"We all have. Besides, I have a cousin who's missing in there."

"Funny you didn't mention it before."

"What was I supposed to do, *announce* it to everybody?"

"Hey," Luke said, stepping into the melee. "Let's remember why we're all here," he said, seizing the overturned coffee urn. "We're talking about a mass grave. How about a little fucking respect." Appalled to the point of wanting to slap somebody, he was also conscious of performing for Corrine, to whom he hoped to appear a figure of stoic dignity, a lone ranger of the downtown canyons. No better than the rest of them, obviously.

At the end of the shift, he walked her to within a block of her door. In the bright light of the morning, just short of the corner of West Broadway and Worth, he pressed her against a doorway and kissed her. She struggled to break free even as she succumbed, and he could tell that her shame at this transgression and her fear of discovery were compounding her excitement.

"We can't," she said, pulling free of him and running to the corner before turning and coming back to kiss him once more. . . .

He was still giddy with the memory when he walked into the apartment and saw Sasha coming down the hallway. He tried to remember what day it was—thinking the two of them were still supposed to be in the Hamptons.

"I didn't expect you back so early," he said, hearing a note of guilt in his own voice.

Her face was pale and drawn, her left eye twitching. "I tried to call you," she said.

"My battery's dead. What is it?"

"Luke, please don't be furious with me."

"What's happened? Where's Ashley?"

"I just left her."

"Left her where?"

"Lenox Hill."

"The *hospital*?"

She threw herself at him and clutched the open collar of his shirt.

"Oh, Luke, I had no idea."

"The fucking hospital?" But if she was in the hospital, he reasoned, feeling Sasha's tears on his neck, didn't that mean she was still alive?

"An overdose," she sobbed.

177

He tried to absorb this information as he led her to the living room, reviewing the recent past for signs and clues. Ashley took drugs? Surely he would know. He lowered Sasha to the couch and sat beside her.

"But she's . . . alive."

Sasha nodded, wiping her eyes.

"I thought you were in the Hamptons," he said, as if by poking holes in this story he might demonstrate its absurdity.

"I was. But at the last minute, Ashley wanted to stay in town with Bethany."

"You went out alone? You *left* her here?"

Her expression then was so frightened and vulnerable that he could almost imagine forgiving her everything in advance, even as he considered the implications of Sasha going to the Hamptons without Ashley. She would hardly have gone out to be alone, not being the sort of girl who believed in the virtues of solitude and reflection.

"And she stayed with Bethany?" He felt as if he were quizzing a child.

She nodded. "I didn't know the Traynors were out of town."

"You didn't even check with Mitsy?"

"I trusted Ashley."

He chose not to challenge this self-serving assertion, wanting to get to the point.

"Bethany called me around three a.m. She was hysterical. She said Ashley was sick and they were taking her to the emergency room." She sniffled and tried to compose herself.

"What kind of drugs?"

She shrugged. "A little of everything. That's what they told me at the hospital."

"A little?"

"I guess not."

He suddenly imagined something worse. "You don't think it was deliberate?"

She seemed shocked. "Why would Ashley want to kill herself?"

"You haven't talked to her?"

"Of course I have. I got there by four. She just kept saying she was sorry."

"How did you get in to the city so fast?"

She looked down at her hands, spread open on her knees. "What do you mean?"

"I don't suppose it matters," he said.

His bitter tone seemed to rouse Sasha to her own defense. "I tried to call you. I didn't know what to do. All that mattered was getting to the city as soon as possible. So I called the only person I knew who had a helicopter at his disposal."

"You're right," he said, realizing he might well have been kissing Corrine while his wife was frantically calling. "I wasn't there when you needed me."

She took his hand and pressed it to her cheek.

"I suppose we need to line up some place for treatment."

"I was thinking Silver Meadows. Gini Danvers just got out a few months ago. She had this huge Vicodin problem and she said it's genius."

He was accustomed to hearing this superlative applied with italicized enthusiasm to shoes, restaurants, new exercise regimens. But in this context, it pissed him off. To his mind, Silver Meadows was the therapeutic equivalent of Round Hill, Hobe Sound, or Saint Barth's, a venerable facility in Connecticut for the treatment of neurotic ailments from which the rich had always suffered.

"Just because your fucked-up friends go there doesn't mean it's the best place for Ashley. Maybe we could break the mold just for once and do what's right for her, instead of what the local narcissists are doing. That's what got us where we are now."

Luke was relieved that she was asleep when he found her in the hospital. He wanted to forgive her, and to love her in the old way, but even as he gently wiped a string of saliva from her cheek, he kept seeing a mask of lust superimposed on her gaunt unconscious face.

Later, as he slept in the chair beside her bed, he saw again the woman of his nightmares, Our Lady of Ground Zero, struggling free of the body bag he held in his arms, faceless beneath the bangs of her dark hair, while the firemen laughed and laughed. When he woke, stiff-necked and basted with sweat, Ashley was regarding him fearfully from the bed.

"You were squirming and whimpering in your sleep," she said.

"Nightmares."

"I'm sorry, Dads."

He nodded. "Help me understand."

She shrugged. "I'm not sure I understand."

"What happened?"

She laughed bitterly. "What didn't?"

"How long have you been doing drugs?"

"You have no fucking idea what my life is like." She rolled on her side, turning her back toward him, jerking the IV tube in her left arm and rattling the hardware on which it was suspended.

"Why don't you tell me?" He sighed, sat in the chair, and waited. If not for the digital readout on the cable box—12:16—he wouldn't have had a clue what time it was.

"It's all so . . ." She seemed to despair of going further.

"So what, honey?"

"I don't know. Just like for example, I'm finally in the upper school, and I'm thinking things will be less stupid and juvenile. But the day before classes start, there's this really stupid initiation where the senior girls make us do all this weird shit—I was locked in a dark closet for like an hour; then I had to call up some boy I didn't know and say dirty things into the phone and then pretend to give a blow job to a banana in front of all the other girls and the seniors—it's kind of stupid, but it's this big tradition at Sprague. I'm kind of amazed the school lets them do it, actually. And then we had to put on these hideous clothes and smear toothpaste in our hair and they made us up to look like cheap hookers and we had to walk fifteen blocks down Third to this place called Manolo's, which is famous for serving anyone who's not in diapers, and we did shots of sambuca in the back room and put spaghetti in our bras. It's all kind of lame, but it's this tradition, and the girls who don't do it—all the upper-school girls will ostracize them and make their lives miserable for the next few years. So we go along with it, and it actually felt kind of cool getting through it and it wasn't that bad. It's all about belonging to a tribe, and not getting pushed out into the jungle, where you starve to death and the hyenas eat you. My friend Kelly—you remember her—she didn't show up for the initiation, even though she said she would, and now I'm worried about her, because all the other girls were cool, and if the seniors put out the word, then we probably won't even be able to hang out with her. It was just so dumb of her. I mean, it's pretty fierce in my class—we've got all these alpha girls like Bethany and Amber and Katrina. Veronica Hanes didn't come back to school this year. They basically drove her away. I told you about her—she was the one who was like really, really pretty, beautiful, I guess you'd say. She used to get home after school and dump out her purse and she'd have like ten business cards—these guys would just come up to her and give her their cards, not just photographers and model scouts but these horny businessmen. Her parents finally got a driver for her, some Polish refugee who drove her around in this beat-up station wagon. But the thing is that the cool girls just turned on her last year. It's like she was *too* pretty, and she was also a really talented artist, but she just never quite fit in. So suddenly Bethany and Amber decided to shun her, and Katrina actually cut off half her hair one day in the locker room. I mean, can you believe it? And finally she couldn't take it anymore—she transferred to Spence, which we just found out when we went back to school."

She stopped abruptly, just as he was becoming lulled by the rhythm of her voice. He sat up and said, "Are you saying you did drugs to fit in?"

She sighed in exasperation. "No, not really. I don't know what I was saying. I guess I was saying, Who wouldn't want to escape all of this shit?" She started to sniffle. "Everything's changing, everything's falling apart. I wish I was still lying on the beach. I wish I was still lying on the beach and I was six years old and nobody had died and the summer still lasted forever. It used to seem like it did, just on and on and on, and nothing bad ever happened."

# 21

Corrine almost skipped the party.

　　None of this ever would have happened, and Russell's life certainly would have been different, and better, if he hadn't twisted her lightly downed and freckled arm, which, he couldn't help noticing at the time, was lately dry and almost powdery to the touch.

　　"It will do us good to get out," he'd said. "Besides, Hilary must have gotten bored with policemen, because she called up this afternoon and offered to baby-sit."

　　"I'm sorry, it just seems weird," Corrine replied. "I'm not in the partying mood. I don't see how anyone could be."

　　"Well, the poor girl didn't plan on spoiling a national tragedy by having a book party. She's not going to sell eight copies. The least we can do is lend a little moral support."

　　"Fine, you go."

　　"You know Nan—it's her book. You like her."

"I like her fine, she's great, but I certainly don't loom so large in her universe that she'll notice if I'm not there."

"I'll notice. I want you to come with me." Oddly enough, this was true. He was acutely conscious of the bifurcation of their social life in recent years. After the kids were born, they'd started to go out separately, ostensibly to take turns baby-sitting. He didn't want to do that anymore. If something else happened, he said, he didn't want to be apart from her on the other end of town, one of them trapped in a building or a subway car full of gas or biotoxins. He suddenly found himself afraid to be alone, even for short periods of time, whereas she seemed somehow more independent.

"Well," he said, "I'm not going if you're not."

"Don't be a martyr. Go. Take Hilary."

"I don't want to take Hilary. What would she do at a book party? I'd have to spend an hour and a half explaining to her what a book is."

"You know she's writing a novel. And if I'm not mistaken, Washington seemed kind of interested, in his perverse way."

"Yeah, and I'm starting a hedge fund. I am not taking Hilary. I want to take my wife." Having expected her to appreciate his change of heart, his new uxoriousness, he instead felt as if he'd returned home after a long journey, only to find the house empty.

"Oh God," she said, with an exasperated sigh of acquiescence. "What am I supposed to wear?"

The checkpoints had been moved down from Canal Street to Chambers, ending the siege of their neighborhood, although the fact that the southern tip of the island was still sealed off reduced the flow of cabs uptown. At the corner stood one of Verizon's mobile phone–transmission vans, which had actually improved cell service in the area.

They waited for several minutes in silence before Russell spotted a cab down the avenue. Corrine had deliberately underdressed, wearing her least sexy jeans and a little TSE cashmere top, to make a statement: She might be at the party, but it was under protest and she didn't feel remotely festive.

"Do you ever think about Jeff?" he asked, after they were settled in the cab.

"You mean lately?"

"I've been thinking about him a lot the last couple weeks."

"I suppose it's not surprising," she said. "It's like an earthquake that suddenly uncovers these ancient ruins. The sediments of memory all stirred up."

"Did I ever tell you I forgave you?" he said.

"I'm not sure you did. I'm not even sure how I feel about that."

He looked over, surprised, but said nothing.

They drove several blocks in silence, long enough to signify that the subject had shifted, not away from Jeff but from the infidelity.

"I think it's partly because of Jim," he said.

"What is?" she asked after a couple of blocks.

It seemed to him she was being intentionally obtuse. Maybe she was punishing him for making her go to the party.

"I mean, Jeff was my best friend, and Jim kind of took his place. Not that you can make the same kind of friends after you're thirty. And they both got taken away in a kind of mass catastrophe."

She nodded.

"Not that it was the same. I mean, obviously there was a self-destructive aspect to Jeff's death."

"Well, *duh*," Corrine said. "Shooting smack and fucking every coke whore in town qualifies as high-risk behavior."

Russell was shocked at her vehemence. Whatever happened, he wondered, to the hazy, romantic glow of memory? "I can't help wondering about Jim," he said finally. "Not that he was self-destructive the way Jeff was, not that he really stopped to calculate the actuarial risks of running into a flaming disaster zone. But I don't know, maybe if his marriage had been happier, if his career had been in better shape, maybe he wouldn't have been quite so . . ."

His voice trailed off. He didn't like hearing what he was saying.

"Precipitous?"

"Well, yeah."

"I think he was just a good guy, with a good heart, who was following his instincts."

Why did he sense a rebuke hidden in this remark?

As they climbed the stairs of the town house—occupied by a prominent literary power couple, a writer and an editor whose enduring marriage was a source of wonder in the publishing world—Russell called Corrine's attention to the lower door, just below street level.

"That's Gay's office," he said. "He gets up every morning, dudes himself up in one of his bespoke suits, has breakfast, waves good-bye to Nan, puts a hat on his head, and a coat, depending on the season, then walks out this door and down the stairs to the lower door and into his office. A ritualistic preparation for his workday, a kind of symbolic commute."

"That's what you always say when we come here."

The party was a somber affair, even by the relatively tame standards of contemporary publishing events, absent the kind of vicious gossip and social swordplay that usually enlivened such gatherings. Everyone on best behavior. Guests were directed outside to the back garden, where a tent had been set up. The turnout was better than Russell would have expected. He realized that they were all probably grateful to have an excuse to convene. Even though the grapevine had long since accounted for everyone in their community, the guests seemed to be reassured to see one another in the flesh. Russell found himself greeting everyone with genuine warmth and affection, most especially the editors with whom he had feuded and the writers he had rejected or bad-mouthed in the past. The usual business chatter had been largely supplanted by current events—the likelihood of war, Judy Miller's anthrax scare, the narrow escapes of friends, the miserable business prospects. Claiming to be acquainted with one of the principals, Dave Whitlock told Russell the story about the Trade Center guy who, after his regular Tuesday-morning tryst at the Plaza, called his wife at eleven o'clock to assuage his guilt and was confounded by her hysteria and relief. Russell glanced nervously at his wife's stony face as Whitlock paused for dramatic emphasis: "'Where are you?' asks the wife. 'In my office,' he lies, while his mistress puts on her makeup in the bathroom."

"That's the third time I've heard that story, Whit."

"Well, it's a small world," he said before drifting off.

Russell kept close to Corrine's side as they moved toward the bar, where they were stalled in a clutch of young assistants talking animatedly about the new Franzen novel. Then he bumped into Buck Calder, with whom he always talked about wine, and introduced him to Corrine.

"Did you hear?" Buck said. "They just stumbled on the wine cellar from Windows. Not a stick of furniture left, but thousands of bottles survived."

Russell lost his composure briefly when their hostess came over and, taking his hands, told him how sorry she was about Jim, who'd once optioned a novel by one of her authors. "Will there be a memorial service?" she asked.

"Officially, he's still missing," Russell said.

"You'll let me know?"

"Absolutely."

As she drifted off to greet new arrivals, he looked up and saw Trisha, his former assistant, hovering just over Nan's shoulder.

Shocked as he was, he couldn't say he was entirely surprised; somehow, he'd always feared that this moment would arrive and, in waking nightmares, imagined versions of it. Trisha looked gleefully deranged, her eyes boring in on him. His initial panic subsided as he considered that her presence was not so unlikely or necessarily ominous. She was, or at least had been, in publishing; she'd probably come along with a friend.

He took Corrine's arm and steered her toward the back part of the garden. Looking back over his shoulder, Russell almost collided with his former boss, Harold Stone, who was standing forlornly beside his wife, clutching a drink, looking more than ever like a great horned owl, with his beaky lips and the unkempt late-life eyebrows that rose into twin peaks halfway up his forehead.

At this point, Harold was such a monument, you could almost imagine the dandruff on his shoulders as pigeon shit. Russell tried to recall how old he might be now—seventy? A junior member of the old *Partisan Review* crowd, protégé of Hellman and Arendt, lover of McCarthy, friend of Mailer, Bellow, and Roth, mentor to Sontag, he'd more or less invented the trade paperback book, publishing serious work in a format that had previously been reserved for romance and detective novels. His deep involvement with leftist politics hadn't prevented him from acquiring a modest fortune, just in time to retire with dignity when what remained of Corbin Dern, the publishing house he'd presided over, was folded into a vast multinational empire. The two men hadn't spoken to each other in years, since Russell had led the attempt to buy the company out from under him in 1987, although they'd crossed paths frequently at events like these. But now Harold greeted Russell with his closest approximation of a human smile, as if he were finally prepared to bury the hatchet. One of the small miracles of the aftermath—although it was hard to be certain, since Harold had always acted as if he considered social grace a sign of intellectual weakness. The smile that Russell conjured up must have looked even more gruesome and artificial as Harold introduced his wife and he, in turn, reintroduced Corrine, who'd met Harold many times, while hoping that the menace at his back would disappear. But as he waited for someone to carry the conversation forward, Trisha appeared, edging into the foursome.

She stood beside them, holding a glass of white wine, while Harold mumbled something about Afghanistan. When Harold paused to take a sip of his drink, she held out her hand.

"Hi, I'm Trisha Wilcox. A real honor to meet you."

Harold reluctantly extended his hand, regarding her with pained forbearance. Another man would have then introduced his wife, but Harold seemed to feel that he had done more than his duty by accepting her tribute. Besides, Trisha had other priorities.

"So, this is Corrine," she said, smiling brightly, "who doesn't give blow jobs."

For a moment, Russell hoped that Corrine's innate poise, her reserves of patrician hauteur, might carry her through this situation. She examined the interloper, looking her up and down as if she were a dog that had sidled up and started to hump her leg. But as she turned to Russell, her composure crumbled into a look of bewilderment that contained a plea for explanation and deliverance. She might have just been shot, gaping at him and then turning again to look at this unknown petite assassin. When she looked back at Russell, her confusion had been replaced with comprehension. Later, he remembered being impressed by how quickly she had grasped the import and meaning of these ugly words and the situation, giving her credit, in retrospect, for understanding it all in an instant—he had always foreseen her clinging desperately to her fondest illusions.

"I don't believe we've met," Corrine said coolly.

"I'm Trisha," she said. "You might remember me answering the phone at the office, although you probably don't, but either way, your husband has been screwing me for two years."

Russell wished to qualify this statement, which was not entirely accurate, and, for that matter, to point out the utter inappropriateness of the moment. It was a time of national mourning, for Christ's sake.

"Or perhaps I should say, not *exactly* screwing," Trisha continued, "but sodomizing. He was actually quite scrupulous about that, mostly, about not fucking me per se. He has a Clintonian construction on the notion of fidelity."

Russell reflexively flinched as Trisha reached into her giant canvas purse. For a moment, he was absolutely certain that her hand was going to come out clutching a pistol, with which she would shoot him. He'd been expecting as much. Her emotional imbalance, her dangerous unpredictability, being somehow an inextricable component of the thrill he couldn't help seeking again and again, though he vowed each morning after to forswear it. He had even dreamed the scene—a movie premiere, an awards ceremony, which ended when his mistress stepped out of the crowd outside the theater and shot him dead.

Now, instead of a handgun, she produced a sheaf of paper, folded in half, which she tried to force on Corrine, who recoiled and drew her hands across her precious buoyant breasts—which, Russell realized with a terrible pang, he might never see or touch or kiss again.

"Maybe you'd like to read our collected correspondence," Trisha said. "After all, this is a literary event. Just printed-out E-mail, I'm afraid, not quite as elegant as handwritten billets-doux on Russell's engraved Crane stationery. I was actually the one who taught him to use E-mail, back when I was his trusty assistant. I guess it's a generational thing. I mean, I couldn't believe it when they put him in charge of that whole E-book disaster, like Russell even knew what an E-book was. It really used to amaze me that after I'd given him a blow job he'd ask my advice about software. It's like there's a whole new reason for men his age to fuck younger chicks—so that they can get help with their computers after they get their ashes hauled. So how about you, Corrine, do you Yahoo?"

Russell lunged for her arm, but she dodged away. Silence had set in among the partygoers in the immediate vicinity, an audience forming around them.

She held out the papers. When Corrine recoiled from this offering, Trisha unfolded the sheaf and leafed through it. "Here's a good one. Oh, definitely one of my all-time faves. 'My dearest Trisha. I can't sleep thinking about you. Corrine is asleep in the other room and all I can think about is you on your knees—'"

Russell snatched the paper away from her. She fixed him with a smile that in other circumstances would have appeared sweet and generous.

"'—in a posture of worship and submission,'" she continued.

"I refuse to listen to this," Harold's wife declared, clutching her husband's arm, although she seemed frozen to the spot.

"You see, Russ," Trisha said, "tawdry and badly written as they are, I've memorized them." She surveyed the audience, which seemed to have expanded in the vast silence around them.

Even as he thought about lunging at her and strangling her, Russell was thinking that Trisha had qualities beyond her complete and abject sluttishness and craven surrender to his filthiest desires, that she was remarkably spirited and clever. But this, of course, was a wildly inappropriate thought.

Trying to imagine what could possibly *be* appropriate in this situation, he reached out and touched Corrine's arm, which she drew back as if snakebitten. He watched as she shrank further and further away from him, though remaining for the moment at his side, the habitual forms of twenty years of companionship having become ingrained, even as lines he'd never seen before creased her forehead and pinched the flesh between her cheeks and her jaw.

Releasing himself from Corrine's excoriating gaze, Russell turned to Harold, whose indignation was similar to, but more modulated than, his wife's. The scowl on Harold's face communicated a sense of outraged chivalry and also, if Russell read it correctly, a hint that he, Russell, this punk who had tried to buy his company, had now betrayed the team and violated the code of his sex by virtue of providing a glimpse, however inadvertently, into the secret room where male lust and misconduct were properly hidden—an expression that reminded Russell of the time, many years before, when he'd burst into Harold's office, only to find him groping his assistant.

He might have been better off if it *had* been a Glock in the bag, Russell realized as he surveyed his life in ruins: the sad bachelor studio in Yorkville, the awkward scheduled weekends with his children, the lonely nights in front of the TV. He could see Corrine receding and fading away as if he were looking at her through the wrong end of a telescope, even before she stormed out of the garden.

He ran after her, catching her just inside the house and grabbing her arm.

Her face was a dry savanna, in which he was already dead—a desiccated corpse, skull in a rictus, half-covered in sand. What could he say? That it was the sordid and one-sided nature of the affair that appealed to him? That as his wife, she lacked the allure of the forbidden? That he wanted love but craved the thrill of selfish carnal indulgence? That lust and respect were inevitably, in his psychology, mutually exclusive? *It's precisely* because *I respect you, honey.* Because you wear white La Perla panties with handmade lace and I wouldn't expect you to submit to my every lurid wish at three in the morning? The fact that all of these propositions were true did nothing now to ameliorate his guilt.

She pulled her arm away. "I'll be going down to the soup kitchen tonight," she said, "so you might as well sleep in the bed and wake up with the kids. I'll call and let you know my plans tomorrow."

# 22

The road seemed to grow narrower, until it threatened to devolve into the ancient game trail that had dictated its sinuous course, encroached upon and overhung with rampant greenery, bordered on one side by a stream and on the other by a crumbling stone wall that tumbled down and rebuilt itself alongside Luke's Range Rover, broached at intervals by a driveway—bright flashes of white clapboard and windowpane showing through the heavy curtain of foliage. He was racing to make it to their appointment on time; as usual, Sasha had been unable to get out of the apartment at the appointed hour and they'd gotten hung up in the early rush-hour coagulation on 95, got off at the New Canaan exit with only twenty minutes to spare, and now were on a deer path, suspended in a green shade from which, it seemed, they might never emerge.

"The Billingses have a house in New Canaan," Sasha said, breaking a ten-minute silence.

"I thought their place was in Southampton."

"They use the New Canaan house on winter weekends so they don't have to schlepp two hours out to Southampton. A lot of people are doing the three-house thing—one place an hour outside the city and another in the Hamptons for the summer. Like the Carmodys just got a place in Locust Valley for the weekends. He joined Piping Rock for the golf. They close the house in the Hamptons in October."

"Huh," Luke said. He couldn't wait to tell Corrine about *the three-house thing*.

"Well, you've got to admit it makes a certain amount of sense."

"I love the way you say 'a lot of people,' as if this were normal behavior. This is why our daughter's in the hospital."

"Ashley's in the hospital because the Carmodys have three houses?"

"In a sense, yes."

"We made this life together, Luke. You used to be more competitive than anyone. Remember how you almost bought that winery in Chile after Jake Steinman got his in Sonoma?"

"Well, I hate to disappoint you, but we won't be getting the winery or that third house anytime soon. We lost a hell of a lot of money in the last few months."

After a suitable and seemly pause: "How bad is it?"

"Frankly, I'm not even sure we can keep the house in Sagaponack."

"You can't be serious."

"You can look at the accounts yourself."

"Have you thought about going back to work?"

"I'm still trying to come up with something useful to do with the rest of my life."

"Many people would consider supporting a family to be useful."

"Are we still a family?"

"That's a terrible thing to say."

A discreet white sign with green letters marked the entrance to the facility—a vast expanse of jade lawn dotted with white houses in the indigenous late-colonial style, a tiny Palladian chapel, and a smattering of modernist structures. It was Luke's first look at this place, which might have been the campus of a New England prep school or college, the kind of school they had always imagined Ashley would attend. She'd been transferred from the hospital to the facility in a private ambulance a few days ago. Luke followed the driveway to the densest cluster of buildings, passing a baseball diamond and tennis courts, then parked in the visitors' parking lot and followed an arrow to the administration building.

"May I help you?" asked the receptionist, a muscular black man whose biceps swelled the sleeves of his polo shirt.

"My name is Luke McGavock, and this is my wife. We have an appointment with Dr. Friedlander."

Minutes later, they were ushered into the office of Dr. Friedlander, who rose to greet them—a woman of indeterminate age with a lumpish figure and a thick salt-and-pepper coif, dressed in loose-fitting blue jeans and a white oxford shirt.

"Luke McGavock. This is my wife, Sasha."

He sensed a trace of hostility in her cool look of appraisal. Certainly she was not the sort of woman who, in his experience, would warm to Sasha, even though she'd done her best to look subdued; her gray turtleneck and gray slacks seemed to him only to highlight the lean perfection of her expensive figure.

"Please, sit."

He scanned the office for clues to her personality and taste, which were scarce among diplomas from NYU and Johns Hopkins, a wall of bound professional journals, and a desk whose surface was pristine. A single painting hung on the wall: black idiogrammatic slashes against a white ground.

"Is that a Kline?" Sasha asked, nodding toward the canvas.

Luke rolled his eyes. Did she really imagine that's what would be hanging in a doctor's office?

"It was painted by a patient," Dr. Friedlander said without turning to look.

"Will Ashley be joining us?" Sasha asked. Luke knew she was nervous, but her tone struck him as impatient and imperious.

"We feel it's important, especially with a younger patient, to involve the family in the therapeutic process, but we don't think Ashley's quite ready for a family conference. In fact, she specifically asked us to postpone your visit. Still, we believe it's important to fill out certain details of her medical and psychiatric history, as well as that of the home environment."

"You mean we can't see her?" Luke said.

"At this time, we feel that would be counterproductive to Ashley's recovery."

"I'd just like to go on record as saying she's not a drug addict," Sasha said. "If that's the diagnosis, I think you may need to reevaluate. I'm not in denial about this. She's been hanging out with a fast group of girls and obviously they've been dabbling. But I think this was more in the nature of a dramatic gesture than a function of any long-term drug abuse or addiction. I mean, let's face it, we're all traumatized by what happened in September. I think it's important to bear that in mind. One of Ashley's schoolmates lost her father and her own father was down there that morning and has been volunteering at Ground Zero ever since. She's scared. Hell, *I'm* scared. Everyone I know is rattled. We're all drinking too much. I've started going back to my own therapist after a year's hiatus. These are scary times. But I certainly don't think Ashley has a drug problem per se."

The pause that followed this speech stretched into an uncomfortable silence.

"Current events are certainly a contributing factor," Dr. Friedlander said. "I can assure you, Mrs. McGavock, our staff is fully qualified to make that kind of assessment. Perhaps you can tell me first of all if there's a history of chemical dependence or alcoholism in your family. Mrs. McGavock, you said just a moment ago that you were drinking too much?"

"I said everyone was drinking too much."

The doctor raised her eyebrows skeptically. "Let's just focus on you for the moment. Is there any history of alcohol abuse in your family?"

Luke was afraid Sasha would betray her indignation, treating the doctor like an impertinent member of the service sector, but he could see her mastering her defensive impulse, drawing herself up in her chair and preparing her story in her mind. He wondered how honest it would be.

"My father was a fairly heavy drinker."

"Was he ever treated for alcoholism?"

This was a sensitive subject and Luke felt an unexpected wave of sympathy for his wife. Sasha seldom spoke of her father, who'd left home when she was three. She liked to portray him as a bon vivant—an aristocratic southern party boy, but the reality, according to her mother, was far less glamorous. He'd ended his days in a flophouse in Charleston.

"Treated? I don't know. He went to Switzerland once. I used to get these postcards of Alpine scenes, edelweiss, gingerbread houses, and girls in Heidi braids. He said he was skiing, but Mom said he was at a clinic."

"Would you characterize him as an alcoholic?"

"He was a good-time Charlie," she said. "He loved saloons and racetracks. It was a different time." She took a deep breath. "But yes, I suppose I would have to say he was an alcoholic."

Luke had never heard her make this admission. He couldn't help wondering if she wasn't sacrificing her late father in order to protect herself. Still, it was a start.

"He's deceased?"

Sasha nodded.

"And what was the cause of death?"

"We never really knew. It might have been alcohol-related."

The doctor made a note on a legal pad. "And your family, Mr. McGavock?"

He shook his head. "My parents were weekend imbibers. We had an uncle who was a drunk, like every other southern family."

"Let's talk about *your* habits. How would you characterize your own drinking, Mr. McGavock?"

"I have a cocktail when I get home." He remembered that he no longer went to an office, or even had a routine. "I mean, I used to. Wine with dinner. I think it's under control."

He was prepared to follow up, to defend the recreational drug use in his teens and twenties, but Dr. Friedlander turned to Sasha.

"What about you, Mrs. McGavock?" There was a note of disingenuity to this inquiry.

Sasha let go of Luke's hand and crossed her legs. "I like my chardonnay. I suppose I sometimes drink a glass or two more than I should. We go out to a lot of benefits and charity events."

"Are you currently taking any prescription medications?"

"Well, nothing scary. The Pill . . . Paxil—"

"You're on the Pill?" Luke said. He thought she'd been infertile since having Ashley—in fact, she'd said as much.

"It's just to keep my cycle regular," she said, not meeting his eyes.

"Have you ever been diagnosed with depression?"

"Well, I've been diagnosed with depressive tendencies." She seemed happy to change the subject. "I mean, hasn't everybody? The Paxil just makes life a little softer around the edges. And Prilosec, for acid reflux. All the P's. And Ambien, for sleep."

"Do you take ephedra?"

"Once in a while, but that's not prescription. Everyone I know takes it. I mean, it's not easy getting into a size four, and we can't very well spend the whole day at the gym."

"I gather Ashley was somewhat overweight until recently. Did you ever encourage her to take any drug for purposes of losing weight?"

"She might have asked me about ephedra, but it's not like she needs my permission to take an over-the-counter medication."

"And Dexedrine?"

She frowned. "I have an old prescription. I haven't taken it in months. Only when I really need to lose a few pounds."

The doctor made a note.

Seeing Luke's expression, Sasha shrugged and tried to look girlishly helpless.

He turned to the doctor. "My wife's a little obsessed with her weight, and it rubbed off on Ashley. The signal she was getting was that her mother loved her when she was skinny."

Dr. Friedlander nodded.

Sasha sat up straight in her chair. "That's ridiculous."

"Did you ever provide her with Dexedrine?"

"I never!"

"And you never noticed that your own supply was disappearing."

"Oh my God," Sasha said.

"Goddamn it, Sasha. You were feeding her speed?"

"Please, let's try to stay calm for Ashley's sake. Now, I need to ask you about Ritalin. It seems that Ashley had two prescriptions, one from her psychiatrist, another one from her physician."

"Two prescriptions?" Luke said. "Why would she have two prescriptions?"

"I gather, Mr. McGavock, that she approached you separately and suggested that it would improve her academic performance."

"Well, yes. But it's not like it's a narcotic, is it?"

"It's essentially an amphetamine, and at higher doses, it creates a euphoric high. Which is why it's so often abused. Particularly in the Manhattan private school environment. I understand she asked you not to mention this to her mother."

This was true. Ashley had told him how she sometimes had trouble concentrating; she had been sheepish about it, explaining how all the smartest girls in the school were taking it to improve their focus, asking him not to mention it to her mother, since her psychiatrist didn't believe in Ritalin. It was their little secret, and at the time he'd been grateful for this little conspiracy between them. Her doctor had agreed to a trial prescription, and after checking in with her once or twice about the beneficial effects, Luke hadn't thought about it since.

"How could you not discuss something like that with me?" Sasha demanded.

"Well, what about the other prescription?" Luke asked. "You must've known about that one. Why didn't you tell *me*? I suppose you thought it would be a good way to lose weight."

"Dr. Rosenblum prescribed it. And Ashley didn't want me to tell you because she didn't want her genius father to know she'd been diagnosed with attention deficit disorder. It had nothing to do with weight loss."

"I think it's clear," Dr. Friedlander said, "that we're dealing with some serious communication issues here."

Luke put his head in his hands. "You think?"

"I'm afraid I have to ask you about so-called recreational drugs. Mrs. McGavock?"

"Why are you asking me? What kind of question is that? Did Ashley say something?" She stood up.

"Please, Mrs. McGavock. It's important that we have all the facts relating to the home and family environment in order to determine the best course of treatment."

Sasha slowly lowered herself back into her chair, a remarkably graceful operation, one that Luke had often admired.

"Okay, fine, I admit I used to do a few lines in a party situation. It was part of the social landscape. It was like, you know, an *amuse-bouche*. So, once in a while, in the ladies' room, I'd do a couple of bumps. I never really thought of it as a problem. I'm sorry, I realize that sounds terrible, but it's true. I know it's no excuse, but it was just part of the world we lived in. I certainly never exposed Ashley to that."

"And now?"

She shook her head. "I realized it wasn't very attractive."

It was a little scary to see how well she lied.

Dr. Friedlander made another note. "Let's talk a little about the family dynamic. Have there been any changes in domestic relations recently, any marital conflict?"

Sasha rolled her eyes. "Oh, for God's sake—why don't you just come out and say it's all my fault?"

"Why would you say that, Mrs. McGavock?"

"Because apparently Ashley mentioned this silly rumor about me, and I suppose that's her excuse for swallowing a bottle of fucking Vicodin. It has nothing to do with the fact that her father spent thirteen years at the office or that our country is under attack and thousands of her neighbors are dead and now they're sending anthrax in the mail."

"Tell me a little more about this *rumor*."

"There was some ridiculous item in the *Post* about me having lunch with a certain . . . with Bernie Melman," she said with the weary air of a celebrity dismissing an ancient canard.

"Well, do you think it's possible that Ashley might have been upset by this rumor?"

"I don't know. You tell me. You seem to know all about it."

"Did you ever talk to Ashley about this?"

"I really didn't think it was worth dignifying with a discussion. And I really don't think it explains anything."

"At Ashley's age, at this stage in life, the mother-daughter relationship is particularly fraught. Issues of sexual competition are bound to—"

"I've always—we've always been open and honest about sexuality. She knows she can talk to me about anything."

"Did she tell you," Luke said, "about the boy I caught her going down on last week?" He wasn't certain what this proved, but he felt the need to pierce through the fog of evasions and prevarications.

"What are you talking about?"

"Maybe if you weren't so goddamned open and honest about sexuality, she wouldn't be blowing strange boys in her bedroom."

"I think we have a lot of work to do on our communication skills," Dr. Friedlander said.

Twenty minutes later, Luke was in the parking lot, waiting for Sasha to come out of the ladies' room, watching little knots of patients straggling up the meadow to a big two-story house, presumably answering a silent dinner bell, some of them moving with the ponderous sleepwalking gait of the heavily sedated. He couldn't imagine his daughter as one of them. If he could just see her, tell her that everything was going to be all right.

Sasha appeared, her makeup repaired. "I don't know about you, but I need a drink. . . . Don't look at me like that. It was just a little joke, sort of."

"I think we managed to provide the answers to the basic question, didn't we? If not necessarily intentionally."

"You mean *I* did."

"I think there's more than enough blame to go around."

"I know you think I'm thick-skinned and cynical."

"I'll take the fact that you know that as a positive sign."

She put her arms around him. "Let's go out someplace quiet, some stupid old-fashioned New Englandy restaurant where they pour big martinis and sell maple-syrup candy at the cash register. Remember when we drove up to the Berkshires to see the leaves and we stayed at that funny old place in Stockbridge?"

"The Red Lion Inn."

"And on the road to Williamstown how you practically swerved the car into the ditch when I gave you a blow job?"

He nodded, refusing to be drawn in.

"We passed a little inn on the way in." She walked up and pulled him close. "Let's just see if they have a room."

Luke could almost see the appeal of this idea, feeling in her embrace a certain nostalgic warmth, a vestigial twinge of affection tinctured with desire. But he was meeting Corrine at a restaurant in the Village, and nothing short of another disaster could sway him from that course.

"I have to go downtown," he said. He would have felt less guilty if she'd remonstrated with him, if she had reiterated her belief that his charitable work was trivial, instead of releasing him and silently retreating to the other side of the car, if she had at least slammed the car door in protest. If saving his marriage were his top priority, this would have counted as a missed opportunity.

# 23

"What kind did you get, Marine Corps or Israeli?"

"The Marine Corps. What, there's a difference?"

"The Israeli masks are definitely better. Plus, they have a child's size. We bought them for the four of us, and the staff. Web went to Choate with the undersecretary of defense, and he bought the Israeli ones for his family. He set us up with his supplier. I could call him for you. I mean, for all intents and purposes, they're impossible to get."

Corrine wondered if the gas masks she'd purchased on the Internet were inferior, putting her family at risk.

"What about Cipro?" Casey said. "I hope you have a stash on hand."

"I called our pediatrician and he wrote a scrip, but all the pharmacies downtown are sold out."

"They still have some at Zitomer's on Seventy-sixth. At least they did yesterday. I was at Minky Rijstaefal's for dinner—you know Minky; her husband's Tom Harwell, the plastic surgeon—and it was so sweet: Folded inside the name cards at the table, we all had prescriptions for Cipro."

"Do you think Zitomer's is still open?" Corrine asked.

"We can call. So, do you really like the new look?"

They were sitting in Casey's living room on Park Avenue with a bottle of chardonnay from an Argentinean winery owned by Web's firm. Casey lived at 740 Park, an address resonant with talismanic significance in her rarefied world. This simple address on an ecru Crane note card consecrated the embossee as an Olympian who had attained the heights of Manhattan social aspiration. Casey had recently had the place redecorated by the hottest new design team in a kind of deluxe Early American folk style, selling off all their eighteenth-century French furniture, seventeenth-century Flemish art, Chinese porcelain, silk damask, and Persian carpets—a look that Casey had recently decided was generic Park Avenue—replacing them with Pennsylvania highboys, braided rugs, antique quilts, tartan and calico patchwork upholstery, and paintings by the Wyeths, *père et fils.*

"It reminds me a little of my parents' house," Corrine said. Indeed, the overall impression was almost farcically reminiscent of the eighteenth-century saltbox she'd grown up in on the North Shore of Massachusetts, furnished with inherited furniture, pewter and brass, and shabby bric-a-brac from her mother's antique store in Salem.

"We wanted it to be homey. Little did we know how appropriate that would turn out to be. Given what's happened, I think ostentation is over." She looked around, admiring her new living room.

At moments like this, Corrine had to struggle to remember the overweight, insecure girl who'd been her prep school roommate, hoping she was still there somewhere beneath the glossy surface.

"How's your mother doing?"

"About the same," Corrine said. "Of course she wants us to leave New York and move to Massachusetts immediately."

"My mother's exactly the same. She thinks we should move back to Wilmington or to the place on Nantucket. As if we could just uproot our lives. Not to mention the kids. I was just talking to Sasha McGavock today—you know our daughters go to Sprague together—and she said that Hampton Country Day got like a couple hundred applications in the past few weeks."

"What's she like, really?" Corrine asked.

"Who? Sasha?"

"I was just, you know, curious."

"Where do I even start?" Casey said, wetting her lips with her tongue.

Corrine didn't want to tell Casey about Russell's chippie until she figured out what she was going to do, since her friend would be only too eager to preside over the dismantling of her marriage; neither was she ready to tell Luke, although at the same time he was the person she most wanted to tell. For the moment, she wanted to segregate her anger at Russell from her feelings for Luke. Of course, that anger made her freer to explore those feelings, but she wished to retain the illusion that the two were somehow unrelated, that beyond the barricades was a world apart.

Over the past few days, she'd minimized her contact with Russell to a couple hours in the evening, between his return from the office and the children's bedtime, not wishing to punish them for his sins. They were already unsettled enough.

The night after the book party fiasco, a chilly formality and domestic routine had prevailed. They ate supper together with the kids, Russell having cravenly cooked one of her favorite meals, salmon with salsa verde, accompanied by an elaborate salad with hazelnuts and about twenty different kinds of lettuce he extolled as "microgreens." As if making a chic meal would compensate for having screwed that girl . . . As if she really cared, the way he did, about what she ate; she supposed he actually might have been mollified, had he been the wronged party, by some extravagant multicourse spread incorporating truffles, caviar, and foie gras. Then, after dinner, he'd bathed the kids and done the dishes.

Corrine had left the apartment as Russell was putting the kids down, in order to avoid him after they were asleep, going uptown to visit Casey before heading down to Bowling Green for her shift, where Jerry gave her a note from Luke explaining that he was at his studio, catching up on sleep. Reading it, she found herself getting all teary—not because she had planned to confide in him that night, but because his presence would've distracted and comforted her and also because she worried about him, his tiredness seeming palpable and almost tragic. Contemplating the long night ahead of her, she realized just how much she looked forward to his company, and how mixed were her motives in turning up every night, how shallow her charitable impulse; she was no better, really, than the voyeurs who came down to glimpse the destruction, and get a war story to carry back uptown.

Corrine worked through the night with the lash of conscience at her back, making coffee and sandwiches, stacking supplies, dishing out chili, uncondensing cans of soup, sweeping out the tent, chatting with cops and Guardsmen and the silver-haired minister from Canada who'd driven down to provide counsel and solace to the rescue workers—all the while imagining how impressed Luke would be if he could see how industrious she was even in his absence. Proving her selflessness even as she wished that Luke could bear witness to it.

She gave a neck rub to a steelworker who'd been on the pile since the first day. The weather had turned, a cold wind gusting from the west, and she felt suitably punished, shivering in her light wind-breaker until Jerry lent her a sweater. She suddenly wondered how it was, since he appeared not to change clothes for days on end, that his head and face remained so clean-shaven. And, for that matter, when and where he slept.

She returned to the loft at seven the next morning, just in time to wake the kids and get them ready for school.

She heard Russell in the shower, then the crackle and pop of squabbling from the children's room. It was way past time to get them their own rooms.

"What's the problem here?" she asked, sweeping in on the battle.

"He hit me."

"I did not. She hit me first."

"Good morning," Russell said plaintively, standing in the doorway with a towel around his waist as she helped them pick their outfits. She was trying to convince Jeremy it was too cold for short sleeves.

She had them at the counter eating cereal by the time he emerged fully dressed, skulking like a stray dog at the edge of the family circle.

"I'll be right back," she said to the kids, heading to the bathroom.

Out of long habit, she didn't think to lock the door. A moment later, Russell burst in on her. "Jesus, Russell, I'm peeing."

"We need to talk."

She wiped herself hastily and stood up, her fury renewed. "We'll talk when and if I ever feel like it."

"Did you read the E-mail I sent you?"

"I glanced at it," she said. "I didn't find anything there that made me feel better about the fact that you'd been fucking some slut for two years."

"I'm so sorry, Corrine. I love you. I promise you I'll make it up to you, whatever it takes."

"I don't know if you can. I really don't. Now get out of here and let me have some privacy." His hangdog expression really pissed her off—as if he somehow thought he was the one who'd been trespassed against. "Just tell me one thing," she said. "I want to know what she could possibly have that I don't." Aware, as soon as she said this, of what a cliché it was, how much she sounded like the victim in some horrible Lifetime movie.

"Do you really want to know? Because she's *not* you. She's different. That's all. Not better. Different. Because—maybe you're right, maybe she *is* a slut. And you're not. You're my wife."

"We'll see about that," she said, pushing him out the door and locking it behind him.

When she finally emerged from the bathroom to join them in the kitchen, Storey looked at her quizzically. "Mommy, were you crying in there?"

"No, honey, I just got something in my eye."

"You look like you've been crying."

"Mommy's been working down where the big fire is," Russell said, "helping feed the rescuers. The smoke gets in her eyes."

She thought then of that old song they used to play over and over, the Bryan Ferry version, how Roxy Music's *Avalon* had been *their* album.

"Mom, you *are* crying," Storey insisted.

"I'm fine, honey."

Jeremy's face balled up in response to his mother's distress, tears now coursing down his cheeks.

"Now Jeremy's crying."

She took him in her arms. "It's all right, honey. Mommy's just tired."

He finally stopped sobbing on her shoulder. "Are the rescuers going to save the people?"

"They're trying, sweetheart. We're all trying."

"Celia's dad is still missing," Storey said.

"Celia?"

"Celia the Fluffy," Jeremy said.

"He woke up twice last night with nightmares," Russell said.

This transparent appeal to her motherly instincts, the thinly veiled protest against her work at the soup kitchen, infuriated her so much that she retreated to the bedroom, before she snapped at him in front of the kids.

She tried to sleep after Russell and the children had left, but her anger had transmogrified into a nagging buzz of guilt. She was a very bad person. A terrible mother. Lost and damned. Because even with the image of her son's contorted, tear-streaked face fresh in her memory, even as she planned her afternoon and evening with the children, hoping to keep the cracks and fissures from undermining their world, she kept anticipating her reunion with Luke, conjuring the look of recognition in his eyes as he glanced up from the grill or the warming trays and saw her walking toward him, an image that continued to play in her mind—after she woke and dressed, as she watched the children play in the park, as she held their mathematics flash cards, as Storey repeated a question she'd failed to hear the first time, and as she bathed them while Russell dined down the street at Odeon with an Italian publisher. What kind of mother had she become, checking her watch as she read to them? It wasn't the minutes to their bedtime so much as the hours until midnight that she was counting. And after she'd finally put their water glasses beside their beds and kissed them good night, she couldn't concentrate on Rushdie's new novel, about a gaudy fin de siècle New York that no longer existed, or on the news, which was all about the terrifying reality that had replaced it.

What powers of dissembling had she suddenly acquired that allowed her, when Russell returned that evening, to discuss the children and ask about his day without summoning up any hostility whatsoever, now that she was counting the minutes till she would see Luke? Russell was almost comically relieved at her civility. Reviewing the schedule for the next day, the mundane details of school drop-off, pickup, and dinner, he demonstrated the earnestness of a dutiful student. Corrine explained that the kids had a play date uptown with Washington and Veronica's kids; she would drop them off after school and he would pick them up at six. He nodded eagerly, repeating everything with the zest of someone addressing the logistics of an adventure holiday. His eagerness to believe in the status quo almost touched her heart, but if she softened toward him a little at that moment, it was only because her mind and her heart were elsewhere.

The burned-plastic stench washed over her yet again as she walked down Broadway. The more closely she approached, the more acutely she felt the presence of the dead—a kind of psychic static. So palpable was this impression that she sometimes feared she might see them, wafting luminously through the canyons of the Financial District. She stopped and glanced behind, feeling a tingling chill on her arms and the back of her neck, though the night was warm and still, and imagined she could feel a current of sadness and regret sweeping up Broadway. What would they tell her if they could speak? Would they advise her against her present course? Or was it a mistake to anthropomorphize the dead? Who was to say they shared our concerns or emotions, or those of their former selves? Perhaps it wasn't their sadness she felt, but only her own.

Luke's absence from Bowling Green the previous night suddenly took on an ominous significance. He might have spent the last thirty-six hours with Sasha. He might have slept with her. Surely she had come to her senses and realized what she risked losing. Corrine knew that after all his trials with Sasha, a little tenderness and affection would act on him more powerfully for having been so long withheld. She imagined Sasha as one of those brilliant coquettes who operated on the belief that male desire was inflamed by competition. Whereas Corrine was disgusted by Russell's infidelity, she wondered if Luke, with the instincts of his gender, might not be incited by Sasha's, seeing her as more valuable by virtue of her being desired, his honor vindicated by reclaiming the prize that had been stolen from him. And whatever Luke said about Melman, the mogul's status, along with the assumption that he could have his choice of women, would reflect a kind of greater glory on the object of his desire and make her seem all the worthier of fighting for. Even if he had withdrawn from the game, Luke had spent his adult life playing in the same league as Melman; she knew these guys, she'd worked alongside them, and when it came down to it, they all respected the player with the biggest pile of chips. They competed for the same trophies. Was Luke really any different?

After she'd first met Luke, she'd found Sasha's photo, svelte in Badgley Mischa, arm in arm with Alec Baldwin on the party page of an old copy of *New York* magazine. Her first impression had been critical: Her prettiness seemed too conventional to qualify as beauty. But as she came to know Luke and listened to him talk about Sasha, her image had acquired a certain retrospective vivacity and mystery in Corrine's imagination. The night before, she had casually asked Casey Reynes about Sasha, knowing they were friends, and the intelligence thus gathered seemed sinister in the light of Luke's absence later that night. Everyone in Casey's circle believed that Sasha and Melman were having an affair, that she'd started exercising her considerable powers as soon as he separated from his wife. But the latest scuttlebutt had Melman flying to Palm Beach, and there was talk of reconciliation.

As she entered the penumbra of light emanating from the ruins, she drew back from this line of speculation, as if awakened by the drone of heavy machinery and the gnashing steel teeth of the heavy grapplers, and asked herself what business she had judging Luke or worrying about his marriage—as if she were free to offer herself. How had she gotten so far gone?

Approaching the bronze bull, she tried to quell her sense of anticipation by telling herself that it was good to know her heart was still pliable enough to have been quickened by this brief encounter with romance. It had been a rejuvenating exercise, this little flirtation of hers. But it could only be fantasy. And she congratulated herself that it hadn't gone any further, that she hadn't done anything she could later regret. Whatever course she decided to pursue with regard to her marriage shouldn't depend on any outside influence. Let Russell be the one to carry that burden of guilt.

She spotted him in front of the tent, smoking a cigarette, talking to Captain Davies. Relieved to find nothing new in his demeanor or his posture, she stopped at the edge of the fence to watch him unobserved. She would have liked just then to take a picture of him. Even more than the cheerful cop, he seemed to project an air of command, to be ready to take charge if he was needed.

As she walked toward him, he caught sight of her and broke into a smile, Davies turning to follow his gaze. Luke swiped his hand across the lower half of his face, a nervous gesture she'd noticed before. One of those little tics—like the way he chewed his cuticles—which, with repetition, became a part of her picture of him.

"You're back," she said.

"I'm back," he replied.

She was afraid she was blushing. "I got your note."

"I needed some sleep."

"I hope you got some."

"I need coffee," Davies said, rolling his eyes. He lumbered off to the tent, clanking at the hips.

"Did I miss anything?" Luke asked.

"I don't know," she said. "Did you?"

"What do you think?"

She could feel her facial muscles spazzing into a stupid smile. Her transparency annoyed her and, in turn, made her annoyed at him. "I think . . . I thought maybe you decided it was time to go back to your real life."

"I'm not sure I have one."

"You have a wife and a daughter."

"That's true."

"God, I'm sorry," she said. "I'm just mad at myself for being so happy to see you."

"I'm happy to see you, too. Should I be mad at myself?"

"Don't you feel guilty?"

"Not really. Well, maybe a little. No, actually that's *not* it. But I think I just feel, I don't know—if I felt a little *less* happy to see you, if you were just some chick I met at the soup kitchen, that cute girl from Ralph Lauren, for instance, then it wouldn't really matter."

"I was ridiculously disappointed last night when I realized I wasn't going to see you."

"I'm glad."

"I suppose I should go sign in and make myself useful," she said.

"I was just going to drive up to Balthazar to pick up some hot food," he said. "Jerry left me his car, and we've got a couple hours till the shifts change. Why don't you join me?"

The cop at the on-ramp to the FDR waved them through. Luke slowed down and lowered his window. "You guys need anything here? Coffee, sandwiches?"

"I don't guess you got any hot calzones in there?"

"We'll pick one up."

The highway was deserted. With the windows up, the car smelled a little too lived in—a funk composed of body odors and food residues both fresh and ancient. He turned off on Houston, driving west, past Rivington, where Jeff used to score his heroin at a bodega Russell had taken him to the morning they did the intervention, allowing him a final hit before they carried him off to rehab. Past Katz's Delicatessen, where she'd become nauseated one afternoon at the sight of all that opalescent pastrami and corned beef. Past Nice Guy Eddie's, where she'd once danced on the bar and Russell had gotten into a fight with a guy who wouldn't leave her alone afterward. Long ago, in another life, she'd been a girl who danced on bars. Suddenly, she felt as if she could do it again.

They parked directly in front of the restaurant, one of Russell's favorite haunts, a place where he entertained his out-of-town writers, because even if they hadn't heard of it, they were likely to see famous faces and feel they were indeed at the center of the universe, that their editor was a player. Although he'd rather die than admit it, Russell was proud to have the private number, to be able to get a table at short notice, or, better yet, a booth; she remembered him pouting and fretting one night when he'd failed to command one of the booths along the far wall; further irked that they were occupied by people he didn't recognize.

At present, a little before one in the morning, the place was half-full of anonymous hipsters. Luke announced their mission to the maître d', the dark one with the goatee who always put her in mind of Lucifer.

"Do you suppose we'll ever go to Paris together?" Luke asked, looking around at the worn silver mirrors, aperitif ads, and distressed tin ceiling.

"I think it's possible," she said, surprising herself.

"I suppose it's a cliché," he said. "Like that picture by Doisneau, the kiss on the street."

"It's only a cliché if you're jaded." Falling in love was a cliché, she realized. It had all been done before, and it looked absurd from the outside.

"I don't feel jaded," he said.

"Me neither."

"Oh shit."

She followed his gaze across the restaurant.

"It's Sasha," he said.

She was sitting in a booth with someone Corrine thought was a rapper turned actor and a slim, glossy blonde who looked as if she might have gotten lost on her way to Le Cirque, although Corrine had to admit that everyone pretty much went everywhere now, uptown or down—the borders had gotten porous, at least until the eleventh, when the word *downtown* had acquired an ominous new meaning. Even from this distance, Sasha was impressive; she had a kind of luminous presence, which made the other blonde at the table look like the Chinatown knockoff version of Upper East Side Barbie.

"Let's just make a discreet exit," Luke said.

"You don't even want to say *hi*?" asked Corrine, who was curious, and also amused at Luke's discomfort—even as she was daunted at the prospect of actually confronting this glamorous creature.

He shook his head, placed a hand on her shoulder, and steered her toward the door.

After two busboys had helped them load the food in the Pathfinder, Luke stopped a few blocks down on Spring Street at Lombardi's Pizza. She stayed in the car while he banged on the door, waving at the man who was sweeping up. Whatever he said seemed to do the trick, and he returned to the car to say the guy was making up a batch of pizzas and calzones.

"She's really quite beautiful," Corrine said.

"I suppose so," he said. "Eventually, it becomes one more thing that you fail to notice, or else it becomes another item on your secret list of grievances. The fact that it allows her to take so much for granted. The disparity between appearance and reality."

"It must be a relief, hanging out with a middle-aged housewife like me."

"Honestly, I think you're more beautiful than she is."

"Now I'm not going to believe anything you say."

He took her shoulders in his hands and shook her gently. "I promise you I'm going to tell you the truth. I have and I will."

213

"I'm sure you mean that," she said, "but you may be too nice to tell the truth all the time. It's too brutal sometimes."

"Then let's make a pact to be brutal to each other."

She checked his eyes for the glint of facetiousness but couldn't find it. "Okay," she said. "Brutal it is."

"Do you think everything will just go back to the way it was?" she asked, as they drove back down the FDR, the Brooklyn Bridge floating brightly against the dark sky.

"It's hard to imagine," he said. "But I suppose eventually it will."

"It just doesn't seem possible."

"The town I grew up in," Luke said, "is one of the sleepiest, most picturesque burgs you could hope to find. Think Mayberry RFD. It was the site of one of the bloodiest battles of the Civil War. Thousands died in the course of a few hours. My great-great-grandmother's house was a field hospital and she had hundreds of wounded under her roof that night. There were four dead Confederate generals laid out on her porch out of the fifteen who fell that day. Nearly fifteen hundred soldiers are buried in what used to be the family cemetery, fourteen hundred and eighty-one to be exact, and they say that my great-great-grandmother wrote a letter to the mothers of every single one of them. When I was a kid, I used to count the bloodstains on the floorboards."

"Don't you think that changed her?" Corrine said. "I'd guess she never felt the same way about gardening or letter writing again. And what about you? You haven't forgotten—even a hundred and fifty years later."

"We had fewer distractions, in the South. New York doesn't have a collective memory."

She didn't want things to be the same, didn't want to go back. She wanted to be with him here in the car, picking up a calzone for a cop manning a checkpoint, just looking at him, watching his eyes modulate from gray to blue and back again. She reached over and ran her fingers through his hair, which was far softer than it looked.

"Do you think we'll ever feel guilty," she said, "that if this terrible thing hadn't happened, we never would've met? I mean, what if some supremely powerful being came to you and said that you could wave your hand and everything would be as it was on September tenth. What would you say?"

"I guess I'm glad I'll never be faced with that dilemma."

"But what if you were?"

"It doesn't bear thinking about."

"I think about that. It's terrible. I think I must be a terrible person."

"I think you're a very good person."

"If I were a good person, I'd know what I'd say."

"Don't think about it, then."

"I try not to. I try not to think about a lot of things, but I do."

"Maybe you should just try to live in the moment."

"I do try. But I can't help thinking."

"I know."

"What are we going to do?"

"I don't know. I'm going to go deliver these calzones. Then we'll go back to Bowling Green. After that, we'll improvise."

"Would it be terrible, after that, to drive up to your studio?"

Half an hour later, they were standing outside the building, a brick town house with a peeling layer of battleship gray paint, stippled with ivy. He unlocked the front door; she followed him up the creaking stairs to the third landing.

The room was conspicuously neat; she wondered if he was fastidious by nature or if he had anticipated her visit. The sleigh bed seemed to take up half the room, the broad white expanse of the fluffy duvet hovering, seemingly taut with suspense. A water glass, two prescription bottles, and a stack of books crowded the candle stand beside the bed. A sofa and two leather club chairs with worn and cracked arms formed a horseshoe around the fireplace. His books and papers were spread across the trestle table that served as a desk; the sleek black Aero chair stood rigidly at attention, facing the PC.

"Cozy," she said.

"Hey, you could be a Realtor."

"Thanks, that's my greatest fear."

After he took her coat, she walked over toward the bed as if to show she wasn't afraid of it, though she was. She was, she suddenly realized, terrified. When she'd imagined this moment, she had pictured them stumbling up the stairs in a passionate frenzy, kissing and groping, pausing between floors to undo buttons, whereas, in fact, they'd ascended the staircase as if approaching the lair of a dragon, silent and grave, struggling upward under their separate burdens of anxiety and guilt, the wooden stairs and the banister creaking portentously beneath their weight.

She examined the books on the candle stand with a semblance of rapt attention, barely able to read the titles. *The Samurai Film*, Auden's *Selected Poems, The Corrections.* "I think if I were ever going to write a novel, I'd call it *The Mistakes.*"

"We haven't done anything yet," he said.

"I didn't mean this. I just meant in general."

"Can I get you a drink?" he asked.

"God, yes."

"Vodka, scotch, white wine?"

"Yes. I mean, whatever. All of the above. White wine."

"All right."

"No, vodka."

"It's in the freezer. Do you still want ice?"

"No ice." She sat down on the bed, hoping to ground some of its charge.

He carried over two drinks, handing her one, and sat down beside her on the bed. He raised his glass, touching it to hers. "You have to look me in the eyes when you toast. The idea is that all the senses are involved—hearing, touch, taste, smell, and vision."

She glanced at him and looked away. "My senses are all a little paralyzed at the moment."

He kissed her on the lips, a little too insistently, thrusting his tongue between her lips.

She pulled away. "I just don't know if I can do this."

He nodded. "I don't know if I can, either."

"Really?"

*"Really."*

"Have you ever done this before? I mean, since you've been married? I'm sorry, it's really none of my business."

"No, that's okay. I want it to be your business."

"So? Have you? I mean, besides the Chinese hooker?"

"Almost. Once. Not really."

She laughed, gratefully, his equivocation seeming hilarious.

"Well, another prostitute story—you're going to think it's my specialty. I went to something called a Turkish bath in Tokyo when I was there on business. One of my clients took me. I didn't really know what to expect. He instructed me what to do. I told myself it was part of the etiquette of doing business. You go in this private room with a bath. The hostess washes you with, you know, with her body. She soaps herself up and lathers you up and down. Then when the first phase is over, she asks if you want the *hon ban*. The *real thing*."

"And did you get the real thing?"

He shook his head. "No."

"You were too guilty."

"Well, yes and no. I don't know what I would have done if I'd been given the choice. But she announced early on, *'Gaijin wa okii, na,'* or something to that effect."

"Meaning what?"

"Meaning that the foreigner was too big."

"Well, you certainly know how to pique a girl's curiosity."

"I'm sorry to say it's the only time in my life I've elicited that comment."

"That's very sweet."

"How about you?"

"Nothing to worry about there," she said. "I've never been told it's too big."

He blushed. God, where was her reserve and decorum tonight? She felt her own cheeks reddening.

"I mean, have you ever—"

"Cheated? Just once. Well, a few times . . . with the same man."

"What happened?"

"He died."

"I'm sorry."

"Not because of me. What is it Rosalind says in *As You Like It*? 'Men have died from time to time, and worms have eaten them, but not for love.'"

"I'm not sure I believe that."

"I don't think you believe that, either. That's one of the things I like about you. For a guy who spent half his life on Wall Street, you seem ridiculously romantic."

He looked as if he wasn't sure this was a compliment. "Actually, our offices were in midtown."

She swallowed the rest of the vodka, wincing at the cold fire in her throat. "Would you mind if we just lay down with the lights out and talked for a while? I'm so tense right now, I'm afraid if you touched me the wrong way, I'd explode right here. I'd just be this flesh and blood smeared on your walls."

He got up and turned off the lights, leaving just enough of a residue of streetlight for her to observe his rangy, athletic body in silhouette as he stripped down to his boxer shorts. She climbed under the covers like a virgin, only then removing her shirt and jeans, lifting the duvet as he slid in beside her, placing his arm beneath her neck.

"Sometimes," she said, curling up into the taut, musky, yielding mound of muscle beneath his clavicle, "I find myself thinking about how close you were to being in Windows on the World that morning."

"I think about it all the time. Such a small, fluky thing—changing the time of that breakfast. Does it mean anything? Was I saved for something better? And what about Guillermo? How can I ever . . ." He left the thought hanging.

"Do you consider yourself lucky?" She felt him nodding.

"Until recently, I took it for granted. But now I realize I've always been lucky. Sure, I've worked hard, but I was given everything I needed to do well, through no virtue of my own. I think I've relied too much on my luck, and to believe in luck after a certain age becomes a form of cynicism. And of course it's a finite commodity, isn't it? We all run out of it eventually. Anyone who makes a lot of money inevitably imagines success as a function of shrewdness and hard work. For some reason, we call them 'self-made men.' The only people you ever hear acknowledging their luck are the poor suckers who've seen so little of it that they're absurdly grateful to have caught a glimpse. The paraplegics who say they feel lucky to have survived the car crash. The concentration camp survivors who lost their entire families."

"Well," she said, "I'm glad you changed the time of your breakfast."

She kissed him, a casual gesture that suddenly turned serious as he parted his lips and pulled her toward him. As she explored his mouth with her tongue, her hands explored his body, squeezing his meaty shoulder and moving down the smooth skin of his back as he stroked her face and neck and breasts, until eventually she lost track of her own physical boundaries and imagined her body and his deliquescing in the warm liquid of pleasure. She loved the smell of him, a pungent musk growing stronger and more insistent as they groped and kissed. She must have responded to it from the start. No one ever talked about smell, but she sometimes thought it was probably the most important thing.

For a moment, she became aware of his strangeness as her fingers discovered the unaccustomed contours of his cock, which, as she explored it, became almost immediately familiar, as if she had encountered it long ago and only forgotten until now. She knew him and it was part of him and it was no surprise that she would love this, too.

She thought she had lost this desire—no, it was more that she'd never even found it until now. She'd never felt such craving, such desire to be possessed and filled, never known she had so much desire inside of her, so urgent a need. . . .

Something primal and alien was stirring within her: Strange pleas, cries like those of a wounded creature, sounded within her and possibly escaped her lips. She pushed herself toward him, again and again, and felt herself approaching that familiar yet elusive destination more rapidly than she ever remembered, racing toward that moment when she would finally break through and absorb his body fully into her own; with each thrust, she seemed to be moving closer and closer to him, even as she found herself stopped short, thrown back into herself as her pelvis collided with his, until finally all at once the membrane that separated them burst, and she possessed him entirely and then lost track of him and of her own body as she hurtled weightless through space . . . before returning to find herself beneath him, his warm body holding her to the earth.

She lay there, pinned, grateful that he hadn't moved, glued to him by a film of cooling sweat, wanting to bear his weight forever.

"I'm sorry," he said. "That was kind of . . . rushed."

"Sorry? Don't be sorry. That was unbelievably nice." How could he even imagine he had to apologize?

"I was afraid I was the only one who felt that way."

"Really?" Oh God, she thought, hating the neediness in her voice.

"Really."

She felt him shifting his weight, starting to leave her. "Don't move yet. Please?"

"Okay."

"Just stay for a minute. I want to feel you on top of me a little longer."

"All right. I'd like that, too."

"You're not just saying that to make me feel better?"

"No. I just, as a man, I don't know. You feel the need to *perform*."

"That would imply a certain self-consciousness, a certain emotional remove."

"I wasn't removed. I was, well, moved."

"I suppose everything might be simpler if it had been lousy."

"It would, wouldn't it?"

"I know I should feel guilty, but I don't." Even as she said it, she began to feel the melancholy of leave-taking, the immanent reckonings in the morning light. "If you think this is just a passing thing . . . if it's already passed, I think you better tell me now. I could live with that. I could go back to my life."

"If you can, then you probably should."

"Is that what you want?"

She lay in the dark, waiting for his answer, waiting even as she wished it might never arrive, that she might just lie there in a state of suspension, having neither to think nor to choose.

# 24

Having abbreviated a business dinner in order to present a case for reconciliation and forgiveness to Corrine, Russell was disappointed to return and find Hilary, who'd been boarding with her cop friend for the past week, on the couch, reading a magazine while images from Afghanistan flickered on the television screen.

"Corrine's at Casey's," she said, glancing up from her magazine.

"Did she say if she'd be back tonight?"

"She's going directly downtown. Said she'll see you in the morning."

He nodded, storing away the elaborate construct of pleas and arguments he'd been assembling throughout the course of the day.

"In case you're wondering, she wouldn't tell me anything, but I gather you fucked up big time."

Looking at her lying like an odalisque on the couch, it occurred to him he'd once feared that she might be the cause of his downfall. It

222

seemed a little rich, getting upbraided for sexual misconduct by Hilary.

"Whatever it is, I hope you can make it right," she said. "I didn't go through all of that just to see you two break up our little family in the end."

That summer, they were still renting the place in Sagaponack, a wood-shingled nineteenth-century farmhouse within hearing range of the surf, cocooned within a mature privet hedge that curtained off the view of gargantuan new houses, which, after a brief hiatus early in the decade, when the economy had tanked, were rising anew in the potato fields around them. It was the summer of '94. The Polanskis, who rented to the Calloways, had worked the land for almost two hundred years, gradually selling off the edges of the farm and becoming wealthy in the process, sending their children to the same colleges attended by the children of the urbanites who'd bought the subdivided lots, while still cultivating a few exorbitantly valuable acres of potatoes. Russell and Corrine had helped steer their daughter to Brown, and Corrine wrote Mrs. Polanski little notes during the year, chatty bulletins from the big city, but after renting the house for a relative pittance for the past seven years, Russell suspected they'd become almost as anachronistic as the farming operation—a sentimental indulgence on the part of the owners, who chose not to modernize the house or the bathrooms or to raise the rent to market value. Even so, the Calloways had come up with the twenty thousand for the season only by selling the last of the stock in Bernie Melman's Magnumedia Corp., shares Russell had accumulated in his failed attempt to take over Corbin Dern. If they pursued their elaborate and expensive scheme to become parents, which would cost at least that much, he didn't see how they would be able to rent again, especially since Corrine had quit her job to focus all of her energies on getting pregnant. Their income would be cut in half precisely when their expenses doubled.

He would miss the house, if not the increasingly frantic social schedule—the premieres, benefits, and the catered affairs with valet parking, which had gradually supplanted the casual clambakes and potluck dinners of an earlier Hamptons era. If anything, the high season in this summer colony was becoming more exhausting than the urban frenzy they were supposed to be escaping.

As August approached, the calendar became even more densely inscribed with cocktail parties and casual dinners for eighty—which was part of the draw for Hilary, who arrived in mid-July. Many of her fellow fashionable Angelenos—directors and actors and the chefs and hairdressers who served them—were now spending August here on the South Fork of Long Island, making Hilary's sacrifice on behalf of her sister considerably less onerous, whereas Corrine seemed to have chosen the time and the place for their mutual project based on quaint notions of rural serenity, fertility, and marine tidal rhythms.

July was devoted to synchronizing the menstrual cycles of the two sisters, August to massive hormone injections. Russell was taking the month off in order to act as the hypo master, Corrine having a lurid fear of needles, not trusting herself to administer the deep intramuscular injections to her sister.

When it became clear that they were going to have to resort to unconventional measures to become parents, Russell had drawn the line at adoption. "Call me vain, superficial, whatever," he'd said, but he didn't want to raise a child to whom he had no genetic connection. If the kid grew up to be a mass murderer, "at least they wouldn't be able to blame someone else's genes." Having set this limit, Russell was staggered at the lengths to which Corrine was prepared to go to have kids. "Is that even possible?" he said when she first proposed the idea.

"Absolutely," she replied.

They were at home, eating Russell's spaghetti *vongole,* watching the carnage in Bosnia on CNN. Russell didn't doubt that she had it figured out; for the past two years, she'd become an expert on fertility and obstetrics. Two miscarriages and one failed round of in vitro had only made her more determined—some might say desperate—to have a child.

"What if the kid gets Hilary's IQ and your mother's insatiable thirst for distilled grain products?" Russell said, avoiding reference to

Corrine's father—a chilly and distant figure who'd decamped from the family home twenty years earlier and started a new family.

"You wanted genetic accountability," Corrine said. "I'm afraid that's part of what's encoded on my side."

The evening she'd asked Hilary to donate eggs was surely one of the most humbling and difficult of her life. It wasn't easy for Corrine to put herself so thoroughly in her younger sister's debt, and she and Russell were both gratified by how readily she'd accepted.

"You should think about it," Corrine had said over the phone, while Russell listened in on the extension.

"I don't have to think about it," she'd said.

"This is a really big commitment," Corrine had insisted, as if she felt she'd won the point too easily, reverting to a habitual mode of trying to prevent her younger sister from acting rashly.

"No, really, I'm honored," she'd said. "I really am. And it's not like anyone else has asked me."

Six months later, they were all established at base camp in the Hamptons, with weekly trips in to Lenox Hill Hospital for blood tests and hormone levels. By the time Russell arrived on the scene full-time, the elevated hormone levels were already wreaking havoc. When Corrine picked him up in the Cherokee at the jitney stop in Bridgehampton, she was near tears after having had a big fight with Hilary about O. J. Simpson—an acquaintance of Hilary's—who Hilary insisted was being framed for his wife's murder.

"She's probably slept with him," Corrine said as they inched along the main street of Bridgehampton in the Friday-evening traffic, "All I Want to Do Is Have Some Fun" on the radio—that summer's anthem.

The fertility doctor had warned Russell to expect mood swings and hormonal surges. Corrine had been on the Pill for the last month, synchronizing her cycle to Hilary's, and she'd just started estrogen therapy the day before.

Oddly enough, Corrine herself had at first believed that O.J. was innocent, on the basis of a personal encounter: They'd been sitting at Elio's, a restaurant on the Upper East Side, when the former football star had come in. The midwestern novelist with whom they were dining was a big fan and had called out, midwesternly, and much to Russell's embarrassment, "Yo, Juice!" at which point O.J. had come over and sat down at their table for five or ten minutes. Corrine, who had no interest in sports, was so entranced by the time he left that she would have followed him into the men's room or out the door. Although Russell couldn't recall what they had talked about, he felt dazzled afterward; like most New Yorkers, he liked to think of himself as relatively inured to celebrity and, unlike the novelist, he wasn't particularly interested in football, but the former running back had a kind of godlike luminescence that left them all stupid with admiration for the rest of the evening. Even so, Russell couldn't help wondering about the beautiful creature he'd abandoned at the bar in order to bask in their admiration. Six weeks later, as they watched the white Bronco leading a school of police cars down the freeway, some of the stardust still clung to Corrine, who was certain that the beautiful man who'd kissed her hand in parting couldn't have been capable of carving up his wife. It wasn't just the personal encounter that inclined her to this view—Corrine was a man's woman by nature, on top of which, she had a morbid fear of coming to resemble her mother, who had railed against male fecklessness ever since her husband had abandoned the family. This, in conjunction with a contrarian turn of mind, tended to make her suspicious of feminist orthodoxy. But over the course of the next few weeks, in the light of mounting evidence, Corrine had gradually and mournfully come to believe in O.J.'s guilt and to take the whole matter personally, angry at herself for having been fooled, suddenly charged with apostate zeal for justice and retribution.

"Hilary's entitled to her opinion," Russell said. "You went to law school. Remember that thing about innocent until proven guilty."

"It's just so typical of her," she said tearfully. "She always sides with the men."

"So do you."

"Not blindly."

"Reasonable people can disagree about this, Corrine."

"Those poor children," she said.

In the last couple of years, even as they failed to achieve conception, her notion of herself as an aspiring parent had infused her worldview. She got sentimental over any advertising that featured children and started to volunteer her baby-sitting services to friends.

As he turned off the highway onto Sagg Main Road toward the ocean, Russell felt his spirits soar, in spite of the new houses rising in the distance, driving past a vestigial cornfield under the limpid marine sky. Turning into the driveway, he felt a melancholy pride at the sight of the farmhouse with its weathered shingles and full-frontal porch, which sagged slightly in the middle. It didn't seem unreasonable to want this simple house by the sea, to have his child spend summers here, playing in the yard and exploring the ramshackle barn and biking to the beach. But it wasn't his and never would be unless he could somehow come up with a couple million. Someday soon, it would belong to some fucking investment banker who'd bought it in cash with his annual bonus, gutted the place, and tacked on a ten-thousand-foot addition with a six-car garage.

Snoop Dogg's "Gin and Juice" was thumping from within, spilling out the screen door.

"And that's another thing," said Corrine, stepping out of the car. "She's got this hip-hop thing going. My sister the homey."

Hilary was standing at the kitchen counter with the phone to her ear, blowing on her nails—undeniably fetching in a bikini top and safari shorts. She blew a kiss at Russell as Corrine snapped off the boom box.

"I'm invited to Ted Field's for dinner," she said breathlessly. "I figured you guys might like some time alone."

"You need to be home by ten for your shot," Corrine said.

"I don't see why we can't adjust the schedule. Otherwise, we'll be running out of parties in the middle of dinner all month."

"She's got a point," Russell said.

"We're not here to party." Corrine turned and walked out of the room.

"Welcome to the egg farm," Hilary said.

He shrugged and exchanged a look of hapless sympathy with her, his sister-in-law seeming to represent everything he would be sacrificing as a father. He'd be leaving dinner parties early soon enough, and for years to come. "Don't worry," he said. "I'll work on her."

"I'm just glad you're here," Hilary said. "Sis is even more uptight than usual. I mean, I don't see why we can't enjoy ourselves a little. We don't want unhappy eggs."

"I really can't tell you how much I appreciate you doing this," Russell said. "I don't know if I've really had a chance to say so."

"Too bad we can't do it the old-fashioned way," she said, giving him a look that made him blush.

It wasn't as if the thought hadn't occurred to him, her points of resemblance to her sister attracting him almost as much as the differences. If you loved Roquefort cheese, it only made sense to crave Stilton. The very nature of the high-tech reproductive enterprise was fraught with erotic and incestuous implications, the taboo attraction that he'd often felt for his wife's younger sister exacerbated by the thought that a month from now his sperm would be united with her eggs, if only in the confines of a petri dish, and that she would, if the project was successful, forever after be the natural mother of his child, conjured so unnaturally and with such effort and ingenuity out of the ether—all of these thoughts hovering around him in the warm, stuffy closeness of the downstairs bedroom that night, in the dim light of a single bulb from the bedside lobster-buoy lamp, as he prepared the hypodermic, slowly drawing from its ampule the thick, expensive, gelatinous hormonal essence, distilled from the urine of menopausal women, while Corrine and Hilary stood in a sacramental hush beside the bed.

"Okay," Russell said, holding the big hypo to the light and checking for air bubbles.

"My goodness, what a big needle you have," Hilary said.

"All the better to prick you with."

"Try not to enjoy this *too* much," Corrine said playfully, her eyes bright, her earlier moodiness dispelled by her excitement over the initiation of this crucial phase of her baroque plan for parenthood. "Even though I know Hilary has a nicer ass than I do."

"I'm only doing it for you, babe," he said.

"For us, you mean."

"Bottoms up," Hilary said, winking at him as she turned away and lowered her shorts, revealing a leopard thong she then tugged down to mid-thigh, lying across the bed, revealing the twin moons that swelled below her tan line. Russell tried to maintain a clinical attitude even as he sneaked a glance below; his hand was suddenly shaking, whether from a sense of the momentousness of the occasion, a fear of inflicting pain, or a sense of guilt at his appreciation of this forbidden vista, Hilary's ass, seeming perfect and unblemished in the dim light that all three had agreed represented a mean between modesty and his need to see what he was doing. He reached down and pinched the cool flesh between his fingers, raising it as he had been instructed and checking for veins, which were to be avoided, lowering the needle and pressing it, feeling a brief resistance—reminiscent of the moment when a paring knife meets a tomato—until it pierced the skin, wincing involuntarily as he pressed it home, the long needle disappearing into the soft mound beneath his fingers.

"Okay?"

"You're very good," she said.

He turned to Corrine, who was looking up at him glassy-eyed, and silently mouthed, *I love you,* recalling him to the purpose of this strange ritual. She turned away as Russell slowly depressed the plunger, forcing the viscous liquid slowly through the tip as Hilary grunted and flinched, squirming beneath his grasp. "Sorry," he said.

He looked again at Corrine, who was staring at the needle, mesmerized, before withdrawing it as gently as he could, watching as a glassy pink tear of blood and pergonal formed on the flesh above the puncture.

Suddenly, he felt exhausted.

Corrine leaned over and kissed his cheek, and he realized, to his relief, that he felt close to her again for the first time in weeks, standing there beside her, the prone and exposed younger sister merely instrumental to their quest for a child.

"Well," Hilary said, reaching down and tugging at the waistband of her shorts. "That wasn't so bad. I can honestly say my ass has experienced more painful insertions."

She raised herself and turned, still lifting her shorts, giving Russell a brief glimpse of the narrow dark stripe beneath the white flesh of her belly while Corrine reached over and swept her into their embrace, Russell hugging both of the Makepeace sisters, grateful to be able to express in some measure the complicated emotions of the moment.

The next night, Corrine cried through most of *Forrest Gump* at the Southampton cinema and paced nervously on the front porch as she waited for Hilary to return home from her dinner party. They had settled on eleven, morning and night, for the shots. At 11:15, the windows of the sitting room were illuminated by headlights.

"Look who I found," Hilary said, throwing open the screen door, towing Jim Crespi behind her. "A friend of yours."

Corrine's fondness for Jim was not on display at that moment. "You're twenty minutes late."

"Sorry, Mom."

"You've been drinking," Corrine said, examining her sister with a cold eye as Russell greeted his friend.

"I had like a glass and a half of rosé," she said.

"Everybody knows rosé doesn't really count," Jim said. "Especially French rosé. Although it may have some bearing on the sex of the child."

"Let's do it," Hilary said. "We're going dancing after this."

"I have it on good authority," Jim said, "that dancing stimulates the ovarian follicles."

"How are Judy and the baby?" Corrine asked pointedly.

"They're visiting Judy's mother in Cohasset, a pleasure I was forced to forgo due to a script conference with a Mr. Alec Baldwin at his stately Amagansett seat."

Her manners reasserting themselves, Corrine stayed behind to entertain Jim while Russell and Hilary repaired to her bedroom.

"It's going to be a long month," Hilary said, stepping out of her thong and lifting her shift, holding it at her waist, fixing him with a haughty, challenging look, before turning her back and sprawling on the bed. "The bitch of it is, these hormones are making me incredibly horny."

Russell didn't trust himself to speak. He tried to focus his mind on the holy purpose of this lurid procedure as he fumbled with the ampule, struggling to insert the needle into the rubber cap. "Reproduction without sex does feel like a terrible cheat sometimes," he finally said.

"Doesn't it just."

Two days before the scheduled egg transfer, Hilary disappeared behind the cultivated hedges of the Hamptons for eighteen hours. She turned up at five in the morning, Russell being awakened from a shallow sleep to hear the sisters shouting at each other downstairs.

"That's it, it's over," Corrine declared when Russell found them in the kitchen. "Finished."

"Don't be so dramatic," Hilary said, her eyes like pinwheels, her wrinkled cotton dress showing a cigarette burn just above her right breast.

Corrine was clutching a grapefruit in one hand and a knife in the other. "Dramatic? Two months, twelve thousand dollars down the drain, not to mention our dreams of having a child. . . . Not to mention that little fantasy. Dramatic would be if I stabbed you right here and now."

"Look, I'm sorry. A few drinks after a month of clean living, what difference could it really make?"

"A few drinks and an eight ball, by the looks of it." Corrine didn't seem to notice when Russell removed the knife from her hand.

"Being cooped up in this house for a month and pumped full of hormones is enough to drive anyone around the bend. Do you have any idea how this is for me? I've never felt so sad, so full of despair in my whole life. I really thought about walking down the lane to the beach and just keep walking right out into the water."

"You and Virginia Woolf, sisters under the skin. Don't make me laugh."

"I'm serious, goddamn it." Tears were welling in Hilary's bright and unnaturally dilated eyes. "I've never felt suicidal in my whole life. Not until the past two weeks."

"So you've told us."

"I haven't even told you the half of it. I was trying to be a trouper. I was trying to be the good sister. I tried to help. If I hadn't had a few lines tonight, I probably would have just driven the car into a tree. It's not natural, what we're doing."

"I don't know why I thought I could trust you," Corrine said, collapsing into a kitchen chair. "You've always been selfish, always been irresponsible. People don't change." She sobbed and buried her face in her hands. "It's all over now."

"It's not over," Russell said. For the first time in months, he knew what he needed to do. Blind certainty, perhaps—but he was determined to press forward. "We're all going to calm down. You two are going to get some sleep. And we're all going to the hospital tomorrow, as scheduled." He lifted Corrine from the chair. Tears were streaming down her face. "We can't," she said, but she offered no resistance as he lifted her and carried her up the stairs and placed her on the bed.

"I don't know what to do," she said, curling up and clutching her knees.

"I do," he replied.

"Do you really?" She looked up at him helplessly, desperate to be persuaded.

"Get some sleep. Everything will be fine."

It was a formula he would often be called on to repeat in the months that followed; a reassurance that turned out to be premature, as were the twins.

# 25

The bottom seemed to fall out of her stomach when she spotted him standing near the gate at La Guardia in a polo coat and jeans, pacing. She stopped abruptly in the middle of the concourse, the man behind her excusing himself after running into her. She resumed her progress toward the gate, trying not to look at him, each step taking her closer to her lover, another step down the path to an irrevocable moment of reckoning.

Recovered from her own surprise, she almost laughed at his startled expression as he caught sight of her and turned away with visible effort, pleased to think that he was not very good at this kind of thing. She didn't want him to be too worldly, to be a man who was accustomed to meeting lovers at airports, although she realized with the feeling you get when a plane drops through a pocket of turbulent air that it was possible, that he might be one of those men she'd met on Wall Street who were known to the clerks of obscure hotels on the

East Side, who had their Visa bill mailed to the office. Did she really know him as well as she believed? What if this was just another fling for him, a short parenthetical passage in the book of his marriage? She wondered irrationally if he'd taken other women to Nantucket, before remembering that Nantucket had been her idea.

She found herself standing at the edge of the departure lounge, watching him perform a pantomime of distracted waiting—running his hand through his dark hair, checking his pockets for his ticket, staring at it and then checking his wristwatch before finally scanning the gate area, until his gaze landed on Corrine, a sheepish expression of relief and gratitude crossing his face before he looked away. Anyone watching him, a private detective, say, would've quickly guessed which figure in the waiting area he was pretending not to notice. And she herself had felt what no one else would have—the spark that passed between them like a kiss. Her crisis of doubt was over as soon as it had begun.

Having restored him in her heart and forgiven him for sins he'd never committed, she had more than half an hour to contemplate her own. She had told Russell she needed time to think and had suggested he take the kids to her mother's house, shamelessly exploiting his guilt and his desire to expiate it. She told him she was going to Nantucket with Casey Reynes, the only truth here being that she was staying in Casey's house. She had finally confided in her friend, her sense of caution overridden by her need to share this secret. Corrine had intended to withhold Luke's identity, but finally she revealed all, in response to the combined pressures of Casey's interrogation and her own desire to share her joy along with her guilt.

Of course, Casey was delighted to become part of the conspiracy, the more so when she learned it was Luke, whom she'd known for years and thoroughly approved of. "He was a star in that world," she said. "They used to call him 'Lucky Luke.'"

Casey had never really believed that Russell was good enough for Corrine, whereas she considered Luke a member of her own plutocratic tribe. Corrine knew her friend wouldn't have been so excited if she'd hooked up with a starving poet or a landscape architect, and also that Casey's professed friendship with Sasha McGavock was not so profound, or untinged with feminine envy, as to prevent her from casting her lot with the lovers. "It would be one thing if she hadn't been cheating on him for years," she said. What was less clear was the status of Sasha's romance with Melman, who'd been sighted several times in recent weeks in the company of his lawful wife. But Corrine would have been ashamed to admit that this was another reason for confiding in Casey—to have a spy in Sasha's camp.

Casey had immediately offered the use of her family's house on Nantucket, where they were unlikely to see anyone they knew in November. The island had the additional appeal of being the site of some of Corrine's fonder childhood memories, before her parents' marriage had disintegrated. Casey's only condition was that Corrine tell her all about the sex. She'd been disappointed so far in her quest for details, incredulous when her friend claimed she wasn't sure whose cock was bigger, Luke's or Russell's. Of course she knew, but she couldn't bring herself to be *that* disloyal. "They're different," Corrine said. "I didn't have my ruler out." Casey just shook her head. "You've got a much better instrument than a ruler for measuring."

The consummation of her desire for Luke, far from sating her appetite, had served to sharpen it. She rediscovered her hunger for the body of another. It seemed like a strange time to experience this rebirth, but suddenly in the fourth decade of her life, she was crazed with lust. She thought about it all the time. She wanted it. She wanted Luke. And she didn't believe she'd ever wanted anyone so much. This experience of an almost overwhelming physical desire had, on the one hand, seemed to render anything else irrelevant, even as it gave her an increased affection for the physical realm that her luxuriously stimulated and craving body occupied, as well as a new sense of wonder and curiosity about the inner lives of all the bodies she passed on the street. Suddenly, one understood that there was a hidden order, a grid beneath the surface. A powerful current of desire ran like an underground river beneath the surface of all human activity. This understanding extended even to her husband. She could comprehend his lust for that trampy girl, if only because she felt the very same thing, albeit on a higher plane. Since she'd started sleeping with Luke, she found herself, to her own amazement, assessing the sexual vitality of men on the street, in elevators, and at the soup kitchen. It wasn't really that she wanted to sleep with any of them—she was devoted to Luke. But she could—and did—imagine it. She now believed she understood *men,* why they so often behaved so foolishly. Her love for Luke McGavock, her thirst for his male body, had made her newly sympathetic to, and appreciative of, his entire sex.

Though she knew what it was like to be desired, she had almost forgotten what it was like to desire . . . the cannibalistic hunger of wanting another's flesh, the smell and taste of him. The Buddhists were right: Desire was what tethered us to the earth, trapping us in this life. But more than ever, she *wanted* to be here, to enjoy it while she could. She wanted to live at this high pitch of awareness, feeling the life in her body, a brimming vitality that connected her with the couple debouched from the cab in front of the building next door as she'd emerged from her door with her luggage this morning into the cool pink dawn—the woman a tawny gazelle in a kind of shiny gold bikini, and her shaven-headed paramour in black leather, leaning against each other out of exhaustion or affection as they crossed the sidewalk to the door, the man fishing in his pocket for keys, the woman casting a wan, makeup-smeared smile at Corrine. She'd wanted to ask if they were in love, feeling a speculative kinship with them as she prepared to meet her own lover, as well as a paradoxical sense of superiority that one who is at the beginning of an adventure feels for the exhausted, sunburned, bug-bitten travelers stumbling down the gangplank at the end of their cruise. Three months ago, she would have envied this young, louche couple. Now she didn't envy anyone.

She wanted desperately to believe that everyone around her could only benefit, since she felt a new sense of affection for all living creatures, even—in fact, especially—for her husband. She would have liked to be able to say that she felt this way after the birth of the children, though in fact she'd been terrified and alienated when they finally came home from the hospital after two months in incubators. After two months of viewing them through Plexiglas, she'd been afraid to touch them, terrified of damaging them. She hadn't felt capable of taking care of them. And if the truth be told, she hadn't felt any sense of maternal connection at first. It had been months before she really believed they belonged to her. Whereas she'd felt that way about Luke in a matter of days.

These considerations could alternately excite her and send her spiraling into a miasma of guilt and despair. How could what she felt for Luke accommodate her love for her children?

Feeling in urgent need of reassurance, she looked for him now. There he was, pacing again with his hands in the pockets of his jeans, adorably collegiate in his polo coat. Tawny and leonine, restlessly prowling the cage of the cramped waiting area. To her relief, her passion flared at the sight of him—it hadn't faded in the minutes since she'd last looked at him, although this thought led her to wonder if it was inevitable that it would, that she would someday fail to be thrilled by the mere sight of him, or he with her.

She made an inventory of the other men around her, deeply satisfied with the favorable contrast he presented, not only in terms of comeliness but also, so she imagined, in masculine authority and vitality. In the event of a crisis—a bomb, another attack—possibilities that hovered at the back of all their minds now—she was confident that he would be the one to whom they looked to lead them out of danger, exhorting them to action, with no thought of his personal safety.

Finally, the preboarding announcement. She gathered her carryons and dawdled toward the gate, falling into line several passengers behind him, staring at the broad expanse of his back, making a note to tell him she loved him in camel and, whatever happened, wanted him to think of her whenever he wore that coat.

"Hello," she said after stowing her bags in the overhead bin and allowing herself to look down at him, seated on the aisle.

"Are you sitting here?" he asked.

"Eleven B. I have the window."

He stood, brushing against her, letting her feel the warmth of his body, and squeezing her thigh before stepping back to allow her to pass.

She hadn't seen any familiar faces in the boarding area, and the seats directly across from them were empty, but she hoped he would stay in character a little longer, so that she might, too. The married woman who flirted with strange men on the plane. Who allowed them to squeeze her thigh. Who might even think about sleeping with them.

"Corrine Makepeace," she said.

"Luke McGavock."

Shortly after takeoff, he invited her to join him for dinner that night. She said she didn't really think of herself as the kind of girl who accepted dinner invitations from strange men. Nor, she whispered in his ear as they circled the island forty minutes later, the kind who gave blow jobs on airplanes, under the tent of a polo coat, but she couldn't say that she wasn't excited by this new version of herself. She would have to tell Casey.

He rented a car at the airport and they drove out through the scrubby dunes to Dionis, her desire to show him around the town overridden by her desire to get him into bed. She contented herself with pointing out historic houses en route, noting the widow's walks that crowned several of them.

"I used to ask my mother why they were called widow's walks," she said, "if the husbands were actually returning from sea. And she always said it was just a figure of speech. But then my father told me that late at night you could sometimes see the wives of the husbands who didn't make it, pacing back and forth up there in the dark."

Brooding against a wan sky atop the highest dune, surrounded by a sickly apron of lawn that seemed to retain only a dim memory of photosynthesis, the gray-shingled house with its unadorned facade conveyed a sense of stoic isolation and Yankee taciturnity. You would probably have to come from New England, and have lived through its winters, to have a taste for this kind of austere beauty. Or so Corrine imagined, trying to see it through Luke's eyes, suddenly afraid that his southerner's heart would find it bleak and unwelcoming, that he would have preferred a softer and more conventionally luxurious love nest. Even though it wasn't hers, she wanted him to like it, to see why she'd chosen it for them—not just because it was offered but because it and the dour, windswept landscape of this little island said something about her taste and her heritage and her vision of the good life.

"My mother would love this house," he said, leaning forward to peer at it through the windshield.

Corrine remembered that his mother had been raised in Marblehead and had summered on the Cape. "It's a little stark," she said.

"No, it's perfect. I love it."

"It was built by a retired whaling captain in the eighteenth century," she explained. "Been in Casey's family for years. I don't often find myself envying my wealthy friends. But I sometimes wish I could own a house like this."

As soon as she said this, she remembered that, in fact, he was wealthy and almost certainly could afford almost any house he wanted; she worried that he'd think her mercenary—imagine that his wealth might be a factor in her attraction.

"Think of it this way," he said. "You can't really own a house like this. A hundred years from now, Casey and her children will be dead and gone, and this house will still be standing on this dune, and we'll be a part of its history. And as long as one of us is alive, it will be part of ours. And afterward, we'll wander its halls as wraiths, calling out to each other and making ghostly love, scaring the hell out of the people who think they own it with our unearthly moaning and yelping. A house like this needs a great love story."

"You say all the right things," she said, leaning across the seat and kissing him.

"Then why do you look so sad?" he asked.

She shook her head, shaping a smile, though in fact she'd had a sudden vision of the future, one in which Luke would be only a memory, when she would look back at this moment with a fond, bittersweet regret. It was as if her mind was too practical and literal to ignore the obstacles that stood between them, to imagine a life they could lead together.

"Hey, don't cry," he said.

"I just had this terrible premonition," she said. "When you talked about how the house would survive, I thought of myself, years from now, mourning you."

She didn't say how she imagined herself reading about his death in the paper, or hearing about it in passing, Casey saying some afternoon, while they watched their grandchildren play on the beach, "Remember Luke McGavock, your great love?"

"I've still got a few good years ahead of me. And we have three whole days in front of us."

"Two and a half."

"Well then, we'd better not waste any time," he said, pulling her toward him and putting the car in gear.

He carried her up the center stairway and followed her directions to the guest room, where he gently pushed her down on the quilt of the four-poster, which, she informed him, was made of tiger maple, now extinct.

"I really don't fucking care," he said, smiling as he unfastened her belt. And she found that she was able to ignore the future and its inevitable extinctions as he drew her back to the present and to the pressing demands of her own vivid flesh.

"I must be morally defective," Corrine said later, lying in the twisted quilt and playing with his penis as if it were her own new toy, even as she found herself weighing her guilt. "Here I am, wanting you to fuck me again, when bombs are raining down on some poor villagers on the other side of the world. I've been reading about how we're all supposed to be ennobled by this terrible thing that's happened, but in the last two months I've started cheating on my husband, lying and scheming in pursuit of my own selfish pleasure. Sending my children away. Running down to Bowling Green every night, supposedly to perform works of charity but actually exploiting someone else's tragedy."

"Your charity, sweetheart, is genuine. Nothing that's happened between us can negate that."

"I wish I could believe that."

"Do you want me to go away?"

She rolled over and put her arm around him. If only she didn't love his scent and the feel of his sweat on her cheek; if only his eyes weren't so beguiling, so boyishly innocent. "No," she said. "That's what's so terrible. I don't want you to go away. I want to be with you. And I feel so guilty about it."

"I don't feel that guilty, honestly. You only do because you still love Russell."

"I suppose that's right. But then why do I dream about going away with you? Disappearing. I keep imagining that there must be somebody who walked away from those towers and just decided to keep walking. Start a new life. Sometimes I wish it were me."

"You couldn't leave your children."

"No," she said. "I couldn't. And I don't know if I can bear to break their world apart by leaving Russell. But I think about it. Keep trying to figure out a way that it would be possible."

"I think about it, too."

"Really?"

"Of course."

Now a new fear seized her. "You realize I couldn't give you another child?"

"I know that."

"You'd be better off with some twenty-five-year-old."

"No way, thank you very much. If nothing else, the idea of lusting after anyone that close to my daughter's age fills me with horror."

"How do you feel about being a stepfather?" she asked, shocking herself.

"I find the idea strangely appealing."

"My God," she said. This nudged the door on her fantasy wide open. The children had always seemed to be the insurmountable impediment; though she had spoken of them often in the beginning and showed him pictures, this had happened less and less as their intimacy progressed.

Down on the beach, the wind raising whitecaps on the graphite expanse of the ocean, leaning into the salt spray, she trudged forward in the sand with her arm laced in his, picturing them as if from the dune, arm in arm against the eternal backdrop of the Atlantic, shuddering involuntarily when she imagined Russell as the hypothetical observer of this elemental scene.

She stooped to pick up a quahog shell sticking up from the sand, running a fingertip over the shiny purple half-moon on the concave inner surface. "We used to collect these when we were kids. We rented a little house on the other side of the island, over in Sconset. My dad would always go out into the surf, swim way out—I remember I used to be afraid he wouldn't come back, that he'd get sucked under. He'd disappear under the surface—it seemed like forever—and my sister and I would start to scream. Of course, then we'd see his head breaking the surface, and he'd swim in with his pockets full of the biggest, most perfect quahog shells and divide them between us."

Luke smiled impishly and started to undo his belt. In a single motion, he slipped out of his chinos and his boxer shorts and then doffed his shirt, sprinting white and naked toward the water.

"Are you crazy?" she called. "It's November."

He ran out into the surf and dived into a shoulder-high breaker. She followed to the edge of the shore and watched as he thrashed out into the water, hugging herself as she felt the frigid salt spray. He went under three times before finally turning back and swimming in, emerging slick and dripping, his shrunken thing sprouting from its dark thicket like a blue mushroom, and then he presented her with a white-and-purple shell on his outstretched palm.

She browsed the bookshelves in the big family room while he crouched in front of the fireplace in his mad paisley bathrobe, laying out logs for the fire. He'd brought Gram Parsons's *Grievous Angel* CD; songs of heartbreak and illicit love wafted through the house.

> *We know it's wrong to let this fire burn between us*
> *We've got to stop this wild desire in you and in me*

Not having had any opportunity to judge them before, she was pleased that his musical tastes were, so far at least, in accord with her

242

own and she admired how they nodded to his southern roots. She kept replaying "Love Hurts," imagining herself as Emmylou Harris singing alongside Luke as the doomed Gram Parsons.

She loved this room, the warm center of a house she'd spent so many hours in since prep school, its fragrant pine paneling impregnated with sea air and stained with centuries of wood smoke. It was an orphanage for odd and broken pieces of furniture from year-round homes, a family museum of accidental and intimate objects stitched together by an underlying nautical theme: the seashells and whale teeth, the lobster-buoy lamps, the iron harpoon tips that served as fire tools; the childish, crudely framed seascapes and the mournful striped bass over the fireplace with its glaze of browning varnish, mounted on a lozenge of pine. It reminded her in many respects of her old house on the North Shore, but without the terrible associations of domestic strife and loss.

She studied Luke's technique, approving of the pyramid of kindling and split logs on the grate, beneath which he was stuffing balls of newsprint, pleased to discover he was a man who knew how to build a fire, surprised to realize it was a quality she valued. She stroked his hair as he poked another wad of paper under the grate. He pressed himself to her and kissed her hip.

Her father had constructed his fires almost as meticulously as the model boats he made in the basement, as if they were meant to be permanent structures, cabins of birch and elm—the old elms succumbing in those years to a foreign parasite—on a foundation of perfect spheres of the *Boston Globe*. She'd often suspected that her dad would have preferred not to touch a match to his creation, and her mother would always complain he'd rolled the newspaper too tightly. A cold man—her mother's refrain; anal retentive. Russell, quite the opposite, was too impatient; he tended to skimp on kindling and paper, too eager to get to the stage of combustion. Come to think of it, that's how he did a lot of things.

She picked out an old edition of Plato she hadn't noticed before, an anomaly among the mid-century bestsellers and *Reader's Digest* condensed books, the almost forgotten names of former best-selling authors: J. P. Marquand and James Gould Cozzens, the Irvings—Stone and Wallace. One of the great pleasures in borrowed vacation homes—and she and Russell had borrowed plenty over the years—was the mad serendipity of the bookshelves ... picking out old volumes, reading the flap copy and the fading inscriptions.

She flipped to the table of contents and saw listed there the dialogues she'd studied so earnestly at Brown.

"Have you read the *Symposium*? You know, I always thought Russell and I were made for each other. I believed there was one person who was meant for each of us, and that Russell was it for me. I always thought of that speech Plato gives to Aristophanes—"

"About the hermaphrodites."

"Exactly!" she said, inordinately pleased that he got the reference, which seemed to confirm her guilty hypothesis—was it possible? was this crazy?—that he, rather than Russell, might be her long-lost twin. "Where he proposes that the earth was once populated by hermaphrodites, and that Zeus sliced the hermaphrodites in half, creating a race of males and females. And these sundered twins walk the earth searching for each other, for their lost half. That's how I always thought of us." She paused, not wishing to go too far. "Did you ever feel that way?"

"I do now. I had a glimmer of that feeling the first time I saw you. Walking out of the smoking ruins. And there you were." He looked up at her with an expression that was just playful enough to ease the awkwardness of the moment, then turned back to the fire and struck a kitchen match against the blue-and-red box in his hand, touched the match to the paper, and watched the flame flare and expand beneath the split logs.

He stood and took her in his arms, clutching her from behind as she replaced the Plato in the bookshelf.

"Books are the most amazing objects, aren't they?"

He looked puzzled, she realized, by the banality of this observation.

"I mean, because they're lumpish objects, they have a physical existence, like we do. But any single book is the instantiation of a kind of Platonic form—the ideal, the creation of an author, which exists independent of the physical object. And here they sit on the shelf: The ideal's latent until we pick it up and connect ourselves with the mind of a man or a woman who may be long dead. And, in the case of a novel, with a world that never actually existed."

"Well, yes," he said, hovering between bafflement and amusement.

"All these books, randomly accumulated over a hundred summers," she said. "Look at this, it's like a history of escapist literature. *Don't Stop the Carnival*, by Herman Wouk. *Back to Mandalay*, by Lowell Thomas. *Night in Bombay*, by Louis Bromfeld. *One Way to Eldorado*, by Hollister Noble. I like that—authors don't have names like Hollister anymore. Here's Thor Heyerdahl's *Aku-Aku; Freedom Road*, by Howard Fast; *The Treasure of Pleasant Valley*, by Frank Yerby; and, of course, *The Shining Trail*, by Iola Fuller."

"And *The Delectable Country*," he said, pulling out a faded volume. "Who wouldn't want to go there?"

"And *Beyond Sing the Woods*, by somebody called Trygve Gulbranssen. *The Far Country* and *Round the Bend*, by Nevil Shute." She opened this last and read from the flap. "'An inspired storyteller writes of the joy that a man gets out of the day's work when he has faith that God is on his side. You will find a ringing note of affirmation throughout this extraordinary novel.'"

"They certainly don't write those anymore," Luke said.

"I think about going away with you." She loosened his arms and turned around to face him, replacing his hands on her back. "I think about us sweating in the sheets under a ceiling fan in Indochina, too hot and exhausted to move after making love."

"I know," he said. "Me too."

It occurred to her that this was one of the nicest phrases in the language: *Me too*. And that the dream of new love, untethered by history or habit, was to go far away, together. A dream that was entirely unrealistic in this case. She extracted herself from his arms. "Tell me something terrible about yourself," she said, moving over to the couch. "Something that will let me go back to my old life."

"I'm a bad father," he said, taking a seat beside her and looking into the flames. "My daughter grew up in the care of nannies. I was too busy to give her the time and attention she deserved and I let my

245

wife do a careless job as a mother. By the time I finally went home to check up on my family, it was too late."

"I'm sure it's not too late."

"My daughter's in rehab, Corrine."

"Which is short for rehabilitation. She's young. She still has lots of chances to shape her life." Which, she realized, might not be true of them, of Luke and herself. Maybe they were too old, too far down the road.

"I haven't even told you the worst of it," he said. "A few weeks ago, I went home and found her in her bedroom. . . ." He faltered, shaking his head.

She picked up his hand and stroked it.

"In her bedroom . . . with some boy. She was blowing him."

"Oh fuck."

"I've wondered since if it would've been better to find her fucking. At least the image wouldn't have been, I don't know, so graphic. What's this shit about blow jobs not really being sex? This is apparently the wisdom not only of our last president but of the Manhattan private schools. If anything, it seems, I don't know, more intimate, more perverse, having your face in someone's crotch."

She tried to stifle the image that flashed into her mind—of taking him in her mouth.

"I can't get the image out of my head. And I know I should probably blame her mother and myself as much as I blame her, but right now I can't quite bear to see her."

She moved closer and put her arm over his chest, pulling him to her. "I wish I could meet her, get to know her. I'd like to look for you, my favorite parts of you, in her."

"Tell me something terrible about *you*. No, actually, I don't want to hear anything terrible about you."

She looked into the flames. "Sometimes, I think I'm guilty of terrible . . . *overreaching,* the way I wrestled my children into existence. It was hubris. Refusing to accept the limits of nature, my own biological limitations. I was tempting fate. Whenever they get sick, I think it's my fault, that I'm being punished because they were premature. And they were premature because I couldn't hold them long

enough and because maybe it was crazy and selfish to stretch reproductive technology to its limits. And there's something else. Sometimes when I see a certain expression on Storey's face, I'm afraid for
her, afraid that I'm seeing my sister, some quality I hate in Hilary. And
I feel so ungrateful, so *unnatural,* that even for a moment I could fail
to love any little part of my daughter."

"I feel the same thing, sometimes. Seeing my wife in my daughter,
this little smirk they both have. Kind of like, *Fuck you.*"

The look he gave her then prompted her to lean forward and kiss
him, made her want him yet again. My God, she thought, where has
all this desire come from, and where has it been hiding all these years?
She reached under the folds of his bathrobe and took his dick, pulling
him toward her even as she launched her body toward his, her excitement compounded by the guilty memory of having made love to Russell on this couch one long-ago summer afternoon.

Ultimately, they had to answer other, more mundane imperatives.
They needed groceries, but it seemed imprudent to go into town together. And they both needed, she realized, to check in on their other
lives, although to acknowledge this awkward fact would break the
romantic spell of their idyll.

"I hate this sneaking around," she said. "I want to flaunt you. I
want to walk down Main Street, down West Broadway, with your
arm around me."

But she agreed to let him go into town alone, and eventually became almost impatient for him to be gone as he inventoried the pots
and pans in the kitchen and laced up the leather tops of his rubber-
bottomed L.L.Bean boots in the hallway. She urgently needed to
speak to her children, something she couldn't comfortably do with
him in the house. She watched from the front door till the car turned
in to the road; then she went inside to call, immensely grateful when
her mother told her that Russell was himself out on a grocery run.

"What's going on with you two?" her mother asked, to the tin-
kling accompaniment of the ice cubes in her glass. "Russell's walking
around here like a whipped dog."

"Nothing's going on," Corrine said, determined not to enlist in her mother's sorority of wronged women. Her husband's decampment with her best friend twenty-five years before had remained the defining event of her life, the creation myth of a bitter and wrathful Amazonian cult. Corrine, newly pledged to Aphrodite, had never been less sympathetic. As much as Jessie liked her son-in-law, she would have taken a certain morbid pleasure in learning that he'd confirmed her low opinion of his sex, and that her daughter had been betrayed just as she had. And even though Corrine was betraying her husband in the flesh—or maybe precisely because she was—she had no desire to rat Russell out to her mother. "I just needed a little time to myself, Mom."

"Speaking of marriages, how's Casey? Did I tell you that Mary Greyson spotted her husband with a floozy at the Ritz-Carlton last month?"

"That was a client, Mom." Jessie still lived in a world that had only one Ritz-Carlton, in which grown women in hotel bars were either wives or whores.

"Is that what they're calling them now? I think we know who's the client of whom in this case."

Finally, she persuaded her mother to summon the children.

"Nana's house smells funny," Jeremy said. "Storey got carsick and threw up on me and then Nana's cat scratched me and it was bleeding like crazy. Dad put on a Band-Aid, but it was just a plain one. Where are you?"

"I'm on Nantucket," she said. "You remember we talked about how Mommy was going to take a girl's vacation with Aunt Casey? You remember Nantucket, don't you?"

"I got a whale's tooth."

"That's right."

"Why can't we come?"

"Well, sometimes parents need their own little time-out."

"A time-out?" he said. "Why, did you do something bad?"

Corrine checked her face in the hall mirror when she heard the car on the gravel drive, hoping he wouldn't notice she'd been crying. In fact, her maternal guilt receded far more rapidly than she could have imagined as she watched Luke striding up the flagstone walk in his Barbour coat, his arms loaded with provisions. At the door, she embraced him as if he'd been gone for days.

"Is that just hunger," he said, "or are you happy to see me?"

She followed him into the kitchen where he displayed the provender—lobsters and soft-shell clams, as she'd requested, a pound of butter, a bag of mixed greens, two expensive-looking bottles of chardonnay. "Too late for corn," he said.

"This will be a streamlined indoor version of the traditional clambake," she said. "We used to take a big pot down to the beach, dig a hole, and build a fire. Onions and potatoes went in first, then kielbasa, clams, mussels, and finally lobsters. My dad would pile kelp on top of the whole thing and Hilary and I would run up and down the dunes while we waited. I can't believe I remember all that."

She'd become more interested in eating since she'd started sleeping with Luke, as if all of her appetites were connected, as if her taste buds had been awakened along with her libido. Perhaps it was just the delight of having another sensual pleasure to share, a ritual communion after they'd briefly sated their lust, but she could swear she felt hungrier lately; and she took an unaccustomed enjoyment in the *taste* of food. She hadn't been able to eat a lobster in years—the idea of them going live into the boiling water making her too sad—but she was eager to share with him this traditional delicacy of her tribe, which, as it turned out, was also his own, at least on his mother's side.

"Are you very close to your mother?" she asked as she rinsed the clams.

"In a sense."

"That sounds . . . clinical."

"We were almost unnaturally close," he said. "Everybody teased her about my being her favorite, about my little brother, Matthew, being an orphan. I used to fake being sick to stay home with her, and she'd pretend to believe me, even though she didn't really believe in illness. Toward noon, I'd miraculously recover and we'd go walking or riding together. Do you ride?"

She sensed a changing of the subject. "I used to, hunters and jumpers. I was on the circuit for a couple years. So what happened to make you less close?" Thinking about the story he'd told her in the first days of their acquaintance, the one about his mother's infidelity.

"Sex, I suppose." He shook his head, squinting out the window at the dark ocean, as if this had just occurred to him. "When I hit adolescence, it was all I could think about, so, naturally, she couldn't be my best friend and confidante after that. That and her own midlife sexual adventure."

"The affair you told me about. With—what was his name? Goose?"

"Duck Cheatham."

"But surely you forgave her for that?" she said, holding an angry lobster in midair. "Eventually, I mean."

"I don't know," he said. "A year later, I went off to Deerfield and then Williams."

"You never talked about it?"

He shook his head.

"Oh my God, your poor mother."

Looking at the flailing lobster, she felt pierced by an intimation of his mother's remorse and suffering over the years—the rejection by her beloved firstborn son. She glanced at Luke and spun away, unable to bear the thought of him causing such pain. She eased the lobster into the sink and took off, walking toward the French doors.

"Corrine!"

Unbolting the door, she almost relented, hearing the bewilderment in his voice, but she was too upset, and confused, to stop herself. She ran down the dune to the beach, turning once to see him outlined in the doorway.

How could she have been so wrong about him? A man so cruel and selfish. Not one word in all those years? She pictured Luke's mother in her own image, her face succumbing to gravity and sadness, half a lifetime punctuated by moments of regret and yearning. Finally, she stopped running, her bare feet turning numb in the cold sand, and tried to find comfort in the rhythmic susurration of the waves.

Why was she so upset? Why hadn't she stopped to consider Luke's feelings, his pain? Was it because it was herself she was feeling sorry for, as much as for Luke's mother? Casting herself in that same role of the scarlet mother . . . imagining her own son eventually and inevitably turning his heart against her? Seeing her as a whore. She didn't think she could bear that. It wasn't fair. She wanted to tell Jeremy—the beautiful little boy who would grow up to judge her and resent her—that it wasn't fair, that she needed them both. She didn't want to choose between Jeremy and Luke, her son and her lover. She wanted to tell Luke that his mother must have felt the same way, even as she wanted to comfort him, the little boy hiding in the closet.

Suddenly, his face in the moonlight reinforced this image—boyishly pained and bewildered.

"I'm sorry," she said, burying her face in his shoulder. "You must think I'm crazy."

He shook his head as he squeezed her fiercely. "No. I think you're right."

"I don't even know why I got so upset."

"And I didn't realize how much you remind me of her," he said.

"Maybe she loved him the way I love you."

"That's what I was thinking when you were gone just now," he said. "I don't want to lose you. I don't want to lose this. Please, don't run away from me."

As they lay in bed that night, she imagined the waves outside to be saying, *Hush . . . hush . . . hush,* absolving them and stilling their mea culpas, their mutual confessions of inadequacy and weakness and guilt. It was as if the innermost battlements of their fortressed souls had been breached and the final intimacy lay in revealing the secrets they'd previously hidden from the world for fear of appearing unlovable. She wanted to strip herself naked before him, even as the ravening desire she felt for him was superseded by a tenderness that was almost maternal. She lay in his arms in the darkness, listening to him talk about his own mother as if for the first time in years.

She must have fallen asleep at some point, because he was talking about something else now and she could see the grid of the windowpanes hovering in the darkness beyond the foot of the bed, and then she realized what he was telling her about.

"Paper's fluttering down from the sky, paper and ash. It's hard to see—visibility is maybe thirty feet—but still I started shaking at what I could see. The front of the Winter Garden is destroyed, a big smoking space, like this ruined cathedral. There's no glass, just debris and dust everywhere. It's like a fucking moonscape. I was with some other guy in a suit. We decided to follow a fire hose into the debris.

"There's a bridge over Liberty Street. We turned the corner; smoke and flames were everywhere. Everything so weirdly quiet. I'd never been anywhere so quiet in the city. You could feel the death. It was just as palpable as the smoke. I didn't think anyone could survive. But I also had this completely irrational notion that I would find Guillermo.

"They say it was a bucket brigade. But the first day, we had no buckets—at least I didn't see any. We used our hands. We formed a human chain, passing along pieces of rebar and concrete, hand to hand. Everyone just fell into place and started working. Eventually, I don't know when, we got these plastic buckets. We were going stone by stone across West Street, digging our way across. By the end of the day, I was five feet over the median divider. There were three lines. Somebody had a lock cutter and eventually there were a few acetylene torches. We were cutting rebar, working in the smoke and the dust while the flames licked up from the hot spots. The strange thing was, out of all these thousands of offices, you never saw a chair or a desk or a fax machine or a computer terminal. You never even saw a piece of glass. Everything had been reduced to powder. And that pretty much told me the chances of finding survivors.

"They found a body ten feet up in front of me. Work stopped while they passed up a body bag. I didn't see that one, just waited in the line until the bag came back to me. We didn't have the Stokes baskets yet to carry out the bodies, so it just went from hand to hand. The bag was so small, so light, I could feel that it was only a torso. No arms or legs. I puked into the rubble and then started digging again.

"Late in the afternoon, Number Seven came down. Suddenly,

people were shouting, 'Run. It's coming down.' There'd been lots of false alarms and we'd already run out three or four times, and you didn't really want to run again because your lungs were aching and the air was like some kind of new element between gas and solid. But this time it was real and I was running down West Street toward Stuyvesant High School.

"For some reason, I couldn't make myself leave, feeling like it should've been me in there, that I'd never done anything in my life to justify my surviving. And maybe this was the first time in my life I had a chance to do something important. So I went back to the pile and joined a line, and pretty soon a body was found twenty feet away from me. Work stopped as we passed up a body bag and it started to come back. When it got to me, I grabbed it and the zipper broke open and I was looking at a face burned beyond recognition. It was black. I'm not sure how I knew it was a woman, but I was sure it was. And I started shaking. A fireman from Long Island who was behind me in the line kind of moved up to comfort me, try to get me to let go. Because I was holding on to it. For some reason, I couldn't let go. Finally, I passed the bag on, and ten minutes later I found myself standing in a puddle of blood.

"We'd find voids, these holes under the debris. That was what you hoped for, what we were all looking for. Voids, pockets of space and air where someone might have survived. That was the worst part for me, when I was at the front of the line—groping into those empty spaces. I felt like a coward; all I could think about was reaching into a void and having a hand grab me. It just seemed terrifying, those holes—like being a kid afraid of the dark space under the bed. Here I am, supposedly rescuing people, and I'm afraid even to reach inside. Those voids are like portals to the underworld. The firemen could do it. But you didn't talk to them. They were righteous. They were angry. We left them alone. I wished I could be fearless, but I was scared shitless half the time.

"I found credit cards, wallets, photos; there was a snap of a guy with his head between a stripper's tits. We passed it along the line. Eventually, all the photos went into a bucket at the end of the line.

"At one point, I got my legs under a beam, holding it up with my feet so they could search underneath. Somehow, it wasn't so frightening, sticking my feet in there.

"After the fumes from the broken gas lines knocked me out, I finally staggered out. I didn't know which way I was going. I felt dizzy and nauseated. I hadn't slept. I could hardly see at that point, from the dust. St. Vincent's had a station set up to wash eyes, and after that I started walking uptown. All of a sudden, this beautiful woman appeared out of the dust and the smoke. And it was you. Whenever I'd closed my eyes, I'd seen that woman without a face. But there you were, giving the world a new face."

She could just make out his features, now, more beautiful to her than ever in the dim light from the window.

"I was so scrambled," he said, "that when I saw you, I thought for a second maybe I had died back there, that you were an angel. Maybe I'd gone down with the towers or later in Number Seven and the digging had just been an illusion, the Sisyphean afterlife I deserved. I thought maybe you were from the other side and that I'd crossed over. Sometimes I still wonder if it was all just an afterimage, because nothing feels very real to me anymore, except being with you. And if I lose you, then I might as well be a ghost walking through the rest of my life without being able to touch or feel anything."

She held him then and listened to the rising sound of his breathing as the light slowly, inexorably filled the room.

After waking in the afternoon, they took a walk on the beach. He laid another fire and she read to him from the *Symposium*.

Later, she fell asleep on the sofa listening to Gram Parsons. When she woke again, the room was dim; the fire had subsided to a pile of embers and she felt a sudden chill of dread. Where was he? She found him out back, smoking a cigarette and gazing out at the sea.

"I was just going to wake you," he said.

"What happened?"

"Ashley's run away from Silver Meadows. Sometime last night. I've booked the last plane for New York."

She wanted to comfort him somehow, to take him in her arms, but she sensed that he was already in midair, beyond her reach, searching the ground below for his child.

"I'll go with you," she said.

"You don't have to."

"Of course I do."

"I'm sorry," he said.

"We'll come back," she said, although just then she feared they never would.

# 26

At La Guardia, Corrine withdrew to a respectful distance as he paced and spoke to his wife.

"No news," he said as he snapped the phone shut.

"I wish—"

"I know."

*He* wished he could say something to lift the pall, to salvage and preserve some portion of the pleasure of their aborted escape. He wanted to comfort her, to tell her that there would be other times, that they would resume where they'd left off, but none of this seemed appropriate. All his concern, he realized, should be directed toward his missing daughter. He shouldn't be missing Corrine, already aching at the thought of her impending absence. She had never looked quite so beautiful; he stroked her chin and examined her face as if she, too, were about to disappear.

"We should probably take separate cars," she said.

"I suppose so."

They trudged in silence past the stream of departing passengers, whose expectant faces were as bright as freshly minted coins.

"You have money?" he asked as they passed the security checkpoint.

"Of course," she said. "But thanks for asking."

At the taxi stand, he reached out and grabbed the sleeve of her jacket. "Corrine, I don't want to . . . I'm worried sick about my daughter. But I don't want to leave you this way. I can't bear this feeling that we're walking away from each other. We'll find Ashley, but in the meantime I don't want you to think that the fact that we were together when this happened . . . I don't know, that it's somehow our fault. That it's an omen. Ashley's problems—they're about what's wrong with me and Sasha. It's not about us. I won't let it be."

She nodded unconvincingly. "I'm glad you said that."

"It's true, Corrine."

"Well, I want you to know, in case you change your mind, I don't know when I've ever been as happy as I was this weekend."

"Twenty-four hours, actually."

"Next time, Mandalay."

After several hours of fruitless phone calls and a nearly sleepless night of self-reproach and recriminations, he'd roused himself and, with Sasha, resumed the search. At nine, he called Casey Reynes to explain the situation, and while he might just as easily have spoken with her daughter over the phone, they both agreed he should walk the few blocks to the apartment for a personal interview. "I think Amber might be more forthcoming if you sit down with her," Casey said, the note of concern in her voice compromised by an undercurrent of conspiratorial zest. "Why don't you pop round now. She's not awake yet, but I'm sure she'll be up shortly. We'll make a list of all of Ashley's friends and see if we can't come up with a lead."

Luke couldn't help feeling grateful for the suggestion, the more so since he'd always considered Casey a vapid socialite. The fact that she was Corrine's best friend, and that she was privy to their secret, inclined him to revise his opinion and he found himself remembering little acts of kindness she'd performed on Ashley's behalf, pickups and birthday presents and solicitous notes.

Standing in front of her building at 740 Park, he thought of how, a year ago, Sasha had informed him of an imminent offering there, and begged him to look at it; even after the apartment ultimately proved to be smaller than their own, on a lower floor with inferior light, she'd urged him to make an offer. But he'd already been thinking of doing something different with his days, scaling back instead of ramping up, so this had been easy enough to refuse. Nor had he been eager to kowtow to the notoriously snobbish co-op board, even though they'd had the good sense, several years earlier, to reject Bernard Melman's application.

"Come in, come in," she said, greeting him as the elevator door opened into her foyer.

He appraised her with new eyes, finding her appearance less brittle than he expected, the porcelain skin of her—according to Sasha—recently lifted face softer and less the Kabuki mask of jaded sophistication he remembered from the fêtes of their thirties. At this moment, it seemed expressive of genuine human concern.

As the door closed on the elevator's wizened, uniformed operator, she hugged Luke and pressed her lips to his. "I can't imagine how you must feel right now."

"Thanks," he said, fighting a sudden wave of emotion. "I really appreciate this."

"Excuse the mess," she said, apparently referring to a neat stack of mail on a trestle table. "Come into my study and we'll talk. Can I get you some coffee?"

He followed her down the long hallway; the apartment, like Casey herself, somewhat confounded his expectations, with its folk art and Wyeths, its hooked rugs and tartan prints in unexpected Fauve colors—a look that might have been diagnosed as psychedelic Early American.

"So," she said, closing the study door behind them, with a great exhalation of breath, as if they'd traveled vast distances and overcome nearly insurmountable obstacles to find themselves alone at last.

The room was a shrine to equestrianism—a theme that reminded him, happily, of his mother. A weathered pine bookshelf displayed trophies and ribbons; the walls were shingled with old English hunting prints interspersed with photographs of Casey on horseback. She walked over to the little Hepplewhite desk and scanned the ranks of photographs. "Here," she said, handing him a faded color picture in a leather frame.

He recognized Corrine immediately, despite the riding helmet and the fact she must've been a teenager, her hair a more vivid carroty shade than he was familiar with, standing beside a younger version of Casey, both of them captured in that transitional stage of adolescence. He gazed at the face, with its smattering of freckles and her thrilling smile, studying it for its predictive qualities, savoring its resemblances to that of the woman he loved, happy to discover that he preferred the latter, which seemed to have gained more in refinement and character than it had lost in freshness.

"I thought you'd get a little kick out of that."

He would have studied it longer had he been alone, but now he returned it to the desk.

Since she had broached the subject, he said, "I want to thank you for the house. I only wish—"

"Please," she said, brushing this away with one sweep of her hand and indicating the love seat with another. "I talked to her last night. I'm sure I don't have to tell you her heart is with you." She took a seat beside him. "This may not be the time or place," she said, putting a hand on his knee, "but I don't know when I've seen her as happy as she's been these last few weeks. I mean, of course, it's been an awful time in many ways, for all of us. The fall from hell, really. You know they lost a close friend, Jim Crespi, the film producer. But aside from that, she's been practically giddy. I've known Corrine since she was a girl, but I've never seen her like *this*."

Luke suspected he should be appalled by this monologue, but he couldn't help drinking it in, as if it were the rarest first-growth claret.

"How's Sasha?" she asked abruptly.

"Well, you can imagine—"

"I feel for her, I really do. But you've got to ask yourself how her behavior might have contributed to this. I'm not one to sit in judgment of my friends, but really, Luke, I think she's treated you shamefully. And it's not as if kids don't pick up these things. I always say they're sponges. I mean, it's no wonder Ashley's . . . having problems; it would be a miracle if she weren't. Hello! I know you: You can't help blaming yourself. But everyone knows what a doting father you are. We all see you taking her to school in the morning and picking her up every afternoon."

"Well, recently, I might have been. But I used to be in the office before she was awake, and some nights I wouldn't get home before she was asleep."

"That's what you had to do to support your family. Web's the same way—sometimes the kids don't see him for days on end. That's his *job*. And it's my job to supervise the kids—along with a million other things. I mean, sure, we have staff, but it's not like I don't make it my business to go to the lacrosse games and help with the homework. I just don't know if motherhood has ever been such a huge priority for Sasha, and I say this as a friend. Sasha's beautiful, she's genius, she's the Nan Kempner of our generation, blah de blah de blah, but I don't see her outside the school at eight a.m. And I'm frankly shocked she left Ashley in town that weekend. Amber tried to persuade me to let her spend the night with Bethany, but I knew the Traynors were in Hobe Sound that weekend and—I'm sorry, call me old-fashioned—but I just don't approve of the idea of unsupervised sleepovers at this age. That's just Parenting one oh one. At least that's the way I was raised. I know *you* thought she was with Sasha," she added quickly. "Corrine told me. I just don't know what Sasha was—"

"Well, be that as it may, she's devastated over this," Luke said, feeling compelled, finally, to rise to her defense. "And I really should be getting back. If you wouldn't mind, I'd really like to talk to Amber."

"Of course," she said, squeezing his knee and rising briskly. "I'll go get her. I know she's eager to help in any way she can." She stood with her hand on the door. "Just between us girls, I've heard that a certain someone is definitely going back to his wife. It seems that he's decided he can't afford a divorce now that his company's worth about half what it was on Labor Day. Just thought you should be armed with that information, in case it has any relevance."

"Thank you, Casey. I appreciate it."

"I'll get Amber. You sure you don't want any coffee?"

He shook his head, wondering how much he wanted this woman—or anyone except Corrine—to know about his life.

Amber seemed more an illustration of the problem than a possible solution to it. She trailed in behind her mother as if at the end of a chain, bleary and sullen, slouching languorously against the door frame for support, as though her long and slender legs, almost entirely visible below the hemline of her tiny pink shorts, were not quite up to the job of supporting her.

"Of course you know Mr. McGavock," Casey said.

Amber nodded sleepily.

"It's very important that you tell him anything you can think of that might help him locate Ashley."

"I really can't think of anything."

"Maybe," Luke said, "if we could just have a few minutes alone."

Amber flashed her mother a panicked look.

"I know you're eager to help," Casey said, taking her hand and tugging her into the room.

Amber threw herself into the wing chair across from Luke, seeming to relax as soon as her mother closed the door. "I feel really bad about Ashley," she said, drawing her knees up to her chin.

"Do you have any idea where she might've gone?"

She shrugged. "I'm probably her best friend, me and Bethany."

"That's why I thought you might be able to help," he said. "I know you weren't at the party that night."

"Well, I did hear about it."

"Was she with anyone I should talk to?"

She stretched like a cat, unfurling her limbs, and shook her head sleepily.

"Do you think she could be with her boyfriend?"

"Boyfriend?"

"You're her best friend, Amber. She must've told you about me walking in on them."

She blushed and clutched her knees closer to her body.

"If I didn't hurt him then, I'm certainly not going to now. But I need his name. Please, Amber."

"I guess you mean Trey Wilbraham. It's not like he's her boyfriend. They just hook up once in a while. He goes to Buckley. But he doesn't know where she is. I talked to him last night. He hasn't heard from her since the night of the party."

Luke didn't know whether he should feel relieved that the boy his daughter was sucking off wasn't really her boyfriend. Was that supposed to be some kind of consolation? "He was at the party?"

She looked down at her knees.

"Are there other boys who might know where she is?"

She seemed to detect an accusation in this. "Just so you know, Ashley's, like, this famous prude. I mean, if it will make you feel any better, she's actually technically a virgin."

As reassuring as this might be, it was merely balm applied to a wound that required stitches.

"'Technically'?"

She blushed, which he took to be a good sign.

"Maybe . . ." she began.

"What?"

"I don't know if I should say."

"Please, Amber."

"Well, you know Anton Hohenlohe?"

"Is he—"

"He's not her boyfriend or anything. He's always telling us all to come over anytime. He's kind of creepy, if you ask me, I mean, we call him 'MP,' which stands for major pedophile, but we sometimes hang out over there. It's like this clubhouse. So, I guess if she was looking for a place to hide out—"

She recoiled when Luke jumped to his feet.

"You won't say I said anything?"

"No, I promise." He started to lean down to kiss her cheek, then thought better of it.

He finally slowed to catch his breath only when he turned east at the corner of Seventy-sixth and Park, decelerating to a fast walk in order to master the surging tide of his righteous fury and to savor the prospect of its possible imminent release. It was a little after ten, a good time to surprise a sybarite sleeping off the revels of Saturday night; but the notion of his daughter as the virginal sacrifice of those rites set him running again, bolting across Madison, dodging a single Sunday-morning cab as he sprinted on to Hohenlohe's town house, the address of which Amber had reluctantly provided.

A brass plaque inscribed HOHENLOHE was mounted above the single buzzer. Luke pressed the bell and waited thirty seconds before pressing it again, holding it down until the tip of his finger was numb.

Finally the intercom crackled. "For God's sake, what is it?"

"It's Luke McGavock."

After a pause: "You'll forgive me, but it's a little early for visitors by my clock."

"You can either come down and talk to me now or wait while I call the police."

Luke was about to press the buzzer again, when the intercom gave another cough. "I'll be down in a moment."

Luke climbed up the steps to try to get a view through the windows, pacing from one side of the stoop to the other. He was envisioning scenarios of escape through the back garden when he heard the click of the inner door bolt.

Hohenlohe threw wide the outer door, presenting himself in a royal blue robe with black facing, attempting to project hauteur in his state of dishevelment. "Good God, man, it's barely morning." His accent, which was sometimes transparent, seemed now a Teutonic version of Oxbridge.

"I'm looking for my daughter."

"What makes you think I'd know anything about your daughter's whereabouts?"

"I hear underage girls are one of your specialties."

"Whatever you may think, I can assure you I haven't seen your daughter in some time. I understand she's . . . out of town."

"You don't know how badly I want to hit you right now," Luke said. "I'm sure you can understand that I'm not going to take your word for it. You can either invite me in to discuss this or I can wait right here for the authorities."

"Very well," he said after a moment's deliberation.

The first set of stairs took Luke up to the parlor floor; the first room he entered showed the remains of the previous evening's party: half-empty glasses, beer and wine bottles, the smeared, hatched surface of a Mapplethorpe flower photo that lay on the coffee table.

"I'm afraid the place is a bit—"

Luke brushed past him and took the steps, two at a time, up the second flight.

"Wait a minute! You can't just barge into a man's home."

On the second landing, he threw open the first door at the top of the stairs to reveal the inner lair, with its king-size bed, a blue velvet duvet entangled with golden sheets on it, matching pillows scattered across the room. On the floor, by the edge of the bed, was a familiar-looking high-heeled sandal.

"See here, I'll call the police myself."

Luke strode across the room and flung open the nearest door. In his agitation, it took him a moment to recognize the terrified figure, swathed in a golden sheet, trembling against the luxurious backdrop of Hohenlohe's wardrobe. He was dimly aware that he should be horrified—and later would wonder about his civic duty—but his relief just now far outweighed his sense of outraged morality.

"Hello, Bethany," he said.

Luke was walking up Madison in the shadow of the protruding brow of the Whitney when Sasha called him on his cell phone to report that Ashley had turned up at his mother's house in Tennessee.

"My God," he said. "How did she get there?"

"She caught a bus, apparently."

Luke realized it was an ungenerous thought, but in his giddiness he wondered which aspect of the story surprised her more, Ashley's destination or her mode of transport.

"And she's fine?"

"So it would seem."

He was conscious of an almost filial sympathy for the mother of his lost and found daughter, even as he felt an exhilarating and impatient urge to share the news with Corrine, whom he imagined to have been restored to him along with his daughter. Because he had been convinced that if anything had happened to Ashley—if the worst had happened—it would have been the end of them, and he had been steeling himself for the loss of the two things that mattered to him the most.

# PART THREE

# Holidays

# 27

The dogs announced his arrival—three adopted strays who met him halfway up the gravel drive and escorted him to the house, leaping and clawing at the window of the Bronco he'd rented at the Nashville airport.

Luke's mother still occupied the Victorian farmhouse in which he'd spent the second part of his childhood, a few miles south of Franklin on the Columbia Pike, along the ill-fated route that had brought Hood's Army of Tennessee from Spring Hill to the southern edge of town, where it was devastated by entrenched Union forces. Although Luke's paternal ancestors had built one of the area's historic estates, it had long since passed out of the family; the farmhouse, dating from the lean years after the war, stopped short of any pretensions to plantationhood. Luke always thought of it as his mother's house, in part because of its resemblance to her family home in Massachusetts— its simple lines and gables closer to the architectural vernacular of rural New England than to the Greco-Georgian vocabulary of the landed southern gentry—and because his father had bought it for her, so she could keep horses and escape the social claustrophobia of what was then more village than town. The first eight years of her marriage had been spent in the rectory of the church, just inside the line of the old trenches. Digging in the garden, she and the children would frequently turn up relics of the carnage—musket balls, rusted belt buckles, grapeshot, and, once, a pitted five-pound ball from a Napoléon gun, which now sat on the mantel of the farmhouse.

His mother rose up now from the autumnal ruins of the vegetable garden, trowel in hand, and waved—the lovely consort of the pumpkin-head scarecrow who ruled over the browning and broken stalks of corn, dressed in a bright orange UT windbreaker. Luke always pictured his mother outdoors like this—on horseback, playing tennis, gardening. Her husband had playfully accused her of being a pantheist, fresh air and sunshine the bread and wine of her faith. *Such a nice day, you should go out and play* was the refrain that haunted his childhood. She hated seeing a tree cut down for any reason and she did not share the ingrained belief of southern womankind in the dangers of the midday sun or of airborne pestilence, nor could she entirely understand why her firstborn was so often hunched over a book, a posture she regarded as both unnatural and unhealthy. Drawn to the light and the air, she could never countenance his need for interiors, his love of books and movies and sheltered reading alcoves.

As she walked out to the driveway, still lanky and slim, he realized with a pleasant sense of surprise one of the reasons Corrine had looked so familiar when he first saw her, standing just beyond the precinct of the ash and the debris, though the resemblance faded as his mother drew nearer; her skin showed the parchmenty texture and piebald spottiness of a blond sixty-three-year-old sun worshiper. It took a moment for him, as always, to recalibrate, to adjust her younger image with the reality of the present.

He pushed his sunglasses to the top of his head as she loped toward him wearing his old Deerfield sweatshirt over a pair of khaki shorts; he was as touched that his castoffs still constituted part of her wardrobe as he was to see the welcome in her smile and the recognition in her eyes—the brilliance of which always startled him anew and made him feel that no one else really knew him, that his encounters with other humans were pale reflections of these sparkling reunions. He mostly forgot this in the intervals in between—a realization that brought on a flood of guilt when he realized how intermittently he treated them both to this pleasure. A week in the Hamptons this summer . . . already three, four months past. Before that, Thanksgiving and his father's funeral. His failures as a father mirroring his shortcomings as a son, although the dogs seemed not to care about either as they bounded and barked around him.

"My handsome boy, you're so thin." This was her highest compliment. "You've lost that horrible business-dinner bloat." She turned her examination to his face. "How are you, Luke?"

Unable to answer this simple inquiry, he felt his composure dissolving, the years falling away, as he buried his face in her hair, its lemon-oil scent always reminding him of sunlight itself. When he lifted his head and tried to speak, he found himself gulping for air, his vision blurred, his memories crowded with fears and regrets.

"It's all right," she said, stroking his back rhythmically.

"You look good," he finally managed to say.

"About like an old saddle that's been left in the sun. Not that it matters. Ashley's out back."

"How does she seem?"

"Well . . ." She sighed. "Pretty fair, considering. Though just now she's nervous as a housefly on a windowpane. She's been kind of a wreck about the prospect of seeing you."

He walked over to the car and checked his reflection in the window; it seemed bulbous and bloated, as if he'd just been pulled up after several days underwater.

"Don't worry, you look fine. Just be sweet to her. This isn't the moment to get all disciplinarian."

"What do you think—I've been beating her?"

"No," she said, "quite the opposite. I think you've let her run a little too free."

"Like you did with me."

"That's true," she said, smiling. "But your dad was always there to crack the whip."

"I'm just grateful she had sense enough to come here."

"She's welcome to stay as long as she wants. Or as long as her mother will let her." She paused. "How *is* Sasha?"

"She's fine, I suppose."

His mother nodded skeptically.

"Actually," Luke said, "I don't really know anymore."

Nora lifted her eyebrows and held her tongue.

Luke was so used to defending his wife to his mother—and vice versa—that it took him a moment to realize he no longer cared to. It was as if the fog of gloom that had enveloped him since he'd first suspected Sasha's infidelity now seemed pierced by a glimmer of relief. For years, he'd felt he had to choose between them.

"I think she's having an affair," he said. "Or at least she was. It doesn't really matter at this point."

His mother was far too generous, and too well-raised, to gloat—to allow that she'd been expecting something like this for years—although neither did she bother to feign surprise. She had done her best to take Sasha to her heart, and to hide her feelings when she found it impossible to do so. "I'm sorry, Luke."

"It's all right," he said. "I'm the one who should be sorry for you. I know what you've put up with all these years."

"I only ever wanted you to be happy."

"I thought I was for a while. And then I got used to being less than happy."

"We can talk about it later," she said. "Right now, you should go find your daughter."

Ashley was in the riding ring, on Scheherazade, the aging Arabian mare his mother had inherited from a neighbor, as she had most of the horses. He opened the back gate and started out across the back pasture, inhaling the rich nostalgic sour mash of grass and hay, urine and manure. The horses lifted their heads from their grazing and turned to watch him, while the pygmy goats rushed from their pen to mob him, grunting and butting one another as they rubbed against his calves, muddying his chinos.

Ashley continued to circle the ring as he approached. She had a beautiful seat, and seemed to him more at ease on horseback than she did on her own newly elongated limbs. When he reached the ring, she changed direction and cut a figure eight. He leaned up against the fence and watched while she completed another circuit at a canter and brought the horse to a stop just across the fence from him.

"Whoa, good girl," she said.

"Does she still switch her leads?" he asked.

"Not as much."

"You both looked good."

Ashley busied herself patting the mare, which stepped forward and shoved its nose into Luke's elbow, discharging a hot blast of breath. Failing to find a treat, she ducked her head to yank at a tuft of grass just outside the ring. Ashley pulled the mare's head up and backed her away from the fence, not yet having looked at her father.

"I'm happy to see you," Luke said. And, in fact, he was relieved to have just discovered a large reserve of love for her, reassured to see this girlishly ponytailed and helmeted figure atop a horse, as he'd seen her in simpler times.

"Are you?" she asked, glancing down at him fearfully.

He was glad that at this moment she had the advantage of height. "Of course I am."

"I didn't think you would be."

"I'm glad you're here. If you had to run away, at least you picked a good place to come to."

She nodded sullenly, rubbing the mare's neck vigorously. "Are you here to take me back?"

"I'm here to talk to you."

She rolled her eyes.

"I don't blame you for anything that's happened, Ashley. If anything, I blame myself."

"I know what you think."

273

"And what do you suppose that is?"

She shook her head stubbornly. "You know."

"I have no idea. Nor do I have a lecture prepared. I don't really even have a plan, to tell you the truth."

She looked down at him skeptically. "I was afraid to see you."

"I know."

"I can't look at you."

He'd imagined this as *his* line, said it to her many times in his rehearsals for this encounter. He removed his sunglasses and held them out to her. "Would these help?"

She shook her head, but then, thinking better of it, leaned down on Scheherazade's neck, plucked the shades from his fingers, and clamped them on her face.

"Why don't you rub the old girl down and put her up. I'll meet you inside."

Nora was at the kitchen counter, pouring water from the kettle into the old silver teapot. He paused at the door, taking in the cypress wood, the olfactory residue of grease, the bright green apples piled high in a wooden bowl on the refectory table. Of all the memories this might have conjured, what he came up with was the day he'd skipped school and had been surprised by his mother and Duck Cheatham.

He took a seat at the table.

"Did she tell you she wants to stay here?" Nora asked.

"For how long?"

"Well, I don't know. Indefinitely."

"I think it's a great idea," he said. "But I doubt Sasha's going to go along with it."

"Ashley seems to have some kind of ace up her sleeve."

"Something on Sasha?"

"It would seem so. But you mustn't say I told you. I want her to feel she can trust me."

"How did I get everything so wrong?" Luke said.

"I've always been proud of you, Luke. Even if I didn't always understand some of your choices."

"Like Sasha."

274

"Well, she's a beautiful woman. I always thought it must be about sex."

He was taken aback, not certain he'd ever heard the word on his mother's lips.

"That was certainly part of it."

"It doesn't last, though. Does it?"

"How long did it last for you?"

"With your father, you mean?"

He shrugged. That was what he'd meant, but now he wanted to know if there were other answers. Not that he actually expected any.

"It was a different era. Women weren't supposed to enjoy sex. We were taught that it was a duty to be fulfilled, a cross to bear for the sake of security and family. It was years before I really came to appreciate it. And by then . . . well, let's just say it was almost too late. Your father had his heart bypass, and something changed in him. Our timing was terrible."

The back door hinges squeaked and Ashley walked just inside and stopped.

"How was Scheherazade?" Nora asked.

"I think her right foot's still bothering her a little," she said. "And she's got a fresh bite on her right flank."

"That would be Billy," Nora said. "He's always harrying the mares. Sometimes I think they missed something when they gelded him."

Ashley winced at this.

"What's the plan for tonight?" Luke asked, secretly wincing himself. "Can I take you two ladies out to dinner?"

"Matthew and Debbie have invited us all over tonight." Nora turned to her granddaughter. "How does that sound?"

"That sounds okay," Ashley said.

"Why don't you go wash up and change, then."

Luke walked out to the back pasture, fending off the goats, the horses approaching in expectation of the evening meal. He escaped into the barn and climbed the ladder to the hayloft, the warm air in the eaves thick with the odor of the old chestnut boards, rotting hay, pigeon shit, and the faint musk of the fox den beneath the hayrick. Motes of dust swam like insects in the shaft of orange sunlight piercing the gloom through the door at the far end of the loft.

She answered on the first ring.

"I miss you," he said.

"God, you don't know how much I was hoping it was you."

"Where are you?"

"I'm home. Let me just get the kids settled and I'll go in the bedroom."

He became aware of the faint lowing of pigeons and looked up to see them lined up on the beam above him, shuffling sideways, regarding him warily, as if they retained a collective memory of the days when he'd carried a pellet gun.

"I'm here," she said. "How are you, my angel?"

"Strangely optimistic," he said. "Ashley seems okay. Our first encounter wasn't a total debacle."

"And your mom? She must be happy to have you. I know I would be."

"I told her about Sasha. That she was having an affair."

"You told her?"

"And that I didn't really care anymore."

"What did she say?"

"She was too polite to say 'I told you so,' but I got the feeling she thought it was the nicest gift I've given her in years."

"That seems like, I don't know, a big step."

"It is. I've made up my mind. Don't say anything; it has nothing to do with you. Well, not nothing. Everything has to do with you. But I'm not asking for any kind of reciprocal gesture. You've just made it easier for me. I realized on the plane that I don't have to be miserable."

"Oh, Luke. I don't know what to say."

"I'm not asking you to say or do anything."

"I know. I know you're not and I love you for saying it. But I can't go on like this. I feel so dishonest. God, Luke, what I want to do is tell him. I don't think I can wait."

He could hardly believe she'd said it, wanting her to want this even as he feared the consequences. But he was sure of one thing. "I'm happy to hear you say that."

"But you don't think I should?"

He ached to hear the note of despair in her voice. "It's not that. You have to think about the children."

"I know," she said. "If it weren't for that—oh fuck, I don't know what to do, Luke."

"I don't expect you to know right now. You don't have to. And you don't have to do anything right now except take care of yourself. I'm not going anywhere. I can wait."

"Do you really want me?"

"I want you so badly, I can hardly stand it."

"Me too."

"We have time," he said. "The rest of our lives."

"I like the sound of that." She paused. "Do you think I'd like it in Tennessee? I have this image of the kids riding their bikes barefoot to school and going fishing with cane poles. Where are you right now? I want to picture you."

"I'm in the hayloft in the barn."

"I wish I could be there with you. Making love in the hay . . . Oh, shit, they're fighting. I'd better go."

"Can I call you tonight?"

"It might be better if I called you."

"I love you."

"You better."

He lay back on the rough flooring of the loft, dazed and exultant, listening to the amorous murmurs of the pigeons and watching the light fade. He felt giddy with the knowledge of his power over Corrine even as he felt unworthy of it. He wanted to be a student of her goodness and decency, a slave to her whims. He wanted to be her protector, though he worried that he was instead the primary threat to her well-being.

.  .  .

Battleground Meadows was a planned community a few miles from the center of Franklin, one of dozens that had sprung up in the old tobacco and cotton fields in the years since Luke had gone off to school. His younger brother, Matthew, had chosen to stay close to home, establishing a law practice in Franklin the same year he married the Nashville girl he'd met his first week at Vanderbilt. He and his bride, Debbie, rented a carriage house in town, a few blocks from his office, moving out to the more spacious subdivision just before the birth of their second son. With its four bedrooms, playroom, and media room, the faux Georgian house sat at the end of a cul-de-sac, where the boys could ride bikes and play ball with their friends. Luke remembered the tobacco field that had been plowed under for this development, a place where he and a friend had shot crows with a .22 while drinking a six-pack of Pabst. You could still see the burlap balls from which the young dogwoods and boxwoods grew.

Luke wasn't one of those for whom southernness was a religion, for whom nostalgia was an emotion more primal than lust. When giving directions, he did not refer to landmarks that had disappeared years before—"Turn left up where the old Swann place used to be"—and he'd never owned a Confederate flag. His mother, after all, was a Boston Yankee, and above all else he was his mother's son—her firstborn, her spoiled confidant and surrogate. His younger brother had embraced his patriarchal heritage, particularly after Luke had left for prep school in the East. Though he returned only intermittently, it irked Luke to see the changes in his hometown and throughout the surrounding countryside—not only the unchecked development but also the fact that regional identity survived mainly as a tool of marketing, the way that their southern legacy was parodied even as it was getting paved over.

He'd gone through a brief period, his freshman year at Williams, of active apostasy. Returning for Christmas break, he'd announced his disapproval of the monument to the Confederate dead in the town square, but as his convictions mellowed, he had come to regard it as an authentic expression of historic memory, unlike the twin cannons sitting on spoked wheels outside the entrance to Battleground Meadows.

"Good to see the artillery is still in place," Luke said after they had exchanged the other formulae of reunion on Matthew's doorstep.

"Cain't never tell when them Yankees might sneak round again," Matthew said, exaggerating his drawl, which had always been thicker than Luke's, smiling serenely with that imperturbable, almost Buddhist mien of his, which caused many to underestimate his intelligence. He radiated an almost maddening sense of being at home in the world, or at least his own corner of it, and feeling comfortable in his skin. Taller and heavier than Luke, he was slow and deliberate in his physical movements and in his mood swings, traits that Luke associated with the South as much as with his brother's bearish solidity. Ashley buried herself in this bulk, wrapping her arms around him. Luke had always envied his ease with children, most especially his own daughter.

"Doesn't look like you're exactly in fighting trim," Luke said, patting his brother's belly, which had grown larger and softer in the year since they'd seen each other.

"Just storing some fuel for the winter. I expect I can still whup your ass on the tennis court."

"Uncle Matthew's just a cuddly bear," Ashley said. "Don't mind Dads. Anorexia is kind of like a religion in New York. Half the girls in my school are bulimic."

"We could use a little of that thinking down here," Nora said, patting her younger son's belly. In her value system, excess flesh was a moral failing, a sign of indolence. It was one of her unshakable prejudices; in addition to fat people, she disliked gum chewers, hunters, self-promoters, as well as cosmetics, public displays of affection, shopping, and dark, airless rooms.

"I guess skinny Uncle Luke won't be wanting any fatty fried chicken," Debbie said, smiling impishly. Marriage, motherhood, and a Talbots wardrobe had utterly failed to supplant Luke's first impression of his brother's wife in a cheerleader's uniform.

"We got sushi out to the mall now, bro." Matthew hoisted Ashley up onto his back as she giggled and pretended to resist. "Thanks to all them Japanese at the Nissan plant."

279

"It's actually really pretty good, Dad," Ashley said from her perch on Matthew's shoulders. "They even have *toro*."

For all his envy of her easy alliance with Matthew, Luke was pleased to see her in this affectionate, childish mode. "When we were growing up," Luke said, "there were only three kinds of fish around here—canned, cat, and sticks."

The six o'clock dinner hour chez Matthew was all clamor and spills: milk carton on the table, plastic glasses . . . arguments relating to table manners and homework, ominous references to starving children in other countries, the house's mod-con sterility ameliorated by the haphazard clutter of family life—the lacrosse stick leaning against the refrigerator, the PlayStation console, videos and discs atop the television set, the chess set on the dining room table.

Sasha had endured these meals over the years with the brittle forbearance of a princess visiting the cancer ward, whereas Ashley had always been delighted to participate in the unfamiliar ritual of parents and children dining together and to learn from her male cousins how to burp, blow milk out of her nostrils, and make a catapult of a fork. For her, this suburban middle-American sprawl was thrilling and exotic.

Davis, the fourteen-year-old, hunched over his plate at the kitchen table beside Ashley, and edited his succotash, separating the lima beans from the corn with his fork; his practice was to confront the horror all at once, eating the lima beans in one or two gulps after everything else was gone.

"Your dad used to do the same thing," Nora said. "Separate his vegetables into little piles and save them till the end." She'd pointed this out many times before.

"Whereas Luke was always sneaky about it," Matthew said. "Hide them in his pocket or slip them to the dogs."

"That sounds like Jackson," Davis said, aiming his tongue at his sixteen-year-old brother, who rolled his eyes, having reached the age where family life proved a constant torment.

"Not that he was really fooling anyone," Nora said, looking fondly at Luke.

Debbie's upturned nose seemed to twitch over her pursed mouth as she studied her mother-in-law, weighing the apportionment of maternal affection.

"Now he sneaks cigarettes," Ashley said. "He says he's going to the newsstand. But really he doesn't want Mom to know he smokes, so he can keep complaining about *her* smoking and feel superior."

Nora turned to the boys. "Your dad, on the other hand, would turn it into a big showdown, a battle of wills. He'd save the vegetables till the end and then he'd force them down in one bite, gagging and retching theatrically."

"That sounds about right," Debbie said.

"Did he puke?"

"One night," Luke said, "he Hoovered the broccoli and promptly threw it up all over the table. After that, I think they stopped insisting that he finish his vegetables."

Davis peered at him. "Did you make the rescue workers eat vegetables, Uncle Luke?"

"We didn't have many vegetables. Although there was a garbage man who was a vegetarian."

"Weird," Jackson said.

"He was actually a very interesting guy," Luke said, conscious of his own eagerness to convey, most especially to his brother, the demographic range of his new acquaintances.

"Did he smell?"

"Davis, don't be a snob," his father said.

"Do you still think Uncle Luke's a snob, Dad?"

Debbie blanched, looking across the table at her husband, whose attention seemed to be absorbed by a delicate operation involving his knife and the skin of his chicken.

"He always has," Luke said, stepping into the awkward silence. For the first time that night, he could clearly make out the white crescent scar on his brother's forehead, signature of a rock Luke had beaned him with one summer.

"Oh my goodness," Debbie said, rising from her seat. "Luke, I know you drink wine with dinner. And here I've forgotten." Theirs was the kind of household in which cocktails preceded dinner, while milk and iced tea accompanied it. "I've got some cheapo Tasmanian

281

chardonnay in the fridge—actually, I think we still have that bottle of Bordeaux you brought the last time you were here."

"Even if it wasn't mature then," Matthew said, "it's bound to be drinking well by now."

"I think I've been zinged by my little brother," Luke said.

Davis was puzzled. "What did you mean, Dad? How did you zing him?"

Ashley, the precocious city girl, got the joke. "He means that wine needs to sit around for a long time before it really tastes good and it's been forever since we were here. It's like—what, two years, Dad?"

"Not quite a year, actually. Gramps's funeral."

"Did you serve wine at the soup kitchen?" Matthew asked, changing the subject. "Lafite-Rothschild? Mouton?"

"Not even wine in a box, I'm afraid. There was a strange moment, the day after, when some of the guys broke into a bar and started carrying beer back to the site."

"You broke into a bar?" Davis asked.

"I don't know if they *broke* in, exactly. It was pretty chaotic down there. The normal rules were sort of suspended."

"I'm sure," Nora said, "the bar owner was happy to have you boys drink his beer."

"Can Uncle Luke come talk to my class about Ground Zero?"

"That's an interesting idea," Debbie said. "Maybe, if he has time before he goes back to New York."

"Did you see any dead people, Uncle Luke?"

"A couple," Luke said.

"Was it gross? Did you have to touch them?"

"I carried a couple of body bags. We passed them along the line until someone put them in a Stokes basket. Everyone stopped working and took off their hard hats."

"What's a Stokes basket?" Even Jackson was now intrigued.

"It's like a stretcher."

"Uncle Luke may not want to talk about this right now," Debbie said.

"Actually," Ashley said, "Dad gets a huge kick out of being the hero."

282

"I think your father's earned a little pride," Nora said, directing a hard look at Ashley, who in that moment discovered one of the limits of her grandmother's indulgence. "And you should be proud of him, too, young lady."

"We all are," Debbie said, standing up to clear the plates. "Just like we're proud of his brother, who's been the president of the Boys Club and chairman of the Cancer Society and a volunteer fireman for I don't know how many years."

"Indeed," Luke said, reminded that his sister-in-law was not as indiscriminately charitable as she might seem; she could not always stifle her sense of resentment that the spoiled firstborn, so she believed, basked in the sunshine of his mother's love, while his younger brother labored dutifully in the shadows, without the recognition and affection that were his due.

"Well, if it comes to that," Matthew said, "Ashley's mom has us all beat on the charity front."

"She's definitely queen of the benefit scene," Ashley said.

"What's the benefit scene?" Davis asked, clearly puzzled by the sudden change in tone among the grown-ups.

"It's where," Ashley said, now on a roll, "you get to show off your latest dress."

"Mom says Aunt Sasha spends more on dresses than we spend on everything put together."

Matthew glanced over at Luke, wearing a look of sheepish contrition.

"I certainly wouldn't dispute that," Luke said.

"Actually, she gets a lot of the clothes for free," Ashley said.

"Why does she get clothes for free?"

"Because," Matthew said, "she's a beautiful woman and the people who make the clothes think she's a good advertisement."

Luke couldn't help admiring his brother's courtliness. Observing Debbie's pinched expression, and Matthew's reaction as he took it in, he imagined that his brother would pay for this observation later. "Ashley," he said, "why don't you help your aunt clear the table."

Luke glanced back at his brother, who, seeing that Debbie's back was turned, put a finger to his ear.

"Brother Luke," he said, "I think I hear the brandy snifter calling."

"Maybe it's just a flirtation," Matthew said, splashing more brandy into Luke's glass.

They were holed up in the den, a Vanderbilt sports shrine–cum–Civil War museum. A refrigerator-size vitrine displayed the brittle gray-and-gold uniform of Captain Percy, an honored, if distant, relation who'd finished the war in a Union prison camp in Nashville. Matthew's comprehensive collection of Civil War literature shared the shelves with team photos, trophies, golf paraphernalia, and relics of the great battle fought a couple of miles down the road.

Debbie had disappeared upstairs with the boys after Nora and Ashley had left to drive back to the farm.

"When I talked to Sasha on the phone the other night—I've got to admit I haven't always been her biggest fan, but she sounded sincere. Between this crisis with Ashley and this other fucking thing—she sounded, well, contrite. Scared. She allowed as how you'd been going through a rough patch, but she said you two were pulling together for Ashley's sake."

"You always think the best of everyone," Luke said. "I love you for it, but still. If Sasha's scared, it's because Melman withdrew from the field. She showed her hand too soon."

"I'm just a country lawyer, bro. But I say wait and see how you feel when the dust settles. You've had a lot of shit come down the last year or so—starting with Dad getting sick. Unless you really think you can't forgive her."

"I can forgive her. I'm enough my father's son in that regard. But that doesn't mean I can live with her."

"Look, it's not exactly like I'm rooting for Sasha. You think it's been easy all these years? We put up with her for your sake. We know what she thinks of us."

He stood up, wobbling slightly, and raised his glass to some unseen entity. "We're just simple middle-class, small-town folk who don't know our ass from a hole in the ground. Yokels. You know who you married, bro? You married Jolene Cheatham. You went all the way to New York fucking City to find a girl just like the goddamn wife of our mother's supposed lover."

Luke sat up straight, indignant, then checked himself. "Whatever happened to Jolene?"

Matthew took a long swig of the brandy and reached for the decanter on the side table. "Have a dividend," he said.

Luke smiled. This was their father's term for a top-up, a piece of period slang that, for some reason, they both found hilarious.

"After her husband shot himself, you mean? She moved to Atlanta and married some poor sap who develops shopping centers. After old Duck went bankrupt and embezzled from his bank trying to pay her bills and assuage—now there's a word for you—*assuage* his guilt about sleeping with our mother. Don't tell me you're actually ready to talk about this?"

"Is that what you think happened?"

"It's what everybody thinks," Matthew said. "The collective judgment of the *community*. It's part of local lore. The biggest scandal since what's-her-name stabbed her husband with that samurai sword. The minister's wife and the banker. I always thought that was one of the things you were so eager to leave behind."

There was some truth in this, and he'd sometimes imagined that it gave his biography a certain veneer of tragic romance.

"Shit, I always thought you knew more than I did."

Luke found himself staring at a row of trophies, tiny figures brandishing golf clubs and footballs.

"Well, hell, whatever happened, Dad stuck it out with Mom and she stuck it out with him. I like to think she did it for us. We moved on, didn't we?" He clapped his arm around Luke's neck and embraced him bearishly. "Some of us further on than others of us."

Duck Cheatham's forebears had been among the first settlers of the area, having come across the mountains from North Carolina in the early years of the nineteenth century, the losing side in some fierce doctrinal schism within the local Presbyterian church. In the early years of the next century, Duck's grandfather had reestablished the prosperity of the Cheathams, which had evaporated in the war, by selling burial insurance to sharecroppers and factory workers around the mid-south region for a small Nashville company that eventually became the ninth-largest insurer, with him as president, and bought his grandfather's house from the descendants of the carpetbagger who had purchased it after the war, a redress of historical injustice that was viewed with regional pride. Everyone knew this history and Duck was well liked for wearing it, and his family's wealth, lightly. He had been sent north to prep at Deerfield and gone on to Williams, where, it was reported, he'd fallen in love with an Irish Catholic girl he met at a Mount Holyoke mixer. Neither family approved of the match, and after graduation he was called back to work at his father's bank, where he brooded on his options until he received a letter from his beloved announcing her engagement to a cousin of the Kennedy clan. After six months, during which he destroyed several automobiles and famously set fire to a suite at the Peabody Hotel in Memphis after a night of revelry—episodes that seemed out of character for the formerly sober and studious Duck Cheatham, if not for southern young men of means in general—he started dating a Vanderbilt girl he allegedly met at a bar in downtown Nashville. This, along with the fact that she modeled for a regional agency and her humble origins—her father owned a used-car dealership in Louisville—was more scandalous to some Middle Tennesseans than car wrecks or hotel fires. His parents were among those who didn't entirely approve of Jolene Colcott, but they feared they'd depleted their reserves of arbitrary parental authority and suspected they had only themselves to blame. So they swallowed their reservations and paid for the wedding, with its 350 guests, rather than trust the great event to the taste and budget of Jolene's middle-class parents.

Jolene Colcott, for her part, could hardly believe her luck, although it didn't take her long to accustom herself to the privileges and honors pertaining to the Cheathams. Everyone had to admit she knew how to dress the part, with her statuesque figure and her mannequin training; she made regular forays to Atlanta and even New York to outfit herself for the Swan Ball and the steeplechase and for the parties she threw at the Greek Revival mansion they bought—the old Hoover place—shortly after the wedding. And even her detractors would acknowledge, over tea at the Belle Meade Country Club, that she restored the place beautifully, stocking it with French and English antiques she'd purchased in New Orleans and Boston, Paris and London.

Jolene was determined to take advantage of every opportunity previously denied her. Duck settled in to work at the bank and Jolene became pregnant with the first of their two children. She also threw herself into the social life of the community, attempting to teach her neighbors what she'd learned on her trips to Europe. As if engaged in some fierce Darwinian battle, she tried far harder than was necessary to win the hearts and minds of Middle Tennessee, losing more than a few in the process.

The annual party the Cheathams threw before the steeplechase was legendary for its extravagance and odd innovations—such as serving the salad after dinner instead of before. It was at the Cheathams' that many of their neighbors first tasted Brie, although, unlike the salad, Jolene served it as an hors d'oeuvre, whether out of ignorance of Continental custom or in deference to local sensibilities. It was also here that many were introduced to the work of such artists as Rauschenberg, Jasper Johns, and Jim Dine. The pride of their collection was a late Picasso, *Le Déjeuner sur l'Herbe*. As a young man, Luke studied this drawing on many occasions, shocked and thrilled at the nudity, trying to interpret the transaction between the two primary figures by studying the expressions on their faces. Were they about to have sex? Or had they just had it? Was this drawing related in some way to the book *Naked Lunch*, which he had seen in a Nashville bookstore but had thus far been afraid to purchase? And who was the other figure behind them? Why were there *three* naked people?

When he saw this picture, Luke was struggling to emerge from his father's conventional Episcopalian worldview, dimly sensing a hidden pantheism in which sex was the connective tissue. Somehow, the drawing seemed to hold the key. And the Cheathams, with their sophistication, were inextricably linked in his mind to this quest for worldly knowledge. More than any of his mother's friends, Jolene excited his erotic interest.

The strange pictures on the Cheathams' walls were a source of consternation in some quarters, but most disapproved on aesthetic rather than moral grounds, finding them not so much obscene as simply unattractive. Ugly pictures on the wall! Salad after dinner! What next? Of course, Jolene, like all avant-gardists, would have preferred that her neighbors took offense rather than finding humor in her collection.

It would be difficult to say where her aestheticism left off and her materialism kicked in, but over the years, Luke began to imagine himself as the Cheathams' disciple, if not their lost son: He developed an interest in the arts as well as a taste for luxury, and was never hence quite able to make the distinction between the two, so that his ambitions oscillated between the poles of creation and connoisseurship. He took up painting and later, when Jolene and Duck started taking him to plays, he dreamed of acting and writing, though when he envisioned his future as an artist or an actor, it was always set in a grand house freighted with museum-quality treasures.

Duck's affection for Nora was so obvious that it seemed ridiculous, at least in the Cheatham and McGavock households, to think anything sub-rosa was going on. Their mutual love of the outdoors expressed itself in Saturday-afternoon rides around the countryside and was eventually consummated in their cofounding a land trust to preserve the farmlands and wetlands around Franklin and Nashville. Their love affair might have started before, or perhaps it grew out of the meetings and the field trips that their positions as co-chairs entailed. The environmental movement was still a freakish novelty in the South, where the chamber of commerce mentality was ubiquitous— every new factory or housing development greeted with boosterish enthusiasm by a population that had retained, more than a century after the fact, a collective memory of wartime ruin and colonial occupation.

. . .

Luke was thinking about their shared cause as, with the deliberate precision of the self-conscious drunk, he drove out through the gates of Battleground Meadows after assuring Matthew that he was fine to drive—past the repro artillery, past the tawdry multicolored light of the McDonald's, Wendy's, Krystal, Shoney's, Pizza Hut, Piggly Wiggly, and Kroger, past Logan's Road House, Circuit City, the Mattress Shack, and the Rite Aid, then through a dark buffer zone into his hometown, circling and saluting the monument in the square to the Confederate dead, whom he decided on the spur of the moment to visit, at what had once been the McGavock plantation.

He came out of the circle into Main Street with its dark Victorian storefronts, which over the years of his self-imposed exile had become a kind of souvenir mall, specializing in postcards, handcrafted quilts and hand towels, scented soaps and candles. Bearing left at Five Corners, he ran a gauntlet of churches, following the pike out past the railroad tracks, passing a bright white police car parked in the lot of an antique store, staring, paranoid, into his rearview mirror until turning with drunken exactitude into what had once been the entrance to the plantation, now a subdivision alongside the country club. But then the vista opened up and he saw in the moonlight not the house itself but the white-columned porches, free-standing against the invisible brick.

He stopped in front of the iron fence, behind which the remains were buried, state by state. His great-great-grandmother had supervised their reinterment on her own property the year after they'd been hastily interred on the battlefield, and kept a meticulous log of the names, which after a winter had already begun to fade on the wooden crosses.

He climbed out of the car, walked carefully to the gate and out among the gravestones, weaving through the narrow alleys separating Texas, Mississippi, Georgia, and Tennessee, each row marked by its state flag, wondering if they had anything to say to him.

Stepping into a depression where the ground had settled above a coffin, he pitched forward and fell facedown into the wet grass. Rattled but unscathed, he sat up between the white stones and listened, waiting for the dead to communicate. It seemed worth a shot.

No one else was going to tell him what to do, and surely these men knew something about duty and honor.

*Night is the beginning and the end.* A line from Tate's "Ode to the Confederate Dead." He was pretty certain that's the way it went. Which suggested there would be no communiqués from the dead.

First he heard the hollow oval query of a barn owl, later the plaintive bluesy call of a coyote. He flinched when an answering yelp came from within the graves, but gradually as the cry was repeated at more frequent intervals, swelling in volume as he crept among the mossy headstones toward its source, he finally recognized it, just before the couple came into view—the sound of human ecstasy.

# 28

The city hauled away the generator the day before Thanksgiving. Corrine arrived for her shift at Bowling Green to find Jerry taking down the tent with the help of two Guardsmen, the remnants of their provisions and equipment boxed and stacked in a wash of litter and yellow leaves, the aluminum skeleton of the jury-rigged shelter like the day-after wreckage of some sad carnival concession.

"So much for services rendered," he said. "They're shutting us down. Not so much as a 'Thanks for everything.'"

Corrine's regret was muted, largely a matter of sympathy for Jerry as well as nostalgia for the urgent, vivid days of September and the predawn intimacies of October. She was ashamed to admit that she was secretly relieved, that she'd grown tired of fattening and caffeinating bored cops and halfheartedly flirting with the homesick Guardsmen. As crisis had modulated to routine, as the delis and shops in the neighborhood had begun to reopen, as the fires had cooled and the jagged pile had sunk to ground level and the sky began to clear above the office towers and the bare trees in the park, her sense of mission had slowly evaporated. They'd stopped going to Ground Zero a couple of weeks ago, shortly before Captain Davies had returned to his precinct. The volunteers had fallen away one by one, and those who remained felt increasingly redundant. But out of stubbornness or guilt, Corrine had persisted in doing what she perceived as her duty, standing around in the cold, making sandwiches and filling the coffee urn between phone calls to Luke in Tennessee.

Surveying the remains of his kingdom, Jerry looked angry and bereft.

"It's a wonderful thing you did here," Corrine told him, wrapping her arms as far as she could around his considerable torso. "You should be proud."

"Then why do I feel so fucking empty?"

"It would be hard no matter when it happened. It's time."

"They could've at least waited until after Thanksgiving," he said, as if he'd envisioned some great communal gathering under the tent.

"I think it's time, Jer," Corrine said, then had a sudden inspiration. "Come to my house. I mean, if you don't already have plans for Thanksgiving."

Russell would probably be put out to learn she'd added a stranger to their table, but she couldn't bear to think of Jerry sitting alone in his apartment on Thanksgiving, and she had a feeling that his girlfriend had flown the coop, if indeed she'd ever been in it. It then occurred to her that he might find a kindred spirit in Judy Crespi, who had become something of a spokesperson for an organization representing the widows of 9/11. Only later did she realize, while she was walking home with her backpack full of peanut butter and jelly jars, that Jerry was a participant in the conspiracy of her secret life with Luke.

"I thought I was being altruistic," she said, talking to Luke on her cell phone an hour later as she trudged up Broadway. "But I think unconsciously I also invited him as a kind of surrogate for you. That's terrible, isn't it?"

"I think you invited him out of the goodness of your heart," he said. "It was the right thing to do."

"I used to trust my motives," she said. "That's the trouble. Now I don't know. I want to be a good person and I want to be with you, and I don't know how to reconcile those two ideas. I feel like Scobie in *The Heart of the Matter*. I can't stay and I can't go."

"I know I've said this before, but you know, you don't have to do anything, not right now. Just take care of yourself."

"I wish I could take care of you. What are you doing?"

"I'm sitting on the fence."

"Please don't say that."

"No, I mean literally. I'm sitting on a three-rail fence out in the pasture, watching my mother work with a pony and an eight-year-old girl with cerebral palsy. Equine therapy. It's her mission, her calling."

"Whereas, unlike your mother, basically, *I'm* the kind of person who'd be working with the little girl by day and fucking her father by night."

"He should be so lucky."

"Imagine what your saintly mother would think. I bet she'd think I'm the whore of TriBeCa."

"No," he said. "I don't think she's ever heard of TriBeCa. Anyway, I'm going to tell her about you this weekend."

"Oh God, are you sure?" This prospect panicked her, although she couldn't say whether she was afraid of his mother's disapproval or of the idea of a definite step being taken. "Look, I'm just outside the door. I'll call you later. I miss you."

Russell took the Jerry news better than she'd expected, still on his best behavior, as if, even with an imperfect understanding of the actual nature of the threat, he sensed by what a slender thread his marriage was suspended. Like some newly ordained Franciscan monk conducting a campaign of good works and penance, he came home straight from the office most nights, devised games and diversions for the kids, and took them to school in the morning while Corrine slept in. He'd become almost absurdly passive and pliable, the perfect wife.

Now he was enacting his role of Thanksgiving patriarch with

even more enterprise and certainly with more good grace than usual, rising at the crack of dawn on Thursday to start the turkey, an organic monster that he'd special-ordered from Dean and DeLuca and soaked in brine for twenty-four hours, pedantically explaining the virtues of the slow-cooking method when she finally joined him in the kitchen at nine. Two years ago, he'd been equally vehement about the fast-cooking method, lately espoused in the food section of the *Times*, smoking them all out of the apartment in the process. The memory made her nauseated, as did, at this early hour, the smell of the turkey roasting in the oven.

"Russell, please. You know I can't stand hearing you rhapsodize about food first thing in the morning. Have the kids eaten?"

"Of course."

"I hope you didn't just starch them up with waffles and crap," she said, immediately realizing how bitchy she sounded.

"We had oatmeal with dinosaur eggs," Storey volunteered from the couch, where she was viewing *The Little Mermaid* for the fifty-seventh time.

"So, I finally spoke to my rival," Russell said. "He called here a few minutes ago."

Corrine paused, steadying the coffee cup she was raising to her lips with both hands.

"Your who?"

"He called to see if he could bring anything."

"*Who* called?"

"The other man in your life. What's his name, Jerry. Sounds like a decent-enough guy. Very apologetic about barging in at the last minute."

"I hope you didn't make him feel like he was ruining your seating plan," she said.

"I was the soul of hospitality and welcome, as ever. I'll sit him next to Judy. Who knows—stranger things have happened."

"I'm not sure I'd wish that on him." Of course, she'd had the same thought the day before.

"She's not the same person, Corrine. Cut her a little slack. After all she's been through."

This had always been one of the things she loved about Russell, his belief in the basic decency of others. Inviting Judy for Thanksgiving had been his idea. Corrine would have liked to imagine that she'd been transformed by the loss of her husband, although she couldn't help feeling that there was a purely selfish and self-dramatizing quality to Judy's grief. In private, she seemed more than anything to be angry at Jim for having abandoned her, even as she took to the airwaves to extol his heroism and to demand her rights as a widow.

A few hours later, Russell was hauling the children out of the tub, drying them off while they thrashed and howled and pretended to try to escape, pumped up with holiday energy and the prospect of company. Corrine watched for a moment from the hallway as he tugged a brush through the stripes of Storey's hair while waving the dryer back and forth with his other hand. Why couldn't he have always been like this, she wondered, and what made him think it wasn't too late?

She went to answer the buzzer and then waited at the elevator, listening to its slow, rattling ascent, trying to summon her dormant sense of hospitality.

The door shuddered open, revealing Hilary and her beau.

"We're here," she said, presenting Corrine with a bouquet of orange and yellow chrysanthemums from the bodega. "You remember Dan."

"Of course."

A massive hand engulfing hers.

"Oh, go on, kiss her," Hilary said. "She's family."

He leaned forward clumsily as Corrine offered her cheek.

"We're very happy to have you, Dan." His awkwardness was almost painful to behold. She regarded him with a sense of wonder—a man who'd left his family for her little sister.

Without his cop's uniform, he could've passed for one of the musicians, actors, or bartenders she'd brought around over the years—dark, muscular, Black Irish handsome, with heavy eyebrows and bright blue eyes. She wondered if Hilary had helped him dress for the occasion, Thanksgiving in TriBeCa. In his jeans, his black leather jacket over a white dress shirt, he could pass for a member of the

Manhattan culture-producing class, although his vowels betrayed his origins across the river.

"And where are my little angels?" Hilary asked.

"Just grooming their wings."

"I've been boring Dan senseless, telling him all about the kids."

"Whaddya saying? I love kids."

On cue, they pattered down the hall, looking plausibly angelic in matching white shirts and gray flannel, hurling themselves at Hilary as Russell followed in their wake.

"Kids, this is Mr. O'Connor. He's a friend of Aunt Hilary's."

The children earnestly shook hands as their father lumbered up to join the group.

"Russell," Hilary said. "May I present my fiancé, Dan O'Connor."

Corrine noted that the man had the sensitivity to wince at this introduction—being, after all, still married.

Russell took O'Connor's hand.

"Dan O'Connor. A pleasure to meet you, sir."

"Russell Calloway."

"Are you really a policeman?" Jeremy demanded.

"Well, yeah, I am."

"He's got the most amazing stories from the street," Hilary blurted. "We're going to collaborate on a screenplay. Not the usual Hollywood cops and robbers crap, but the real thing about life on the narcotics squad. I've got a call in to Michael Mann—my friend Rowena works for him and he's coming to New York next week. Dan has a real storytelling gift—you should talk to Russell, honey; he's brilliant with story. If there were any justice, he'd be rich and famous. He edits all these Pulitzer Prize–winning authors."

"Do you have a gun?" Jeremy said.

"Well . . ." O'Connor directed a questioning look at Russell. "I don't know if—"

"I don't think it would hurt to look at it," Russell said, much to Corrine's annoyance.

O'Connor pulled aside his jacket to reveal a holstered automatic.

"Wow," said Jeremy. "Cool. Do you get to shoot it?"

"Only on the firing range," he said.

"Dan took me out there last week," Hilary said, squatting down to take Jeremy in her arms. "When you're older, maybe Dan can take you out to the range."

"Much older," Corrine said.

Hilary frowned. "Corrine doesn't let any toy resembling a weapon in the house. Which, if you ask me, just increases the lure of the forbidden. Trying to protect kids can backfire. It's like any kind of taboo—like making a big thing out of alcohol or s-e-x. In the end, it just makes it more attractive."

"What's s-e-x spell?" Storey asked.

"It spells never mind," Corrine said.

"No it doesn't."

She found Hilary's opinions on child-rearing comical, when she didn't find them intolerable, and she was mildly revolted by the look of cute complicity passing between Hilary and Dan.

"Can Aunt Hilary play with us?" Jeremy asked.

"I think Aunt Hilary probably wants to talk to the grown-ups."

"I'm always ready to play," Hilary said. "You know me." Showing Dan how easy, how good she was with kids.

"I've got a new Transformer," Jeremy told her.

"I love Transformers."

"You have to see the Fluffies," Storey said. "They have a tiny little turkey on a little table."

"The Fluffies," Hilary explained, "they're like fairies, with their own little house and furniture and their own tiny tea set, and they come out at night when everybody's asleep."

"One of the Fluffies is missing," Storey said solemnly. "His name is Bevan. We made a poster for him. A missing poster."

"Can I get you a drink, Dan?" Russell asked as Hilary followed the children to their bedroom.

"A beer, if you've got it," O'Connor said. "They're great kids."

"I hear you've got a couple yourself," Russell said, blundering in where Corrine would have feared to tread, though it occurred to her that he might be heading off the whole question of the kids' conception, about which Hilary had undoubtedly briefed him.

"Yeah, they're terrific," O'Connor said mournfully.

He reached into his wallet and showed Russell the snapshots, a newborn in a pink dress and a round-faced, gap-toothed boy with his father's eyebrows. "Bridget was born in June, and Brendan's three. Right now, she's not letting me see them. My wife—Mary-Margaret. She's taking it awful hard."

Even if Russell had left her for that ridiculous bimbo, Corrine thought, she never would have kept him away from his own kids. No matter what happened, they'd be civilized, the two of them, and protective of the children. She conjured up a vision of a future Thanksgiving, at which Russell and Luke debated the merits of a Napa cabernet sauvignon while the children vied for the attention of their new teenaged stepsister. The scenario, in all fairness and plausibility, demanded a new mate for Russell, so she generously bestowed on him a worshipful young thing, the kind of girl you saw at downtown poetry readings—or at coffee shops in Williamsburg—an aspiring memoirist or an assistant editor at *The Paris Review*, thirtyish and nerdishly pretty, with serious black rectangular-framed glasses. She would ask Corrine's advice about a Christmas present for Russell, and in the summer they would all move freely between two households in the Hamptons. Hilary, too, although in this fantasy the little sister was an infrequent visitor, having taken her act back to the West Coast. The fact that their family had been so unconventional from the beginning—starting with what Russell liked to call "the immaculate conception"—seemed to lend plausibility to this rosy scenario: a community of caring adults and well-loved children.

The loft was soon full of little people, a cacophony that might've been distracting to the childless guest but was for the most part inaudible to the parents until some note of distress or dissension broke out. Washington and Veronica arrived with pictures of the house they'd just closed on in New Canaan, Washington dressed city sharp, a black suit over a crisp white shirt, whereas Veronica seemed to be girding herself for their new life with a lime green cardigan over a red tartan wrap skirt. Not very good at reading fashion, Corrine couldn't tell if this was intended to be ironic or not, neosuburban or whatever. Jerry was like the bear who came to dinner, hulking in shyly with a six-pack of Heineken, overdressed in a too-tight suit and an old skinny tie from the eighties. Corrine introduced him to Judy, who arrived with her new Icelandic au pair in tow—a vanilla and butterscotch sundae of a girl, who introduced an undercurrent of suppressed hysteria that coursed among the middle-aged men and surfaced intermittently during the afternoon; Russell struggling heroically to appear oblivious . . . Judy in her beige cashmere twinset, confessing to Corrine that she never would've hired the girl if Jim were still around.

Corrine, meantime, was struggling against her own sense of disengagement, her mind drifting off to Tennessee, trying to picture his Thanksgiving. . . . She felt as if she were watching the scene in her own loft from a distance, from a great height; she kept finding herself parachuting into the middle of conversations.

"I really don't see why compensation shouldn't be based on the projected earnings of the victims," Judy was saying. "I mean, it only stands to reason."

Hilary flushed at this. "Do you really think a fireman or a cop's life is worth less than a bond trader's?"

"What are you—a fucking socialist?" Washington said, putting his arm around her, cleverly diffusing the situation by dragging her off for a private chat as Jerry took up her part of the argument.

Corrine took this opportunity to seek refuge with the children, involving herself in a game of house with the girls and then corralling them, with the help of Miss Iceland, for the children's sitting, trying to maintain order as Russell served and Jeremy initiated a burping contest. As a sign of his long-standing devotion, Dylan Crespi pressed mashed potatoes into Storey's hair. In between sobs for her ruined coif, Storey informed Dylan that there was a policeman in the house, a special friend of her aunt Hilary. Hilary's beau, chatting with Jerry in the no-man's-land between the adults and the children, heard himself invoked and came over to investigate the assault.

"Did somebody here call for a policeman?" he asked, kneeling beside Storey, who apprised him of the facts as Corrine extracted mashed potatoes from her hair. "Sounds to me like misdemeanor assault."

At which, the perp burst into tears.

When Judy Crespi rushed to the aid of her son, Corrine retreated to the bedroom and closed the door behind her, doubtful of her own patience, on the verge of some inappropriate outburst. She lay down on the bed, listening to the muted clamor, yearning for sanctuary. On a sudden impulse, she reached for her cell phone on the bedside table, feeling an illicit thrill as she dialed, the recklessness of the act rousing her from her torpor.

He answered with his public voice.

"I just wanted to tell you I missed you," she said.

"I echo that sentiment."

"If I said I wanted to fuck your brains out, would you echo that sentiment, too?"

"Absolutely."

"It would be more convincing if you actually said it."

"Let me just—"

"I know you can't talk. I shouldn't even be calling. I'm in the bedroom, hiding. I just needed to hear your voice. To verify my existence. I feel like I'm underwater. As hard as I try, I can't seem to connect to anything that's happening out there." She saw the doorknob turning, the shiny ring of brass worn through the paint, the door swinging open to reveal Russell holding a weeping Storey.

"*Here's* Mommy," he said.

Feeling her own face betraying her, she said, "Anyway, just wanted to say Happy Thanksgiving. We'll check you later."

Had Russell asked her who the hell she was talking to, she might have been relieved, but his failure to do so was as telling as the change in his demeanor—as if he had been running through an open field and suddenly collided with an invisible barrier. She even had her lie prepared, she was going to say she was talking to her mother. But he didn't ask.

"Your daughter was looking for you."

"What's the matter, honey?" she asked, avoiding Russell's gaze as she took Storey in her arms.

"Dylan's mom was yelling at Aunt Hilary's friend."

"It's a fucking madhouse out there," Russell said, staring down at Corrine's cell phone, inert on the bed.

Tempers had cooled by the time Corrine returned to the gathering, Dylan and his mother having been mollified with the promise of a ride in O'Connor's squad car. Corrine threw herself into the role of hostess, energized by fear and by an irrational hope that she might somehow stretch the day out and postpone the inevitable moment when she would be alone with Russell. She detected a new note of formality in his manner toward her, even as he became more sentimental and theatrically gracious—like a manic politician—under the influence of alcohol. He was particularly solicitous of Judy, whom he placed on his right at the table, and apparently had deputized as his drinking companion. Corrine wished Russell would stop monopolizing her so she could talk to Jerry. If she weren't uncertain of her own authority, Corrine would have taken him aside and scolded him about his drinking—they'd had these conferences before—but as things stood, she felt helpless as she watched him toss back the zinfandel. Sitting beside Corrine, the sober-as-a-judge Washington remarked, "Old Crash Calloway has strapped on his drinking helmet."

"I've never understood that expression. What does it mean?"

"Way back, when we first came to town . . . You remember William Holden, the actor? Big booze hound? About that time, he had a skinful and keeled over, banged his head on the edge of the fucking night table, and bled to death right there in his bedroom. So it became kind of a joke—when we were going for a night on the town, we used to talk about strapping on the William Holden memorial drinking helmet."

"I'm sure it must have been amusing at the time," she said, "but it isn't now. Maybe you could say something, Wash."

Washington responded with that special laugh of his that made one feel especially uncool. "If you understood anything about male friendship, or about drinking, you'd realize why I can't possibly honor your request."

"You sound like Russell."

"QED, babe."

"What are you two conspiring about down there?" Russell boomed from the other end of the table.

"Your husband's just the greatest fucking guy," Judy said, throwing her free arm around him as she raised the other in a toast. "I just hope you know that. He's been a real comfort to me in my time of need. Such an amazingly great, wonnerful . . . support."

Was it possible? Corrine wondered, looking at the two of them. Living in the double world of infidelity, she possessed a newfound respect for the unpredictable and treacherous capacities of the heart. She had acquired the melancholy wisdom of the guilty; Russell's frequent protestations of dislike for Judy might count as evidence to the contrary. She suddenly flashed on what he'd said that morning: "She's not the same person." How did he know she'd changed? Had he been comforting her in those long hours when Corrine was downtown? What could be more natural than to fall in love, or lust, with your fallen friend's wife? She'd heard of cases of that very thing among the firefighters. With a guilty thrill, she realized this scenario absolved her of her own sense of culpability, and provided the solution to her insoluble dilemma.

"You know he's drunk when he starts flirting with Judy fucking Crespi," Washington said drolly.

And all at once, as she examined them across the table, she dismissed this suspicion as too implausible, the fantasy as too convenient. "You don't think it's possible?" she said, trying to sound playful.

"Are you insane?"

"God, I don't know. Lately, almost anything seems possible. You in the suburbs, for instance."

"It's more a question of my children in the suburbs," he said. "I've had my time."

"Do you really think you can be happy sacrificing your own needs for theirs? I mean, if you're not happy, will you be a good father? Does being a parent mean you stop yearning and striving for your own happiness?"

"It's a question of balance, babe."

She never thought she'd see the day, Washington as the spokesman for moderation and family values.

This debate was interrupted by the dinging of Russell's fork on his glass as he rose to his feet in full toastmaster mode. "I'd like to give thanks that we're all here together today . . . on Thanksgiving. And I'd like us to pause for a moment to remember those who can't be with us. I'm grateful that you're all here, family and friends, and I'm sad . . . just so incredibly sad that Jim isn't with us. . . ." He paused, uncharacteristically at a loss for words. "I miss Jim. I miss him every day. All over the city, there are family gatherings like ours, with empty chairs, with missing loved ones. Out there"—he gestured toward the window, which had framed an oblique view of the towers—"there's a hole in the sky. And in here, in all of us, there's a wound that will never heal. I'm just glad we're together. And I'm also so goddamn angry."

Corrine was shocked at the sudden trickle of tears rolling down his face.

"I just hope," he continued, "we all remember to try to make our lives count, and appreciate what we have together, our friends and our families." He looked across the table at Corrine. "I realize now how easy it is to take your blessings for granted. I've been careless, some of you know . . . not proud to say I've made some careless mistakes along the way. Corrine knows. But I hope I've learned, hope I won't forget how goddamn lucky I am, how precious and fragile our time together really is . . . how goddamn blessed we are. I hope we'll all be together for many, many years to come."

A ragged tattoo of clapping filled in the silence that followed this speech as Russell slumped to his seat and Judy tearfully embraced him.

Corrine was stunned; even allowing for his intoxication, she hadn't seen him this emotional in years, not in the black days of September, not even in the days following the revelation of his sordid little affair, when he'd begged her forgiveness on pain of death, and she couldn't help feeling, guiltily, that the outburst had been triggered by a sudden intimation of impending loss.

Precariously attaining verticality, Judy stood, holding her fully refreshed glass aloft. "I just want to say you guys, Russell *and* Corrine, you guys are like family to me."

Corrine looked down at the table, at her plate with its opalescent slick of congealing gravy, embarrassed by this effusive exaggeration. She looked over at Jerry, wincing apologetically.

"It's been an awful time," Judy said, "a terrible, terrible . . ." She sobbed, struggling to regain some semblance of composure. "But I feel like I'm where Jim would want me to be. I know he's looking down on us." She glanced up at the ceiling and took a deft step backward, recovering her balance. "All of you . . ." She looked around, her eyes, glassy with emotion and booze, coming into focus on Hilary. "Even Hilary, who I know . . . You know what I know; I won't say it in front of the children. . . ."

Corrine instinctively checked the landscape . . . the kids all comatose in front of the television.

"But it's okay, it doesn't matter anymore. I've learned how to forgive. And . . . I don't know. I just wanted to say I love you all."

"Now I remember," Washington whispered in Corrine's ear, "why I quit drinking."

Judy was the last to leave, strewing declarations of love and fealty as her children stood wide-eyed, holding hands with the stoic au pair. Corrine felt terrible about Jerry, the first to leave, whom she'd barely had a moment to talk to. Russell opened another bottle of zinfandel, the ninth by her count, on top of the two bottles of champagne. The presence of the children circumscribed communication between the host and hostess as they cleaned up the physical wreckage. Corrine swept up the remnants of the glass from the wineglass Judy had dropped, while Russell loaded the dishwasher.

At 8:30, she announced, as if to a large audience, that she was going to put the kids down. She read *Madeline* for Storey and *Captain Underpants* for Jeremy. No matter that she had tried to raise them according to good feminist principles—from the start, they'd seemed determined to represent the most primitive of gender stereotypes.

"Why did Dylan's mommy fall down?" Storey asked after Corrine had turned out the bedside light.

"She was drunk," Jeremy said.

"Well, maybe she had a little too much to drink. But you have to understand, she misses her husband, Dylan's daddy. Sometimes she just gets sad."

"Because her husband died in the big fire," Storey said.

"That's right."

"Is Daddy sad?"

"I suppose so. Of course he's sad. Dylan's daddy was his best friend and he misses him."

"I'm glad Dad didn't fall down," Jeremy said.

"Is Daddy drunk?"

"Daddy doesn't get drunk," Jeremy said loyally.

"He gets happy," Storey said.

"Daddy's fine. Now go to sleep."


After performing her ablutions, Corrine slipped into the bed, grateful for the sound of the television in the main room. If she were lucky, he might pass out on the couch and the reckoning could be postponed for another day.

She was almost asleep when he climbed into bed and rolled over to lie against her, his sour breath—brandy now, atop the wine—rancid in her nostrils, hand stroking her thigh.

She pushed it away. "Russell, it's been a long day and you know I don't like to do it when you're drunk."

"You don't like to do it, period." He thrust a dry, rasping tongue in her ear.

"Russell, please."

He took hold of her left breast and squeezed it. "Are you getting it somewhere else—from someone else? Is that it?"

"Don't turn this on me," she said, trying again to dislodge his hand as he tried to force her legs apart. "You know why I haven't been sleeping with you."

"Are you saying there's no one else? That it?"

"Ow, Russell, you're hurting me."

He removed his hand and licked it ostentatiously.

"Stop it! We'll talk about this when you're sober."

"We've talked enough."

She tried to turn away as he rubbed his hand across her mons and probed roughly with his middle finger, thrusting his other hand beneath her ass and turning her toward him.

"Are you saving yourself for someone else?"

That was exactly what she'd been doing for almost two months now, though she hadn't admitted this to herself before now. But at the moment, she was protecting something far more basic. She couldn't believe this was happening. Struggling against him in earnest now, she was amazed by how strong he was, how ineffectual her own strength in comparison.

The battle apparently excited him, his erection growing and hardening against her thigh. She thrashed and tried to scratch at his face, but he pinned her arms back against the bed as he pulled himself on top of her. He could, she realized, overpower her. And if he did, she would never be able to forgive him. If he—she could hardly bring herself to think the word—if he *raped* her, she would have no choice but to leave him.

As she considered this, she suddenly stopped struggling. Yielding up her body, she tried to empty her mind so as to preserve two irreconcilable ideas—that she was surrendering of her own will, and that in resisting up to that point, she had remained true to Luke. She choked back her tears as he thrust his pelvis at her, probing with his cock between her legs, thrusting himself half an inch into her ass before he retreated and probed again.

The act itself took less time than its violent prologue, and when he rolled away from her, she lay rigid, determined not to move or to speak, imagining his postcoital remorse, calculating her moral advantage, contemplating the stark vista of her new freedom. Whatever she decided now, her decision would be unclouded by guilt or sympathy for Russell.

After twenty years of cohabitation, they had become experienced at ignoring elephants in the loft, and parenthood had only refined their skills at concealing resentments beneath the surface of domestic routine. A casual observer might have discerned a certain sheepishness in Russell's demeanor—something more than the chagrin of a hangover—when he finally staggered into the living area that morning, and a distinct chill in his wife's manner. The children, with their acute sensitivity to parental relations, responded to the tension with ostentatious displays of cuteness.

Corrine, for her part, was scrupulously correct with her husband, almost solicitous of his hangover. She even offered to cook eggs for him. The fact that Russell accepted her offer was a sign of abject contrition; Russell was absurdly prissy in his epicurism, and it was an old joke between them that she was unable to coddle eggs.

She had decided it would be easier to get through the holidays in a state of truce. It was surprisingly easy, she found, to be nice to him—much, much easier than she'd feared it might in the three hours that she waited for him to wake—now that it didn't really matter, now that she'd decided to leave him.

# 29

They traipsed out into the dewy pasture in the flat light of morning to catch the horses, tacked and trailered them, and set out for a farm down the road, as they had done so often before he'd left home.

"I think I'm in love," Luke said as he turned the Suburban out into the pike, taking a cigarette from his shirt pocket, knowing she would disapprove. He wanted to prevent himself from succumbing to the easy sentimentality of the occasion and to dilute her maternal sympathy, hoping to avail himself of a more objective vein of understanding and wisdom.

Predictably, she plucked the cigarette from his mouth and threw it out the open window, smiling at her own audacity. "Okay," she said. "Tell me about her. I guess we can assume she's a damn smoker."

"You'd like her. In fact, I think that's one of the things I liked about her, imagining your reaction."

"I always used to think you liked Sasha for the opposite reason."

"That's quite possible. She's kind of the opposite of Sasha."

"Good with children and animals, doesn't like to shop?"

This sudden burst of candor surprised him. "All of the above."

"Does she have a name?"

"Corrine."

"Wow," she said.

"Wow *what*?"

"The way you say her name."

He found himself pleased by this observation. So much, he thought, for playing to her objectivity.

"We met at the soup kitchen. No, actually, I met her before that, on September twelfth. I walked out of the smoking ruins and there she was. I can't tell you what it was like that day. It was like the world had come to an end. You can't believe some of what I saw down there. There was a woman with her face burned off. And suddenly there was this new face. It was like seeing Botticelli's Venus in the Uffizi, like the reinvention of the world. I actually thought, in my delirium, she might have been an angel. That sounds idiotic, I know, love at first sight, but everything since then has confirmed that flash of intuition, made me feel as if I've never really been in love before. And I can't go on living the way I've been living."

"Sounds like you've definitely made up your mind. Does she love you?"

"I think so." He contemplated another cigarette. "But it's not that easy. She's married—with two kids." He turned and looked across the seat to gauge her reaction—a slight pursing of the lips.

"I don't know what I could tell you, Luke, that you don't already know yourself."

He glanced back at the road. "You could tell me about you and Duck."

He was almost afraid to look across at her, so long had he saved the question, to the point he was almost convinced that he'd forgotten all about it. When he finally turned to look at her, she was nodding her head thoughtfully, looking straight ahead at the road.

"I suppose I'm glad you finally asked," she said as he turned into the service road to the farm, and the conversation was postponed until they backed the horses out of the trailer and mounted up.

"Let's follow the fence line out to the trail along the ridge," she said, pulling her hair back from her face and clipping it behind her. "Are you sure you want to hear this?"

"I think it's time."

"Don't let Billy do that," she said when his horse leaned over to chew the top of the fence rail. "He's a cribber."

He wrestled the gelding's head away from the fence. "If you'd been as much of a disciplinarian with me as you are with horses, I might've turned out better."

"You turned out fine," she said impatiently, as if she were accustomed to defending him, and tired of having to do so. "Your father and I thought so. I'm sure Corrine would agree."

He liked the sound of her name on his mother's lips, which seemed to confirm his instinct that they would approve of each other.

"You raise horses to accept bondage and service. You raise children so they can eventually run free."

This was such a generous notion, so genuine an expression of her beliefs, that he didn't have the heart to parry it with the more sophisticated notion that children grew up to become slaves of the same imperatives that bound their parents. "Did *you* ever think about breaking free?" he said as they trotted along side by side.

"You mean did I ever consider leaving your father? Of course."

"Did you love him?"

"Duck? Or your father?"

"Either. Both."

"You surely know I loved your father. If nothing else, I'd hope you're certain of that." She regarded him with a censorious frown, as if he'd crossed a line—as if to say that flippancy has its limits.

"Did you love Duck?"

She seemed to consider this as they approached the back gate of the pasture. "Yes," she said. "I did. I truly did. If I hadn't, I never would have let it go so far."

He dismounted to open the gate, pausing with his hand on the latch.

"It would take a long time to explain how that happened, how I let myself do that. I always wanted to tell you, but I felt that if I did, it would be betraying your father—further betraying him, I mean. And I'm not sure even now that I'm willing to do that. But I can tell you when it changed, when I decided that I couldn't leave your father. Or rather, that I wouldn't."

"When?"

Her body seemed to deflate slightly, her posture to deteriorate. If she'd been standing beside him, on the nibbled-down pasture, rather than six feet above him on a horse, he would have made some physical gesture of comfort.

"You were in the house that day, weren't you?"

A year or six months ago, he might have protested that he didn't know what she was talking about. "Yes," he said. "I was."

"In the bedroom?"

He nodded.

"I always hoped and prayed that I was wrong. I remember it as if it were yesterday, coming into the house after saying good-bye and finding the peanut butter and jelly on the counter, the glass of milk on the table. And then I remembered hearing something in the closet, earlier . . . thinking for a moment that someone was there. This is terrible, really. . . ." She paused to wipe at the corner of her eye. "At that moment, I hoped it was Matthew. That he was the one. I prayed it wasn't you, my firstborn. My favorite—there, I've said it. Everyone else was always saying it. It's true, I suppose. But when you came down to dinner that night, I could tell. I so wanted to pretend that it wasn't true, but we were so close, I could read you like a book. At least I could until that moment. And everything afterward confirmed that you'd . . . you'd seen us."

She blushed, all these years later, at the memory. As if in sympathy, the mare whinnied and shook her head.

"And I was so mortified and so ashamed of myself. When I felt you turning away, I tried to convince myself that it was adolescence, a natural process, a boy pulling away from his mother. Wishful thinking, though I suppose it would've happened anyway, to some extent. We couldn't have stayed that close. The ironic thing is, I wanted you to go north to prep school, to get out of this poky town and out of the South, to play and win on the big field. But I didn't want you to do it because you wanted to get away from me."

He lifted the latch and walked the gate backward, holding Billy's reins, nudging the gelding's wet snout—an operation that in its relative simplicity seemed to emphasize the complexity of processing and addressing this information. He looked up at his mother on the Arabian, silhouetted against the crisp blue sky, a tableau that was suddenly, achingly familiar. "The best days of my life," he said, "were the days I pretended to be sick, and you pretended to believe me, and I'd stay in bed reading while you came up to check on me, until we agreed I'd somehow recovered enough to go out riding with you."

"I thought you must've forgotten," she said.

He dodged around behind Scheherazade and slapped her flank, urging her through the gate.

"Does she ride?" Nora asked.

"Does who ride?"

"The love of your life."

"She used to be on the circuit, hunters and jumpers. She's from the North Shore."

Her face brightened at these simple phrases from her native dialect.

"Let's see if you can still ride," she said. "Race you to the ridge."

"We used to come up here," Nora said, halting at the top of the ridge ahead of him, looking down on the black ribbon of the pike bisecting the yellowing pastures and the tributary roads with their ganglia of housing developments and industrial parks. "The view was much prettier then, before all the building."

"I remember."

"That was one of the things that we had in common, loving this landscape, and trying to save it. It started innocently, like I suppose these things always do. Your dad and Jolene were happy not to be dragged outdoors over hill and dale. At first, I was able to talk to Duck because it seemed so . . . well, *because* he wasn't my husband. And he was a good listener. I never really felt as if your father was entirely listening. He had everything worked out, all the great questions of life, God and sin and redemption, and I never felt I could contribute anything. And I certainly couldn't tell him I didn't share his faith, that I wasn't even sure I believed in God, at least not the God he believed in. Duck had some of the same doubts and questions and he did seem to care what I had to say. The conversation went on for years. I loved that he didn't care about his family's money or Jolene's social ambitions any more than I did. He told me he always wanted to be a teacher, either that or a vet."

"I guess I always assumed you were swayed by his more obvious charms, the things Dad didn't have."

"You mean *money*?" She seemed vastly amused by this supposition. "Well, I'll admit I loved watching him play polo."

"Well, yes, money and everything that went with it." Luke pressed on, even as he started to suspect the weakness of his case. "His worldliness and sophistication, all the trappings of the good life."

"I think those were the things *you* admired him for, sweetie. Why else did you follow in his footsteps, all the way to Deerfield and Williams. Even into banking, for God's sake. I always thought that was a little ironic, Luke, because he hated the bank."

Of course she was right. Duck had always been an attractive alternative to his distant, pious father—even after Luke had discovered their secret. Perhaps *especially* afterward. It occurred to him, not quite for the first time, that he had wanted to be like the man she loved, but apparently he had chosen the wrong qualities to emulate.

"I might have found those things appealing, though I don't think I loved him until I realized he didn't really care all that much about them."

The horses were restless, shifting positions and shaking their heads in some primitive power struggle, snorting, eyeing each other warily. Billy suddenly thrust his head forward and nipped at the mare's flank. Luke yanked on the reins as Scheherazade wheeled away, whinnying in protest.

"The law of the jungle," his mother said, "is so much simpler." She started her mare down the other side of the ridge, into the hollow, glancing back over her shoulder. "Let's have our breakfast down by the stream."

They tied the horses at the edge of the clearing, a wedge of moss and grass in the woods, which the deer had grazed short, and walked down to the bank where the water tumbled six feet over a ledge of shale into a pool just large enough to submerge a midsize car. A nest of fresh Budweiser cans in the crotch of a cedar beside the bank completed the pastoral scene.

Nora sat down on the carpet of yellow-green moss and fished a pair of sausage biscuits from her pockets and handed him one—a ritual almost as old as he was.

"You must have come here with him," he said, pitching a stone into the pool.

"Not at first," she said. "I saved this spot. I always thought of it as our place, yours and mine."

"That's okay." He nodded at the beer cans, sitting down beside her and unwrapping his biscuit. "I think it's been discovered."

"It was a long time before I realized I'd fallen in love, and when I did, I tried to break it off. But it wasn't so easy. The ironic thing is that I'd never really had a big sexual appetite. Your father used to complain about it, but I never really got it. Never felt it. I was raised to think that sex was something a woman endured. It was the fifties. I was a virgin when I married your father. I saw *From Here to Eternity* that year and didn't even suspect Deborah Kerr was a prostitute, because I didn't know what a prostitute was. Your father wasn't exactly a prude, but he did believe in chastity. We never got any further than what was then known as making out until our wedding night. And I can't say I saw any fireworks go off that night. I put up with it because I loved him, because it was part of the deal. My primary impression was blood, sweat, and pain." She paused. "I'm sorry, is this more than you want to hear?"

"Jesus, I don't know," Luke said. "I'm kind of morbidly riveted."

"And then, I don't know, news of the sexual revolution reached us here, about five years after the rest of the country, and Jolene formed that women's consciousness-raising group. How ironic was that? Jolene encouraging me to get in touch with my body and my womanly needs. And suddenly one day, I did. My body called me, and for the first time it seemed like a local call."

The familiar and soothing sound of the water was like distant background conversation—the higher voices of the shallow riffles, the deeper murmur of the stream plunging from the ledge into the pool.

"It was as if I woke up and understood what all the fuss was about. Maybe it was just a natural process. I was thirty-three or -four, just the age that the books Jolene was lending me said a woman comes into her sexual maturity. Well, I was ready to roll, but your father seemed to have lost interest. Maybe it was his bypass operation. Maybe it was age. Maybe it's impossible to really maintain desire for the same person after a certain number of years. At any rate, it wasn't happening. But Duck had been waiting all those years. And conveniently, I suppose, I was already in love with him." She paused, stood up, and walked down to the bank, rinsing her hands in the water. "So. How's the sex with Corrine?"

Even in the context of the current conversation, this question, coming from his mother, was shocking. "Who said we'd had sex? Or that I'd want to discuss it with my mother if we had?"

"Oh, come on. We're both adults. Hell, I'm an old woman. I don't have time for decorum. I wish I'd had less of it over the years. Funny—that's one of the things I used to like about the South. The sense of decorum, the exquisite formality of the social code. So much sugar on everything. I thought it was all just lovely. But in the end, you realize you're all alone in a double bed, where a little more sincerity might've served you better. Your father and I—there were so many things we should have said to each other. At the end of the day, I'd like to feel I didn't make the same mistake with you."

"I don't really know how to describe it."

"Well, try."

"Fireworks."

"Better than Sasha?"

"I don't think I want to do a comparative analysis. It's just different."

"I always imagined Sasha was great in bed."

"I'm not even thinking of dignifying that with a reply."

"After all these years—still the southern gentleman."

"You're my *mother,* for Christ's sake."

She turned to face him. "That must be one of the things she loves about you. It was a big part of what attracted me to your father. The accent, of course. And those wise, sleepy eyes. But his courtliness, his old-fashioned sense of family. That sense of knowing where he came from, and honoring it."

"But it obviously wasn't enough," he said, standing up and walking down to her.

"No, that's not true. You're old enough by now to know that love isn't so simple, that you can love more than one person. Certainly you can desire more than one. You seem to forget that I stayed with your father. I thought about leaving him, but in the end, I chose to stay. And I know I made the right choice."

"Would Duck have left his family for you?"

She hesitated. "He wanted to, yes."

"So it was your decision."

She nodded.

"Because of us."

"Oh, God, there were so many reasons, Luke. I'm not sure I can sort it out after all these years."

"And you don't regret it?" He was looking for some lesson he might apply to his own life.

"A part of me has missed him every day since. I miss the romance, the passion, the intensity of feeling so alive. But that would've faded. It always does. But there's something else, something your father understood. He asked me flat out once if I wanted to leave, and told me he'd still love me if I chose to go. Loving isn't the same as wanting, Luke. And it's certainly not the same as having. It's not about desire and self-fulfillment. In the end, it's about wanting what's best for the other person. It's about giving and even, sometimes, letting go. Sometimes I think love is more about renunciation than possession."

His dissatisfaction must've been visible to her, because she quickly added, "I'm just saying, if you love her, and the choice is yours to make, try to do what you think is best for her."

Then she looked at her watch—a plastic thing, black and white, the sight of which made him self-conscious about the expensive piece of hardware on his own wrist, a Rolex Yachtmaster, which he had once imagined to be a tasteful and masculine accessory. "I've got a session at eleven," she said. "We'd better get going."

The little girl arrived with her mother as they were unloading the horses.

The dogs, previously engaged with barking and harrying the horses, rushed off to greet the white Suburban crunching up the driveway.

"That will be Celeste," Nora said. "I don't think you've ever met her. She's five, though you'd never guess it. Subdural hematoma at birth. She has some movement in her arms. Talk about your angels. I don't know if she'll ever walk, but I wouldn't be a bit surprised if she just up and flies someday." Nora delivered this fantastic prediction in a dry and clinical tone. Whatever modicum of sentimentality she'd been apportioned in the beginning had been worn away over her years of working with the handicapped, like the fuzz from a peach, without eroding the firm core of hope and human sympathy.

Luke carried the tack back to the barn while his mother went out to greet the visitors. In equine therapy, Nora had found her calling. If she was more attuned to the horsey world than the human, as her family sometimes suspected, she'd discovered this perfect point of intersection between the two when she read an article about the Feldenkrais Method and immediately started working with a paraplegic niece.

The idea that there might be a sympathetic communion between the bodies of a horse and its rider struck her as tautological. After a year, her young patient took her first step on crutches and word spread across the state. The local hospital began referring parents, who knocked on the door, carrying damaged children, like pilgrims searching out the rumor of a rural saint.

Emerging from the tack room, he watched them approach across the pasture, the young mother with an unearthly child in her arms, the girl's body proportioned like that of an infant, her torso and frail limbs dangling like an afterthought from the skull, with its wispy halo of hair.

"Celeste, Ronnie? This is my son Luke."

With her hand cradling the girl's head, the mother directed her daughter's gaze at Luke. In contrast to the helpless body, her eyes were animated with vivid curiosity.

"Hello, Celeste."

She worked her shiny lips, calling forth cheerful, birdlike syllables of greeting.

"Celeste is riding Little Jimmy Dickens," Nora explained.

The very name evoked a squeal of recognition from Celeste.

"May I watch?" Luke asked.

Another seemingly happy response. "She'd love to perform for you," her mother said, interpreting her daughter's response.

He was sitting on the fence along the side pasture, watching as Nora walked her on the shaggy pony, when Ashley, groggy and stiff from her teenage slumber, climbed up on the railing beside him. Grateful for her company, he decided not to tax it with speech.

Basking in the late-fall sunlight, he risked slipping an arm around her waist. She adjusted her position and laid her head against his shoulder. When he glanced over at her, he saw that she was crying. He pulled her closer.

She sniffled and buried her head in his shoulder. "Oh, Dad, I feel like such a loser."

"We all do, honey."

"How can you say that? You have everything." She freed herself from his arm and slipped over the back side of the fence.

"Let's take a walk," he said, jumping down beside her.

She nodded tearfully. "That little girl," she said.

"I know."

The horses in the back pasture raised their heads to observe their approach as they walked out behind the barn.

"I don't want to be a selfish bitch," she said. "I want to be a good person, like Gran."

"You've got her blood in your veins. And you are a good person."

"I don't know how you can—"

"I can say it because I believe it. Of course I'm biased. The thing you might not realize is that I'll still love you, no matter what you do. Although I hope you won't push that proposition to the limit."

"You could really forgive me?"

"I already have."

She buried herself beneath his arm. He held her and looked out across the brown fields, watching a hawk circle the pasture beyond the fence line.

"You know," she said finally, when they started walking again, "I thought it was pretty cool that you quit your job."

"I thought you were annoyed to have me hanging around the house all the time."

"Yeah, well, I was." She kicked at a steaming pile of manure wreathed in a cloud of tiny flies. "I want to stay here," she said.

"What about school?"

"I could go to the high school with Jackson and Davis. And it would just be for the rest of the school year. Next year, I'll be at boarding school anyway, if I get accepted."

"Well, your mom and I haven't quite decided on that one." This was a reflex. He realized as he said it that in his imagination he'd already taken up residence with a woman other than Ashley's mother; his reluctance to send her to boarding school, as she and her mother wished, had been based on the myth of an intact family. But in the wake of this unexpected reconciliation with his daughter, he was reluctant to concede to this plan, even when it so blatantly served his selfish interests.

As if she could read his mind, she said, "I mean, come on, are you and Mom really going to stay together?"

He was surprised and grateful in equal measure that she had so casually broached the subject.

"I've been wanting to talk to you about that. How would that make you feel if Mom and I weren't together?"

"It's not like half my friends' parents aren't divorced."

"That's not the same as your own parents divorcing."

"I've heard them on the phone, Dad."

"Heard whom?"

"Oh, come on. Who do you think? Mom and Bernie. It's not just sex. He's been giving her financial advice. I mean, sure, I wish things could be like they were a thousand years ago when I was a little kid and we used to come here for Christmas and Fourth of July and you guys still acted like you loved each other. But it's not. That's one of the reasons I want to stay here. I know you and Mom don't think Uncle Matthew and Aunt Debbie are the most exciting people on the planet, but I like them and I like it here. The high school's supposed to be one of the best in the state, and it's just for the rest of the school year and I'd have Jackson and Davis to show me around."

"Are you sure you could be happy here? Big-city girl like you?"

"It's not so bad. Davis is in this speed-metal band and he says maybe I could do some singing. I could help Gran with her therapeutic work. She's been showing me some stuff, and I really think it's something I'd be good at. Not to mention that I'd be safer," she said. "I mean, the drug scene isn't exactly rampant here, and Franklin, Tennessee, has got to be pretty near the bottom of the hit list for the terrorists."

"Is it because you feel ashamed to go back?"

She kicked at a clump of fescue. "It's not just that."

"What do you think your mother will say?"

"Speaking of being ashamed."

"I don't think you give her enough credit."

"It's nice that you're a gentleman, Dad, but Jesus, don't be a schmuck. Don't you think she'll be relieved to have me out of the way? I could visit her on weekends. And you could write here. Or do whatever. It's not like you have any pressing reason to be in New York."

Somehow, even as he'd been warming to this plan, he'd failed to fully consider his own part in it. "You're going to have to follow through on your treatment," he said.

"There's a place in Nashville," she said eagerly. "It's supposed to be really good—all the country-music people swear by it. Johnny Cash used to go there. I could do outpatient therapy after school. Gran and I already looked into it. And I could help her out with the farm—work with the kids and the horses. I mean, don't you think that's a lot more useful than hanging out at Bethany's house and Bungalow Eight?"

"When did you ever go to Bungalow Eight?"

"There's a lot you didn't know, Dad."

"I know."

"Like the last time I went to Bungalow Eight, who do I run into but Mom. She's with, like, Courtney Love and that English painter Damien Hirst. Great! Just when I'm getting old enough to go downtown. I got out of there before she spotted me. I was with Amber and this older guy—"

"Hohenlohe."

"Yeah, Anton. I'm not even sure she would've minded all that much, but partying with my mom at the next booth isn't my idea of a great time. And I'm thinking, Great, now that I'm finally getting out and having fun, my mom's having some second childhood, so I have to, like, call up all the cool places in advance and see if she's there before I go out every night. Talk about a small world. I mean, how am I supposed to feel when she's like Ms. Social Queen and all the men act like they want to, you know, sleep with her? And *she* acts like that might be okay. I don't know how you put up with it, actually. Except you weren't really around enough to notice before. And now she's—"

"Ashley," he said. "I don't want you to say anything else about your mother. You don't need to. Let's just leave it, okay?"

"Okay."

"As you said, I wasn't really around much before."

"So here's your chance," she said.

# 30

The pre-Christmas lunch at "21" was a family tradition, one that Sasha was determined to observe this year, despite Ashley's objections. The mother's enthusiasm, like the daughter's reluctance, was based on the public nature of the venue, "21" being a kind of clubhouse for the tribe. It was obvious to both Luke and Ashley that Sasha was eager to make a show of unity and concord. "It's *especially* important this year," she'd insisted when they discussed it on the phone before the two of them flew back from Tennessee.

"It's *so* bogus," Ashley concluded. "Like if you go through the motions, everybody's supposed to pretend everything's normal. We can all pretend I didn't go to rehab and you and Mom are still the poster couple for *W*. It's like Katie Cathcart's mom's big Fourth of July party in Southampton, remember? How she went ahead with the party and said Mr. Cathcart was in Europe, even though everybody knew that he'd tried to hang himself in the bathroom two days before the party and he was lying in a bed in Lenox Hill Hospital with rope burns after the maid cut him down."

"You heard about that, did you?"

She turned her head with an air of heroic exertion and rolled her eyes. "What do you think—we just talk about hooking up and homework?"

"No, actually, that particular illusion has been pretty well shattered over the last few months."

As he drove in from the airport, the sudden sight of the skyline etched against a milky sky filled him with anticipation and melancholy, all of its rich personal and historical significance reduced to a vague melancholy shot through with a single yearning. Even the absence of the twin monoliths, and the ghostly smudge over the tip of the island, seemed inextricably linked in his mind with Corrine.

"It's weird, isn't it?" Ashley said, gazing out the window of the Town Car. "I never really noticed them until they were gone."

Shortly before noon, they arrived at the apartment, where Sasha's assistant informed them that she was running a few errands after her Pilates class and would meet them at the restaurant. Luke, relieved that their first encounter would take place in public, retreated to the library, closing the door behind him.

Corrine picked up on the sixth ring, the one just before it went to voice mail.

"I'm here," he said.

"Wait a minute. . . . No, honey, the blue one. I'm sorry, let Mommy get it."

"I hate that I can't just come to you now."

"I hate it, too. . . . Jeremy, stop that right now!"

"But I guess that's out of the question."

"Mommy doesn't hate anyone; she's just talking to a friend. *Hold on.*"

He waited as the din receded.

"Oh hell, I'm sorry. Where are you?"

"I'm at the apartment."

"It's almost worse, knowing you're so close."

324

"I know."

"I can't get away until three. And I have to be back by five. Kid Christmas thing."

"Maybe I could meet you downtown. It will give us more time. I could get a room at the Grand."

"I don't know, I think that would almost be harder." In a whisper, she added, "If I take my clothes off, no way am I going to make it home on time. You're going to have to wait till tomorrow night. Gotta run—I'm hearing major combat out there. Meet me at Evelyn's. Around three-fifteen. Love you."

"This should be fun," Ashley said drolly, as they drove down Fifth in the cab, passing the skating rink, the Plaza looming on one side, FAO Schwarz on the other.

Shoppers and tourists swarmed the sidewalks, but for Luke the Christmas spirit had yet to kick in. "Let's just try to keep your mother happy," Luke said.

"You wait. I guarantee you the first thing she'll say is I've gained; then she'll make some crack about southern cooking."

"You look great," Luke said. Although it occurred to him that if she'd wanted to court her mother's approval, she would've worn something a little dressier than a turtleneck over cargo pants and those big Eskimo-style boots—Uggs. He'd almost said something, then selfishly decided to leave the provocation intact; he cherished his new intimacy with his daughter and was unwilling to squander his capital. For his part, he'd changed into his old uniform: a bird's-eye suit from Dunhill; a spread-collared shirt with red, white, and green stripes that he thought of as his Christmas shirt, and a solid red Charvet tie.

Shawarma, the official greeter, shook Luke's hand and steered them gently toward the coat check. "Mr. McGavock, Miss McGavock, we haven't seen you lately."

Luke felt that there was an elegiac note to the occasion—as if somehow this were to be his last such visit. Coats safely checked, Shawarma led them the few short steps to the desk, where Bruce, the severely tailored, thin-lipped captain, greeted them and led the way into the front room, where a waiter pulled out their table, which was jammed up against its neighbors. Space was at a premium here in the front room, where the term *rubbing elbows* became literal and where those unfamiliar with public transport experienced at least a simulacrum of its intimate charm.

"You want the inside?" Luke asked.

Ashley shook her head, choosing to have her back to the room, the next best thing to being absent, leaning back in her chair to take in the ceilingscape.

"Boys and their toys," she said, shaking her head at the overhead collection of miniature planes, trains, trucks, boats, and sports memorabilia that commemorated the empires and accomplishments of patrons past and present.

"What does that mean, exactly?"

"I don't know. It just makes you think that maybe there's not much difference between men and boys."

Luke took in the crowd, the overfed men in their Savile Row suits, the svelte women spangled with gold and gemstones, all bearing gifts—fat robin's egg blue boxes from Tiffany's and flat black boxes from Gucci sitting on the tables and piled beside the chairs. He waved to Charlie Braithwaite, a colleague from his Morgan days. It all seemed a little unreal to him, like some tableau from the distant past; the center of Luke's city had shifted south, to a downtown loft he'd never seen but which he'd measured and furnished in his mind, to a bar on Ninth Street called Evelyn's, where they had trysted before and where he would be meeting her in two hours. His current surroundings came into sharper focus when he spotted Casey Reynes at a table of blondes in the middle of the room, sitting between Nina Griscom and Patricia Duff, rising as she spotted him and bouncing over.

"Hello, Luke, Ashley. You're looking wonderful, sweetie. I didn't know you two were back."

Luke did his best to rise, pinned as he was behind the table. "We just got in," he said, mildly fearful that some indiscretion would escape Casey's carmine lips. "Sasha's joining us. The annual Christmas lunch."

"Isn't it festive?" she said, gesturing around the room. "Ashley, you look . . . super. Amber will be so happy to see you. You must call her."

Ashley nodded miserably, having already announced her intention to avoid her friends for the duration of the visit.

"Come over and say hello to the girls when you get a chance," Casey said to Luke, fluttering her hand in farewell.

"That's exactly why I didn't want to do this," Ashley said, sucking on a bread stick.

"She means well."

"She doesn't even have a clue," Ashley said.

"Did I ever tell you my dad brought me here, the first year I was at Deerfield?" He had, of course, but he was groping, and Christmas-time allowed for formulas and bromides; at any rate, she seemed inclined to indulge him.

"I miss Grandpa Mac," she said.

"It was a kind of rite of passage in our family. Your great-grandfather used to come here when it was a speakeasy. Dad always ordered the chicken hash, which his father had always ordered. I ordered the steak tartare just to be different and because a character in some sophisticated novel I'd read had ordered it and I remembered the name. When my dad asked me if I knew what it was, I said I did, which wasn't true, so he held his tongue. They brought a plate of raw beef to the table and I choked the whole thing down, then went to the bathroom and threw it all up. I realized later that he must have known, but he didn't say a thing."

"You never told me that part of the story."

"Later, when the choir came around to sing carols, I thought it was all kind of corny. Dad singing 'Hark the Herald Angels Sing.' And then the choir sang 'Dixie'—you know how they do sometimes—and when Dad stood up, I was so embarrassed, I wanted to crawl under the table. I thought I'd die of mortification. Here we are at the most sophisticated restaurant in New York, and Dad's standing up for the old Confederate anthem."

"What did you do?"

"Nothing. I slid low in my banquette and pretended I didn't know him."

"That was kind of creepy of you."

"I'd think my teenaged daughter, of all people, might empathize with my creepy teenage self."

"Wrong."

"It was the sixties. Well, the seventies. Close enough. Neil Young was singing 'Southern Man.' Peter Fonda had been blown off his chopper by southern rednecks."

"Your dad was cool. You told me yourself he was all involved with civil rights and stuff. I don't know why you're so ashamed of being from the South."

"I'm not ashamed."

"What's the matter?" she said, turning around, following his gaze, only to see Bernie Melman standing in the doorway with his wife and daughter. "Oh fuck."

Luke was too distracted to chastise her; as the Melmans were easing themselves into the front booth while accepting the hearty obsequiousness of the staff, Sasha appeared in the doorway, an arm's length away—a potential collision had Bruce not been chatting with the billionaire.

A hush descended like snow, almost imperceptibly at first, as Sasha took them in, and gradually whitened the room. Luke couldn't help being impressed with how she followed through, stepping forward rather than retreating, kissing Caroline, Melman's daughter by his first marriage, on both cheeks before the courtly captain stepped in and offered Sasha his arm, nodding toward her family. She smiled and waved semaphorically while he led her across the attentive room.

As he observed the broad stylization of her expression and her theatrical wave, Luke's suspicion that Sasha'd somehow engineered this coincidence gave way to an unexpected pang of sympathy for his wife, who had clearly been caught off guard by the encounter with the reunited Melmans. Sasha's social mask was impeccable, but he could read discomfort in the stiffness of her posture and the lack of fluidity in her gait as she crossed the room, reminding him somehow of a young model taking her first nervous stroll down the runway. He imagined she was more surprised than others in the room to have found her putative lover dining with his wife.

The awkwardness was briefly dispelled by the rituals of greeting and the mechanics of moving the table.

Their daughter allowed herself to be hugged.

"Ashley, you look wonderful. Hello, Luke."

"Sasha, you're looking beautiful, as always."

Eventually, they were seated, Sasha sharing the banquette with Luke and waving to her friends and rivals at the middle table. She was dressed conservatively, Upper East Side matronly, in a tweedy vintage Chanel suit, accessorized with a single string of grape-size pearls.

"Here we are at last," she said, beaming across the table at Ashley.

"Now can we leave?" Ashley said.

"Don't be ridiculous. I've been looking forward to this for weeks. So tell me everything. How's Nora?"

"Gran's cool."

Sasha waved to the waiter. "Could I get a glass of chardonnay?"

"Catch that buzz," Ashley said.

"It's called social drinking, darling."

"No wonder they call you a socialite."

"Better to light up a room than cast a pall over it, my sweet."

"Shall we order?" Luke said, hoping to accelerate the pace of the ensuing trial, which threatened to become contentious shortly after the arrival of the appetizers, when Sasha asked about the status of prep school applications.

Ashley glanced across the table at her father. "I was kind of thinking I might postpone that decision for a year," she said. "Don't look at Dad that way. I haven't even told him about it yet."

"I think it would be lovely to have you at home for another year," Sasha said.

"Well, actually—"

The arrival of the choir, a quintet of uniformed Salvation Army officers, blessedly interrupted this debate. Luke wasn't quite ready to catch Sasha up on all the news: that her daughter wanted to go to the high school in Franklin, for instance, or that he planned to move out of the family residence.

*Peace on earth, and mercy mild*
*God and sinners reconciled . . .*

A wave of sentimentality engulfed Luke as he listened to "Hark the Herald Angels Sing" and "Silent Night," a strange cocktail of joy and melancholy that stirred a hundred bright and fading memories and associations—as if he had just opened a box of ornaments for the tree. Whatever contentment he felt was compromised by sadness for the lost family of his childhood and for the broken promise of this one. He felt his eyes welling, charged with nostalgia for Christmases past, even as he experienced an unholy yearning to share the rituals of this and future seasons with someone not present—someone with her own family, with her own history and traditions, all of which seemed at this freighted moment to weigh more than his own selfish desire.

In the wake of "Silent Night," a restless buzz of conversation rising against the clatter of flatware on china seemed to indicate a general consensus in the front room that enough was enough. The choir pressed forward bravely with "Battle Hymn of the Republic" and followed up, evenhandedly, barely pausing for breath, with "Dixie."

To Luke's astonishment, Ashley rose and stood at attention—this seemed out of character for a girl who'd spent most of lunch trying to shrink under the table. Across the room, Isaac Caldwell, the publisher, did likewise, saluting her and placing his hand over his heart.

Ashley then held out her hand. "Come on, Dad."

Sasha was not amused. She clenched her teeth, a pained expression manifesting itself through the serene paralysis of Botox.

Luke gestured toward the table, to indicate the difficulty of standing, before relenting under the pressure of his daughter's pout of entreaty. He pushed the table forward and climbed out, silently mouthing an apology to the vaguely familiar gentleman on his left, and took his stand beside Ashley, putting his arm around her as the choir looked away, looked away, looked away. . . .

"For Grandpa Mac," she whispered.

Luke glanced back at his wife, shrugging sheepishly. With a jaunty snap of his head, he invited her to join them, but Sasha shook her own head almost imperceptibly, forcing a smile of tolerant indulgence. Relieved when the final bars died away, he quickly resumed his seat. Look away indeed.

"Well, aren't we the rebels," Sasha said.

"Come on, Mom. It's your heritage, too."

"There's a time and a place," Sasha said. "Not to mention that I saw Al Sharpton checking his coat out front. He's probably sitting right behind us."

"Don't worry," Ashley said. "I saw them escort him to Siberia back there. They certainly wouldn't want him sitting up here with the regulars."

"Since when do you care about Al Sharpton?" Luke asked.

Sasha shrugged. "He's actually very amusing."

Her attention was suddenly diverted by the sight of Sylvia Melman kissing cheeks at Casey Reynes's table, making a real show out of it, the twittering sound of her laugh piercing the room.

A young uniformed chorister was moving down the row of banquettes, collecting money. Luke found a fifty in his money clip and dropped it in the tambourine just as Sylvia loomed up behind Ashley, smiling over at him with her bone-china face and her bobbed nose, the tendons of her birdlike neck throbbing like suspension cables holding up multiple strands of black pearls.

"Luke, you're an angel, really you are," she said, her voice pitched to a volume that exceeded the demands of private conversation. "I just wanted to say my heart goes out to you." She paused, placing a ropy diamond-studded hand on Ashley's shoulder.

Luke glanced over at his wife, whose face was frozen in a gruesome smile. Was it actually possible that he'd just been publicly congratulated for being a stoic cuckold?

"Of course I heard all about the wonderful things you were doing down at Ground Zero. You're an example to us all in these difficult times."

He nodded, feeling a flush rise on his face as Sylvia patted Ashley's shoulder. "Welcome back, dear," she said to her. "We're all pulling for you." She blew Luke a parting kiss that completed her snub of Sasha and returned to her table, waving broadly as she went.

"Now I *know* I'm back," Ashley said.

Luke felt for Sasha's hand under the table as the room buzzed like a hive of wasps. "Anybody for dessert?"

"Oh, why don't you just order me a fucking glass of hemlock," Sasha muttered, "and get it over with."

"What's hemlock?" Ashley asked.

"It's what the Greeks used to poison people," Luke explained.

"At least that would solve the problem of how to get out of here."

"That's very supportive, Ashley," Sasha said.

The conversation seemed more than a little bizarre to Luke, predicated as it was on certain facts and suppositions that had never been openly acknowledged among the three of them. He signaled the waiter. "I think we should order a bottle of champagne," he said.

"Yes, sir?"

"A bottle of Krug, please. The 1989," he added, "if you have it."

"Very good, Mr. McGavock."

"What exactly are we celebrating?" Sasha asked.

"Well, the fact that we're alive, to start with. Looking back on the events of the fall, I'm feeling pretty lucky that the three of us are all sitting here."

Sasha did not appear convinced.

"Of course, anyone who doesn't necessarily feel the same way might at least want to go through the motions of being in a festive and celebratory mood for the benefit of the room."

A glimmer of comprehension now crossed Sasha's face.

"I think it would be much cooler," Ashley said, "if we just flipped them all the bird."

"Your father's right," Sasha said. "We should have a toast."

The sommelier arrived with the champagne, complimenting Luke on his choice and making due fuss in its presentation, unwiring the cage and deftly twisting the cork, which debouched with a resonant, satisfying pop. He hesitated with the third glass, holding it in the air as he gave Luke an interrogatory look.

Luke nodded toward Ashley. "Just a splash," he said.

When the glasses had been poured, Luke raised his own and held it aloft. "To a merry Christmas," he said, "and a happier New Year."

"A-freaking-men to that." Sasha raised her glass high, smiling gamely. They all clinked glasses. After sipping, Sasha tipped her glass toward Luke. "And I'd like to propose a toast to my husband," she said. "I'm sorry, Luke."

He was taken aback. She seemed to be apologizing for everything that had led up to this bad lunchtime theater; he wasn't sure he was prepared for that, especially given what he'd been preparing to say to her. It would have been easier if she'd continued to behave in character.

Luke excused himself to go to the men's room, noticing, on the way out, that Melman's seat was empty, although his wife and daughter were still seated; only as he was pushing the men's room door open did the likely explanation become obvious. There was nothing to do but take up a position at the vacant urinal beside the mogul, who at first failed to register his identity, staring straight ahead at the colorful mural depicting a Rubenesque flapper bent from the waist, the skirts of her dress lifted above her ample hips, peeing in an unlikely trajectory into a goldfish bowl several feet away while her dapper morning-coated consort did the same from the other side.

Unzipping, Luke turned conspicuously to his left and stared, an act of aggression sustained and blatant enough that Melman reflexively turned his torso away and concealed himself even as he snapped his head toward the voyeur, his outrage modulating to confusion and then embarrassment when he recognized Luke—directing his attention downward, aborting his mission, and hastily arranging himself for an exit.

Melman yanked the flush and turned away while the attendant flipped the taps of the sink and held out a towel for him.

"If those hand towels come in different sizes," Luke said, "he'll take the smallest."

Luke glanced over his right shoulder to see Melman tossing his towel to the floor, grabbing for the door before the attendant could manage to get around and open it for him. When the door had finally wafted shut, the man stole a glance at Luke, shaking his head in amazement.

"Childish of me, I know," Luke said. "But the man fucked my wife." After washing his hands and drying them thoroughly, he left a fifty in the tip basket. "That's for the both of us."

"Merry Christmas to you, sir. I'm sorry for your troubles at home."

"Thanks," Luke said. "But the New Year's looking much happier."

# 31

To descend the stairs beneath the tattered awning and muscle through the double doors of Evelyn's was to leave behind the social contract along with the crisp, lung-prickling air of a December afternoon and to enter a kind of permanent twilight in which an extramarital affair—or even a conspiracy to sunder and rearrange the components of two families—seemed like a minor breach of etiquette. Or so Corrine liked to imagine, thinking this the perfect place for an assignation. Luke had said that he could meet her downtown and she'd immediately thought of this place, scene of half-remembered debauches as well as several stolen hours with Luke before he decamped for Tennessee.

Inside, she blinked and waited for the interior to resolve itself from the murk, two milky faces at the end of the bar turning like lilies toward the flash of daylight as she entered. The frat-house stench of stale beer and cigarette smoke washed over her, a skyline of premium bottles glinting above the dark, pitted plane of the bar. Corrine took a stool near the door as the ghostly bartender, with skin as gray as his hair, materialized in front of her. She didn't really feel the need for alcohol, but neither did it feel appropriate to order a soft drink. "Heineken, please."

Behind her, the susurration of the door announced his arrival; he paused, framed in the entryway, his face in shadow, a few renegade wind-whipped strands of hair tipped with the golden residue of daylight from the street.

His face was chilled and scratchy when he crushed her in his arms, and she rooted in the folds of his cashmere scarf for the scent of him before pressing her lips to his as he lifted her off of her feet; seeking the essence of their kiss—a kiss she had seemed to recognize that very first time, like some memory from a distant, golden age, the familiar earthy taste of him beneath a sweet, vinous residue. She felt like a princess awakened by a magical kiss—as if she'd been sleepwalking through the weeks since she last had seen him.

"I was so nervous," she said after he lowered her to the floor. She pulled her head back to look at him, finding the reality even more satisfying than the image in her memory. The boyishness of his face and his grin emphasized by the sophisticated counterpoint of the expensive-looking shirt and bright red tie. It was as if he had somehow perfected himself in his absence.

"Me too."

*The nicest phrase in the language*—had she said that to him once? No, but she'd thought that. QED. Me too. "I wondered if it would be different."

"But it's not."

"No, it's not."

He took off his big drapey camel coat, the one she'd pictured him in ever since the trip to Nantucket, and folded it over the stool.

She smiled. "I was almost hoping it would be different."

"I know."

"But I'm glad it's not."

"You look beautiful."

"So do you. I've never seen you in a suit. You look very, I don't know, very Cary Grant."

"An illusion created by a skilled tailor."

In her eyes, he was one of those men who redeemed the idea of the suit, which emphasized his masculinity even as it somehow underlined his superiority to the lumpish herd of the facelessly uniformed. Strange to imagine that this is what he would have looked like for most of his adult life—all those years before she'd known him. She thought about all the other women who had looked at him in a suit—on the street, in conference rooms, across the lobby of a hotel in Paris or Hong Kong. When he removed his jacket, she ran her hand across his chest.

"I've been waiting to feel the Christmas spirit," she said. "Seeing you in your stripy shirt with your tie like a big red ribbon—you look like a present waiting to be unwrapped."

"*Precisely* the effect I was hoping to achieve."

"I don't know how I'm going to get through the holidays," she said. "It seems so hypocritical just going through the motions, the rituals of Christmas and family harmony. And I'm so self-conscious, I feel like everything I do and say now could have some enormous consequence later. I keep thinking, Should I be supernice, or—"

"I know."

Trying to think of a gift for Russell, for instance, was paralyzing her. What was an appropriate gift for a husband you were about to leave?

The bartender drifted over and hovered; Luke pointed to her Heineken.

She held it to his mouth, licked the stray flecks of foam from his lips. "Now I wish I'd let you get that hotel room," she whispered.

"Friend of mine has a little place around the corner on Patchin Place."

"Don't tempt me."

"No?"

"Where's your friend?"

"Out of town." He fished in his pocket and came up with a fresh-cut brass key on a carabiner, dangling it before her like a forbidden delicacy.

"Pretty damn sure of yourself, aren't you?" She drew her head back in a mock pose of offended dignity.

"It was just a thought."

"I like the way you think."

The bartender placed a sweating green bottle on a coaster.

"Shall we?"

Leaving a fifty on the counter, he winked as he slipped the two Heinekens in the pockets of his coat—the boyishness of the second gesture just about balancing out the grandiosity of the first—and held the door open for her.

Outside, bedazzled by the daylight, she groped for her sunglasses in her purse. He took her arm and walked her west on Ninth Street toward Sixth Avenue through the chilly, vivid air of the December afternoon, her awareness heightened by the cold and by the perfect transparency of the flat light in which the facades of the nineteenth-century town houses seemed as precisely etched as architectural models, in which at any moment she might herself be exposed in her illicit and naked happiness, drinking a beer like a teenager, to the scrutiny of a friend or an acquaintance. She didn't care. She almost hoped she'd see someone she knew, then suddenly worried that there must be some flaw in what should have been a self-sufficient state of bliss, because otherwise she wouldn't feel the need to flaunt it. She felt selfish and vain, realizing that even as she floated above the concrete on the arm of her man, envying no one and, in fact, pitying all around her, some part of her secretly courted the envy and admiration of passersby.

"What's the matter?"

"What do you mean?"

"You looked worried."

"I was just worrying that there was something wrong with feeling this happy." He looked at her as if she were loony.

"What's so funny?"

"You are."

The pout she served up to him was essentially theatrical, the reflex so familiar that she didn't know at first why this little exchange felt strange, then realized that it mimicked a thousand she'd had with Russell over the years—Luke's expression of fond exasperation almost identical to Russell's habitual reaction to what he called her "earnest non sequiturs."

"Now what?" he said, looking down at her. "You look like you've seen a ghost."

"It's just . . . nothing."

He engulfed her shoulder with his gloved hand and pulled her closer. She was afraid he was going to try to kid her out of her mood—already she could picture herself drawing farther away as he tried to jolly her up.

"Tell me," he said, passing Balducci's windows with their stacked wheels of Parmesan and aging sides of beef, the sky opening out above Sixth Avenue. "We have too much at stake not to be honest with each other."

Dodging a jogging young couple in matching warm-up suits, the man pushing a bundled infant on one of those tricycle rigs, the name of which she tried to remember. They'd once bought two of them, used them all of five or six times—now collecting dust in the closet dedicated to good intentions and unrealized ambitions. That's right: a baby jogger.

Luke held the beer bottle to her lips as he steered her gently up the avenue.

"I wish I could come to you all fresh and dewy," she said. "Without all this history. I'm suddenly afraid I don't have anything new and original to bring to you. How many people can you love in your life? I wish you were my first love."

"I don't think it's very logical to wish your history away, since I love you the way you are now."

"Middle-aged, married, with children?" She didn't know why she was playing the devil's advocate. Part of her wanted to postpone this kind of reckoning, to simply savor his presence. But suddenly it felt as if they'd largely managed to avoid facing these most salient facts.

"You love your children; therefore I will love your children." He was guiding her gently across Sixth, his arm under her elbow.

As much as she welcomed the sentiment, it terrified her to hear it expressed. "Are we really going to do this? Change our lives?"

"I am."

"It seems impossible now to imagine living without you," she said, passing through the chilly shadow cast by the hulking, fortresslike Jefferson Market Library. "But it seems just as impossible to leave. What I was thinking of back there, when you asked me if I'd seen a ghost—you sounded exactly like Russell."

He was silent as they finally came to a halt in front of the iron gate of Patchin Place—a narrow mews of dollhouse tenements, vaguely connected in her mind with Greenwich Village poets.

Looking into his eyes, seeing his sadness, she was overcome with a kind of tender remorse, which transmuted, almost immediately, into desire. She reached for his shoulders and kissed him with a carnal hunger as surprising to her as it seemed to be to him.

They stumbled into the alley, clutching each other and kissing, Luke fishing in his pocket for the key as he pressed her up against the door of one of the little gray houses, turning the key in the lock while probing her mouth with his tongue, pressing his body against hers until the door yielded and they staggered into a hallway. She took her bearings long enough to notice a kilim on the floor of the front room and to pull him down on top of her as he wrestled her coat from her shoulders and tugged at her panty hose while she unzipped his fly and freed his cock, imagining herself as a rutting creature with neither history nor memory, with no obligations beyond the imperatives of her own instincts and desire. At some point, she realized the rhythmic thump she was hearing was her head banging on the floorboards. She felt as if she were drifting in and out of her own body.

When at last he collapsed on top of her, she gradually began to regain a sense of her surroundings. His hot breath, a warm smudge of saliva from his cheek on her shoulder. Three white strands in his brown sideburn, and dust swimming in the remnants of the daylight above her. She stroked his hair back across his ear and heard the clink

340

could live for her own desires, but now she worried that this anxiety was a permanent condition, that she would never know the untroubled sleep of youth, that she would always be hovering near the surface of consciousness in the perpetual light of the restless city, alert to the sound of a cough, the thump of a falling body, the drone of a plane overhead.

# 32

uke?"

"Earth to Dad. *Hello?*"

They were in a Town Car, assailed by faux balsam air freshener, crossing through the park to the West Side: the family, he and his wife and daughter—of this much he was certain. He tried to recall if some fragment of current conversation had filtered through the reverie of his afternoon idyll with Corrine. "Sorry," he said. "What was the question?"

"Sometimes," Sasha said, "I think you got hit on the head or something back in September."

"In a sense," he said, "I did."

"Well, maybe it's time to move on."

"Mom was just talking about next semester," Ashley prompted, pinching him on the thigh.

"I was saying to Ashley," Sasha said, "what I just said to you— that it's time to get back to normal. Move on."

"That depends," Luke said, "on what you think is normal."

"We can't run and hide from our problems forever. Ashley's place is open at Sprague—we paid the tuition in full. And it's not as if we're going to pick up and move to Tennessee, for God's sake."

"Why not?"

"Ashley, *puh-lease*."

"There's life outside of New York, Mom."

"There's life on the bottom of the ocean, Ashley, but fortunately for us, our ancestors crawled up on the beach and developed lungs and feet, not to mention hand-stitched Italian footwear."

Ashley turned to face her mother. "You know," she said, "last year, I used to think that having the right Steve Madden shoes and shopping at Infinity for baby tees and teddy-bear backpacks and knowing a tenth-grade boy at Collegiate, that those were the only really important things. But you know what? I grew out of it."

"*Girls,*" Luke pleaded. Torn between loyalty to his daughter's wishes and his own desire to set up house with Corrine, he found himself arguing Ashley's case against his wife. "Have you forgotten," he said, "that our daughter was hospitalized for a drug overdose last month?"

"Of course I haven't forgotten. But she can get treatment in New York. I mean, if anything, she can get far better treatment here than she can down there in Dollywood."

"You're both aware, right, that I understand English and that I'm sitting directly between you?"

"This is kind of a huge discussion," Luke said. "Maybe we can finish it after the ballet."

The annual trip to *The Nutcracker* had for many years been a highlight of the holidays for Ashley, until last year, when she'd attended under duress, declaring *The Nutcracker* childish and the ballet elitist. But when he broached the subject the week before, she'd surprised him by embracing the outing, deciding that it would be "kind of cool, like old times," as if childhood was now distant enough to have taken on a rosy, nostalgic glow. He wasn't sure how she had so quickly reconciled herself to the taint of elitism, the very quality that in her mind defined her mother—a charge against which Luke had defended her. The fact that Sasha was a snob didn't negate her genuine passion and connoisseurship; she'd been on the board for a decade and she was furious when, two weeks before, Luke had declined to fly back from Tennessee to attend the opening-night performance of *Stars and Stripes*, chosen as the season opener more or less at the last minute in deference to the national mood of patriotic mourning. Somehow, Luke felt he owed it to her to follow through on *The Nutcracker*. She in turn had helped him put together the memorial service for Guillermo two days hence.

Their car having finally pulled to the curb amid a school of lumpish yellow cabs, they disembarked and strolled up the long plaza toward the theater. Luke took Ashley's hand as they pressed into the crowd, which coagulated as they approached the doors.

"Where's Mom?"

"I don't know, pressing the flesh."

Standing on his toes he surveyed the throng of dark coats and bright holiday faces, finally spotting Sasha in the middle of the plaza, smoking with Biff and Mimi Pulver. Not five feet to her left, Corrine was striding toward him with a seraphic towheaded child and waving at him—or so it seemed until he saw the couple off to his right, a black man and a white woman with two café au lait children, waving back in Corrine's direction.

Properly, almost primly, attired and groomed after the shambolic dishevelment of the afternoon, she was buttoned into a tailored Black Watch tartan coat, her coppery mane brushed back and tamed by a black velvet headband—a preppy princess. Disoriented and nervous as he was, it struck him as odd that she hadn't specified the nature of the engagement that had foreshortened their afternoon assignation. But neither, he realized, had he. It was as if they'd both observed some scrupulous interpretation of a boundary between lust and its biological raison d'être. "Some friends coming over," she'd said, looking him in the eyes. And he'd likewise dodged the question. Even as he was about to dissolve his family, he'd felt, it seemed in retrospect, protective of its rituals, reluctant to mention it; she must have felt even less inclined to let these two worlds interpenetrate.

She paused and looked behind her, awaiting her husband, for such he clearly was, carrying a second child as he fumbled with his coat pocket. Russell Calloway lowered the little boy to his feet beside the girl, his twin, the two standing at attention in their double-breasted navy coats, with their flaxen hair and matching expressions of cautious bedazzlement. Storey and Jeremy. He'd known their names for months, but until this moment their existence had been somewhat theoretical. The girl reached over and took the boy's hand; his expression, the exasperated moue with which he reacted to this gesture, suggested that he did not in general approve of holding hands with a girl, especially if she was his sister, but he grudgingly acquiesced with an air of making an exception just this once, indulging his sister amid this surging crowd of tall strangers—or so it seemed to Luke from his vantage across the plaza. Studying their half-formed faces, he told himself the twins favored Corrine, even as he scrutinized Russell, who was searching the inside pockets of his overcoat.

Luke had to admit this man was not an entirely unworthy rival in the physical sense—tall and commanding, if a little lumpy in the middle. His hair could be criticized as unfashionably long, almost foppishly so for a man his age. And strictly speaking, his tweed overcoat was unsuitable for evening. Luke might have discerned additional individual faults, but his critical focus kept shifting to the group portrait: Russell leaning over to brush his son's hair away from his eyes as Corrine held out to him the tickets she'd pulled from her purse, these overlapping gestures creating a harmonic composition around the still center of the luminous twins.

If there was any constraint between the parents, he was unable to detect it as they started up the plaza with the solemn twins between them, an enviably handsome family that appeared, from this distance, to illustrate some cosmopolitan ideal. Luke watched, transfixed by the children, searching their excited faces for traces of their mother.

. . .

Seeing Corrine in this context reminded him of something his mother had said—that if love is something more than wanting, it involves putting someone else's well-being ahead of your own inclinations and desires.

"What's up, Dad?" Ashley was regarding him with skeptical curiosity.

"Nothing," he said, just as it occurred to him that they should move out of the path of the approaching Calloways.

Sasha had extracted herself from the Pulvers and started toward them, tossing away her cigarette and falling into step just behind Corrine. Spotting Luke, she waved and walked the fingers of one hand across the palm of the other to signal her good intentions.

Luke raised his hand dutifully, waving back, his gesture drawing Corrine's attention. She blanched at the sight of him, pausing in mid-step, upsetting the delicate rhythm of the familial quadriga, the twins stumbling into her as she recovered herself, helping them to right themselves and making a clownish face of self-reproach.

Luke found himself standing beside the mixed couple with their two stunning bronze children—apparently the Calloways' friends. He knew he should move, but he felt paralyzed as he watched Sasha and the Calloways converging, Corrine directing her attention ostentatiously toward the children as she advanced, smoothing her son's hair, performing a methodical and unnecessary adjustment of her daughter's overcoat, just as Sasha drew abreast of her, brushing up against her shoulder as she pressed her way forward, an entitled New Yorker in a hurry.

"The Pulvers send their love," Sasha announced, cutting in front of Corrine and nearly colliding with the children as she reached for Luke's arm, simultaneously looking down. "Oh, I'm so sorry. Look at these little angels. . . . I almost stepped on you." She touched Storey's head as if for luck, to the obvious horror of her mother. "Oh my God, they're gorgeous," she said to Corrine. "They are just *to die*. Twins? In their little matching Bonpoint coats. To *die*!"

Corrine managed to nod and shape a facsimile of a smile as the other couple called out greetings, Russell waving to his friends even as he paused to check out the attractive and imperious stranger who was fawning over his children, who looked frightened, especially Storey.

Corrine knelt beside her daughter. "What's wrong, honey?"

She seemed on the verge of tears. "That lady said we're going to die."

"No, honey, it's just an expression."

Sasha crouched down, bringing herself face-to-face with the girl while Corrine sneaked a helpless, frightened glance at Luke.

"Oh, sweetie, I just meant you were *beyond*."

"Beyond what?" the boy said, showing his courage.

"How *old* are you two little angels?" Sasha asked in an exaggerated singsong tone.

Storey looked up at her mother for guidance.

"They're six," Corrine said.

"Almost seven."

"In Feb'uary."

"Such a brilliant age." She stood and turned to Luke. "Don't you miss it, honey?"

He nodded skeptically; something in his expression caused his wife to turn her attention back to Corrine just when she might've let the encounter die a natural death.

"We haven't met . . . have we?" she said, looking back and forth between Corrine and Luke.

Russell extended his hand. "Russell Calloway. And this is my wife, Corrine."

"Sasha and Luke McGavock. And this is our daughter, Ashley."

"Actually," Corrine said, smiling at Luke as if she'd almost failed to recognize him, "Luke and I worked at the soup kitchen together this past fall."

"So you were the one keeping my wife out all night," Russell said cheerfully.

"Well, it was all for charity," Sasha said in a crisp, icy tone, the import of which was lost on Russell, if not on his wife.

Luke and Corrine exchanged a glance freighted on both sides with recognition and loss. He felt as if he were watching her disappear. Almost from the start, they'd had a kind of transparency to each other. Now he saw only sadness, and her embarrassed recognition of what had just happened—an event that in its outward aspect was as subtle as a shift in the breeze, but which was even now carrying them away from each other like two small craft on separate currents.

"You'll excuse us," Russell said. "Our friends are waiting."

Her lips drawn and quivering, Corrine gathered her children around her as she greeted the other couple. In her wake, Luke caught a faint trace of the sunny coconut perfume of her hair, and it carried him back to the first time he'd smelled it, infused with the acrid scent of death, kissing her as dawn broke over the harbor.

In that moment, the nighttime plaza with all its swirling throng blurred and faded as if engulfed in a sudden storm of sand or snow. Even as she glared at him, Sasha's features grew fainter and less distinct, perhaps a preview of a future when her image would be hard to conjure except in a general way, like the graduation-day and prom-night faces staring out from telephone poles, from the walls outside hospitals and fire stations. What he *would* remember, picturing it again and again over the years, was Corrine's stricken face turning away, like a door closing on the last of his youthful ideals and illusions.

He stood there under the scrutiny of his wife and daughter, struggling to maintain his balance and composure against a wave of vertigo, as if he'd found himself standing on some precipitous slope, having crested a summit somewhere back there without quite realizing it at the time—sharing a bench in the singed morning air of October or a four-poster bed on Nantucket—and looking down now into an abyss. Everything hereafter would be a gradual descent, faster or slower, from regret to oblivion.

She was his lost twin, his sundered other half, and after half a lifetime he had found her, and now would let her go. Of course they would speak again, tomorrow or the next day, in the park or on the brown lawn under the bare trees of Bowling Green, if only to try to comfort each other and flagellate themselves. And perhaps they would meet again, in the years to come, randomly, as one does in New York, on a midtown sidewalk or at the bar of a restaurant in the Village—or, rather, as one used to, before the idea of the protean city as eternal and indestructible had been called into doubt. It seemed to him both hopeful that he could once again imagine the city as a backdrop to the dramas of daily life and sad that the satori flash of acute wakefulness and connectedness that had followed the initial confrontation with mortality in September was already fading behind them. For a few weeks, they had all found it impossible to believe that anything would ever be the same again. As he sat beside his daughter and watched the "Dance of the Sugar Plum Fairies" for the tenth or twelfth time, he took comfort in that vision of the city as the setting for a future encounter with Corrine, and in the fact that he could imagine it now. He was grateful, sitting there in the theater, to be participating in this ritual of family and community, if possibly for the last time. And even in the slough of his sadness, he found himself conjuring brighter scenarios, and seeing his virtuous renunciation rewarded in the end.

How are you? he would say after they'd expressed surprise at their chance encounter and he had told her she looked beautiful and she'd squinted at him and complained about how her hair frizzed in the rain.

And when he politely inquired after Russell, she would admit she was separated, or divorced, or widowed. She would recount sadly the emotional withdrawal, the habitual lying, the ugly affair; or the slow wasting as the cancer spread outward from the lungs, or what was known of the unexplained plane crash. He would tell her how sorry he was as they stood on the sidewalk, oblivious to the fine mist of rain and the hiss of car tires on the avenue. I thought about calling you, she would say, her coppery hair glistening, spangled with tiny droplets of rain.

Well, here we are, he'd say, at once awkward and exhilarated.

Yes, she'd say, her face sad and hopeful—so he imagined—even as she rolled her eyes at the banality of the situation, the stiltedness of their exchange. Here we are.

# ACKNOWLEDGMENTS

For bucolic shelter and rooms with view I want to thank Dominique Browning and Will and Cissy Akers. I'm also very grateful to Anne and Amanda Hearst and to Helen Schifter, Paul Schrader, and Kim Tipaul for anthropological background. I'd like acknowledge the amazing dedication and inspiration of Bruce Grilikhes and Jeff Stafford, formerly of the Bowling Green Relief Station. Once again, Gary Fisketjon's editorial advice was deft, insightful, and indispensable. And without Amanda Urban's advice and encouragement I seriously doubt I would have completed this book. Thank you, Binky. Finally, I would like to thank Barrett and Maisie McInerney for their patience.

# ALSO AVAILABLE BY JAY McINERNEY

## BRIGHT LIGHTS, BIG CITY

'A rambunctious, deadly funny novel that goes for the right mark – the human heart' Raymond Carver

You are at a nightclub talking to a girl with a shaved head. The club is either Heartbreak or the Lizard Lounge. All might become clear if you could just slip into the bathroom and do a little more Bolivian Marching Powder. Then again, it might not ... So begins our nameless hero's trawl through the brightly lit streets of Manhattan, sampling all this wonderland has to offer yet suspecting that tomorrow's hangover may be caused by more than simple excess. *Bright Lights, Big City* is an acclaimed classic which marked Jay McInerney as one of the major writers of our time.

'The seminal novel of the 1980s'
**NEW YORK TIMES**

## BRIGHTNESS FALLS

'A funny, self-mocking, sometimes brilliant portrait of Manhattan's young literary and Wall Street crowd, our latest Lost Generation'
**TIME**

Corrine Calloway is a young stockbroker on Wall Street, her husband Russell an underpaid but ambitious publishing editor. The happily married couple head into New York's 1980s gold rush where prospects and money seem to be flying everywhere, and all vie for riches, fame and the love of beautiful people. But the Calloways soon find out that what goes up must come crashing down, both on Wall Street and at home.

'McInerney has a gift for the simultaneous perception of the glamour and tawdriness of city life and the novel pulsates with his trademark sense of excitement about living in New York'
**EVENING STANDARD**

BLOOMSBURY

# STORY OF MY LIFE

'Line for line, it's one of the funniest novels I have ever read'
**LONDON REVIEW OF BOOKS**

It's party time. Alison lives for the moment in a carnival of gossip and midnight sessions of Truth or Dare, and her cocaine-bashing friends crave satiation. Young and beautiful, sex-crazed and alcohol-fuelled, Alison juggles rent money with abortion fees, lingering lovers with current conquests and is the despair of her gynaecologist. Story of her life right? But in a world of no consequences, Alison is heading for a meltdown.

'McInerney has proven himself not only a brilliant stylist but a master of characterisation, with a keen eye for the incongruities of urban life'
**NEW YORK TIMES**

# RANSOM

'McInerney is one of the most gifted writers of his generation'
**OBSERVER**

Living in the ancient capital of Japan, Christopher Ransom seeks a purity he could not find at home, and tries to exorcise the blur of violence and death he encountered at the Khyber Pass. Supporting himself by teaching English to eager Japanese businessmen, Ransom feels safe amongst his fellow expatriates. But soon he is threatened by everything he thought he had left behind, in a sequence of bizarre events whose consequences he cannot escape . . .

'Cleverly written, intelligent, lively, concise and humorous'
**GUARDIAN**

B L O O M S B U R Y

# MODEL BEHAVIOUR

'A fast-paced, funny tale of true love gone wrong, full of McInerney's wit and style'
**COSMOPOLITAN**

Connor's girlfriend is off to California, allegedly on a fashion shoot, but something tells him she might never come back. His friend Jeremy has a dog being held to ransom for reasons too Machiavellian to blurb. Connor's sister Brook, genius and anorexic, is busy anguishing over Rwanda and Bosnia. His editor at *Ciao Bella* is only concerned about the celebrity of the month. Thanks goodness for Pallas, a knock-out table dancer with a heart of gold.

'*Model Behaviour* does for the '90s what *Bright Lights, Big City* did for the '80s ... New York, New York: so good he nailed it twice'
**INDEPENDENT ON SUNDAY**

# HOW IT ENDED

'Sharp, spare, exquisitely observed writing'
**DAILY MAIL**

Discover a world of sex, excess and urban paranoia where worlds collide, relationships fragment and the dark underbelly of the American dream is exposed. A transsexual prostitute accidentally propositions his own father. A senator's serial infidelities leave him in hot water. And two young lovers spend Christmas together high on different drugs. McInerney's characters struggle together in a shifting world where old certainties dissolve and nobody can be sure of where they stand.

'McInerney is the type of American novelist to whom English readers instinctively warm ... *How It Ended* is the work of a fine writer on the top of his form'
**SUNDAY TELEGRAPH**

B L O O M S B U R Y

of the iron gate and footsteps in the alley; she wondered if they were visible through the front windows, but, pinned as she was, she couldn't turn her head. The footsteps passed on by, the turning of a key, the click of the latch next door as clear and proximate as if she'd had her ear pressed against the door. The musty smell of the place, pierced with the pungent tang of sex.

When he pulled out of her and rolled onto his side, she was filled with a sense of loss. She listened as the tempo of his breathing slowed, as the light suddenly dimmed, and on a sudden inspiration she extracted herself from his arm and the wreckage of her clothing and twisted around, taking him in her mouth. This was something new, something that hadn't been worn out with repetition, that she'd never done before, never wanted to taste herself fresh on anyone's cock, and indeed it was strange but also weirdly exciting, this commingled essence of his own juices and hers. She felt incredibly wicked sucking him, Luke groaning and cupping her head in his hands.

The second time was like an entirely different act, a gentle merger, his breath in her ear like the lapping of waves, and when she came, it was a gradual deliquescence rich with tenderness and melancholy.

"I wish I could just lie here and watch the night fall."

For a few minutes, she suspected he'd fallen asleep, until he raised himself on his arms and looked down at her.

"What are you doing tonight?"

"Nothing really," she said. This was not exactly true, but she wasn't quite ready to contemplate her other life. "Some friends coming over." All at once, she felt terrible lying to him. It was the first time she could remember being less than truthful with him. In fact, they were going to *The Nutcracker,* but it seemed profane to speak of her family in this setting; she couldn't quite reconcile the separate realities of Sugar Plum Fairies and blow jobs. She stroked the hair back away from his face. "You?"

"About the same."

"I should probably think about getting up soon," she said, testing an idea utterly at odds with her inclination.

"Should I let you up?"

"I don't really want you to."

He bent down and kissed her and then rolled away, sitting up beside her.

She found herself lying in a small parlor with a lumpy slipcovered couch, a couple of Shaker chairs with woven seats, a rattan coffee table populated with half a dozen incarnations of the Buddha in bronze and wood. Two bookshelves sagging with faded paperbacks. Crude, colorful school of de Kooning canvases adorned the walls.

"Who's your friend? Last of the action painters?"

"Do you like it?" he asked.

"The house? It's adorable. I've always looked in from the street and wondered about these places. I feel like Djuna Barnes is going to knock on the door any minute and ask to borrow some gin, or e. e. cummings to say, 'Kisses are a better fate than wisdom.'"

"I've leased it, with an option to buy."

It took her a moment to absorb this and sort through the implications.

"If you like it."

"If I like it?"

"It's got four rooms upstairs," he said. "And it's a ten-minute walk to school."

For a moment, she wondered which school he was talking about. "You mean St. Luke's?"

"Am I freaking you out?"

"A little. Just give me a few minutes to catch up." She looked around with a new eye, trying to see herself living here. The two of them—no, the four of them. Or was it five, with Ashley? What was he thinking?

"It needs work, obviously. It wouldn't even be ready till late spring. I need to redo the kitchen and the bathrooms. Come see the rest of it."

"Oh my God, Luke." She leaped on his back and made him carry her up the stairs, eager to give form and shape to her misty vision of this future, projecting herself and her children into these rooms, almost believing it possible, and wanting desperately to believe, but unable to imagine the in-between . . . the tears, the bewilderment of the children, the meetings in lawyers' offices and the sorting of possessions, the sad cardboard boxes stacked beside the bedroom door.

Standing in the mews half an hour later in the flat afternoon light as he locked the door behind them, she stared at the misty cloud of her own breath and prayed for a sign.

With his arm around her shoulder, they walked over the cobblestones to the gate. She wished he would say something, specifically the one thing that would dispel all her doubts.

Ahead, in the shadow of the old women's prison tower, a flash of red and then another—two Santas marching up Tenth Street, one fat and the other skinny. Approaching the street, she spied two more and two more behind them, one showing what she supposed was Desert Storm camo beneath his red coat and talking on a cell phone, one carrying his red-and-white hat in his hand. A cavalcade of Santas, ten, fifteen, more than twenty in all, some festive and springy of step, others dragging their tails behind them, one visibly drunk, tacking between the edges of the sidewalk, half a dozen shades of red represented in their costumes—scarlet, ruby, and vermilion. Here was a Santa with bright ermine fur trim on his coat, and another with a ratty browning fringe. One balding pinkish Santa wore jeans and carried a bulging red sack slung over his shoulder. Several were appropriately portly, while a gaunt, sickly-looking one marched beside a beanpole who appeared to be pregnant.

Luke and Corrine stopped just inside the gate to observe and marvel at this manifestation of the season, watching in silence as the herd of Santas turned up Sixth Avenue and disappeared around the corner. They followed, closing the gate behind them, but by the time they reached Sixth Avenue, there wasn't a single Santa in sight.

"Can you believe that?" she said.

"Never seen anything quite like it in my life."

Seeing Famous Ray's on the corner of Eleventh Street, she realized she was ravenous and asked if he would buy her a slice. Somehow, she wasn't quite ready for the afternoon to end.

"God, I haven't been here in twenty years," she said as they stood at the counter, waiting for their slices to warm.

"My first time, I'm afraid."

"You've never been here?" she said, astonished.

"I've been to other establishments bearing the name."

"No, no, this is the *real* Ray's. Forget about all those Original Ray's. I can't believe you've never been here. You haven't seen much, have you? What the hell have you been doing the last twenty years?"

"I was working."

"And eating at 'Twenty-one' and Le Cirque."

"Actually, I was looking for you."

"No wonder. You needed me."

He walked her to the subway, past St. Vincent's Hospital with its wailing wall of MISSING posters. She looked down at her feet, dazzled by the whiteness of the sidewalk, spangled in the sunlight. It had been years since she'd noticed the way that, on certain winter days, the sidewalks are bedizened as if studded with diamonds.

Already she felt herself separating from him, unable to keep herself from lifting away, making the transition to her other life, a process that accelerated when she saw a boy about Jeremy's age in a puffy blue parka slip on a patch of ice and fall to the ground, his bare head hitting the salt-stained sidewalk, and though he recovered quickly from his fright, his mother lifting him upright and dusting him off, she couldn't help worrying about his head, imagining the shock of the impact and thinking of her own children, in whom she would sometimes see the ghostly image of their newborn eggshell skulls, remembering how she had cried when she'd first seen them, intubated under glass, their tiny writhing bodies and their translucent pink skulls veined with blue, blaming herself for the precariousness of their existence, guilty about the lengths she'd gone to in order to satisfy her craving for offspring when nature had demurred, despairing of her ability to protect them from pain and harm.

She had hoped that someday she might take their existence for granted, and this afternoon she'd been lulled into believing that she